GLIMMER VALE CHRONICLES

Books *1-3*

MICHAEL KINGSWOOD

CONTENTS

GLIMMER VALE

OUT-DWELLER

TOLLARD'S PEAK

INTRODUCTION

I initially wrote Glimmer Vale, the tale of two fighting men on the run from their past who become unlikely heroes in a remote mountain town, as a one-off story for National Novel Writing Month (NaNoWriMo). As I was preparing for the month of writing, I had the idea of doing something like Seven Samurai in a medieval fantasy setting. Then the name Glimmer Vale came into my mind. Shortly thereafter, the scene where Julian and Melanie first meet appeared, and would not go away.

So I wrote the book. And I liked it. I liked it a lot, so much that I decided to revisit Julian, Raedrick, and Melanie. And then do it again. And again...

It became a series that, as of this writing, is five novels and one short story long. And I plan to continue their adventures for many future books to come.

Thanks for reading! I hope you enjoy these books as much as I have enjoyed creating them.

Michael Kingswood
San Diego, California
January 2019

Enjoy the book! After you're done, please come to my website and sign up for my mailing list at www.michaelkingswood.com/newsletter-signup/. Guaranteed to be spam free, I use it to announce new releases and special promotions for my fans. I look forward to hearing from you.

MAP OF GLIMMER VALE

GLIMMER·VALE
Northflow
To Mangin City
Holbar's Pass
Glamor Wood
Saddleback
Lydelton
Mountains
Silver Falls
To Calas
Garret's Gorge
Cascade River
Lake Glimmer Mere
Eastflow
Mountains
The Hook
Saddleback

GLIMMER VALE CHRONICLES #1

GLIMMER VALE

MICHAEL KINGSWOOD

GLIMMER VALE

On the run from their past, swordsmen Raedrick Baletier and Julian Hinderbrook search for a place of refuge where they can start over.

That search sends them through a remote mountain valley called Glimmer Vale, where unbeknownst to them, dark forces threaten the population's lives and fortunes.

With their hopes of quiet passage through the Vale dashed, and facing a deadly conflict against overwhelming odds, Raedrick and Julian will need all of their wit, courage, and skill just to survive, let alone prevail.

❧ I ☙

GARRET'S GORGE

Cold wind whipped past Julian, making his cloak furl out behind him. Biting back a curse, he clutched at the flapping cloth and pulled it back in tight around his body, but not before the momentary exposure had done its damage. What small warmth he had been able to retain was gone, leaving him to shiver in his saddle. The mail shirt he wore didn't help matters, but he had learned the hard way not to go without it.

It was supposed to be getting on into spring. Down below, in the lowlands many miles behind him, farmers were tilling their fields in preparation for the first planting. Trees and bushes were beginning to show their first buds. And people could go about their business in less than three layers of clothing. But not here, among the peaks of the Saddleback Mountains. Here, winter still clung to the land like a young maiden to her first crush.

"Tell me again why we're taking this route?" he muttered with anncyance.

Julian's companion looked sidelong at him and rolled his eyes. Raedrick was a hand taller than Julian and thin as a stick, with shoulder-length black hair that was tied into a short ponytail at the nape of his neck. Like Julian, Raedrick wore a cowled brown cloak of thick wool over his mail, and calf-high leather riding boots. Beyond that their fashion sense deviated, for while Raedrick usually picked shirts and pants of blue and grey, Julian preferred greens and browns; they went with his short brown hair and hazel eyes better.

Or at least that's what the ladies told him.

When they first met, Julian thought sure he could break Raedrick in half with one hand. He had quickly learned the folly of that. Raedrick was quick, and a lot stronger than he looked. And he could wield the saber that hung from his saddle horn with deadly efficiency.

"I don't feel like getting caught, do you?" Raedrick said. "Not many people come this way anymore since the southern passes became viable. Plus, it's faster."

"I'd almost rather take my chances down south," Julian replied.

It had been a hard week since they departed Calas. The army did not generally chase deserters, but all the same if a chance patrol happened upon them, they were done. So they took pains to remain out of sight, which meant they mostly traveled at night.

That had been bad enough, but once they made it into the foothills of the mountains, past even the most distant picket lines, the journey had gotten steadily worse. At first Julian had thought riding in the day again would be easier, but as the terrain became more rugged their progress slowed and the day's ride grew more exhausting.

Then, the day before yesterday, they passed through the last of the trees and emerged onto the bare flank of the mountains, leaving them completely exposed to the elements. Fierce gusting winds and lowering temperatures conspired to create a thoroughly miserable day and a restless night. They finally got a bit of relief yesterday afternoon as they put the first few peaks behind them, and then again this morning when they entered Garret's Gorge. But that was a respite only compared to the bitter cold of the mountain range's flanks, as the last wind gust revealed.

At least they had a nice view. Julian had to concede that.

About ten feet to his left, the road abruptly fell away. A sheer cliff, and another one a tenth of a mile away facing it, formed the walls of the Gorge. At the bottom, a couple hundred feet down, the Cascade River flowed, a long series of rapids that only subsided in the foothills far to the west, where it merged with the River Lonaylay on its way to the Tymor Sea. Between the Gorge and the mighty peaks all around, there was always another awe-inspiring sight here. But right then Julian would trade it all for a nice fire and a warm mug of mulled wine. And a warmer maiden.

"Quit complaining," the other man said. "We're almost to the falls. From there it's just barely a half day to Lydelton."

Julian only grunted in reply.

They rode in silence for another hour. Slowly, almost imperceptibly, a low noise began to intrude on Julian's consciousness. At first it was easy to not notice it, a low rumble that could just as easily be his imagination. But the rumble grew over time until eventually it became impossible to ignore.

"What's that? The falls?"

Raedrick nodded with a wry grin. "Just around the next corner. Brace yourself."

Julian snorted. He had seen plenty of waterfalls before. One was much the same as... They rounded the corner and Julian abandoned the thought as his jaw dropped in amazement.

The falls were about a quarter of a mile ahead. Spilling over the side of a jagged mountain peak that rose high above all the others nearby, the falls had to have measured a thousand feet from the dropoff to the bottom of the Gorge, where the river began to flow. Mist billowed off the water as it fell and rose in a great cloud at the falls' base. The rocks on either side of the Gorge and on the adjoining flank of the mountain gleamed, frozen mist reflecting the mid-morning sunlight that shined from the west. Julian instantly understood why they were called Silver Falls; if he didn't know better, he would have thought the ice was precious metal from the way it reflected the sunlight.

"Gods be good," he said. Or at least, he tried to say it. Even at that distance, the roar from the falls was tremendous. He could barely hear himself speak.

"We'll need to protect our ears as we get closer." Raedrick leaned over close to Julian's ear as he spoke. Even still, it was hard to understand him.

Julian nodded and flipped open one of his saddlebags. After a moment of digging, he found a small lump of wax. Breaking it in two, he held the two pieces in his fists for a moment to soften them up. Then he pressed them into his ears. The roar was immediately muffled, though it was still distinctly noticeable.

The two men continued forward. The great mountain peak rose on their side of the Gorge, blocking their path like a colossus. But the road shortly veered away from the Gorge and the peak itself, instead climbing the mountain's flank on the other side of the peak from the falls. Julian considered, as they turned on the first of what would probably be many switchbacks designed to lessen the road's angle of ascent, that it was probably for the best. He didn't want to think about how difficult the road would be to follow if it was covered in ice from the mist. So the extra few miles to go around the peak were probably worthwhile.

Just before noon, after more switchbacks than Julian wanted to count, they reached the road's highest point and paused for a moment. Looking down from their lofty perch, Julian was struck by the beauty of the valley before them.

The road descended across the face of the mountain and made its way back to the river just above the falls, then followed the river to a large lake shaped like a kidney bean that dominated the center of the valley: Lake Glimmermere, if Julian remembered his maps correctly. Still except for the wakes from a number of boats making way around the lake, the water reflected the mountains on the other side of the valley with near-pristine clarity.

Off to the north of the lake, the valley was wooded all the way up into the mountains. To the south, a few copses punctuated the rolling hills, but for the most part there was only grassland except for a narrow spur of mountains that pushed north almost to the shore of the lake. Two rivers flowed into the lake: one from the north and one from the east. A number of what Julian assumed were farming hamlets clustered in the grasslands surrounding the eastern river. Almost directly opposite the two men on the other side of the valley, Holbart's Pass led away off to the northeast.

But the thing that truly drew Julian's eye was the fair-sized town on the north shore of the lake. A sprawling collection of buildings large and small surrounding a half-dozen piers that protruded into the lake like the fingers of some great grasping hand, the town of Lydelton might as well have been the most opulent metropolis in the world. Down there were warm Inns, home cooked meals, and wenches aplenty. He could hardly wait to get there.

"Glimmer Vale," Raedrick said in a soft tone. "I've not been here in years."

"Looks like a nice enough place."

Raedrick nodded. "The people are friendly and hospitable, and they have a local recipe for the fish from the lake that is to die for."

"Then what are we waiting for?" Julian spurred his horse to motion and began the descent. Behind him, he heard Raedrick chuckle before doing the same.

Going down was faster than coming up. Before long, they reached the base of the mountain. The road met the river a few hundred yards above the lip of the falls, near a small copse of evergreens. The river was narrow there, maybe a hundred feet across, but flowed swiftly toward the dropoff. Julian was struck by how much quieter it was here than down below. Oh, the falls' roar was still plain to hear, but it was nowhere near as deafening as it had been on the other side.

"I guess the Gorge makes it louder," he murmured to himself, earning a curious glance from Raedrick. Julian shrugged in response and gestured toward the falls.

Raedrick nodded. "A good thing, too. Can you imagine trying to live next to all that racket?"

Julian shuddered.

The road ran into the copse about twenty feet from the rocks overhanging the river. It was a pleasant change from the bare rock of the last couple days, and Julian found himself grinning as they passed beneath the trees' canopy. The smell of pine was soothing, reminding him of pleasant days from his past. He lost himself in enjoyment for a moment.

Which made the harsh voice that barked out at them all the more unpleasant.

"That's far enough. Stop right there."

Julian shook himself back to attention and groaned. Half a dozen men stepped out from behind the trees lining the road ahead. They were unshaven, wearing dirty cloaks and leggings that had seen better days. But they also had on what looked like high-quality leather breastplates that were lined with iron studs, leather gauntlets and bracers, and greaves on their shins. Five of them arranged themselves in a loose arc in the road ahead, while the sixth stood a few feet back and, nocking an arrow to his bowstring, drew back and sighted in on them.

Brigands.

Julian and Raedrick reined in their horses, and a burly man with a vicious-looking scar on his chin who stood in the center of the ring of five spoke. From his voice, he was the same man who spoke before. That made him the leader. "Your money or your life, boys," he said.

Nice welcome.

❧ 2 ☙

A WARM WELCOME

Julian and Raedrick shared a brief look. This was annoyance they did not need. Julian raised one eyebrow and began inching his hand down toward the pommel of his sword, which hung in its baldric from his saddle horn, a far more comfortable place to keep it while riding than on his hip. Plus, it was easier to draw from there.

Raedrick saw the movement and gave a slight shake of his head. He always wanted to try to talk first. Of course, considering the numbers in this particular encounter, Julian couldn't really blame him much. He pulled his hand back and looked back at the brigands, waiting for Raedrick to take the lead.

"We don't have much money," Raedrick said.

A loud snort was the brigand leader's initial reply. "And yer gonna have a lot less. Hand it over!"

Raedrick sighed and looked back at Julian again. With a shrug, he said, "Alright. Hand it over, Julian."

Julian wore a small pouch tied to his belt. Moving very slowly, he untied it and held it up for the brigands to see. It was filled to overflowing. The leader's expression changed to one of satisfaction. The fellow to his right, wearing an expression of open greed, stepped forward and reached out for it.

"Here you are," Julian said and moved to toss it to the fellow. He breathed a curse as he apparently lost his grip earlier than he planned and, instead of landing in the brigand's hand, the pouch flopped onto the ground near Julian's horse's feet. "Sorry about that." He managed a sheepish grin.

The brigand bounded forward and bent over to collect the pouch at the same time as his leader shouted, "No, you idiot!"

The brigand stood back up, Julian's pouch in his hand, and looked back at the leader for a heartbeat. That was the opening Julian was looking for. He kicked with his left foot, catching the brigand square in the face as he was returning his gaze back to Julian.

With a crunch of breaking bone, the brigand went down, clutching at his nose and jaw.

There was a moment's shocked pause while the other brigands looked wild-eyed at their comrade. Julian drove his heels into his horse's side, urging him into a run. The gelding bounded forward, but only made it a few feet. A second brigand, more quick to recover than the others, grabbed at the horse's bridle and pulled for all he was worth. The world lurched beneath Julian as the horse stumbled and then began to fall.

He cursed again as he launched himself out of the saddle and off to the side. Tucking his shoulder as he hit the ground, Julian rolled to his feet and drew his belt knife. Then he spun around.

Raedrick was on his feet, laying about with his saber. The brigand Julian had kicked was still down. Another had fallen beneath Raedrick's blade, and the brigand he faced wore an expression of panic as he parried, then ducked, then leapt backwards away from Raedrick's relentlessly fluid assault. Julian almost felt sorry for the man, having been on the receiving end of Raedrick's fencing prowess more than once in the sparring circle. Almost.

The archer was nowhere to be seen, though a single arrow was buried deep into a tree trunk not far from where Julian stood. Hopefully Raedrick had taken him out, or they were in trouble. But Julian didn't have the time to look around for him, as the brigand who grabbed his gelding was charging at him, followed by the scar-faced leader of the brigands.

Julian adjusted his grip on the knife and settled into a loose, ready stance. He forced down a surge of fear as his fighter's mind calculated the odds of survival for a man who brought a knife to a sword fight. They were not good, in his experience.

Then the brigand reached him and, drawing his arm back, attacked with a powerful cut from Julian's left to right. It probably would have spilled his guts, but Julian bounded forward inside the brigand's swing.

The brigand's sword arm struck Julian in the ribs and he wrapped his left arm around it, pinning it in place.

At the same time, Julian stabbed upward with his knife. The brigand wore an expression of disbelief as the blade entered his neck, severing his carotid artery and trachea. Julian withdrew the knife and the brigand fell to the ground, spasming out the last of his life.

Ten feet away, Scarface came up short, his expression suddenly a mix of wariness and eager anticipation. Behind him, Raedrick was nowhere to be seen, though Julian heard the noise of more fighting somewhere off to the left.

The leader of the brigands smiled, his grin causing the puckered scar on his chin to expand. For a second, Julian thought sure it was going to swallow the other man's face whole, it grew so large.

"This could be fun," Scarface said. "Pick up the sword." His voice was steady and calm despite the grin of excitement on his face. He gestured with his sword point toward his comrade's weapon, now lying at Julian's feet.

What was this? Either Scarface was very confident or very stupid. Or maybe both. But Julian wasn't about to question the sudden generosity. Slowly he lowered into a crouch and, replacing his knife into its sheath, he took hold of the sword.

Scarface came on in a rush, his weapon singing through the air as it descended toward Julian's neck.

Desperately parrying upward, Julian flung himself away from the assault. The clang of steel striking steel was still in the air as he completed a full backward roll and rose to his feet.

Just in time to meet a second attack from the brigand leader.

Another quick retreat left the cut to whistle harmlessly through the air.

Julian tried to counterattack, but Scarface's assault was relentless and he found himself driven backward again. And again. The man was good!

Parry, dodge, retreat.

Julian gave up more ground, and found himself leaving the copse and treading on the bare rock near the riverbank. Bending his knees to avoid a high cut, he attempted a riposte.

Somehow Scarface's high cut became a descending parry that knocked the thrust aside. Then Julian found the wind driven from his lungs as the brigand leader spun around and drove the heel on his boot into Julian's lower ribs.

He tumbled to the ground, unable to breathe and awash with pain from his ribs. He felt as much as heard Scarface's blade descending toward him and forced himself to roll over and raise his own sword.

Steel met steel again as the force of the cut's momentum drove the two hilts together in the air above Julian's body.

For a moment, the two men looked at each other through the frame of their entwined blades. Finally able to draw a breath, Julian saw that Scarface had barely broken a sweat and was breathing normally. He smirked, a mocking twist of the lips that carried no small amount of disdain, and leaned in, driving the two blades slowly downward despite Julian pushing upwards with all his strength.

"Ready to die?" he asked.

Julian knew he wasn't going to be able to keep the sword from falling for much longer. Already his arms were shaking from the strain of resisting.

Julian abruptly stopped fighting it and rolled with the force of Scarface's push, driving the swords to the ground beside himself. At the same time he kicked upward and to the side, catching Scarface on his hip. Now it was the brigand leader's turn to tumble to the ground.

In the brief respite, Julian bounded to his feet and backed away, gingerly feeling at his ribs with his left hand. The brigand leader flipped to his feet easily and assumed a ready stance, his blade held loosely in both hands with the tip pointing at Julian's eyes. He inclined his head in salute for a moment, the mocking smirk gone from his face.

Then he attacked again, and again Julian was driven back.

He gave ground with each exchange and only avoided severe injury on one occasion because of the mail shirt he wore. All the same, he accumulated several small cuts where his parry or dodge wasn't quite fast enough.

Scarface remained untouched.

The roar of the falls was louder now. Between parries, Julian glanced over his shoulder and was shocked to see that he had retreated almost all the way to the edge of the river, only twenty yards or so from the drop off.

The glance cost him. Julian barely hopped back from another attack, but still took a deep cut in his thigh. He was running out of time and space, and now his balance was off as his thigh protested every movement. Julian attempted another counter, a rising cut toward the brigand leader's armpit.

He found his eyes growing wide with surprise as Scarface executed a highly stylized, spiraling parry that ended with the tip of his sword hooking beneath Julian's hilt. A flick of Scarface's wrists pulled the sword from Julian's hand and left him with a deep cut in the meat of his thumb.

The sword clattered away somewhere off to the right. Stunned, Julian took a half-step back and raised his hands. This couldn't be happening!

The brigand leader sneered and snapped off a quick salute with his sword. "Well fought," he said before he began to move forward.

Frantic, Julian retreated again. Wait. Raedrick, where was Raedrick! Julian looked back toward the copse, but there was still no sign of his friend.

Scarface swung at him, and Julian leaned far backwards to avoid a cut that would have taken his head off. All the same, he felt the tip of the sword cut a line across the bridge of his nose.

He stumbled back and suddenly found he had nowhere else to go as his heels reached the edge of the rocks overhanging the river. Pinwheeling his arms for a moment to regain his balance, Julian glanced down at the swirling, frigid water as it rushed to the lip of the falls.

This was it. He never once imagined it would end this way.

He looked up again just as Scarface attacked with a backhanded swing that was again headed for his head.

In desperation, Julian moved forward and raised his right arm. Scarface's wrist struck the bones of his forearm.

Julian cupped his hand over the brigand leader's wrist and drove his palm upwards toward the back of his elbow.

The sharp CRACK of breaking bone preceded Scarface's scream of surprise and pain by a heartbeat. His hand spasmed open, dropping the sword at Julian's feet, and his eyes went wide with shock, then wider still with dread as Julian pivoted about his rear foot and, using the arm as a lever, hurled the brigand leader over the edge of the rocks.

His arms and legs flailed at the empty air for a second, then the brigand leader splashed into the river. He bobbed to the surface quickly, but just as quickly began to sink again. Heavy boots and armor made swimming difficult, Julian thought with a certain satisfaction. He watched as Scarface splashed with his one good arm, trying with all his might to avoid being pulled under.

"Help me!" Scarface cried, to whom Julian couldn't guess since *he* certainly had no intention of lending a hand.

The current swept the hapless man toward the drop off. His swimming attempts became more frantic as he looked with horror toward the approaching edge.

"Help! Please!" he screamed.

Then he reached the edge and dropped out of sight. His last long scream of despair carried over the falls' roar for a moment, but was quickly overwhelmed.

"Well fought," Julian said.

$\maltese$ 3 $\maltese$

GLIMMER VALE

Julian limped back to the ambush site and found Raedrick tying up the bandit Julian kicked at the beginning of the fray. He didn't have a scratch on him, naturally. As Julian approached, Raedrick looked up and, upon seeing his condition, winced.

"You look like hell."

"Feel like it, too," Julian said. "Where did you go?"

"This guy hightailed it. You looked like you had things under control, so I went after him."

"Don't do that again. I really could have used the help."

Raedrick gave him a long, searching look, then nodded. "Sorry."

Hobbling over to his horse, Julian fished through the saddlebags until he found his medical supplies. Consisting of a few rags for bandages and a needle and thread, it wasn't much, but it would be sufficient for this job. "My leg and thumb are going to need stitches before we move out," he said.

Raedrick did the stitching once he had the prisoner secured.

Getting stitched up was never a fun experience, but having to lie there without pants in the chilly air just made it worse. The cold numbed Julian's leg a bit, so the stitching itself wasn't as unpleasant, but taken as a whole, Julian would have preferred to do the deed in warmth. Fortunately, Raedrick was a good hand with a needle, so before too long he finished stitching and wrapped both wounds in snug bandages. Julian got dressed again and took a few ginger steps. The stitches seemed to hold well, but he would have to take it easy for a few days.

They took a few minutes to search the dead brigands. Julian was not surprised to find they had little money on them. But their armor and weapons were of good quality and would probably fetch a decent price, so he and Raedrick strapped those items down on their horses as well as they could. Their saddlebags were already full, so it was a very awkward packing job, but it would do for a short journey.

"What are we going to do with him?" Julian said, nodding toward their prisoner. "I'd say tie him to a tree and leave him for scavengers."

The brigand's eyes widened and he shook his head vigorously, but before he could speak Raedrick beat him to it.

"No. There's a Constable in Lydelton. He'll see that justice is done properly."

Julian frowned. "That's still a long way."

"About four, maybe five hours."

"We'd better get moving then if we want to get there before dark."

Raedrick nodded. While Julian slowly pulled himself up onto his saddle, his friend fished a length of rope out of his bag and tied one end into a knot around the brigand's neck. The other end he brought back to Julian. "Do you want the duty?"

Julian grinned and accepted the rope. Removing his baldric, he looped the rope around his saddle horn, making several turns to ensure it was secure. Then he draped the baldric over the saddle horn again and looked back at the brigand. "Hope you are a good runner, friend."

It was perhaps heartless, but Julian got a lot of satisfaction from the brigand's terrified expression.

They set off at a slow trot, just barely above a jog, but after a half hour or so Julian heard a thud behind them, and the brigand began screaming. Reining in to a walk, he turned around to find the fellow dragging on the ground behind his horse. Julian rolled his eyes and pulled his horse to a full stop.

"I figured he'd be in better shape," he quipped to Raedrick, who shrugged. In a louder voice, Julian called back to the brigand, "On your feet! You're slowing us down!"

The brigand slowly pushed himself upright. It took a while, but Julian figured it was probably difficult with his hands tied behind his back. Beyond that, he was a mess. The right side of his face was scraped and bruised, his clothing was torn in several locations, he had a big red welt around his neck where the rope dug in, and he was panting heavily. Served him right.

As soon as the brigand was up again, Julian spurred the horse forward, at a walk this time. It was slower, but he had no real desire to torture the brigand to death. Killing a man in a stand-up fight was one thing. Dragging him behind a horse? That crossed the line into senseless cruelty.

The road followed the south bank of the river as it made its way east toward the Lake. Though the terrain to their right was mostly rolling hills, the road was, for the most part, level and made for an easy passage. So despite only moving at a quick walk, they made good time.

As they traversed the valley, Julian was again struck by the picturesque nature of the place. Everywhere he looked was another amazing view. When Raedrick told him of his plan to take this route, he had at first scoffed. Lydelton was a flyspeck of a town in the middle of nowhere. Why would anyone want to visit, let alone live there? Now that he had seen the valley, though, he was beginning to understand how it could be appealing.

If only it was warmer.

As advertised from their high vantage point on the flank of the mountain, this part of the valley was mostly rolling grasslands, punctuated every so often with the occasional copse, some large enough to almost be rightly called forests themselves.

There was no habitation as yet, but plumes of smoke in the distance announced fires from chimneys or forges.

After a couple hours, they drew near to the spit of mountains they had seen from above. The road became more wandering, to avoid the worst of the hills, as the mountains drew nearer. Until finally there was nothing for it but to go nearly straight up one side of a hill and down the next. The mountains came almost to the river; the main peaks could not have been more than a mile to the south. But from this vantage point, Julian could see that the peaks, which thrust northward from the main range to the south, bent to the east for a while before turning south again.

"The local's call this area The Hook," Raedrick said, seeing Julian eyeing the mountains as they rode. "Supposedly if you look at a quality map of this part of the Vale, the line of peaks forms a hook that bends off to the east and makes its own little concealed valley within a valley."

"Impressive," Julian replied.

Past The Hook, the land slowly flattened again until, by the time they reached the southeast corner of the lake, the hills were mostly gone. There, they began to see the first farmsteads. A single farmhouse here, a small cluster there, at first they were few and far between, but as the afternoon wore on, they became more frequent. All as he would have expected.

Then, about an hour and a half before sunset, not far from a ford across the river that flowed down to the lake form the mountains to the east, they encountered a farm that had been burned out. It had happened several days earlier based on the lack of smoldering and the general state of the place, but it was clear that the burning was not an accident. The front door was cloven in two as though by an axe or sword. Peeking inside, the remains of a large table had distinctive cut marks, as did one chair that somehow escaped the fire and stood pristinely in the midst of the destruction.

But the confirmation came when they stopped, at Raedrick's urging, to investigate the ruins more closely. There, within the husk of the burned house, lay two charred bodies: one larger and one small. The larger body, the mother Julian presumed, was clutching the smaller body as though to shield it from the flames and smoke. He supposed the fact that two people perished didn't rule out an accident. Until they then found a man's corpse, beheaded with his hands tied behind his back, in a small ditch not far behind the house.

"Hopefully they killed him first," Raedrick said, his tone carrying the same revulsion that Julian felt. "Can you imagine if they'd made him listen to his wife and child screaming inside the house before finishing him?"

"Who would do this?" Julian asked aloud. He looked back at their prisoner and found him close-mouthed, unwilling to look even in the same general area as the bodies. "Do you know, friend?" Julian asked, tugging at the rope as he did so.

The brigand jerked and turned a baleful eye on him. "Not a clue," he replied in an oily tone that just screamed the man was lying.

"Oh you know alright," Julian said. "Friends of yours, weren't they? Did they brag about it?" Anger began to well up within him and he found his voice rising. "Or did you go along for the ride, to have a little fun? Did you enjoy it, you sick bastard?" He began walking his horse back toward the brigand as he spoke. The brigand's expression grew frightened, then terrified, as Julian approached.

"Enough, Julian. He'll get justice from the Constable," Raedrick growled as he spurred his horse in front of Julian. "Remember?"

Julian took a long, deep breath to get himself back under control. After a moment, he nodded to Raedrick and turned his horse away. "Then let's get moving. The sooner we dump this fellow off, the better."

❦   4   ❦

LYDELTON

As they rode into Lydelton, Julian was surprised to find the road paved. He had expected dirt streets, or at best cobblestones, but the main street into the town was paved with what looked like squares of flagstone.

"How did this happen?" he asked Raedrick.

The other man shrugged. "There's a rock quarry a little ways up in the mountains east of here. Back before I first came here, some folks got the idea to use some of that rock to pave the streets. They only got the main street done before deciding it was too much effort, or something."

Julian chuckled.

But his humor faded quickly as he looked from the paving stones to the people in the town. A dozen, maybe twenty, townsfolk were walking the main street as their horses began clopping down the road. One and all turned toward the sound of the horses' hooves with expressions of dread. A woman nearby clutched her small child and pulled him close as though unwilling to let him come near them. The weight of all those fearful eyes was nerve racking.

"What gives? I thought you said these people were friendly?"

Raedrick shook his head slowly. "I've no idea." Turning his gaze toward a young man, barely old enough to need to shave more than every other day, who had stopped in the street not far from them, he nodded in greeting and smiled. "Hello there. Can you point us toward the Constable's office?"

The young man blinked and for a moment looked as though he was going to bolt. But then he looked from Raedrick's smile to the brigand trailing behind them, and the rope tied around his neck, and he swallowed then answered. "Three blocks down, then make a right. First building on the left." He paused for a moment as though unsure of himself, then spoke again. "You're not with...him...are you." Gesturing toward the bound brigand, his voice sounded almost hopeful.

Julian snorted.

"Him?" Raedrick replied. "He and a few others tried to rob us on the road here. We're taking him to the Constable for justice. His friends weren't so lucky."

The young man's eyes widened and a large grin spread across his face. Looking around, Julian could see the tension leave the other people on the street in a flood. As they spurred their horses forward and moved on down the street, the eyes continued to follow them, but the murmur of hushed discussions sprang up among the townsfolk as well. Julian caught the word "heroes" a few times. What was that all about?

They found the Constable's office right where the young man said it was. Just off the main street, on a side street that was paved, if that was the right word for it, with assorted rocks and gravel, it was a small, functional place. Short stairs led to a porch and a wide set of double doors at the front of the building. A simple sign, reading "Constable", hung over the door.

"Looks like this is it," Raedrick quipped as he dismounted and tied his horse off on a hitching post in front of the building.

"You are a master of the obvious," Julian replied with a grin.

He made quick work tying his horse off. Then he grabbed his baldric from around his saddle horn and, donning it, walked over to the brigand. "Time to face the music, friend," he said as he untied the knot around the brigand's neck.

The rope dropped to the ground and for a second Julian thought the brigand was going to try to make a run for it, no matter how exhausted and beaten-down he was. But with his hands bound and the pair of them ready to chase him down he wouldn't get far. Apparently he knew it, because his shoulders, already slumped from fatigue, drooped further and his gaze lowered to the ground, defeated.

Julian grabbed him by the arm and pulled him toward the building. "Let's go."

Raedrick led the way, swinging the doors open to allow Julian and the brigand to follow easily. Inside was a simple office. Two desks, one on either side of the room facing each other, and a pair of benches on either side of the entrance were the only furnishings. Mounted on the wall behind one of the desks was a rack holding a small collection of swords. A similar rack holding several unstrung bows and an equal number of full quivers hung behind the other. A pair of lamps on wall mounts burned merrily, adding light to the room. A door made of iron bars was set in the wall directly across from the entrance. Julian could see a number of other, similar barred doors in the corridor beyond. Holding cells, no doubt.

A slender man of medium height, with a narrow face and unruly hair the color of hay, sat behind the desk on the left, reviewing a leather-bound ledger. He looked up at once, his eyes widening in surprise, as they walked in. He collected himself quickly, closing the ledger and standing up to greet them.

"Gentlemen. What can I do for you?"

"You the Constable?" Raedrick asked.

The man shook his head. "I'm Deputy Fendig. Constable Malory is off dealing with an issue right now."

"Good enough. This man," Julian pushed the brigand forward as Raedrick gestured toward him, "and several others tried to rob us on the road earlier today. We've brought him here for justice."

Fendig did a double-take and looked the brigand up and down. "Is that right," he said quietly.

There was a long silence as Julian and Raedrick looked at each other. Something very odd was going on, Julian thought.

"That's right," Raedrick said slowly as he looked back at Fendig. "About an hour after noon on the road just above Silver Falls. He and five other..."

"*Five?*"

"Yeah, five," Julian replied.

Fendig looked doubtful, but he nodded. "Alright." Moving back over to his desk, he pulled open one of the drawers and removed a large iron ring hung with a number of keys. As he stepped past them and unlocked the door to the cell block, he said, "Bring him along."

They followed Fendig into the cell block. Once inside, Julian saw it contained eight cells, four on each side of the corridor. They were all unoccupied. Each cell had a pair of cots and a bucket, no doubt to use as a chamber pot. Narrow windows, too small for a man to squeeze through, let in light. It would be paltry even at noon, but now with dusk coming on the light was virtually non-existent. Only a pair of lamps mounted at either end of the corridor provided illumination. Fendig led them to the last cell on the right and opened the door. It squeaked on its hinges, making Julian wonder how long ago it had been used last.

"In here," Fendig said, gesturing toward the cell.

Raedrick, who was bringing up the rear, stepped forward and pulled out his knife. A quick cut removed the rope that bound the brigand's hands. Then Julian shoved him forward.

He stumbled into the cell and fell over onto a cot. For a moment, he just lay there. Then he turned over and sat up. Rubbing his wrists to help restore circulation, the man looked up at Fendig.

"If I were you, I'd think hard about letting me go, Deputy," he said. "I'm with Farzal."

Fendig went pale, and he swallowed audibly. But his voice was steady when he spoke. "That'll be up to the Constable," he said, and he shut the door and locked it. The brigand chuckled softly, a laugh of sadistic amusement.

As Fendig walked back to the front office, Julian lingered for a moment to study the prisoner. He did not look half as defeated as he had outside, when he was in Julian and Raedrick's custody.

Back in the front office, Fendig pulled out another ledger and dipped his quill into an inkwell on his desk.

"I'll need your names and where you're staying in town. The..."

"Who or what is Farzal?" Julian asked.

Fendig paused, his quill poised over the paper. Then he sighed and looked up at the two of them. "A band of outlaws has been making trouble in these parts for the last month or so. From their look, they're mostly deserters from the army. Small wonder they turned to thieving, right? Men like that will do anything. Farzal's their leader."

"You're afraid of them," Raedrick said, his tone flat with disapproval.

"Of course not. He's all bluster, that's all." Even if his body language and expression hadn't screamed that he was lying, the speed of Fendig's reply made it plain as day. "Now then, as I said I'll need your names and where you're staying in town. Constable Malory will want to talk to you about this incident."

"Does Molli Millens still run The Oarlock down by the docks?" asked Raedrick.

Fendig looked surprised again, but he nodded. "Yes. Has been for years."

"We'll be staying there."

Raedrick and Julian gave their names, and Fendig thanked them and showed them out with promises that the Constable would contact them first thing in the morning to take their statements.

As the office doors swung shut behind them, Julian shook his head. "Three to one that guy releases our boy before dawn. I'm amazed he even locked him up. Probably wouldn't have if we weren't there."

"I don't know," replied Raedrick. He looked as troubled as Julian felt. "Nothing we can do about it though. Let's go get settled and warm up."

It was hard to argue with that idea.

THE OARLOCK

The Oarlock turned out to be a fair-sized Inn a block and a half away from the docks. Two stories tall, it was a simple building, and far from new, but it had obviously been well-maintained over the years by a very conscientious owner. A simple sign, showing a bearded man in foul weather gear pulling on the oars of a rowboat in rough seas with the Inn's name written in the waves, hung from a wrought-iron stanchion on the street.

Raedrick needed no directions to find it. He led Julian to the Inn's stables as quickly as if he had been going between the Constable's office and the Inn every day for his whole life. Julian thought he knew what made Raedrick tick after all the time they had spent together at the front, but his familiarity with the Vale and its inhabitants had come as a surprise. He reminded himself to ask about it after they were settled and nursing a tankard.

The interior was not very much different from any other Inn Julian had visited. A long wooden bar rested along the wall to his right as he walked inside. Tables with chairs for four lay scattered around the room, and there were a half dozen booths built into the wall to his left. A set of swinging doors in the back no doubt led into the kitchen and a stairwell in the left rear corner led upstairs. Two fireplaces, one in each of the front corners, provided warmth and some light. About two dozen customers sat around the various tables or on stools at the bar. One table in particular, in the right rear corner of the taproom, was particularly popular. Seven men and a lone woman clustered around it. A dice game, unless Julian missed his guess. Two powerfully built men sat on stools at either end of the bar. The fact that they were facing away from the taps and toward the rest of the room screamed that they were bouncers.

Raedrick made a beeline for the bar. Julian followed more slowly.

The bartender was a balding man in his early middle years. He had the bland look of a man who had listened to enough drunkards to no longer pay any mind to what they have to say. Raedrick waved at him, but he took his time in coming over.

When he finally arrived, the bartender looked Raedrick, then Julian, up and down and sniffed.

"Looking for a room, eh boys?"

Raedrick looked around the room again before answering. "Is Molli here tonight?"

The bartender nodded. "She is. She's dealing with something right now, though, but I can set you up."

Raedrick shook his head. "We'll wait for her, thanks."

The bartender shrugged and turned away. That wouldn't do at all. Julian spoke up. "We'll take a drink while we wait."

"Yeah? What'll it be?" The bartender sounded annoyed. His expression as he looked back at them over his shoulder confirmed it.

Julian said, "Mulled wine." He glanced at Raedrick and added, "Two of them."

The bartender nodded and moved away to the center of the bar, where several tapped casks sat on their sides. He returned a short time later with two steaming tankards and sat them down on the bar in front of Raedrick. "Two pennies," he said.

Raedrick fished a couple coins from his pouch and paid the man, then handed one of the tankards to Julian. The aroma of the mulling spices combined with the wine's natural nose made Julian's mouth water, and he suddenly realized how hungry he was. Not surprising considering their small, hurried lunch earlier. "Probably ought to get some dinner, too," he said before taking a drink. The wine was just as good as he anticipated, bringing a smile to his lips.

"Yes, definitely. But first I'd like to..."

Raedrick broke off as a portly woman with grey hair tied in a bun atop her head stepped into the room from the kitchens. She wore a simple dress with a bright white apron over top and took a moment to survey the taproom before heading over to the bar. She conferred with the bartender for a moment. He gestured down the bar toward Julian and Raedrick and she looked over at them, her expression one of curiosity. Then she said something else, which the bartender acknowledged with a nod, and made her way toward them. She stopped along the way to exchange pleasantries with a group of customers and was still chuckling from something they said when she reached Julian and Raedrick. Wiping her hands on her apron, she looked them up and down for a moment before speaking.

"I'm Molli. What can I do for you?"

"We're looking for a room..." Julian began, but Raedrick cut him off.

"You may not remember, but you used to do business with my father. Roland Baletier?"

"Baletier." Molli repeated the name slowly, as though she was tasting every syllable. Then her eyes widened. "Woodworker who traveled with Crispin Thunderly." She smiled, a broad grin that changed her expression from severe and businesslike to warm and inviting. "Why, you wouldn't be little Raedrick would you?" At his nod, she laughed and clapped him on his arms then pulled him in for a hug. "Well look at you, boy. All grown up! What brings you back through these parts?"

"Heading home from the front."

Molli's mirth faded. "Well. I'm glad you're able to. I've heard it's brutal out on the front lines."

She had no idea, Julian though. If she knew half of what had happened out there... Well, she didn't, and he had no intention of describing it. Neither did

Raedrick, apparently, as he simply shrugged and looked away. Julian knew him well enough to recognize the guarded expression that hinted at emotion ready to burst out in a torrent.

Clearing his throat, Julian said, "Mistress Millens, I'm Julian Hinderbrook," and offered her his hand.

Molli turned to him and shook his hand with a warm smile. "My pleasure, Julian. Call me Molli. You and Raedrick know each other from the Army, I assume?"

"Yes, ma'am. We finished with the Army at the same time, and he told me so many good things about Mol Teribor that I decided to come along to see what the fuss was about."

"Is that where your father keeps himself these days?" she asked, looking back at Raedrick. "I haven't heard from him in...ten years? Fifteen? I hope he's well."

Raedrick had his emotions under control again. He smiled and made a dismissive gesture. "He always finds a way to do well. I haven't heard from him in six months or so, but last I heard he was on the verge of making a killing in some business deal or other."

Shaking her head, Molli laughed merrily. "That sounds like him." Stepping back, she looked them over again. "Well. Looks like you two could use a bath, a meal, and a bed. You're in luck: I have one more room empty. Follow me."

Molli led them up the staircase at the back of the taproom. It was a tough climb, with every step painfully straining the stitches in Julian's thigh. He took his time, but even still he wasn't at all certain he hadn't pulled some of the stitches out by the time he reached the top. Molli eyed him askance as he stepped, breathing hard from the pain, off the landing.

"A strapping young man like you shouldn't have so much trouble with one flight of stairs," she quipped. "What's wrong with your leg?"

"Brigands on the road," he replied through gritted teeth. "Got me in the thigh."

Molli's eyes narrowed as she looked down at Julian's leg. "Where did this happen?"

"Just above the falls," Raedrick replied. "We brought one of them in to the Constable before we came here."

Molli mumbled something under her breath. Julian was not really surprised to hear a few salty curses in there, ladylike or not. She did run a tavern, after all. More loudly, she said, "Farzal's bunch?" They nodded. "Figures. Well, you're safe now. Come on."

She set off down the hall, leaving Julian and Raedrick to look quizzically at each other.

"That was awfully fatalistic," Julian said.

Raedrick nodded. "The Molli I remember was no-nonsense. Wouldn't tolerate trouble from anyone." His eyes moved to follow Molli as she moved down the hall. "First the deputy and now Molli. Who *is* this Farzal fellow?"

"Dunno. But it's not our problem, is it?" Julian limped down the hall after Molli. He glanced over his shoulder several paces on. Raedrick hadn't moved from an inch, and he wore a very troubled expression.

Their room was all the way at the end of the hall on the left, just before the hall made a turn to the right. It was about the same as every other room Julian had ever rented out. It had two narrow beds against the wall on opposite sides of the room, a locking chest at the foot of each bed, a chest of drawers beneath the window, a hanging wardrobe in one corner, and a washbasin and mirror in the other. The window was curtained and constructed so the lower half could be opened outward. All in all, not too bad.

Molli smiled apologetically as she showed them the room. "I wish my premium rooms were available for you boys," she said, "but they were rented out two days ago. I hope this will be ok?"

"It's perfect, ma'am," Julian said. Raedrick echoed him, and Molli smiled a bit more broadly.

"The baths are across the hall, and the privy is around the corner," she said. "When you've cleaned up, come downstairs and I'll have dinner ready for you."

"Thank you, Molli," Raedrick said.

"It's great to see you again," she replied. She turned to leave, but before closing the door behind her, she looked over her shoulder and gave Raedrick a conspiratorial look. "Don't be too long. Lani should be back soon, and I know she'll want to catch up."

Molli pulled the door shut. The click of the latch sounded solid and, for some reason, comforting.

Julian tossed his saddlebag onto his bed and began removing his belongings from the pouches. "Who's Lani?" he asked.

Raedrick was still looking at the door. At Julian's words, he gave a start then, smiling abashedly, set about unpacking. "She's Molli's daughter. We used to play together when my father and I came through here. She used to say I was her best friend." He paused for a moment. "I always liked her, but..." Raedrick looked over at Julian and shrugged. "She was also a bit odd. I didn't understand how I could be her best friend, since we came through so infrequently."

Julian shrugged. "Girls are hard to understand sometimes."

"That's an understatement."

"I thought you said your father owned a ranch in the hills above Mol Teribor. How did you come to pass through here so often?"

Raedrick paused again. "He does now. For a long time, though, he made his living as a woodworker. He made high quality tools, furniture, and toys that his friend Crispin sold from city to city. After my mother died, he couldn't bear to stay in our town anymore. So he convinced Crispin that they could make more money if he joined the caravan and made his products continually on the road. And he was right. The money flowed like never before. But more than money, we made many great friends, like Molli and Lani. Of course, we eventually got tired of traveling all the time. In truth, I think he tired of it before I did." Chuckling softly, Raedrick looked back at Julian and grinned. "But that might be because he met a lovely young widow whose late husband was a big-time rancher."

Julian chuckled as well. "I can understand that. Glad to hear it all worked out."

Raedrick nodded. "It did."

NIGHT LIFE

After a bath, Julian felt much better. The previous few weeks had been draining, and had filled him with tension he almost hadn't realized. To say nothing of grime from the road and his physical injuries. He could have soaked all night and to blazes with going back down to the taproom, but eventually the bath water cooling and his stomach growling forced him to get up.

Raedrick had already finished dressing and gone back downstairs when Julian returned to their room from the baths, so he lingered just long enough to change out his bandages and don a fresh set of clothes before heading downstairs himself.

It was a lot easier on his leg going down than coming up. No big surprise there.

He found Raedrick sitting at a table not far from the bar with Molli and a pretty blonde-haired girl. They spied him as he approached and waved him over with a trio of smiles. As he took a seat at the table, Raedrick spoke in an excited voice.

"Julian, this is Lani Millens, Molli's daughter."

Lani was even prettier up close than she had been from afar. She was not terribly tall, best as he could tell with her sitting down, but her warm smile, rosy cheeks, full bosom, and intelligent gaze was enchanting. Julian smiled broadly as he shook hands with her and brought his lips down to the back of her hand.

"The pleasure is all mine," he said.

Lani giggled, glancing aside at Raedrick. "You weren't kidding," she said in a melodic alto.

Julian looked askance at his friend. "What did you say to her?"

"Only that you're a rascal who likes to flirt," Molli said.

"Great. Well, that's not true." He smiled a bit more broadly. "I'm not at all a rascal."

Both ladies laughed merrily for a moment, then Molli stood up.

"I'll go check on dinner. It should be ready by now. Please make yourself comfortable, Julian. Tonight's on me."

That was music to his ears.

Dinner was outstanding. Braised beef atop seasoned rice, with steaming bread fresh from the oven and a very nice bottle of wine from the Pyreen Valley, followed by a large slice of a kind of cake Julian had never eaten before. It was unbelievably delicious, though, and was a fitting end to the meal.

Conversation was muted at first, since Julian and Raedrick were both famished and did little more than shovel food down their throats. But eventually, after the plates were all pushed aside, the talk picked up a bit.

Unfortunately for Julian, however, the conversation quickly degenerated into Raedrick and Lani exchanging cherished anecdotes from their childhood dalliance. Or whatever it was. Julian quickly began to feel that his presence was no longer needed, especially after Molli left to tend to business, so he begged off to run to the privy. Neither Raedrick nor Lani objected.

In truth, he *was* feeling the call of nature. But when he returned to the taproom after satisfying that particular need, he looked over at the table and saw the two of them engrossed in conversation and lost in each others' eyes, and he turned away toward the bar. Far be it for him to block his friend's chance to do well with a pretty lady.

Julian slid onto a stool next to an older man in a faded wool cloak and tried to flag down the bartender. The man was busy at the far end of the bar, though, so Julian was forced to wait.

"You're one of them two newcomers, the ones who brought the thief in this evening, right?" The man sitting next to him had turned to look at him, and addressed him in a tone of friendly curiosity.

"Sure am. Julian." He held out his hand and received a good firm handshake in response.

"Horace. Damn good to meet you, boy. 'Bout time someone did something about them scumbags."

"It's wasn't much, really. Just defending ourselves is all."

Horace snorted. "Way I hear tell, you two boys fought off a dozen of them bandits without taking a scratch. Don't sound like nothing to me."

Julian looked incredulously at him for a moment, then burst out laughing. "First of all, there were six. Secondly," he gestured toward his thigh, then held up his bandaged right hand and pointed to his nose, "I took more than a couple scratches. Now, my friend over there," he nodded in Raedrick's direction, "he got off without a hitch. But I had the tougher task in that fight."

Horace snorted again. "Well, whatever. Point is, you boys did real good, and I'm proud to know you."

"Thanks, Horace. I appreciate that."

The bartender finally made it over to Julian, and he ordered another tankard of mulled wine. But when the bartender brought the drink, Horace spoke up again.

"I'm paying for that, Rolf. In fact, this boy and his friend don't pay for another drink tonight, understand? It's on me."

Rolf looked quizzically at Horace, then shrugged. "However you want to play it, Horace. I'll put it on your tab."

"That's really not necessary..." Julian began, but Horace waved him to silence.

"The hell it ain't. You boys did us a public service today. Least I can do is buy you a couple drinks."

Julian realized arguing any further would be futile. Besides, who was he to pass up free drinks, especially if they were for doing something that really wasn't anything special at all. Smiling, he raised his tankard to Horace and said, "In that case, thank you, kind sir. I..."

A movement at the other end of the room drew Julian's eye, and he lost track of what he was about to say. The woman descending the stairs from the second floor was hard to miss. Long, wavy dark hair, a perfectly hourglass-shaped figure, and a pretty face, she would have stood out anywhere. But here, the fine fabric of her dress and the glitter of precious metal and gems reflecting the firelight from her wrists, ears, and neck stood out and marked her as a lady of means. Julian couldn't help but stare.

Horace noticed, of course, and followed Julian's gaze with his own. Then he burst out laughing.

"Forget about it, boy. That girl ain't got no interest in the likes of you and me."

"Is that so. What makes you say that?"

Horace looked at him as though he was daft. "Well look at her!"

Rolling his eyes, Julian returned Horace's gaze with one of incredulity. "That's it?" he asked, and realized that he had just let a healthy dose of annoyance slip through into the tone he was using to address the man who was buying his drinks. He cleared his throat and looked away. But if Horace was put out or offended, it didn't show in his demeanor or in how he treated the question.

"A well set-up lass like her probably comes from nobility, has a rich husband, or is looking for one. *That's* it."

The woman walked, or rather flowed, over to an empty table near one of the fireplaces and sat down. Julian noted with interest that she sat with her back to the wall. She was a careful one, or so it seemed. She had barely settled into her chair when a server hurried over. They exchanged quick words then, making a slight curtsy, the server made her way quickly back to the bar.

"Let's see if your theory is true," Julian said to Horace. Then he stood and moved over to where the server stood waiting for the woman's drink.

Horace chuckled. "Your funeral, boy."

Julian reached the server as she was reaching for the drink. Moving quickly, he got his hand in ahead of her and snatched it up then tossed a few coins onto the bar.

"Hey!"

"I've got this one, thanks," Julian said over his shoulder as he moved away from the bar. The mixture of chagrin and bemusement on the server's face was classic.

He reached the woman's table quickly, only having to pause once to avoid being run over by a large drunk fellow on his way to the privy. She was reading from a small leather-bound book as he approached. From a distance, she looked attractive. Close up, she was gorgeous. Stunning, even. Suddenly struck by a big case of nerves, Julian almost turned around and went back to Horace at the bar.

None of that.

Taking a deep breath, Julian squared his shoulders and strode the last few paces to the woman's table.

"Your drink, my lady," he said as he placed her glass onto the table in front of her.

The woman didn't look up. She just murmured, "Thank you," and held out a coin. A silver coin. Again, Julian was tempted to just walk away, after pocketing the money, of course. Instead, he sat down in an empty chair at her table.

"No need for that. I covered this one."

She looked up from her book and frowned. Julian moved ahead before she could say anything.

"I'm Julian Hinderbrook. And your name is...?" He put on his most charming smile as he spoke, the one that normally made the maidens swoon.

"None of your business." She inserted a place mark, snapped her book shut, and cast it down on the table with an expression of disgust. "It's bad enough I'm stranded in this flyspeck of a town in the middle of nowhere. I don't need to be accosted by every bumpkin in the place. Thank you for the drink. Now, off with you." She made a shooing gesture that carried entire levels of contemptuous dismissal.

Julian had to force his smile not to compress into a scowl. Why that conceited little... "I'm no bumpkin." He knew his tone was frosty, but he couldn't help it and, frankly, she deserved it.

The woman rolled her eyes. "Yes, of course. How could I have missed it? You're a cultural minister from Tyrash." Sarcasm dripped from her words. It didn't help that Julian had no idea where Tyrash was.

All of a sudden he felt stupid, and from her expression he looked the part, too. She shook her head slightly then picked up her book again and opened it up to her place. Making another shooing gesture, she began to read again.

A lesser man would have departed at this point. Julian decided to make one last attempt.

"Look, I'm just trying to be friendly here. I..."

As he began speaking, the woman looked up at him through narrowed eyes that sparkled with irritation. She cupped her hand in front of her mouth as though she was going to blow him a kiss. But when she blew out, instead of a kiss a plume of flame leapt out toward him.

Julian shouted a curse and pushed himself backwards, his hands flying upwards to protect his face. He leaned way back and his chair teetered for a moment, then fell over onto the ground, taking him with it.

The flame burned out very quickly; it did not even reach his position where he had been sitting. But the flash of heat was real. Very real. Julian lay there on the floor for a moment, stunned.

A sudden silence descended on the taproom as Julian pushed himself up to his feet. Every eye was fixed on him and the woman. His face warm with embarrassment and from the brief heat from the flame, he fixed the woman with a glare as he brushed himself off. Then he turned and walked away. From the corner of his eye, he saw her give a mocking little wave as he left. He did not look back.

Horace looked as stunned as Julian felt when he returned to the bar. All the same, he managed a smirk as he said, "Told you so."

"You could have warned me she was a mage," Julian replied angrily before he downed a large drink of his wine.

Horace sniffed. "She ain't no mage. Women ain't allowed to study magery, boy. Wonder how and where she picked that up."

Julian shrugged and drank again, finishing off his tankard. Slamming it down onto the bar, he scowled over at the woman for a moment. "Whatever. I've had enough for one day. Good meeting you, Horace."

Horace chuckled and shook Julian's hand again. "Don't let it get to you. Good night."

Julian nodded slowly and made his way to the stairs. As he began to ascend, he looked back over his shoulder for a moment. The woman was still there, looking just as pretty as before, and just as separate. For a heartbeat, he imagined their eyes met and she smiled briefly.

❧ 7 ☙

OPPORTUNITY KNOCKS

Julian and Raedrick awoke with the dawn the next morning. When they came downstairs, Julian was surprised to find the taproom all but deserted. A young man stood behind the bar and a single serving girl lounged on a barstool near him. Besides them, one man sat alone in one of the booths and another two sat together at the same table the mage lady used the night before.

It took a few minutes after they sat down for the server to notice Julian and Raedrick's presence. She sauntered over hurriedly, her hips making a nice swaying motion as she moved, and spoke in an apologetic tone.

"Good morning. I'm Celine. I'm sorry to keep you gentlemen waiting. We don't get very many customers this early."

"No worries, Celine," Raedrick said with a smile. "We're just looking for some tea and breakfast."

Celine returned Raedrick's smile and nodded, then swayed away to the kitchens. It was hard for Julian to move his gaze away from her hips, but she soon passed out of sight as the kitchen door swung shut behind her. Ah well. He looked back at his friend instead.

"So Raedrick, what's the deal with Lani?"

"What do you mean?"

"She was pretty into you last night."

Raedrick snorted and waved off Julian's remark. "We were good friends for a long time and had a lot of catching up to do. Of course she was excited about it; so was I."

"Whatever you say."

Celine returned then, carrying a tray that held a teapot, two cups, and a jar with two spoons. Smiling professionally at them, she set a cup in front of each of them and placed the teapot and jar in the center of the table. Then she said, "Your breakfast will be out in a moment," and left them to return to the bar.

Curious, Julian opened the jar while Raedrick poured the tea. It was full of honey. Perfect. He took two dollops and set the jar back down where Raedrick could use it, then stirred his cup.

Getting back to the subject at hand, Julian asked, "So you're saying you'd tell her no if she offered to... you know." He left the rest of the thought go unspoken, instead grinning at his friend as he raised one eyebrow meaningfully.

Raedrick flushed but didn't say anything. The silence spoke volumes.

"I didn't think so."

The room brightened noticeably as the front door swung open, admitting the morning's sunlight far more effectively than the few windows in the walls did.

Julian turned in his chair, his eyes drawn to the glow of the doorway as two men stepped inside. Both were tall men; they easily had a hand on Raedrick, and he wasn't short. But he wasn't able to make out much more about them until the door swung shut and the glare from outside subsided.

The man on the right was plump, with carefully trimmed hair that had gone grey at the temples. His clothing was plain, but the fabric was obviously of high quality, and he wore a golden pin of some sort over his left breast. The other man was more lean. He was bald and wore the clothing of a working man, except for the silver pin he wore over his breast and the baldric that hung across his body from shoulder to hip, which housed a short weapon of some sort. Probably a sword breaker, from its shape.

The two men paused inside the front door and surveyed the room. Then the lean one nudged the other and nodded in Julian and Raedrick's direction. They moved toward the table in a deliberate, businesslike pace.

"Who are these fellows?" Julian wondered aloud, earning a shrug of ignorance from his friend in reply.

He didn't have long to wait to find out. The two men arrived at the table quickly. Up close, he could see that the plump man's pin was in the shape of a fish jumping out of the water. The silver pin the other wore was shaped like a pair of scales dangling from a clenched fist.

"Raedrick Baletier and Julian Hinderbrook?" It was the leaner of the two who spoke first.

The two friends nodded in unison.

"I am Lucian Malory, the Constable. This is Wil Brimly, the mayor of this town." Constable Malory gestured to the two empty chairs at the table. "May we join you?"

Julian and Raedrick exchanged glances.

The Constable wasn't a big surprise, but what did the mayor want with them? From all the hints the previous evening, Julian knew Raedrick was curious and troubled about what was going on in town. And, truth be told, Julian was as well. It wasn't often he got called a hero for stringing up a single robber. What could it hurt to hear what these two had to say?

Julian shrugged, and Raedrick replied, "Please do."

The two men settled into the chairs and collected themselves quickly. Mayor Brimly wasted no time in getting to the point.

"You gents did a great thing for this town last night when you brought that thug in for justice."

"Oh?" Raedrick affected a surprised tone, though Julian was sure he was no more surprised than he was himself. Enough people had made a fuss over that fellow already, after all.

Mayor Brimly nodded emphatically. "Absolutely. You two are the first who've been able to strike back at Farzal's gang in any meaningful way. I can't tell you how much higher people's spirits are this morning, since the word of your deed spread around."

Constable Malory looked sidelong at the Mayor as he spoke, his expression a bit less enthusiastic. When the Mayor finished talking, he cleared his throat and cut in, looking back at Julian and Raedrick. "Fendig passed your story on to me, but there are a number of details that need to be filled in, if you don't mind answering a few questions."

"Why would we mind?"

Julian could think of several reasons without straining, but they had decided on how to answer certain questions a long time ago, so there probably wouldn't be much harm in it. All the same, he wished Raedrick didn't sound so eager.

Constable Malory inclined his head, in a gesture Julian was sure was meant to portray gratitude, but it ended up appearing condescendingly superior. Irritation rose within Julian, but he forced it down. This wasn't a time to go off half-cocked.

"You say the attack occurred just above the falls, on the river road. How many attackers were there?"

"Six."

The Constable looked down his nose at them, doubt plain on his face. "That's what you told Fendig. He didn't believe it, and neither do I. Four, maybe, but six? Farzal's men are too good for that."

Julian snorted, not waiting for Raedrick to reply. "Good? They were careless. Sloppy. Only one of them was worth a damn."

"The man you brought in?"

Julian shook his head. "No. He was the first to fall, and he's damn lucky all I did was kick him."

The Constable and Mayor exchanged long looks. The Mayor's eyes gleamed with an eager light, but Malory held up a calming hand, silencing him before he could speak.

"What brings you boys into town?" the Constable asked as he looked back to Julian and Raedrick. "Not many folks come through this way anymore. Hell, almost no one does unless they're part of a merchant's caravan, and most of them take the southern routes now too."

"It was time to come home from the Army, and I didn't want to take the extra time to circle around to the south. Julian's heard me talk about Mol Teribor enough that he decided to come along since he was leaving at the same time." Raedrick told the tale quickly, but in an earnest enough tone that Julian found himself halfway believing it, even though he knew better.

The Constable's eyes narrowed. "You boys been out on the front?"

They both nodded.

"I heard they were canceling people's release from enlistment until the end of hostilities. How is it you got out?"

"We heard that too, a few days after we left," Julian replied. "We've been thanking our lucky stars that we didn't leave a week later than we did."

Constable Malory pursed his lips in thought for a moment, then he nodded and leaned back in his chair. He turned to look at Mayor Brimly and gave a little nod.

Beaming, Mayor Brimly moved his chair closer to the table. "I'd like to hire you boys."

"I beg your pardon," Julian replied.

"The town needs good men on our side if we're going to get rid of Farzal's gang. You two seem like ideal candidates for the job. What do you say?"

❧   8   ☙

EMPLOYMENT

Julian was speechless. How was he supposed to react to that?

Raedrick, as usual, was quick on his feet. "Why don't you start with telling us who this Farzal person is."

Mayor Brimly looked disappointed as he sat back in his chair, but the Constable's eyes were understanding. In point of fact, Julian could swear the doubt he had seen in the man's eyes faded when Raedrick asked the question. What, did he think they were a couple of rank amateurs, who would take a job without knowing what it entailed? Apparently, he had. Or at least he had feared they were. Julian wasn't sure which was worse.

"A month and a half ago," Malory said, "a merchant caravan pulled into town with one carriage burned and two men dead. They told of being attacked by robbers in Holbart's Pass. A few days later, a delivery man working for one of the craftsmen in town discovered one of the outlying farmsteads had been burned down. Since then, the attacks have come more frequently, and against larger targets. Last week, they hit a farm not far from here, down by the Eastflow. A calling card at the scene claimed Glimmer Vale in Farzal's name and said that unless we paid a regular tribute, things would get worse. Then four days ago, a merchant caravan was completely destroyed on its way through Holbart's pass. There were only two survivors: a lady who managed to escape the battle and a caravan guard who we found barely clinging to life."

Malory's eyebrow rose. "And yesterday you were attacked. This is the first time we've seen activity from them on that side of the Vale, and it proves they are becoming more comfortable with their position. It's also the first time anyone has managed to defeat them to date."

Mayor Brimly spoke again. "Lydelton lives and dies by the traffic coming through the passes. Our population has dwindled in recent years as merchant traffic has shifted south. If these bandits are allowed to continue unchecked, before

35

long no one will make the transit at all and we will lose everything we have. We *must* put a stop to these attacks. And we need your help to do so."

"Why don't you just pay the tribute?" Julian asked.

Mayor Brimly looked shocked. "Give in to these thugs?"

"It's better than being burned out."

He shook his head vigorously. "No! Even if we had the funds they demanded, it's a question of honor!"

"But the fact is we don't have the money," Constable Malory interjected. "Even a large city would be hard pressed to come up with the sum they demanded on a monthly basis, and we are far from being a large city."

"Have you tried negotiating with them?"

Malory snorted. "With whom? The man you brought in is the first of Farzal's band anyone has seen and lived to tell of it."

"Then you don't really know what you're dealing with," Raedrick said. "For all you know, it could have only been those six fellows lurking in the pass this whole time. Six men with bows can do a lot of damage in the right place."

The Constable again shook his head. "No, the survivors of the last merchant caravan described an attacking force of at least thirty to forty men."

"So you see why we must have your help?" Mayor Brimly's voice trembled slightly.

"No," Julian replied, "I don't see that. You don't really know what you're up against yet. If you want my advice, I'd say you should give that man we brought in a counter-offer, one you can afford to pay, and have him deliver it to Farzal. Unless he's a total fool, he'll take it, and you can avoid a major confrontation." He looked from the Constable to the Mayor and back. "Or do you think you can win a pitched battle against them?"

The Constable shook his head. "It's just me and Fendig here in town. In the summer months, I sometimes hire some of the tougher lads from the nearby farms or off the fishing boats to help keep order while the caravans are in town. That's all we've ever needed until now."

"Then you're in no position to not pay. I -"

"We'll do it," Raedrick said, to Julian's chagrin but not to his complete surprise.

"I'm not sure..." he began, but Raedrick cut him off.

"We'll do it." Raedrick gave him a firm, no-nonsense look as he repeated the words.

Julian met Raedrick's stare for a moment. He knew that expression. Raedrick always wore it on the way into battle.

"Will you give us a minute, gentlemen?" Julian asked, not looking at the Constable and the Mayor. Out of the corner of his eye, he saw them nod and leave the table. He gave them a minute to walk out of earshot, then he spoke again.

"What the hell are you doing?"

"These people need our help, Julian."

Julian rolled his eyes. "No, they need help from a company of soldiers, not..." He looked around quickly. No one was close enough to hear. All the same, he leaned closer and spoke in a whisper. "Not from two guys on the run. We need to be putting as many miles behind us as we can. We can't afford to get caught up in this sort of thing."

Raedrick's eyes flashed with anger. Julian raised a placating hand and continued quickly.

"Look, I get it. You've got nice memories of this place from when you were a kid. But it's not our problem. And even if it was, the two of us can't make a difference here. Not against forty men."

"We can and you know it. We just took out six of them without much trouble."

Julian snorted. "I'm out of action for a week or two thanks to that little meeting, in case you forgot," he said, pointing at his thigh. "Yet another reason we can't and shouldn't do this."

"Rubbish," Raedrick replied. "You heal quickly. And it's not like we're going to charge off to fight them all at once, right this minute. It'll take time to get intel and prepare before we can expect any action."

Julian opened his mouth to reply, but Raedrick spoke over him.

"I'm going to help. You can leave if you want, I suppose. But do you really think you'll make it out of the Vale?"

"What are you talking about?"

"They're ambushing people traveling through the passes, remember? I doubt they'll just let you go."

Raedrick's words hit like a ton of bricks. Julian had to admit that hit upon a point he had not considered. He took it as a given that the two of them could just move along. But if Raedrick was right, they were stuck here.

Son of a bitch.

"Hadn't thought of that, had you?" Raedrick asked. He didn't have to sound so satisfied about it.

Julian shook his head.

"The way I see it, if we can't leave, we're now part of this community. So yes, this *is* our problem. And I'm going to help solve it. This is the sort of thing I *thought* I'd be doing in the Army, but never did. Didn't you?"

Julian looked away from his friend. As his gaze panned around the taproom, he noted the tension, and the hope, in the Mayor's face. The suppressed fear in the bartender's. The determination, tinged with hopelessness, in the Constable's. Yes, this was exactly the sort of thing the Army claimed to do, and was supposed to do. Defending those who could not defend themselves.

Damn it all.

"Ok, I'm in. Hope we don't live to regret this."

Raedrick chuckled. "Don't worry. If it goes wrong, we won't live to do anything at all."

That was not very comforting.

❧   9   ❧

WORKING ARRANGEMENTS

Mayor Brimly bubbled over with enthusiasm when Julian and Raedrick announced their acceptance of the offer. He shook both their hands repeatedly, fairly bouncing up and down each time he did.

"Thank you, gentlemen. Thank you! The people of Lydelton will honor your names always."

He sure was laying it on a bit thick, considering they hadn't really done anything yet. Julian found it understandable to an extent; the town had been living in fear for weeks. But still, he couldn't help but wonder how true the Mayor's gratitude really was.

Constable Malory was more reserved, merely nodding with a small smile. Again, appropriate. It was the Mayor's place to be boisterous, and from what Julian had seen they all tended to enjoy it. The Constable had a serious job, though, and that tended to attract more serious, business-minded men to it.

Finally, Mayor Brimly took a step back. "You'll report to Lucian on this, but I'll be keeping tabs on how things are going. For now, I'll leave you to get better acquainted." He beamed a smile at them and added, "Good luck to us all!" Then he turned and strolled out of the Inn.

"Well he's plenty enthusiastic," Raedrick quipped.

"Mayor Brimly cares very deeply for the people of this town," Constable Malory said.

Just then, the waitress came out of the kitchen, carrying a tray with two plates, a pitcher, and two cups on it. She approached the table, but paused when she saw the Constable standing next to them. She looked between Julian, Raedrick, and Malory with a questioning expression on her face.

The Constable noted her presence and gestured for her to get about her work, saying, "I'll not interrupt your breakfast any longer. Come by my office after you've dined and we'll discuss the situation in more detail."

Breakfast consisted of chopped up fried potatoes, a hunk of bread smeared with butter, and fish meat baked in a sweet batter, along with spiced cider. Julian had noticed in their short time in town that the locals seemed to put fish into just about everything. That was understandable, he supposed, considering the proximity of the lake and its obvious contribution to the local economy. Still, fish for breakfast struck him as odd.

It was tasty though. He couldn't complain about that.

"I hope you know what you're doing," Julian said as he and Raedrick tromped upstairs to retrieve their equipment. His thigh began to sting again, causing him to question his decision.

Raedrick responded with a soft snort and a shrug of his shoulders. "You know as much as I do."

Julian rolled his eyes. Yeah, this was going to end up being a bad idea.

A few minutes later, after they donned their mail and strapped on their weapons, the two friends headed out.

In midmorning, Lydelton was markedly different than it had been the previous evening. More people were out and about, conducting the errands of the day. Looking to the right as they exited the inn, the road became more congested quickly as it descended to the lakeshore and the docks. A trio of boats were tied up along the lone pier in sight. A line of men stood around next to each boat on the dock, helping offload large bundled items in a daisy train leading off of pier, and out of sight to the right.

The scene struck Julian as a bit odd. "A little early to be offloading isn't it?"

Raedrick followed Julian's gaze toward the dock. A confused expression on his face, he shrugged his shoulders before replying. "I would think so. I wonder what's going on?"

There was no particular hurry to get to the Constable's office, so the two men set off toward the docks. The road descended quickly, and before long they reached the reached the head of the pier. From there they could see five more piers stretching out into the lake, each with a couple of boats tied up and similar lines of men hauling bundles. The lines of workers converged on a large wagon that waited at the head of the second pier, one street over from where Raedrick and Julian stood.

As they watched, the wagon reached its capacity and a balding man with a bit of a paunch waved off the lines of men with their burdens. Then he hopped into the front of the wagon and shook the reigns. His team of two horses began moving, and the wagon departed up the street. Moments later, a second, identical, wagon appeared from the same street and came to a halt before the pier, and the lines of men commenced to fill it.

That was curious. Julian and Raedrick hurried past the newly-arrived wagon and up the next street. A block up the road, the first wagon was parked next to the side entrance a nondescript building that could only be a warehouse. Additional workers were offloading the wagon and bringing its contents within.

The two friends walked past the wagon to the corner of the warehouse, where another door that looked to be the main entrance was situated at the head of three short stairs. Julian looked at Raedrick questioningly and received a shrug in response, so he led the way to the main entrance and then inside.

Within, the warehouse was larger than it appeared from the outside. The ground level consisted mostly of a single large room with a vaulted ceiling. A number of large bins stood at intervals around the room. The workers came in through the side and walked to specific bins. There they unwrapped their packages and dumped the contents, fish of course, into the bins. As Raedrick and Julian watched, one of the bins became filled to capacity, and a man standing near it pulled on a rope. A bell rang overhead and, a moment later, another pair of workers entered the room, pushing a bin before them. It was only then that Julian noticed that each bin was wheeled. The two new men replaced the full bin with their empty one and pushed it toward the rear of the warehouse, where a wide pair of swinging doors separated this room from another.

"Hey, what are you doing in here?"

The voice, gruff and businesslike, drew Julian's eye to a tall stocky man who was approaching from the left. The man was in his early middle years and wore his greying black hair cut short. He wore work boots and coveralls like the other men, but his shirt was red while theirs were blue. Julian surmised he was the foreman.

"We were just curious about your setup here," Julian said, putting on a friendly smile. "Seems a bit early to be offloading the boats. The day's not even a third done."

The foreman scowled. "It's almost done for this shift. Fish don't jump except at twilight, so the boats go out before sunrise and at sunset to catch them." He looked them up and down, his eyes lingering on the sword at Julian's hip and Raedrick's saber. "Don't see what that matters to you. You don't have the look of men looking for a job."

"We're not."

"Then get out. This is a business, not a tourist attraction." He pointed with authority toward the door they had entered through.

There wasn't any point to objecting, so they left.

It took about ten minutes to walk to Constable Malory's office from the fish warehouse. By the end of the walk, Julian's thigh was throbbing again. Each step caused him to grit his teeth. This was no way for a big hero to start off his job as savior.

Constable Malory was seated behind the desk to the right as they walked in the door, perusing a small collection of official-looking papers. He looked up as they entered and nodded in greeting.

"I was just going over the reports of all the raids to date. I thought maybe you would like to review them as well. Might be there's something we missed."

That made sense, Julian supposed. He moved over to the desk to pick up one of the reports, but Raedrick's words brought him up short.

"Where is the prisoner?"

Julian turned to see his friend looking into the cell block. His eyes widened when he noticed what Raedrick was talking about: all the cell doors were open. Julian turned back to the Constable, a simmering anger beginning to well up within him. What had these people done?

Then Constable Malory spoke, dousing Julian's anger as quickly as it flared up. "Fendig has him down at the courthouse for his preliminary hearing with the judge. They should be back in an hour or so."

"I didn't realize you have the resources for a full inquiry and trial here, as remote as you are," Raedrick replied as Julian picked up the stack of reports.

"Due process is still due process, wherever you are," Constable Malory said, his lips turning downwards into a slight frown.

"I didn't mean to imply..." Raedrick began, but Constable Malory cut him off.

"You did more than just imply it. You flat out stated that..."

The argument faded into the background as Julian picked up the reports and began reading.

The first was the deposition from a month and a half ago by a fellow named Modrin Gilanty, of Holis, over by the Great Sea. He owned a trading company and had been traversing Holbart's pass when he was accosted by half a dozen men who were equipped similarly to the brigands Julian and Raedrick encountered the previous day. Gilanty reported that his guards had repelled the attack but one of his carriages had been burned to the ground, along with all of its wares, and two of his men killed. Total loss: 200 marks, including contractual reparations he now owed to the families of his lost men. Julian winced; that much money would keep twenty families eating for a year in many areas of the kingdom.

That was bad. The next report was worse. Julian knew what to expect from what Malory had told them back at the Inn, but the deposition went into more details. Lev Harpwell was the man who discovered the burned out farmstead during a run to deliver horseshoes from Gil Aberdyn, one of the two blacksmiths in town. What he described... It made the burned out farm Julian and Raedrick came across seem civilized, by comparison. What was wrong with these people?

The reports continued, almost a full dozen of them spanning the time between the first caravan attack and the attack above the falls yesterday.

Julian replaced the last report before his and Raedrick's back down on Constable Malory's desk and suppressed a slight shiver. This was not going to be easy. He looked over at Raedrick, who was reading an earlier report, and shook his head.

"All of a sudden I've got a bad feeling about this."

Raedrick looked up, one eyebrow moving upward as he responded. "You had a good feeling before?"

"You know what I mean. The lady who gave this last report said there were dozens of attackers. We'll need a bloody army to fight them off."

Constable Malory nodded. "Aye, I'd come to a similar conclusion. I asked the fishing foremen to lend me some of their boys like they do in the summer, but they refused." With a sigh, he settled back into his chair. "I'm hoping they'll come around if you can add a few smaller victories to what you did yesterday, and get these cells filled."

"Let me guess, you and Fendig won't be coming with us for these victories."

He shook his head. "We will help as we can, but you must understand my primary duty is to maintain law and order within the town limits."

"Great."

Raedrick picked up the final report and scanned it quickly. "Did the wounded guard from this last attack pull through?"

Constable Malory shook his head. "Alas, no. He passed not long after we got him to town. The Guildsmen from the Healers Circle tried their best, but they say he lost too much blood."

"That's too bad. What about the woman? Is she still in town?"

"Oh yes," replied the Constable. "And complaining every minute about it. She's holed up over at The Oarlock. Word is she tried to hire every coachman in town to drive her down to Calas, but none of them would take the job."

Julian felt his interest piqued. "How come?"

Malory shrugged. "Too dangerous." A sudden grin appeared on his face and he chuckled, adding, "'Course, I can think of two men offhand who said they were willing, except for her attitude."

Julian had a feeling he knew who the Constable was talking about. "Good looking?"

Again Malory shrugged. "They don't seem to have problems with the ladies..."

"Not the drivers, the woman!"

The Constable blinked, and flushed slightly. Clearing his throat, he nodded. "Yes, quite striking in fact."

Julian grinned. This was turning out to be his lucky day. Giving Raedrick a little punch in the shoulder, he said, "I think I know where we can get some help."

10

MAGERY

Julian knocked on the door, making a firm staccato series of thumps against the wood. A muffled voice from within indicated the occupant would be with them in a minute, so he stepped back and waited. Beside him, Raedrick smirked slightly but said nothing.

A short while later, the door swung open, revealing the woman Julian met the night before in the taproom. She was, if possible, even more lovely than he recalled, garbed in a dark green dress that was just as well-crafted as her clothing from last night. Recognition flashed across her face as she saw him, and she frowned.

"You again. I thought I made myself clear last night: I don't want to be bothered by the likes of you."

Julian fought down a surge of irritation. "We're here on business, Mistress Klemins."

Her frown deepened as he spoke. "How do you know my name?"

Readrick interjected. "I'm Raedrick Baletier, Mistress Klemins. This is..."

"Jules Hiddenstrap. We've met."

Julian ground his teeth in irritation. "Julian Hinderbrook."

"Oh, I'm sorry." She didn't sound like it, and from the sweetly innocent expression she wore, she sure didn't look it either. Silence hung awkwardly between the three of them for a moment.

Finally, Raedrick cleared his throat and got back to it. "We're working with Constable Malory, Mistress Klemins. He told us about your encounter while you were with the caravan that was attacked, and we wanted to ask you a few questions about it."

"Law men, huh?" she replied. "You don't look the type."

"That's because we're not."

She smirked. "Hired swords then. These yokels must really be getting desperate." With a sigh, she gestured for them to come into her room. "Fine, let's get this over with."

Room was inaccurate. She had a suite. A sitting room, larger than the room Julian and Raedrick shared, lay beyond the entrance. A couch and two padded chairs sat in a loose circle around a low table in the far end of the room, near a crackling fireplace. Two other doors led out, one on either side of the room. A taller table stood near the door on the right with a decanter filled with dark red wine and several glasses resting on top. Next to the table stood a small shelf that was filled with books. Julian recognized several titles from one afternoon of liberty that he spent within a bookstore in Calas. He normally didn't have the money to indulge in many books, and a man in his position couldn't afford to get overly encumbered. But he had always enjoyed reading a good story, so he found himself envying the collection.

"Can I offer you anything?" she asked.

Julian shook his head.

"No thank you," replied Raedrick.

"Suit yourself." Taking a moment to fill a glass for herself, she moved over to the couch and sat down. Taking a sip of the wine, she smiled faintly and said, "What is it you want to know?"

"Mistress Klemins," Raedrick began.

"Melanie."

"Alright. Melanie, how much of the attack were you able to see?"

She looked at Raedrick as though he was daft. "All of it, of course. At least, all of it until I slipped away."

"So what did you..."

"There were thirty-five of them, ten with bows. They started shooting and the wagon drivers tried to make a run for it. At first it looked like we were going to get away, but we turned a corner to find they had felled a tree across the road, so the horses could not carry us onward if they wanted to." Melanie shrugged her shoulders. "You can imagine what happened after that."

"Thirty-five. That's a fairly precise number."

Melanie gave Raedrick a long-suffering look. "I have a very good memory," she replied.

"I'm sure," Julian said. He didn't try to keep the irony of her statement out of his tone at all. "So did you get a look at their leader?"

Melanie shook her head. "They were split up into three groups, and each of them had a leader. I couldn't even hazard a guess which of them, if any, had overall command."

"How did you escape?"

She shrugged. "When I need to be, I'm very good at not being seen."

"I've heard you mages have some tricks that can help with that."

Melanie made a soft tsking sound in response to Julian's statement. "You are mistaken. I'm not a mage. The Magestirium does not admit women as students."

Julian snorted. "After what you did last night, do you expect..."

"A simple carnival trick, nothing more." Melanie's tone was casual, dismissive. But her expression had become guarded and wary.

"Like hell. I've seen that trick, and I know how it's done. You didn't touch your drink at all, and you sure didn't have time to suck down anything else. And the only fire nearby was the candle in the center of the table. So you can claim not to be a mage, and maybe you didn't go to the Magestirium. But you learned a thing or two about magic somewhere."

Melanie was silent for a time, meeting Julian's gaze with a level stare of her own. Finally she shrugged and looked away. "I suppose it is hypothetically possible that a young lady might encounter a certified graduate of the Magestirium, that the two of them might fall in love, and that he might pass on what he'd learned to her despite the rules against it. But if such a thing were to happen, she would have to be very careful never to let her ability become common knowledge, because the Magestirium's wrath is legendary in its viciousness." She looked back at the two men, an unspoken plea in her eyes.

Julian and Raedrick exchanged glances. *Everyone has secrets, it seems,* Julian thought. *He wouldn't want his betrayed any more than she wanted hers.* He gave Raedrick a small nod, which the other man returned with a quick grin.

"Your secret is safe with us, Melanie," Raedrick said.

"Who said it was *my* secret?" she replied, but Julian could not mistake the gratitude in her eyes.

"One thing I don't understand," Raedrick added. "If such a hypothetical lady existed and she was in a situation where her traveling companions were attacked like you were, why wouldn't she try to help? Surely her companions would keep her secret in exchange for their lives."

Julian nodded. "Yeah, we saw the mages assigned to our division wreak some serious havoc in battle. Lightning from the sky, fireballs...it was impressive."

Melanie sniffed. "Well, speaking hypothetically, the sorts of things you're talking about require more than just waving your hands around. There are incantations to make and very specific gestures and stances that must be performed in time with the incantations. Also, there are material items that are used up in the spell. If the lady in question found herself in a situation similar to mine, she would have two problems. First, the only spells that could have conceivably helped take several minutes to cast and would have left her exposed to harm for the entire time. More importantly, though, the material components involved... Well, some of them are worth more than that entire caravan and all its contents. She would have been foolish to expend them under those circumstances."

Julian supposed he could understand Melanie's point, but at the same time... To figure the cost of her spell components against the lives of her companions struck him as particularly cold-blooded.

But then, he thought about several decisions his officers had made on the battlefield. Decisions that he had understood even if he had not always completely approved of. They all came down to math: don't risk twenty men to rescue one who was probably dead, things like that. Was her decision all that different from theirs?

Raedrick spoke again. "You've made it more than clear you don't want to be here. So where were you going?"

"Away."

"Away from what?"

"Let's just say it was time to leave."

That was suitably vague. And not that dissimilar to the thought process that got them started on their own journey. Julian looked over at Raedrick and saw from his expression that he was thinking the same thing.

Raedrick continued, "Well, as long as these thugs have the passes blocked, you're stuck here, you know."

"That's been distressingly clear for days. But thank you for confirming the obvious."

"You know we're working to drive the brigands off," Julian interjected.

Melanie nodded. "I assumed as much."

"If the group that attacked you numbered thirty-five, there's probably at least forty to fifty total. Pretty long odds for the two of us. But if there was someone in town who had knowledge of magic and could even the odds a bit, that might make all the difference."

"What would be in it for this person?"

Raedrick replied before Julian could. "The satisfaction of helping people in need. And," he added as a smirk began to form on her lips, "freedom. Once the brigands are gone, there's nothing stopping you from going wherever it is you're planning to go."

Melanie pursed her lips in thought. Leaning back on her couch for a moment she considered the two men. Julian felt as though he was being weighed and measured under her gaze. Finally, Melanie shrugged and nodded.

"I may be able to do something to help. What is your plan?"

THE PLAN

"That is the stupidest plan I've ever heard."

There was never any mystery where Constable Malory stood on an issue, that much was certain. Not that Julian necessarily disagreed on this particular point, but as far as he and Raedrick could tell after talking it over all afternoon, there was no other way to go if they wanted to find out more information about the brigands.

"What's so stupid about it?"

Julian almost snorted out a laugh at Raedrick's reply. He knew the plan's flaws exactly; hell, he was the one who envisioned the basic premise of the plan in the first place.

Constable Malory looked at Raedrick as if he were daft. "You want me to just release the man who attacked you, give him back his arms and equipment, and let him go back to his friends? Why, so he can wreak more havoc out there?"

They were talking in one of the booths in The Oarlock. They had picked one near the corner of the room, as far from the other patrons as possible. It wasn't that he didn't trust his fellow townsfolk, Malory had said, it was just that secrets get more difficult to keep up as more people learn them. So they kept a close but unobtrusive watch on the other patrons to ensure they weren't discussing sensitive topics in the open.

Raedrick shook his head as he responded to Constable Malory's question. "It wouldn't be some charity project. He's leverage..."

"Damn right he's leverage. And that's wasted if he makes it back safely and lets his boss know what pushovers we are."

"Actually," Julian added, "that's what we want. The easier they think the target is the less likely they'll expend a lot of resources to keep the pressure on. Why bother risking it if we're just going to fold anyway?"

"Near as I can tell, Farzal's pretty confident as it is."

"True, but if we're so scared of him that we release one of his men and make an example of the two guys who injured him and killed his companions..."

Constable Malory snorted again. "What, you want me to whip you or something?"

Raedrick shook his head. "Not for real. But you can put on a show of punishment or something. Then you release him and he rides out of town feeling smug and superior."

"And then we follow him back to his base camp," Julian added.

Constable Malory nodded slowly. "I understand, but it's still a dumb plan."

Julian opened his mouth to reply and so did Raedrick, but the Constable cut them off.

"There are too many things that can go wrong. And then we'll be without a prisoner and Farzal will think we're cowardly *and* incompetent."

"So what would you do with him?" asked Raedrick.

"Have a nice show trial and then hang him. Leave his head on a pike where Farzal's sure to find him and negotiate from a position of perceived strength."

Now *that* was stupid. "If you consider Farzal riding into town with his whole gang in a towering fury to be negotiating from a position of strength, who am I to dissuade you?"

Constable Malory looked taken aback for a moment. Then he flushed and nodded, the wind leaving his sails noticeably. "Hmm. Maybe that wouldn't be the best idea after all."

"So we're a go then. When are you going to release him?"

The Constable sighed and shook his head. "Tomorrow, I suppose. The mayor is not going to like this at all." With that, he slid out of the booth and stood up. He took a step away, then looked back over his shoulder at the two men. "This better work."

"This is just the first move in the game, Lucian. Trust us." Julian had to hand it to him, Raedrick could be smooth and reassuring when he needed to.

Constable Malory sniffed, but Julian noticed he cracked a smile as he turned again and walked out of the Inn.

The door swung shut behind the Constable and Raedrick looked quizzically at Julian.

"Ok, you want to tell me how we're going to follow this guy across the grassland around here without him or his teammates noticing?"

"I've been thinking about that."

"I hope so, because I have also and I'm not coming up with anything."

"That's what we have Melanie for."

Raedrick's expression was almost comic in its lack of comprehension.

Melanie met them shortly before noon the next day on the outskirts of town. She was dressed down from when Julian last saw her. Her dress was simple enough to pass unnoticed in most situations, but a closer look revealed that it was divided for riding and was made from the finest material. It also accentuated her curves in a very pleasing way as she walked toward them.

"I wouldn't go there if I were you."

Julian glanced sideways to see Raedrick giving him a knowing look. "What do you mean?"

"I know that look. She's not someone you want to go down that road with."

"Yes, yes. We're in business together."

"That's not what I mean."

Julian didn't answer for a short while. He knew exactly what Raedrick meant, and pretty much agreed. That didn't mean he wanted to admit Raedrick was right. Finally, as Melanie reached their side, he said, "I know."

"What do you know, bumpkin?" Melanie asked, looking curiously between the two men.

Irritation welled up within him. Bumpkin? He almost told her off, and to hell with the plan. Almost. Instead, he took a deep breath to calm himself and replied, "This is a big risk. If your trick doesn't work..."

"It will. As long as you don't screw it up. So you better do exactly what I tell you to."

Raedrick cleared his throat. "Ok, are you going to explain what this master plan is now?"

Julian laughed, both at Raedrick's words and at the incredulous expression on Melanie's face.

"Really, you haven't figured it out yet?"

Raedrick shook his head.

"I thought you said he was clever," Melanie quipped to Julian, receiving a shrug in return. Rolling her eyes, she addressed Raedrick and spoke very slowly. "I'm going to use the same spell that I used to get away from the merchant caravan when it was attacked. The spell makes it very difficult for someone to notice a thing unless the person knows exactly what to look for and where to look for it."

"You're going to make us invisible?"

She shook her head. "That's actually impossible. It is more of a suggestion to the mind that encourages people to not notice or pay attention to what they see."

Raedrick whistled softly. "That's a neat trick. How long does it last?"

Melanie shrugged. "That depends on the spell caster and what she puts into it. Anywhere from a few minutes to several hours." Both Julian and Raedrick opened their mouths to reply. That was not going to work. But she raised a calming hand and added, "But I will use the extended incantations and the strongest components in this casting. That typically gets me six to eight hours' effect."

"That should be enough," Julian said.

"I hope," Raedrick added. Glancing up at the sun, he moved his lips for a moment.

Julian suppressed another chuckle. He would bet good money Raedrick was doing sums. He always had trouble with numbers, even the simple formulas used to convert the sun's angle in the sky to the time of day.

Finally, Raedrick nodded to himself and said, "Malory should be releasing our prisoner in a few minutes. We'd better get a move on."

Melanie nodded and, opening her satchel, withdrew a large leather-bound tome and a stoppered jar made from opaque glass. She placed the jar carefully on the ground and opened the tome. After leafing through it for a short time, she tapped her index finger on one particular page and nodded in satisfaction. "Here it is."

"What do we do?" Julian asked.

"Stay right there and don't move until I tell you," Melanie replied absently as her eyes scanned the page. After a moment, she closed the book and deposited it back into her satchel, then picked up the jar again.

Slowly, carefully, she worked the cork until, with a soft pop, it pulled free. Then she closed her eyes and stood still for a time, the jar pressed to her chest, as she breathed in and out in long, slow breaths. She began chanting softly. It was almost too quiet to hear at first, but quickly her chant became louder until she reached her normal speech level.

Then her eyes opened and she began to move. It was as if she was dancing with an invisible partner; her feet landed in precisely chosen places as she turned a circle in front of them. Her chanting continued, becoming more rhythmic, in time with her footsteps. She turned a circle again and her voice became louder. As she turned to face the men, one at a time, she reached into the jar and cast part of its contents into the air above their heads and those of their horses.

Dust of some sort, sparkling in the sunlight from small reflective pieces that were entrained in it, puffed around them and gradually settled onto their heads, shoulders, and torsos. Julian had to forcibly restrain the urge to dust himself off. Next to him, it looked like Raedrick was desperately trying to hold back a sneeze.

All at once, Melanie's chanting reached a loud climax. Then she stopped and once again clutched the jar to her chest.

"It is done," she said in a somber, dramatic tone.

"That's it?" Julian asked. "I don't feel any different."

"You don't look any different either, more's the pity," Raedrick quipped.

Melanie rolled her eyes as she re-stoppered the jar. "Of course he doesn't," she said. "You're both under the spell, so you'll see each other normally. Other people, though..." She shook her head. "I cast the spell, and I have to concentrate to notice you two. But even that might not work if I didn't know for certain that you were there. Believe me, you are both quite un-noticeable." With a pronounced smirk, she added, "Which is, I suppose, not that big a change."

With that, she replaced the jar into her satchel and turned away. "Good luck. Try not to get killed."

"I don't know about you," Raedrick said after she walked out of earshot, "but I've never been so inspired."

❧ 12 ❧

A WALK IN THE GRASS

A quarter of an hour passed.

Julian sat in his saddle next to his friend and tried not to grow impatient. The Mayor and Constable Malory were supposed to have brought the prisoner out by now. Where were they? Just then, he began to think maybe Melanie was right, and the people in Lydelton were just a bunch of yokels.

But then the sound of horse hooves clopping on flagstone drew his eye. Three men, one of them leading a saddled horse, were walking down the main street toward where Julian and Raedrick waited.

At last!

They drew nearer and their conversation slowly became audible. "...terribly sorry about this. We cannot control what drifters who happen to pass through do. You understand?" The Mayor was good. He actually sounded nervous, terrified even. His voice dripped with sycophantic pleading. Julian *hoped* he was just acting.

The brigand wore a deep scowl, but his eyes glittered with contemptuous amusement. "Of course I understand, Mayor Brimly. But I can't guarantee Farzal will. Those two killed some of our brothers, and you gave them shelter here. That will cost you."

"But..." The Mayor wiped his brow as his eyes darted toward the brigand nervously. "We didn't know..."

The brigand snorted and turned his back to the Mayor. Holding out a commanding hand to Constable Malory, he said, "My horse?"

The Constable's face was a storm cloud, but he handed over the reins without comment. The brigand smirked, a distinctly unpleasant sight considering the scabbed-over scrapes on his cheek and chin, the swelling around his eyes and nose, and the broken teeth in his mouth. In spite of the man's smile, Julian felt a certain satisfaction in seeing the results of his kick.

The brigand mounted the horse and adjusted the reins. He took one last look at Mayor Brimly, who bobbed his head and wrung his hands nervously.

"You will remember to give Farzal our offer?"

The brigand shrugged. "I'll tell him. He'll say no, but I'll tell him."

"That's all we can ask."

The brigand snorted again and dug his heels into the flanks of his horse. She surged forward into a canter and quickly carried her rider away out of earshot.

"Laid it on a bit thick, didn't you?" Constable Malory said, disapproval plain in his tone.

"I hate this. I hate it." The Mayor mopped his brow again. You would think it was the height of summer, as much as he was sweating. The Mayor looked around, his frantic expression making it apparent he wasn't acting much at all. "Where are they?"

"They said they were going to follow at a distance and avoid being seen. They wouldn't wait right here for him."

Julian grinned and exchanged glances with Raedrick. He hadn't doubted Melanie's word, precisely, but it was nice to get confirmation that her spell had worked. Raedrick returned the grin and nodded toward the brigand, now several hundred yards away.

They kicked their horses into a fast trot and set off after the fleeing man.

The brigand slowed after a quarter mile or so. His horse could only canter so far, and it wasn't like she was a racehorse or battle-trained. Truth be told, Julian was surprised she went that far before having to walk. It was just as well, because he had no desire to waste his and Raedrick's horses to follow the thug.

For the rest of the afternoon, they followed about a tenth of a mile behind the brigand as he rode south. From their position behind him, he appeared wary, looking behind himself every few minutes. Julian couldn't blame him. The Mayor was clearly spooked, but Constable Malory hadn't even tried to pretend to be scared. Considering the brigand's line of work, treachery was probably second nature to him, so Julian was sure he more than expected the Constable to have some trap set.

An hour after leaving town, they reached the ford across the Eastflow, near the burned out farmhouse that had almost cost the brigand his life. The bastard didn't even give it a second glance. He did glance backwards again, though, while Julian and Raedrick were in the middle of their crossing.

"Stop!" Raedrick cried.

"What? Why?"

"The splashing."

"Son of a..."

Julian reined in, bringing his horse to a quick halt. He hated to leave his steed with his hooves in the flowing, cold water for long, but Raedrick was right: their invisibility, or whatever it was, that Melanie had bestowed probably would not conceal the splashes from their crossing.

Were they blown already?

The brigand stopped also, looking back over his shoulder for a long few minutes. It was impossible to see his expression from that distance, but Julian imagined he wore a mask of concentration as he studied the ford. A sudden chill went down Julian's spine. The swirling of the current around the horses' legs was probably distinctly visible as well. He was just about ready to kick his horse forward, certain that they had been spotted, when the brigand shrugged and turned around again, then nudged his horse into motion.

Julian exhaled, letting out a breath that he didn't even realize he had been holding. "Let's get going," he said, and urged his horse forward.

They quickly exited the ford and rode up to the burned out farmhouse.

"We'd better stop," Julian said, "and rub down the horses. We don't want them getting cramps."

Raedrick nodded. "Not here, though. I don't want to look at this farm."

"Me neither."

The brigand turned to the left, veering southeast toward the hills leading to the mountains. They followed and soon found themselves riding over a small hillock. In the miniature valley between it and the next rise, they stopped and dismounted.

It took several minutes to dry the horses' legs and rub the circulation back into their feet. Julian grew more concerned by the minute as they worked. For one thing, the horses' lower legs were extremely cold. For another, the brigand was getting farther away every second, and in this hilly terrain it would be very easy to lose him. Finally, he and Raedrick determined they had done the best they could for their mounts and got moving again.

They reached the top of the next rise, and Julian breathed a curse. The brigand was nowhere to be seen.

"He's got to be here somewhere," Raedrick said in a concerned tone.

"Let's give him a minute, hope he climbs a hill."

And so they sat. And sat. After ten minutes, there was still no sign of the brigand. Where was he?

"Could be he's sticking to the low areas between hills," Julian said.

"If that's true, we may never find him. Damn it."

"Let's head out and see."

The next hilltop revealed more rolling hills ahead that gradually got larger as they ran up to the mountains that ringed the Vale. But no brigand. They looked around carefully, then moved off again. The story was the same at the next rise as well. And the next.

The sun was beginning to sink lower on the eastern horizon and the shadows grew longer. As they crested yet another rise with no sign of their quarry, Julian reined in his horse and turned to look at his friend.

"Well what do you think?"

Raedrick shook his head and made a gesture of hopelessness. "We'll lose the light soon, and there's no way we'll find him then." He punched his thigh with a clenched fist. "How the *hell* did we lose him?"

"We'd better get back to town. I don't want to spend the night out here. It's bloody cold."

Raedrick let out an extremely colorful curse, but he nodded in agreement. Without another word, they turned back and nudged their horses into a trot. With luck, they might make it back before full dark.

❧ 13 ☙

RESTART

The barstool was hard, but that was the least of Julian's problems. His injured thigh hurt like no one's business from the afternoon's ride, but that wasn't his biggest problem either. His ears rang from the laughter of several burly fellows off of one of the fishing boats down at the docks, and his cheeks flushed with embarrassment. But that, too, wasn't his big problem.

A glass on the bar in front of him lay on its side, its dark contents spreading slowly across the top of the bar as they drained out. It was almost enough to make him cry.

"The winner!" shouted Horace as he raised the arm of the man next to Julian up over his head.

Julian should have known Horace was a fishing man from his attire the first time they met. And being a fishing man, Julian also should have figured he could more than hold his liquor. And so could all of his fishing friends.

The winner grinned and shook his raised hand in a clenched fist of victory, then turned toward Julian. "Pay up," he demanded in a slightly slurred voice.

Julian nodded and reached for his belt pouch. Or rather, he tried too. It took three attempts to get the laces untied, then another two to get the proper number of coins out. At least, he hoped they were the proper number; it was hard to remember what their bet actually had been.

"Here y'go," he said and held out the coins, which the winner snatched away quickly. What was that fellow's name again?

"You alright, boy?" Horace asked.

Julian waved him off. "Fine, jus' fine. I'm..." He wanted to say something else, but all that came out was a loud belch.

The fishing men around him burst out laughing again.

"Bugger me," he muttered and pushed himself away from the bar.

He must have pushed harder than he intended because he found himself stumbling backwards. The taproom swayed and spun around him, and he began to get a queasy sensation in the pit of his stomach. That wasn't good.

His grasping hands found the back of a chair, and he smiled in relief. He managed to maneuver himself around the chair and collapse down onto the unpadded seat with a sigh. The room instantly slowed down, and he was able to at least somewhat regain his equilibrium.

Water. He needed some water.

"Right here," Horace said, pushing a cup into his hand. How had he known what Julian needed?

That was a worry for another time. Right then, all Julian cared about was getting that water down his gullet. When he finally came up for air, he let out a great sigh. His head still spun and he was still a trifle queasy, but that was fading quickly and at least he was less thirsty.

"Thanks," he said.

"Pleasure's mine." Horace pulled a second chair around and sat down. "What's got you so wound up, boy?"

"Whacha talkin bout?"

"You don't normally tie one on this way."

Julian spluttered. "Hey now.. You don't know me tha well..."

Horace chuckled. "I know when a man can hold his liquor and when he's gone well past his limit."

Julian waved off his words with a dismissive gesture. "I'm fine."

"You can barely stand. Really. What's the problem?"

Julian looked away from the old fishing man and toward one of the fireplaces. Pushing down a surge of queasiness from the suddenness of the change in his field of view, he swallowed hard before replying. "My friend an' me... Wer helpin Malory with the attacks."

Horace's eyes narrowed. "That so?"

Nodding, Julian replied, "Ya. Thing is... There's what, fifty of um? If we knew where they were based, that'd be one thing, but..." He threw his hands out in an overly exaggerated gesture of helplessness that sent the last of his water flinging out of his cup and into the face of a passing waitress.

"HEY!" she exclaimed.

"Oh, I'm so sorry," Julian stammered as he stumbled to his feet. He had a hand-kerchief somewhere... Ah there it was. "Here...let me help."

Julian held the handkerchief out and tried to help sop up the water on her shirt. She screeched and pushed him away. He found himself stumbling backwards until he struck something solid. Looking back over his shoulder, his spirits sank as he realized that the something solid was a large man with an unruly black beard who had just stumbled forward into his equally large friend, spilling both their drinks.

"Gents, I'm real sorry..." was all Julian was able to get out.

The bearded fellow growled as he spun around. Then, from out of nowhere, a very large fist struck Julian in the cheek and he saw stars. He didn't stumble; he toppled to the floor in a heap. There he lay for a long moment, tasting blood as he tried to figure out what the gaping hole he was staring into was. Finally it came to him: he was staring into his now empty cup, which lay on the floor beside his head.

"Stay down." The deep gravelly voice could only belong to the bearded fellow.

It probably would have been smarter to do what the large man said. But Julian wasn't in the mood to listen to the smart thing. Anger and a bruised ego demanded he get up and trounce the man.

That was easier said than done, however. Julian got his hands below his torso and pushed himself up onto his hands and knees. But there he stopped as another wave of nausea swept over him. He swallowed again to avoid losing his dinner and took a deep breath. Then, equilibrium restored, he forced himself erect.

Or rather, he tried to. But as soon as his hands left the floor, he collapsed again. Undaunted, he tried a second time, with the same result.

Somewhere above himself, he heard voices but he could not make out the words. Then suddenly he felt hands on his upper arms and someone hauled him to his feet. Two someones, in fact. Looking slowly left and right, Julian saw that he was being supported by two of his new drinking buddies, one of them the fishing man who won the bet.

The two men guided him to a table and helped him into a chair, then set another cup of water in front of him. As he sat down, he looked back over his shoulder and saw Horace talking with the two large men. A waitress, a different one, came by and delivered drinks, which the men accepted. Then Horace clapped the bearded one on the shoulder and, with a friendly grin, turned and walked away from them toward Julian's table.

Horace's smile faded as he sat down across from Julian. "Those boys are touchy, and they drink top shelf liquor. You just cost me a fair amount of money."

"I didn't ask you to help."

Horace snorted. "Didn't need to did you?" Drawing a deep breath, he paused for a moment. Then, making a dismissive gesture, he said, "Don't think anything of it. Now," he leaned forward and clasped his hands together on top of the table, "you were sayin'?"

"Bad day today is all."

Horace did not reply; he just fixed Julian with a flat stare.

With a sigh, Julian explained what happened, how they failed in their pursuit of the prisoner. He almost found himself telling Horace about Melanie's role, but caught himself at the last moment and instead took a drink of water.

"Long story short, we're back to square one, except that now they know who we are. And they'll come looking for us. We're screwed."

"Hmmph. Your buddy agree with you on this?"

Julian shook his head. "No. Rae's never one to accept reality, even when it slaps him in the face."

"Funny thing about reality, boy. How you look at it changes what it is."

Maybe it was just the alcohol, but Julian couldn't make sense of what that was supposed to mean. Reality was, well, reality. It didn't change.

Horace chuckled softly. "From the look on your face, I just lost you." He stood up suddenly. Walking around the table, he clapped Julian on the shoulder and said, "I'll explain in the morning. When your head's not full of mud."

Horace walked over to the bar and spoke with the bartender for a short time, making some gestures in Julian's direction. Then he left the inn. His fishing men friends left with him.

Julian awoke to sunlight streaming in through the window in his and Raedrick's room and instantly wished he hadn't opened his eyes. His head pounded and his mouth was so dry as to feel gravelly on his tongue. He felt more than a little queasy as well, and the bright light did not help matters one bit.

Pressing his palms to his forehead, Julian groaned softly and lay still for a long moment. This was not going to be a good day.

He glanced aside to the other bed and was not surprised to find it empty. Raedrick almost never slept in. But then, they couldn't really afford to be late risers.

Knowing that didn't make it any easier to sit up and swing his feet over the side of the bed. Or to stand, grab a towel, and shuffle across the hall to the privy and the baths for his morning routine.

A bath left him feeling slightly more human. And as he tromped down the stairs, the ache in his head helped him ignore the twinges of protest from his wounded thigh. Maybe a hangover was good for something, after all.

The taproom had more patrons than usual in the morning. Maybe it was just that it was later than he normally came down. He limped over to a table near the bar, scanning the crowd as he went. Raedrick was nowhere to be seen, but Julian recognized several men who stood in a cluster at the bar: the fishing men from last night.

He ordered tea and the standard fish breakfast, then slouched forward at the table and rubbed at his temples with his fingertips, wishing he could rub the ache out.

Sooner than he expected, he heard footsteps approaching his table and looked up. But instead of the waitress with his tea, Horace stood there. His weathered features were rested and alert as though he hadn't been up well past midnight drinking with the younger men at the bar.

"Morning, boy. Looks like you could use some help."

Julian winced. "Not so loud, please."

Horace chuckled and sat down in the chair across from him. The old man reached inside his coat and pulled out a small vial. He set it on the table and pushed it across to Julian, saying, "When that tea gets here, put some of this into it. It'll do wonders for your head."

"Is that right." He picked up the vial and held it up to the light from the nearby window. Within was an orange-red fluid of some sort. "I've heard of plenty of hangover cures. Tried them all." He raised an eyebrow at Horace. "None of them work."

Horace leaned back in his chair and scratched at his chin. "You this cynical about everything?"

"I'm not cynical. I'm realistic."

"Sure," Horace replied with a snort. "Well, how's this for realistic." Leaning forward, he tapped at the top of the table with his index finger. "Me and my boys are going to help you and yer friend. Just call and we'll be there to put the fear of the gods into those thugs."

Julian blinked in surprise and looked from Horace to the other fishing men. They numbered a dozen in all, all weathered from days out on the lake, all solid and strong. And every one of them was watching him and Horace from across the room, wearing the resolved expressions of men ready for a hard day's work.

"I don't understand. Malory told us you were leery about lending a hand."

"That's just the management." Horace spat to one side as he said the word. "I'm head of the Guild, though. If I say we don't work so we can help you defend the town," he grinned and spread his hands, "we don't work. And ain't a damn thing management can do about it, unless they think they can man the boats themselves. Cause they sure won't find anyone else in these parts to do it. We'll see to that."

Julian's jaw dropped. "How..."

"'Course, if I were to do that, management might just decide running a fishing company is too much trouble, close up shop, take their money, and run." Crossing his arms over his chest, he continued, "Me and my boys can run the boats, but we don't have the money or the contacts with the merchants outside the Vale to make it worth a damn. So it's a balancing act. Management knows I can shut them down, but they know I'm buggered if I do."

"So you're saying...?"

"I'm saying, boy, that those men there," he jerked his thumb in the direction of his men at the bar, "volunteered to help you two out, and I got management to keep paying them while they do it."

Julian looked from the men at the bar to Horace in disbelief, and found himself speechless for a moment. Finally, he managed to say, "Horace, I don't know what to say. Thank you."

The old fishing man grinned. "Reality looks a bit different in the morning, don't it?"

❧ 14 ☙

NEW BLOOD

Raedrick walked into the taproom a bit before noon. Spotting Julian almost immediately, Raedrick strode quickly over to where he was chatting with the new recruits near the bar.

Breakfast had helped settle Julian's stomach, but Horace's hangover cure was as miraculous as he claimed. His headache reduced to a barely noticeable throb, he smiled cheerfully as his friend arrived. Raedrick's opening comment removed his smile quickly, however.

"Good to see you're up and about. I've just been at the Mayor's office."

That could not have been fun. "Was it bad?"

"You could say that. I thought sure he was going to pull his hair out. He's terrified, convinced that we've brought more harm than good already."

"Does he want us to leave then?"

Raedrick shook his head. "I offered, but he practically begged us to stay." He sighed. "I'm not sure he knows what he really wants, except for this whole episode to be over. So we still have a job."

"That's good, I suppose."

Raedrick shrugged, then looked past Julian to the fishing men. "Who are these guys?"

Julian grinned broadly. "My dear friend," he made a sweeping gesture as though he were a herald introducing an arriving dignitary, "may I introduce our army?"

Julian had thought the morning could not get any better. The confused expression on Raedrick's face proved him wrong. "What are you talking about?"

Julian laughed. "These fine fellows have pledged to help us against the brigands." Wagging a finger at his friend, he went on. "I keep telling you, staying up late and drinking with the locals always reaps benefits."

Raedrick's eyebrows rose high onto his forehead. He turned to regard the fishing men for a long moment, his veteran eyes taking their individual measures in

63

a silent appraisal. Finally, he cleared his throat and said, "Have any of you ever used a sword?"

One hand went up, from a swarthy fellow in his middle years near the back of the group.

"A bow?"

Three more hands went up.

Raedrick rolled his eyes and gestured for Julian to follow him. The two friends moved several paces away. Raedrick spoke softly, even though it was all but certain they were out of earshot.

"What the hell good does it do us to have amateurs backing us up?"

Julian knew this was coming. "I've thought of that, Rae. All these fellows are strong and know how to work hard. They can learn."

A soft snort was Raedrick's initial response. "It takes months to learn the sword to the point where you won't accidentally stab yourself in combat. We have days. Maybe a week or two."

"But the brigands don't know they can't fight, do they? They look impressive enough to help with any negotiations we may do."

"And when Farzal calls our bluff, then what?"

Julian shrugged. "The bow's a lot easier to learn than the sword. Long as they stay out of reach..." He spread his hands. What did Raedrick want? This was far from an ideal situation, and beggars couldn't be choosers.

He could tell Raedrick did not like the idea at all, but he also recognized the necessity of increasing their numbers. After a brief pause, he nodded acquiescence. As Raedrick moved back toward the group of fishing men, Julian heard him mumble, "Lambs to the slaughter," under his breath. He hoped his friend's assessment was wrong, even though he secretly shared it.

More loudly, Raedrick said, "Alright gentlemen, it's time to learn a new trade. Meet us at the Constable's office in a half hour. If you have anything that can pass for armor - a leather apron, gloves, boots - or any actual armor maybe passed down through the family, bring it. Same goes for weapons. Questions?"

Several of the men shook their heads, but all remained silent.

Raedrick nodded. "Alright. A half hour."

With that, the men quickly dispersed, exiting the inn alone or in groups of two or three. All moved with a sense of purpose, and a serious demeanor. It was hard not to be impressed by their attitude, at least.

Constable Malory appeared surprised when Julian asked him for the use of his bows and swords.

"How many?"

"All of them."

His jaw dropped. "Why?"

Raedrick grinned at him. "We've got some new recruits. I don't suppose you have a place to shoot around here?"

Malory nodded. "Down this street, just past the edge of town. Fendig and I set up a few targets for practice away from where most people travel. Who are these recruits?"

Just then the swarthy man who had claimed knowledge of the sword walked into the office. Though Julian still had his doubts about him, the man had on a leather breastplate that looked at least passable and wore a curved sword with a hand-and-a-half hilt on his hip. He looked the part, at least.

"We're here," he reported, then he turned to go.

"Wait," Julian said. "What's your name?"

"Selam."

"Have the others come in and grab a bow and a sword, Selam."

The swordsman nodded and exited the building. Constable Malory shook his head in surprise.

"I didn't know he had a sword. Hell, I didn't know he knew anything besides knots, currents, and tides. He spends more time on the boats than anyone." Malory smirked slightly, then looked at the two friends and shook his head. "How on earth did you convince the Covington brothers to let their men off work?"

"I take it they own the fishing company?" Julian asked.

Malory nodded.

Julian grinned at him. "Don't need an in with the owners if you drink with the workers."

The fishing men began trouping in and collecting weapons. Grinning a bit more at Malory's renewed expression of confusion, Julian clapped him on the shoulder and followed the first pair of recruits out onto the street. It was time to figure out what he and Raedrick had to work with.

———

Three hours later, Julian's spirits were quite a bit lower.

Despite experience having taught him to expect poor performance from beginners, Horace's pledge of support combined with the fishing men's eager attitude conspired to make him forget that lesson. Julian thought sure they would be, if not skilled, at least passable.

It was a struggle to claim even that much.

Not that the entire group was a loss from the start. The men who earlier claimed experience with the bow all managed to get arrows downrange without difficulty, and even hit the targets a time or two. Everyone else, though... Julian winced just thinking about it. Most of the men had bandages on their forearms from their bowstrings. Almost all were quite a bit less enthusiastic than they had been at the beginning.

"They *did* make progress," Raedrick whispered into his ear.

"A little." More loudly, Julian said, "Alright, gentlemen. That was a good start. Obviously, we've got a fair bit of ground to cover before you'll be ready for combat. We'll meet here at sunrise every day to work on it, and we won't quit until sundown, except for lunch. Before you know it, you'll be hitting bulls-eyes with ease." He managed not to sound ironic as he said that last. He seriously doubted many of them would progress beyond merely competent. But that was all he needed them to be.

"Are we going to work the sword too?" asked one of the younger fishing men. Julian would have called him slender except for his bulging stomach; everything else about him was thin as a rail. He had been the closest to promising of any of the men who had no previous experience.

Julian shook his head. "Yes, but one thing at a time. Once you can get arrows downrange with some accuracy, we'll teach you how not to stab yourselves. But your default should be the bow. A sword is a lot more difficult, and we frankly won't have time to make you proficient with it."

The young man nodded, disappointment clear in his eyes.

Raedrick spoke up. "You're dismissed for the evening, gentlemen." The men nodded and began to disperse when Raedrick added, "Selam, Hiram, Rolf, and Gilroy, please remain for a moment."

The swordsman and the three practiced bowmen lingered as their fellows departed. Julian waited until the others were out of sight before addressing them.

"Since you have more practice than the others, we're going to lean heavily on you when the time comes. Are you up for it?"

Selam looked uncertain. "I'm no good with a bow." That was an understatement, from what Julian had seen this afternoon. However, Raedrick spent some time with him and walked away impressed with his swordsmanship. No mean trick, that.

"That's why you're going to teach these three the basics of the sword while Rae and I focus on the others."

Selam blinked in surprise, then grinned broadly and nodded. The look he gave the other three was almost predatory. Julian made a mental note to keep an eye on him.

"In that case, we'll..."

"Raedrick! Julian!" Fendig's voice sounded as though he was in a near-panic. What was he doing here?

Julian turned around just as the Deputy came to a halt and bent over, placing his hand on his knees and panting heavily. He was sweating as though he had just sprinted the entire distance from town.

"What's wrong, Fendig?" Raedrick asked.

Fendig coughed and took a deep breath, then forced himself to stand up straight. "Farzal," he managed between breaths. "He just rode into town with a bunch of his men. He's going to the Town Hall for the Mayor!"

"Bugger me," Julian breathed. "We're not ready for a showdown."

Raedrick nodded in agreement. "Let's hope it doesn't come down to that." Looking at the four remaining fishing men, he said, "You guys spread out on the street and be ready to cover us if it comes down to a fight."

The four newcomers swallowed hard and nodded. Only Selam looked truly calm; the others looked ready to jump out of their skin. Julian couldn't blame them. It was far too early in the game for this sort of confrontation. And him all but crippled, too! It was enough to put the notion of flight into *his* head for a moment.

Then he met Raedrick's eyes and saw the same dread that he felt, but it was suppressed beneath a steely resolve. If he didn't know Raedrick as well as he did, he would not have known he was anxious at all. But then, he always had been good at projecting calm.

The two friends exchanged nods, and Raedrick smiled thinly. "Let's get it done."

Loosening his sword in its scabbard, Julian set off at a trot toward Town Hall, trying his best to jog through the twinges from his thigh.

✽ 15 ✽

DIPLOMACY

Julian tried to shake off the shiver that always came when his adrenalin began to flow while also licking his lips in a vain attempt to wet a mouth that had suddenly gone dry. He had long since stopped trying to figure out how it was possible to be exhilarated and terrified at the same time; by this point in his life he had come to recognize both as a soldier's constant companions on the eve of battle. That he felt them now, as he and Raedrick hurried to follow Fendig to intercept Farzal with the four fishing men following, should not have been special at all.

Yet for some reason it felt different this time. Perhaps it was the eyes of various townsfolk, their expressions terrified beneath a facade of confident hope, following them as they rushed past. Or perhaps it was the protests from his injured thigh, reminding him that if the meeting did come to blows he was not equipped to make a good showing.

Regardless, when they rounded the corner and emerged onto Main Street near the Town Hall, Julian's heart was in his throat. Seeing twenty men on horseback, all armed with quality blades and wearing good thick leather breastplates with steel plates sewn on or, in a few cases, mail similar to what he and Raedrick wore, did not help the situation.

The Mayor, Constable Malory at his side, was standing on the steps of the Town Hall, his hands clasped in front of him as he clearly tried not to appear terrified. He was addressing a pale-complected man who couldn't have been much older than twenty-five, thirty at the absolute maximum. He had sandy blond hair and a lean, muscular body with very broad shoulders. A scar crossed his forehead from his right temple to the brow of his left eye, and he wore a mocking smile on his face.

Julian recognized him immediately.

"Son of a bitch," Raedrick murmured. He recognized the man also.

Very quickly they were within earshot, and it was clear Mayor Brimly was at a disadvantage. Hardly a surprise, considering. However, upon seeing them, and the fishing men behind them as they fanned out along the width of the street just as Julian and Raedrick had directed them to, the Mayor squared his jaw and stopped whatever he was saying.

The brigands noted their arrival as well. Though they looked disdainful, particularly as they regarded the fishing men, they nonetheless adjusted their formation to keep the new men in plain view.

For his part, the blond fellow looked over everything Julian's and Raedrick's men did with a measuring eye. Julian noticed his smile slip somewhat as he studied the fishing men. He was no fool.

Then the blond man's eyes alighted on Julian and Raedrick, and he burst out laughing companionably. "Well, well. Baletier and Hinderbrook. What brings you to this fine township?"

"I think you know what, Isenholf," Raedrick replied.

The blond man laughed again as he shook his head. "Name's Farzal now, Corporal." He looked from Raedrick to Julian and back quickly. "I assume you're to blame for the men I lost down at the falls."

Farzal did not phrase it as a question, so neither Julian nor Raedrick bothered to reply. He sniffed at their silence.

"I'll take that as a yes." He sighed and shook his head. "Now normally, I take the skin off a man who kills one of mine. But I'll tell you what. For old times' sake, I'll let that slide, just this once."

"Very kind of you," Julian quipped.

Farzal nodded. "It is."

"You obviously know each other." The Mayor's tone was confused.

Farzal laughed again. "Oh we know each other, all right. We're closer than brothers, aren't we, boys?"

"We *were*," Raedrick replied. Turning to address the Mayor, he continued. "We served together in the Army. He was a squad leader in the other platoon in our company."

Constable Malory's expression grew even more severe than it had been before as he processed Raedrick's words. If anything, the Mayor looked more worried than ever. Farzal ignored them, though, focusing his attention fully on Raedrick and Julian.

"And it looks like I was wrong about you two." His mocking grin returned as he spoke. "I thought you had swallowed the propaganda completely. But look at you now!"

Julian got a sinking feeling in his stomach. This was about to get ugly. Glancing aside at Raedrick, he could see that his friend had the same thought. If Farzal suspected...

"What are you talking about?" The Mayor's worry and confusion was obvious from the trembling of his voice. His eyes flitted back and forth between Farzal and the two friends, and he mopped his brow with a trembling hand.

Farzal's grin only deepened as he looked at the Mayor. "They were no more released from their enlistment than I was. No one was to be released." Looking back at the Julian and Raedrick, he spat out, "You left of your own accord, didn't you? You deserted."

There it was, out in the open for all to hear. The sinking feeling became a cold lump of dread that radiated chills throughout Julian's entire body. There was no denying Farzal's accusation; it was the truth after all.

In the long silence that followed, all eyes turned onto them. Julian felt the urge to run away, not out of fear but out of shame. The Constable's stare, the respectful look of a colleague earlier, now held contempt. The Mayor's was worse, because his face was that of a man who had abandoned hope for despair, and was ready to do violence to the one who had taken that hope. In this case, Julian was painfully aware that he was the one.

Farzal laughed again and turned his attention back to Mayor Brimly. "So those two were to be your mighty saviors, were they?" He shook his head and snorted. "Payment is due in two weeks. Don't be late."

He nodded and his men began turning their horses away. A trio set off down Main Street; two columns of five spread out to either side of the street and began moving at a slower pace. Outriders and flankers taking station, Farzal looked back at Julian and Raedrick briefly.

"You two boys really ought to think about joining up with me. The authorities won't treat you any better for trying to play hero here when they catch you. There's strength in numbers, my friends. We can make very good money together. You won't find a better deal this side of the grave."

"Not a chance," Raedrick replied, taking on the stern tone he saved for green men under his charge who were making trouble. "I'll make *you* a deal. Ride out of here now and don't come back, and we won't put you down like a dog."

Farzal looked, if possible, even more amused than he did before. As he rode away and the rest of his men followed, his laughter echoed in his wake.

Julian watched the brigands grow steadily smaller until, not long after they rode past the town limits, they turned to the right and rode out of view. Swallowing, he braced himself then looked back at the Mayor and Constable. Disbelief, disapproval, hope, despair, terror, anger...all those and more were contained in their expressions.

"I suppose you'd like an explanation," he said.

They both nodded. Mayor Brimly gestured toward the Town Hall. "In my office."

Mayor Brimly's office occupied most of the second floor of the Town Hall. Which wasn't saying much, considering the entire Town Hall took up less area than The Oarlock's taproom. Despite being small, it was well appointed, with ornately carved furniture made from darkly-stained wood, no doubt harvested from the forested hills north of town. The desk was particularly impressive, a massively constructed, ornately carved piece that had clearly been designed to intimidate people on the receiving end of its occupant's attention.

Julian certainly felt intimidated, or if not intimidated at least threatened and judged. It was only natural, considering. But he still didn't like it.

The Mayor sat in his chair and looked at them over steepled fingers. Constable Malory, a grimly disapproving expression on his face, stood beside the desk with his arms crossed over his chest. The fingertips of his right hand drummed rapidly on the muscles of his left forearm as though from anxiety. He probably couldn't wait to put them in irons; local law enforcement often received generous compensation from the kingdom for capturing deserters.

As though he was reading Julian's mind, Mayor Brimly said, "Why should I not lock you both up right now?"

Raedrick replied, "We're helping you..."

"The hell you are. You've not made any progress; in fact, you've made things worse for us." The Mayor leaned forward in his chair and scowled. "Farzal raised his price, to, as he put it, compensate the families of the men he lost. The men *you* killed."

"Before we knew anything about what was going on here."

"So you say," Constable Malory interjected. "Why should I not think you've been playing us from the start? For all we know, you could be in league with him."

"How stupid do you think he is?" Julian asked.

"What are you talking about?"

Julian sighed. "If we were working together, why would he tell you about us?"

Malory blinked and scowled then nodded with obvious reluctance.

"Fine," said the Mayor. "That doesn't change the facts about you, does it? Why should I trust you at all?"

Julian and Raedrick shared a long look. Then Julian shrugged. "Tell them, Rae." Mayor Brimly knew most of it already. He might as well know it all.

Raedrick nodded. Julian could tell his friend was as reluctant as he was, but there was little choice in the matter at this point.

Drawing a deep breath, Raedrick began talking.

❧ 16 ❧

LAWFUL ORDERS

Raedrick's heartbeat filled his ears, the thudding so loud he almost couldn't hear the screams of wounded and dying men all around him. He paid neither sound any mind; his only focus was the man in front of him and the movement of the man's sword.

They had danced around each other for an eternity. Three passes and still neither had struck home with his weapon. Through the prism of his concentration, Raedrick felt a grudging respect for the man. He was the enemy, yes, and his nation had waged brutal war against Raedrick's homeland. But he was skilled and he fought with honor. It was hard not to appreciate that.

All around him, men on both sides of the battle had stopped their fighting. Those in the immediate vicinity formed a loose ring around him and his opponent. All eyes watched as though entranced; all enmity was forgotten before the spectacle of the mighty duel.

Flexing his fingers on the grip of his saber, Raedrick advanced slowly. The man circled to the left, and Raedrick pivoted to follow. He feinted upward, but pulled back from the true attack as the man simply countered, a lightning-fast cut at waist level that forced Raedrick to leap backwards to avoid having his guts spilled.

Landing lightly on the balls of his feet, he had to dodge aside immediately as the man followed his cut with a rising thrust toward Raedrick's chest. He barely avoided the tip of the man's sword by twisting his torso as he moved to the left, but he felt the blade tug at his mail for a heartbeat before he pulled clear. Slightly off balance, the only counter he could muster was a quick kick upward with the ball of his right foot.

A soft grunt accompanied the satisfying feeling of his boot striking the man's side, and the man stumbled. Grasping his side with his left hand, he fell to the ground.

Raedrick moved in, but again the man's reflexes nearly proved his better. Rolling onto his back, Raedrick's foe made a wide cut at ankle height, forcing

71

Raedrick backward just long enough for the man to spring onto his feet in a single fluid move.

They paused for a moment, eyeing each other carefully. Raedrick's opponent removed his hand from his side and returned it to the hand-and-a-half hilt of his sword. Then he inclined his head, a gesture of respect that Raedrick returned in kind.

Just because they were trying to kill each other didn't mean they couldn't be civilized, after all.

Then the man advanced. His blade flicked upward, then abruptly descended toward Raedrick's front knee. Nearly taken by the initial feint, Raedrick froze for half a heartbeat. Too late, he pivoted backwards, moving his front leg to the rear, but not before taking a deep cut to his thigh above his kneecap.

Grimacing at the flash of pain, and ignoring the cheers from several enemy soldiers as their fellow finally drew blood, Raedrick cut downward with his saber in time with his pivot. The razor-sharp edge of this weapon arced toward his opponent. The man's eyes widened and he pushed backward off the balls of his feet, his only defensive option with his blade still whistling downward in follow-through from his cut.

Blade and man both were a blur of motion that suddenly stilled. A fine spray of red flicked from the tip of Raedrick's saber, which was otherwise unstained. The man blinked and his jaw dropped open in bafflement as he raised his left hand to the side of his neck. As his fingers touched the skin of his throat, blood began flowing from the cut. At first it was a slow seep, then it became a spurting rush. The man's eyes widened and he stumbled backward a half-step.

Then his sword dropped from the suddenly limp fingers of his right hand and he fell to the ground in a heap.

A low sigh seemed to emanate from the enemy forces as Raedrick's foe fell. One and all, those nearby all wore expressions of stunned disbelief. As he watched, their fighting spirit seeped out of them, almost in time with the last of his opponent's lifeblood as it left the wound in his neck.

The momentary lull ended as Raedrick's comrades took up a loud, enthusiastic battle cry and surged forward, passing him on either side as they charged. The enemy fell back before their renewed onslaught. Entire platoons fell before anyone in the enemy camp tried to rally the troops, but by then it was too late. Inside of a half hour, the kingdom's army swept the field, leaving only a few of the enemy wounded alive to see the sunset.

"Besting the enemy army's champion in single combat, Corporal Baletier single-handedly dealt a devastating blow to enemy morale, enabling our forces to win a decisive victory. Corporal Baletier's unflinching bravery, unrivaled skill at arms, and stalwart example reflected great credit upon himself and were in keeping with the highest principles of service to the Throne."

The Brigade's Executive Officer finished reading the citation as the Colonel pinned a medal, green and blue fabric separated by a strip of gold from which dangled two miniature crossed swords made of silver, onto the breast of his dress uniform doublet.

"Congratulations, Corporal," he said.

"Thank you sir."

The Colonel returned his salute then turned to the assembled troops and led them in a round of applause. Raedrick stood at attention and tried not to blush at all the attention.

Soon enough, the official ceremony was over and Raedrick limped down from the podium. He was eager to get back to his tent and change into less formal and more comfortable attire. And for a bath and a good night's sleep, followed by a week of leave back in Calas. It wasn't often that a soldier could partake in such luxuries, but the High Command tended to pull out the stops after a great victory. And by any measure, last week's battle had been just that.

His squad intercepted him at the bottom of the stairs. The five men he knew best in the world clustered around him, offering their congratulations along with good-natured quips, then walked with him back to their tents. It was a slow journey, and not just because of his injury. Throughout the camp, men he knew by name, by face, or not at all stopped to wish him well. One and all, they wore the exuberant expression of men who had not just survived, but conquered, in the face of what they all thought going into it was almost certain death.

The mood at their Company's tents was more subdued though. Men were hurrying about, putting their gear in order as though getting ready for action instead of preparing to go on leave. What was going on?

The platoon Sergeant answered the question as soon as he saw Raedrick and his squad. "Leave's cancelled. We're heading out."

Raedrick's spirits, soaring high a moment ago, sank like a stone. "Where to?"

"The scouts uncovered an enemy outpost about twenty miles from here. We're to take it out."

* * *

The Company assembled on the crest of the hill overlooking the enemy outpost. To Raedrick, it didn't look like much more than a country village. It consisted of fifteen or twenty buildings clustered around a central green. There was a small encampment of some sort on the east side of town, halfway around the town from their hill. Maybe that was the target.

"Doesn't look like much, does it?" Hinderbrook said.

Raedrick looked sidelong at him and grunted. "The scouts say it's a key outpost. Is everyone else ready?"

Hinderbrook nodded.

"Good. You know the signal."

Little else needed to be said. The men in Raedrick's squad were well drilled at this point. Months in combat conditions had melded them into a team that was second to none. Sometimes, it almost seemed like they were reading each others' thoughts, the way they fought as a unit. It was a beautiful thing to see in action.

There was not long to wait. Maybe ten minutes later, the word passed down the line to make ready. Raedrick gripped his reins more tightly and forced down his growing anxiety. He needed to be cool and collected to lead his men correctly. It would be all the more important since he was not at his fighting best.

Then a whistle sounded from the center of the line and was picked up by the platoon leaders. Advance at a trot. Raedrick dug his heels into his horse's flanks and began to post in time with her steps.

Again into battle. Would there never be an end?

Where was the enemy?

Everywhere Raedrick looked, old men, women, and children fled before the Company's advance. But not a one of them had a weapon of any kind. Confusion reigned on the faces of his squad members as well. They had their weapons at the ready, but there was no one to use them on.

The scouts and intelligence people had fed them bad information before, but never this bad.

At the Platoon Leader's order, Raedrick veered away from the main column and led his men to investigate a collection of outbuildings. Eager to actually accomplish something, his men fanned out as they neared the buildings. Dismounting, they quickly kicked in all the doors and conducted a search.

Their faces when they returned were more confused and almost dejected.

"Just a few kids hiding out. Other than that, there's nothing here at all, Corporal," Laremy reported.

"Better bring the kids along so we can muster them with the others. We don't want them getting hurt by mistake."

"Right."

It took a few minutes to get the kids out of their hiding spot. In the end, Hilbredth had to sing a song to coax them out. He had a fine singing voice and a kind nature, so these sorts of things always seemed to fall on him. Soon enough, though, they were all formed up with the smaller kids riding ahead of them on their saddles and the bigger kids walking alongside.

They made for the town commons, or whatever the locals called the central green. Standard procedure was to muster civilians there, where they could be accounted for, while the unit finished its sweep. That had the dual affect of preventing surprises during the search and minimizing the chance of harming the civilians.

Suddenly a plume of smoke began to rise from the other side of the village. Then a second, and a third. Screams reached Raedrick's ears, coming from the direction of the Commons. What was going on? Raedrick reined in and turned to his men. They all looked as nervous and confused as he did.

"Let the kids down." Raedrick looked for the oldest of the children and pointed at him. "You there! Do you know a better hiding spot than those buildings we found you in?"

The youth nodded, his eyes wild with fright.

"You're in charge. Take the others and go there. Do not come out again until you see me come back and tap myself on my head with the flat of my sword. Do you understand?"

The youth nodded again and began herding the other children together. Seeing that he had things in hand, Raedrick turned to his men. "Let's go. Keep on the alert."

Weapons drawn, his squad charged into the village at a canter. More smoke plumes were rising now and the screams and shouts were louder than ever. Biting back a curse, Raedrick turned into the Commons.

And cursed out loud.

The Commons was a scene right out of a slaughterhouse. Everywhere he looked lay hacked civilian bodies. Soldiers, mounted or on foot, chased down fleeing people and cut them down without hesitation. Some unfortunate women did not get that mercy. Several had been stripped naked and were being raped by soldiers. On the far side of the Commons, a large group of civilians was being herded into a large building, the Town Hall maybe.

Sitting on their horses in the center of the Commons, the Company officers pointed and shouted orders.

"What in hell is going on here?" Raedrick demanded in a fury. Just then, the soldiers finished herding the civilians into the building. They then chained the doors shut and backed away.

The Company Commander, a grizzled older Captain, glanced at Raedrick and scowled. "New orders from High Command, Corporal. Scorched earth: take no prisoners and leave no support for the enemy. Send a message that continued resistance means death for everyone." Though his tone of voice was strong as always, his posture and expression said he was as troubled by this change as Raedrick was. That did not stop him from turning to the soldier leading the contingent who had just herded the civilians into the building and ordering, "Burn it."

The soldier looked a bit sick, but saluted and turned away to carry out the order.

Was he serious? Raedrick barked, "No! Sir, we cannot do this!"

The Captain scowl became deeper. "We can, and we will. More specifically, you will. Private!" The soldier who received the order to burn the building turned, flaming torch in hand. The Captain gestured to Raedrick. "Turn the duty over, Private." To Raedrick, he said, "Burn it, Corporal. Do it now."

The Private handed the torch over, looking relieved to be rid of it. Unable to believe what was happening, Raedrick looked down at the torch in his hand, then back at the officers. Behind him, the members of his squad murmured amongst themselves. He knew they were as discontent as he was.

The officers noted his hesitation and turned their horses to face him. The Captain leaned forward and spoke in an even, cold tone. "Light the fire, Corporal, or I'll have you up on charges for disobeying a lawful order and hanged this very night, decoration or no."

COURSE CORRECTION

Mayor Brimly sat back in his chair, stunned. Beside him, Constable Malory's expression had softened. He and the Mayor looked at each other for a long minute.

"We did not set out to desert. But when High Command gave those orders..." Raedrick shook his head. "I would not execute such an order. Nor would I order my men to."

"No. No, I imagine you could not."

"The rest of us in the squad left with him," Julian interjected. "And some others from the platoon as well. Disobeying an order gets you the gallows. Not reporting a desertion gets you almost as bad. But weren't none of us who could stomach staying with the unit after that."

The Constable nodded slowly. "What about Farzal? Or..what was it you called him?"

"Isenholf," Raedrick replied with a sigh. "Theobald Isenholf."

"He was a rat from the beginning," Julian said, earning a look of reproach from Raedrick. "What? He was. You just didn't see it because you were a Squad Leader as well." Looking back at the Mayor, Julian went on. "He had a cruel streak, and took matters too far even before things began going downhill. Then the officers found out that he had been stealing. They were going to make an example of him, but he left before they had the chance. Took a few of his cronies with him."

"And now here they are," Mayor Brimly grumbled. Grunting, he stood up and turned around to look out his office window. "This town cannot survive under Farzal's domination. He'll drain us dry. And we do not have the resources or know-how to deal with him on our own." Taking a deep breath, he turned back around. "Very well. The job is still yours, if you will do it."

"Your Honor, I..." Constable Malory began.

"Would you have done differently in their place, Lucian?"

Malory took a moment in answering. He looked sidelong at Julian and Raedrick and frowned. Then, finally, he shook his head. "No, I suppose not. But still..."

"We can worry about the rest after this crisis has passed," Mayor Brimly replied.

Malory nodded, clearly not happy even if he did understand.

For his part, Julian didn't much like the sound of that. The only thing he could think of that they had to worry about later was turning them in, and damned if he was going to risk his life for them just to be repaid like that. He was just about to open his mouth and say that when the Mayor spoke up again.

"You understand the Constable and I are bound by oath and duty to turn in deserters that we come across. However, if you will rid us of these criminals, we will pretend we did not learn of your past. Are we agreed?"

Raedrick nodded and Julian followed suit.

"Very well then. I'll leave you to get on with it."

———

Julian and Raedrick descended the steps at the front of the Town Hall. Their men, waiting in the street at the foot of the stairs, perked up when they returned.

"Is everything alright?" asked Selam. He did not truly sound concerned.

"No problem. The Mayor is calm again at least."

Julian's words evoked chuckles from the fishing men.

"Brimly is high strung, that's for sure," Rolf quipped. "But he means well. Now what?"

That was the question, wasn't it? Julian looked to the east, where the sun was beginning to dip below the mountains. The day was about done.

"Change in plans, Julian," Raedrick said suddenly. "You're running the training on your own tomorrow. Rolf, Hiram, and Gilroy will assist."

"Say again?"

"Selam and I are going to take an excursion tonight, and I doubt we'll be back in time to meet the others in the morning."

Selam blinked in surprise. "Where are we going?"

Raedrick pointed toward the end of Main Street, where the brigands had turned right after leaving town. "Twenty men on horses leave a trail that should be easy to follow. We're going to find their hideout."

"But Rae, I..."

"You're still hurt, Julian. You'll slow us down, and you'll be a liability in a fight right now."

"Now hold on."

"You know it's true, my friend."

Julian wanted to deny Raedrick's words, but he could not. Even going up and down stairs was a strain, and would be for a number of days yet. Reluctantly, Julian nodded.

Raedrick smiled and clapped him on the shoulder. "Don't worry. We'll leave a few of the scum for you to handle."

With that, he and Selam set off down the street. Julian couldn't help but chuckle at his friend's bravado. All the same, he felt a pang of something that felt disturbingly close to jealousy as he watched them depart.

Twilight was nearing its end as Julian stepped into the taproom.

Even though he had been in the Vale for a number of days, he still found it strange how quickly night descended in the valley. He was just as happy to get indoors, since the night's chill was beginning to set in. That was one advantage to not going on Raedrick's excursion; it felt like it was going to be a cold one.

The taproom was more crowded than usual. Men sat at every bar stool, and most of the tables were taken. It took a moment of thinking before Julian realized why: tomorrow was Godsday. No work on Godsday, so there was no reason for people not to stay up a bit later than normal, and maybe indulge in a little extra fun. Molli was behind the bar this evening, a change from her usual routine. Lani was probably around somewhere too, but Julian couldn't see her anywhere.

Instead of lingering in the entryway, Julian decided to go say hi to Molli at the bar. She was always good for a chuckle, and maybe a discounted drink. But as he hobbled around a full table and barely avoided getting run down by a hurrying waitress, he spotted another lady he had not seen in a while.

Melanie sat, impeccably dressed and alone as usual, at a table for two near the fireplace on the right.

Julian altered his course without thinking twice.

The lady mage, or whatever she wanted to call herself, noticed him coming long before he arrived beside her table. He chose to believe the little toss of her head came from happiness to see him rather than something else, but it was hard to not notice the way she rolled her eyes as he continued toward her table.

Well, they say if you want to get close to a woman it's better to get her dander up than to not cause any emotion in her at all. Julian had always seriously doubted how wise "they" really were about women, but just then he clung to that thought like a drowning man to a twig.

"Good evening, Melanie," Julian said.

"Why do you insist on bothering me, bumpkin? You and your friend got your help, so can you leave me alone, please?"

"Yes, well, about that. First, I'm not a bumpkin. I was born and raised a city boy, if you must know. Second..." Julian cleared his throat softly. "Our plan didn't turn out so well."

"No." If sarcasm were gold, she would be able to live like a queen for the rest of her life.

"No, really, it didn't. But we're moving on to plan B. There is a chance we'll need to ask for more help, though." She rolled her eyes again, her expression even more annoyed than it had been. "But that's not why I'm here."

"Then why *are* you here, city boy?"

He simply could not catch a break with her. "Well I'm on my own tonight. You clearly don't have any company." He put on his most winning smile and gestured toward the empty chair at her table. "Eating with company is always better than eating alone."

"Not always."

Feeling slapped across the face, Julian had to force the smile to not become a snarl. "Well if you're going to be rude about it..." He turned to leave.

He could hear the eye roll in her tone as she spoke to his back. "Oh sit down,

Julian. Honestly, it's no wonder you men are always fighting duels and starting wars, as thin skinned as you are."

Julian had half a mind to just walk away, but looking back over his shoulder, he was struck by the color of her skin in the firelight and how the flames reflected off her eyes. She really was stunning. And so, against his better judgement and the commands of his ego, he sat down in the proffered chair.

And had no idea what to say next.

The silence had become almost unbearable when their waitress finally came by to ask for his order. Silently blessing the waitress for her timeliness, he looked questioningly at Melanie.

"I've already ordered."

Nodding, Julian said, "Ale. And to eat, fish and chips."

The waitress nodded and made a note on her tray, then hurried off toward the bar.

"You're a true gourmet."

Now it was Julian's turn to roll his eyes. "Really, do you have to mock *everything* I do?"

Melanie sipped at her drink and smiled innocently. "You make it very easy." He opened his mouth to protest, but she stopped him with a raised hand. "But I'll try to be more gentle."

How kind of her. He half-snorted, half-chuckled. "Thank you."

They were silent for another brief period, during which the waitress brought Julian's drink. He gulped down a mouthful of ale and relished the flavor for a moment.

"Which city?"

Swallowing another mouthful of ale, he raised an eyebrow at Melanie. "Come again?"

"Which city are you from?"

"Oh." He set his tankard down and shrugged. "Taris, on the coast of the Tymor Sea."

"Very cosmopolitan."

Irritation welled up. It must have been visible on his face, because Melanie rolled her eyes again and said, "I'm serious. It's one hell of a lot more worldly a place to grow up than my little village."

"Really. And where was that?"

She shrugged. "It's called Vernon's Passing. Not even a one horse town, in the middle of nowhere. I got out of there as soon as I was able."

Julian supposed that explained a few things. "You've come a long way."

"You've no idea."

❧ 18 ☙

SKULKING

A s Raedrick expected, the twenty horses had indeed cut up the ground fairly well. He found it hard to believe that Isenholf--he could not bring himself to call the criminal by his assumed name--neglected to think about that. So he halfway expected to find the rear guard lying in wait somewhere on the trail.

But when he and Selam reached the Eastflow ford without incident, Raedrick began to rethink his assumption. Maybe Isenholf had *not* thought about the trail he left. Or worse, maybe he simply did not care. He had not bothered to hide his contempt, even of his former comrades in arms. He had always been cocky, but not sloppy.

"He must be very sure that his advantage is unassailable," Raedrick said to himself.

"Or he's just an ass," Selam offered.

Raedrick blinked in surprise. He had not realized he spoke loudly enough to be heard. He shook his head and chuckled softly before replying. "Always has been."

Selam chuckled as well, and the two men exchanged grins.

They had opted against horses for the pursuit. For one thing, riders were easier to spot, and this night's excursion required stealth. For another thing, Selam did not own one. And Raedrick did not feel right about loaning out Julian's without asking. So instead they had taken a few minutes to retrieve warm cloaks from their rooms and wading boots from the fishing company's warehouse, then set out after the brigands as twilight was beginning to settle over the Vale.

Even with the wading boots, crossing the ford was uncomfortably frigid. Raedrick shuddered in sympathy for the horses who had to cross it and made a mental note to get a few extra cubes of sugar for his mare. She had earned it crossing this three times in the last few days.

It was full dark when they emerged from the ford and discarded their wading

81

boots behind an outbuilding at the burned farm. "It's going to be tough following even this trail in the dark, you know," Selam noted.

"I know. The moon should be up soon; that will help." Raedrick glanced to the west toward where he expected the nearly full moon to rise and was gratified to see a faint glow on the horizon beyond the mountains. Any minute now.

Selam was right. Even after the moon rose above the mountains, it was slow going. It helped to have some notion as to where the trail would lead. And sure enough, at around the same place the prisoner had turned southeast the other day, this large group made the same turn. At least that was not just a ploy.

As before, the riders moved into the hills, climbing the first several and then descending into the small valleys between them. After doing that several times, Raedrick was beginning to become irritated; how did he and Julian lose that guy the other day if he had gone on like this?

The question answered itself a moment later. As they descended the back of yet another hill, the trail abruptly turned to the left, heading due east down the center of the valley between two hills. The valley continued a fair distance, slowly veering back to the south. About a quarter of a mile further on, as the curve of the valley brought the first hill out of sight, the hill to the left became rougher, more boulder-strewn. Then suddenly a cleft in the hillside came into view: a narrow chasm between adjoining hillsides that stretched east and slowly rose higher into the hills.

"I never heard of a formation like that in this part of the Vale," Selam said, sounding and looking surprised.

"There hasn't been a farmstead in a while. How often do people come out this way?"

The fishing man shrugged. "Not too often that I know of. But then, I don't know all the ins and outs around here."

Raedrick looked sidelong at him. "I didn't think you grew up here."

"What gave me away?"

"There don't seem to be very many trained swordsmen in this town." Raedrick chuckled and added, "And you drop your r's. Folks from here don't do that."

Selam frowned as he looked away from Raedrick and back toward the chasm. "Even with that moon, it will be hard to see anything in there."

Ignoring the change in topic, Raedrick glanced up at the moon, now almost directly overhead. "We won't get any better light until morning. Might as well get moving."

"I know. Just saying."

Sure enough, it was extremely dark within the chasm. The passage was narrow; maybe two people could ride side by side, but it would be uncomfortable. Also, it looked as though the walls of the chasm actually narrowed toward the top. That all resulted in very little light making it down to the floor where Raedrick and Selam walked.

Fortunately, the floor of the chasm was smooth and devoid of loose rocks. No doubt the brigands had cleared it out to make for easier passage. All the same, both men stumbled on occasion and their progress was very slow.

At one point, Raedrick looked back and was surprised to see that they had ascended a hundred feet or more. Glancing upwards, it did not look as though the chasm walls were much lower than they had been before. That meant the hills the chasm cut through were large indeed. He racked his brain, trying to recall seeing any hills high enough to conceal a feature like this when he and Julian had been here in the daylight, and came up lacking. What was going on?

The chasm continued to rise for a several hundred yards, then abruptly came to an end. One moment, Raedrick and Selam were walking in near pitch blackness. The next, they stepped out into a large open area that appeared chiseled out of rock. Or at least, Raedrick surmised it was open. He couldn't see very far ahead, but there were no distinguishing features except behind them. Rather than rolling hills, sheer cliffs, a couple hundred feet tall, rose on either side of the chasm and stretched out in either direction as far as Raedrick could see in the gloom.

Raedrick blinked. It was only marginally less dark here than it had been in the chasm. Confused, he looked up to find the moon. And saw only darkness, along with what looked like a smoky mist not far above the top of the cliffs. There was not even a hint that the moon was in the sky.

"Where is the light coming from?"

"I was just wondering that," Raedrick replied. Selam was quick on the uptake. He liked that. "I'm not sure what's going on here, Selam. Do you want to go back?"

The fishing man looked at Raedrick with offended eyes and shook his head. "Haven't found what we came for yet."

Raedrick grinned.

They moved forward, away from the chasm. The riders' trail was no longer visible, but there was no doubt which way they had gone. After a short while, Raedrick looked over his shoulder and felt a surge of dread. The cliffs were no longer visible. It was as if reality ended in a dark haze an indeterminate distance behind them.

"Stop, Selam."

The fishing man looked at Raedrick in confusion. Then he looked back also and his eyes widened. For the first time, Raedrick saw fear in the man's eyes. He was not sure his own did not show the same thing.

They hurried back the way they came. After a moment, the cliffs, and the chasm opening, suddenly emerged from the gloom. Raedrick was surprised at how relieved he felt when that happened. He found himself letting out a breath he had not realized he had been holding.

"Well at least we can get back."

Selam snorted. "We can also get turned around completely without realizing it and lose our way."

Raedrick pursed his lips. He hadn't thought of that. "Isenholf's bunch must have a way to safely get back and forth. Maybe we missed something."

They went back to the chasm opening and spent several minutes looking carefully around. The cliff walls, the ground, the swirling mist above, nothing escaped their attention. There *had* to be a way for them to know how to get back.

It was Selam who found it, by chance. He stepped back from the cliff face to look at the walls at a different angle. After a moment, he shook his head and threw up his hands. Raedrick bit back a curse and turned away. Maybe there was something inside the chasm itself...

"Raedrick!"

He spun around, his hand going to the grip of his saber. But Selam was alone, squatting down not far from where he had been looking up at the cliffs. He vigorously waved for Raedrick to come over. Once he reached Selam's side, Raedrick's spirits lifted.

Seen from the angle Selam took while squatting, there was a fine silver inlay in the rock floor. It outlined a path about as wide as four men walking abreast which stretched from the chasm exit, straight ahead for twenty yards. There it turned abruptly to the right and stretched away out of sight into the gloom.

"We weren't going the right way at all," Selam said, a slight quaver in his voice.

"It's a good thing we turned back when we did. Good job."

Raedrick stood and found he could still see the path's outline. It was almost as if, having found it once, he was now allowed to see it completely. Allowed by whom was not clear, especially since there was no one else around. But he couldn't shake the feeling that it was designed thus, for some reason.

"Do we go on?" Selam sounded a bit less certain, less confident, than he had before when Raedrick asked that question.

Raedrick nodded. "Haven't found what we came for yet."

Selam chuckled.

❦ 19 ❧

BASE CAMP

It was difficult to determine how long Raedrick and Selam followed the path through the gloom. Without the moon overhead, Raedrick had only his own internal clock to figure the passage of time, and he knew well how imprecise that could be. Also, very soon after setting out, the cliffs again vanished from sight. Without a reference point, it soon became impossible to judge distance either. It was almost as if time had stopped and distance had lost its meaning. Even though he knew it to be an illusion, Raedrick still found that notion extremely uncomfortable to consider.

So he was relieved when, out of the gloom ahead, shapes appeared: two columns flanking an open doorway were set into a rock wall. At first, Raedrick thought the wall was just another part of the cliffs, but it was too smooth and not nearly as tall. The gloomy mist swirled the same distance above this wall as it had the cliffs, however. Very strange.

Biting back a yawn--it was well past midnight--Raedrick drew his saber and ran toward the column to the right of the doorway.

The whole setup made the hair on the back of his neck stand up. It wasn't just the oddness of the place. Where were the sentries? He half expected arrows to begin raining down from atop the wall, but none came.

He reached the column and pressed flat against it. On the other side of the doorway, Selam had done the same. It was good that he hadn't needed to be ordered to do so; Raedrick was becoming more and more impressed with him as time went on.

And with his sword. This was the first time Raedrick had seen it unsheathed, and he found himself doing a double-take.

The blade was standard length, but curved almost as much as Raedrick's saber. Its edge was sharpened on the convex side of the curve and on the last half-foot of the concave side just below the point. Nothing unusual there except that it was obviously high quality workmanship.

It was the flat of the blade that drew Raedrick's attention. Stylized symbols and

85

designs were etched into the metal down the entire length of the blade: game animals, fantastic creatures, stars, the moon in its various phases, and all manner of strange letters and symbols that Raedrick did not recognize. Done poorly, such a collection of inscriptions would have been cluttered, awkward. Not so in this case. Every symbol or picture flowed flawlessly into the next so that the whole became a beautiful work of art that captured the eye and would not let go.

Selam noticed Raedrick's study and moved the blade so he could more readily examine it. "A family heirloom," he said in a whisper that just reached Raedrick's ears, "It has been passed down from father to son for many generations."

"I can see why."

Selam teeth flashed in the gloom as he grinned.

Back to business. Raedrick slid around the column until he could just peek through the doorway. Again, Selam followed his lead without needing to be told.

There was not much to see at first glance. The path turned to the left beyond the doorway and sloped upward along the outside of another wall. Raedrick presumed it reached another level area above somewhere, but that was obscured by the gloom.

For a moment, he wondered if it was more cheerful here in the daylight. Given the lack of moonlight, he would wager no. Talk about a depressing place to lair, if that were the case.

"I imagine we'll come upon some sign of them before much longer," Selam offered. "Sentries, horse pickets...something."

"You'd think. Keep alert."

Raedrick noted Selam's expression from the corner of his eye as he slipped through the doorway: the annoyed look of a man who has just been told the obvious.

The trail started out ascending at a shallow angle, but before long the grade increased and the climb became more difficult. Raedrick imagined it would be even more difficult on horseback. Maybe they made a practice of walking their horses from this point. The slope made for a good way to slow an assault, regardless.

After an indeterminable climb, shapes began to emerge from the gloom ahead and above. Squared off like blocks, it was hard to make out what they were for a long moment. Then he and Selam ascended a few more feet and the structures came clearly into view.

It was a gatehouse, complete with crenelated walls, a portcullis, and a thick wooden gate. And a pair of guards with torches on the battlements on either side of the gate.

"Cover!" Raedrick pressed against the wall and slowly edged his way backward down the trail until the torches and battlements were only just visible.

"That will be difficult to breach," Selam observed. "At least from this approach."

Raedrick nodded. "But are there any other approaches? I wouldn't want to try to find a different way through this place to find it, would you?"

"Not in this life."

Raedrick hesitated. This was, without a doubt, Isenholf's lair. But they only knew marginally more than they had before coming. He was loathe to leave without getting more information. Perhaps they could scale the wall... But no, it was shear and smooth, with hardly a seam between the stones it was built from.

It was useless. They had learned all they could this night. "It's time to go," he said with a sigh.

Selam nodded and began moving down the trail. With one last look up at the gatehouse, Raedrick followed.

———

They made better time going out than coming in. Partly because they knew the way already, but mostly because of relief. Raedrick was not about to admit it to Selam, but the thought of leaving the oppressive gloom of this place, wherever or whatever it was, lent extra speed to his stride.

Before long, they stood before the chasm opening in the side of the cliffs. Beside him, Raedrick heard Selam breathe a sigh.

"Not a moment too soon. This place makes me nervous."

Smirking, at his own cowardice in not admitting similar feelings more than anything else, Raedrick replied, "I know what you mean. Let's get out of..."

The sound of metal striking stone echoed down the chasm toward their ears, causing Raedrick to stop talking mid-thought. He froze, sudden anxiety flooding through him. Then, far down the chasm, a glow appeared. Flickering and bouncing, the glow could only be from a torch that someone was carrying.

"Son of a bitch," he breathed.

He and Selam exchanged glances and Raedrick was again impressed by the other man's calm. They exchanged nods, then darted to the cliff face beside the chasm mouth. Just as they had at the columns, Raedrick took the right and Selam the left, blades drawn. There they waited.

Slowly, more noises began to emanate from the chasm. Footsteps, metallic clinking, and voices. It was hard to make out the words at first, but before long, the conversation became more clear.

"...good take."

"Ya. Farzal was right again. Didn't even try to put up a fight."

A short pause followed, then the conversation continued.

"Ain't it s'posed to be brightening up in here? Sun came up a while ago."

A loud snort followed, along with mocking laughter.

"Things don't line up here, you know that."

"Whatever. It's unnatural, I tell you."

A general murmur of agreement followed.

Raedrick glanced across the mouth of the chasm toward Selam and held up four fingers. The other man nodded agreement: there were four distinct voices in the conversation. If they got the drop on the brigands, it should be an easy fight.

If.

Though maybe a minute passed, it felt like an eternity, waiting there. His heart rate increasing rapidly from tension, Raedrick took a deep breath. Then another. He forced himself, in spite of becoming more and more keyed up, to breathe slowly and deliberately; he had found over the years doing that helped him to focus. It did not do anything for his nerves, though.

Just when Raedrick thought they were never going to show up, a pair of brigands stepped out of the chasm mouth walking side by side. They were armed and armored the same as the others Raedrick had seen so far, though they looked weary, with bags under their eyes. *I probably look even worse,* Raedrick thought with an inward smile.

The two brigands looked neither left nor right, but continued straight ahead on the trail. Raedrick met Selam's eyes and nodded.

The two men sprang into action as soon as the next pair of brigands stepped from the chasm. Raedrick darted in with a backhanded rising cut from his saber at the same time Selam attacked his foe. The brigands both wore nearly identical expressions of shock as they fell, spurting blood from their throats.

The first two brigands had just begun to turn around when Raedrick and Selam spun and advanced on them.

Selam's man managed to duck beneath his cut and roll to the side away from him.

Raedrick's man also had quick reflexes; he turned all the way around and had his sword half-drawn when Raedrick's cut reached him. Only luck saved his life. Raedrick's saber struck his sword on its blade just above the hilt, sending the brigand staggering backwards but leaving him otherwise unharmed.

Shrugging off the sounds of fighting to his right, Raedrick advanced, feinting low and then cutting high in an attempt to end the fight quickly. But his foe was skilled and recovered his equilibrium faster than Raedrick expected, leaping backward to avoid the true attack as he finished drawing his blade. Then he countered, a straight thrust that should have run Raedrick through his midsection.

Except that Raedrick was not there. He lunged far to the left, lowering his weight fully onto his left foot as the thrust passed harmlessly through the air where his torso used to be. Then he followed up with another backhanded cut.

The brigand screamed as Raedrick's saber cut through the tendons in the back of his right knee, and he fell to the ground.

Desperate fear and agony contorted the brigand's face as Raedrick moved forward, and the brigand made an awkward attack to ward him off. But Raedrick simply stepped within his swing radius and grabbed his sword arm by the wrist.

"Please no," the brigand begged.

Then Raedrick's saber tip entered the hollow where his jaw met his neck. The brigand spasmed once and went limp.

Raedrick turned around to assist, but found Selam's foe already dead and the fishing man standing there calmly with his arms folded across his chest.

"Why do you toy with him?" Selam asked.

Taken aback, Raedrick was not sure how to respond at first. Bending over to wipe the blood off his saber using the brigand's cloak, he looked askance at Selam. "What do you mean?"

"You let him counter twice. You are skilled enough he should not have been able to counter at all. So...why do you toy with him?"

Raedrick had no answer.

❧ 20 ☙

RIFTS

Melanie whistled softly and leaned back in her chair.

Julian had never seen her so impressed. He and Raedrick sat in the couch across the coffee table from her. Raedrick had just finished telling the tale of his exploits the night before last. Her eyes had grown wider and wider the more he spoke.

"I've heard of this sort of thing."

"Oh?" Raedrick replied.

Melanie nodded. "Timon told me about it. It's called..."

"Timon?"

Melanie looked at Raedrick with the sort of expression Julian had seen teachers use with particularly dense students. "Remember the hypothetical mage I told you about?"

He nodded.

"If that had really happened, Timon would be the mage in question."

"Ah."

Melanie rolled her eyes and shook her head quickly. "As I was saying, Timon told me about it. It's called a trans-planar rift. It allows passage from our world to one of the higher planes of reality."

Higher planes of what? What the hell was she talking about?

Looking over at him, Julian could see that Raedrick was just as confused as he was. That helped. A bit.

Melanie must have seen the confusion on their faces because she looked at the ceiling and sighed, then stood up. A small writing desk stood over by the window. She retrieved a pen and inkwell along with a piece of paper from the desk and returned to the coffee table.

"Look. The material world we live in is not the sum total of existence." She looked down her nose at the two of them, adding, "You should have learned this from your school teachers, or at least from your priests, at some point."

89

Raedrick nodded.

Julian spread his hands and shrugged. "Yeah the priests always used to talk about how the gods live in the higher realms, or some such drivel. Didn't mean much to me."

To his surprise, Melanie smiled. "Or to me either, to be honest. When Timon explained this to me, I thought he was putting me on at first. But it turns out to be true." With a little shrug, Melanie looked down at the paper and drew a line on it. "Let's say this is our material world."

"The world is not two dimensional," Raedrick pointed out.

Melanie gave him a long-suffering look, making Raedrick shut his mouth and slouch back in the couch, looking chastened. Julian found himself grinning. She could be a handful, but he found himself admiring her more and more.

"If we assume our three dimensional world can be represented by this line," Melanie said in an annoyed tone, which Raedrick responded to with a nod, "we can also represent the other planes of existence with lines." She drew several more lines on the paper, some above the world line and some below. "All have their own rules. Some are very similar to ours and can be visited. Some are different enough that to enter them means instant death. A few are so dangerous that even opening a portal to them could destroy wide swaths of the material world."

"How do we know that?"

Melanie looked at Julian and shrugged. "Trial and error. From what I hear, members of the Magestirium have experimented with accessing the different planes for years. Centuries, maybe. And they aren't the only ones." Her eyebrows rose high on her forehead. "Do you remember the tale of Ciril Eremot?"

Julian nodded. Who hadn't heard that story? How the ancient kingdom had come to a sudden end, destroyed by the gods in a fit of rage. How the kingdom's entire existence had been wiped away, leaving only a deep crater that was filled by the inrushing water from the world's oceans.

Wait...

"Are you saying the Ciril Eremot was destroyed because someone there accessed one of these...places?"

Melanie nodded. Julian felt a chill go down his spine.

"A trans-planar rift is a junction between our material world," Melanie placed the pen on the material line and drew a second line connecting it with one of the other lines on the paper, "and one of the other planes. If the plane in question is habitable, people can go visit. It's tricky, but it can be done. Even more tricky, it is possible to establish a permanent connection to part of a nearby plane and then create a bubble, if you will, of the material world within it. I'll wager that is what you and Selam encountered, Raedrick. It would explain why time was different there, as well as the strange perception you experienced."

"How..." Raedrick stopped and swallowed. He looked as confused, as disturbed, as Julian felt. "How is that sort of thing accomplished?"

Melanie shrugged. "I've never seen or heard the incantations for it. If Timon knew them, he did not share. He did say that only the most powerful mages, wielding the rarest of compounds, could create a trans-planar rift."

"Bugger me," Julian said. "That means Farzal..."

"Isenholf," Raedrick corrected.

"Whatever. That means he has a big-time mage on his side. And we're supposed to fight that how?"

Melanie looked askance at him.

"No offense, Melanie. I'm sure you're totally capable. But you just said you don't -"

"I know what I said. You did not listen."

"Sure I did. Only the most powerful mages can do this sort of thing."

"True, but you did not stop to consider the implications of that fact. When I say only the most powerful can do it, I mean less than a dozen men in the entire world."

"So?"

"So, everyone knows who those men are. And where they are. These are not the sorts of people who tend to associate with criminals. Or to go somewhere without people knowing about it."

Raedrick interjected, "Alright. So if it wasn't one of those famous mages, who could have made this place?"

"Could be it's been there for a long time and we just didn't know about it," Julian offered. "There are a lot of old ruins everywhere."

Melanie considered his words for a moment, then shook her head. "It's possible it was there before, but these aren't the sorts of things you can just walk into by mistake. Sometimes they are tied to an object of some kind, a focus for the magical energy. He would have to have obtained the precisely correct object linked to that particular rift, and then known the correct procedure to activate it, in order to access the rift."

Raedrick frowned. "That leaves us with the fact that he has help from a mage."

Melanie nodded.

"Hang on a second. You just said -"

"I said he wouldn't have help from one of those particular mages, Julian. If the rift was activated through an object, a large number of lesser mages could make it work."

"Could you?"

She did not answer immediately. Looking down at her sketches of the planes, she picked up her teacup and sipped it, a thoughtful and troubled expression on her face. Finally, she looked up at them.

"I'm not sure. If I found the exact procedures associated with the object...maybe."

Julian and Raedrick exchanged troubled looks. This just got better and better.

"That means that Isenholf's mage is probably more skilled than you are," Raedrick said. It was not a question.

Melanie nodded. "Looks like you're definitely going to need my help again."

"Told you so," Julian said with a broad grin. That earned him an annoyed look that turned, after a moment, into a small smile and a nod from her.

Raedrick looked between the two of them, a thoughtful expression on his face. "Well we have one advantage. Isenholf probably doesn't know we found his lair."

"How's that?" Melanie asked. "You killed four of his men."

Raedrick nodded. "True. But Selam and I drug the bodies a few hundred yards into the mist, away from the trail to the fort, and cleaned up or covered as much of the blood as we could. So it's possible they just think those fellows deserted."

"You hope."

He nodded again. "Yes, I hope."

"Another advantage," Julian said. "With your adventure, that puts him down nine men. If he started out with forty -"

"Thirty-five," Melanie corrected.

"He probably did not send all his men to the raid on your caravan," Raedrick explained. "He probably had at least forty men at that point."

Melanie frowned, but nodded. Then her eyes opened wide. "He's taken twenty percent casualties in less than a week! That's got to have some of his men thinking about whether they want to keep doing this."

"Exactly. If we can whittle away at him a bit more, maybe we can force his hand, get him to do something foolish."

A sudden thought occurred to Julian. "Melanie, what would happen if the object controlling the rift were destroyed?"

She pursed her lips in thought for a moment. "Most likely the rift would close forever. Although, I suppose there's a chance of something more dramatic happening."

"So best case, whoever was in the rift at that point would be trapped, Is there any way they could come back?"

Melanie shook her head. "No. There are an infinite number of planes of existence. Even if a highly skilled mage consented to recreate the rift, to target the exact place on the exact plane where they were located without a guide of some kind would be all but impossible."

"Well that's it!" Julian bounded to his feet, unable to contain his excitement. "We don't need to worry about fighting all of them. We just need to find that object and..." He made a gesture like he was breaking a stick in two.

Raedrick's eyes widened. "You might be on to something there."

"No."

Melanie's emphatic statement took the wind out of Julian's sails. He looked back at her in confusion. "Why not?"

"Any object chosen to be imbued with this sort of power would have to be extremely durable, for the reason you just stated. I doubt you could just simply break it. But even if you could...where is it?"

"I don't know. That's why we need to find it."

Raedrick sighed ruefully. "No, Julian, she's right. They've probably got it hidden in their fort. Or Isenholf keeps it on him. Or the mage does. Either way, we'd still end up having to fight our way through his men to get it."

Julian nodded reluctantly. He hated that they were right, but he couldn't deny it. It would come down to a pitched battle after all.

Wait a minute.

"Melanie, why can't you just, you know," he waved his hand around in a way that he hoped looked mystical, "bring the chasm down and block the rift that way?"

Raedrick rolled his eyes. "Really, Julian? She's not a god."

"Didn't say she was, Rae. But mages can do some impressive things."

Melanie replied, "Julian, while that is theoretically possible, it's not practical."

"How come?"

"Well for one thing, like I told you before, the incantations for a spell that would actually move the earth would take a couple hours and the components would likely cost more than this town." Julian blinked, his initial enthusiasm blunted by her response. It got worse as Melanie continued. "But more important than any of that...I don't know any spell that could do that."

"Rubbish. We saw the mages in the Army do things like that."

Melanie nodded. "I didn't say the spell doesn't exist. I said *I* don't know it."

Julian sighed. "Well maybe we could roll a bunch of rocks down manually. You know, get a bunch of men from the town to -"

"Julian." Raedrick was eyeing him in his patented 'stop being stupid' manner.

And he was right. There was no way they could get enough stones moved in to block up the chasm without the brigands noticing it somehow. Then they would just have a fight on their hands, and they were not ready to face all of Isenholf's brigands yet.

So be it.

Julian sighed again. "Alright. Let's figure out how to whittle him down some more, then."

OBSERVATION

Melanie met Raedrick and Julian after the morning's archery instruction, and they all walked to Constable Malory's office. Unlike the last few times Julian had been there, both Constable and Deputy were present. They sat in their respective desks looking over paperwork of some sort or other. For a town that was normally quiet, those two seemed to have a lot of paperwork.

Malory looked up as they walked in and nodded in greeting. "Gentlemen." Then his eyes widened and he smiled with what appeared to be pleasure. That was different. "And Mistress Klemins! To what do I owe this pleasure?"

"Have you been able to find the answer to that question from yesterday?" Raedrick asked.

The Constable frowned and made a non-committal gesture. "I'd rather we talk about it in private."

Melanie's lips compressed into a frown. If what Julian had observed from her so far was any indication, she was about to let fly. Raedrick beat her to it, though.

"Melanie is working with us now. You can talk freely with her."

Constable Malory blinked in surprise. "Oh? That is...surprising."

"I don't see why it should be, Mr. Malory," Melanie said cooly.

"Well it's just that..." Malory trailed off as Melanie's stare became more and more icy and her frown became a scowl. Apparently not a total fool, he cleared his throat and gestured toward Fendig. "We haven't learned much yet. Fendig's been on it."

Fendig coughed, looking uncomfortable as their gazes turned to him. "We have not received any reports of additional raids or robberies since Farzal met with the Mayor. Are you sure they had just attacked someone?"

Raedrick replied, "That's what they said. And they had enough money on them, so it certainly looked like it."

Fendig frowned and looked through his documents again. He shook his head, looking confused. "I don't know where the attack could have taken place, then. No one has reported any trouble at all."

"That is odd," Julian murmured.

Raedrick shrugged, however. "Well whatever. We'll figure it out eventually." Turning back to Malory, he cleared his throat. "We've been making better progress with our recruits than I expected. I think they're almost ready to take into action."

"Well that's good. What did you have in mind?"

"Now that we know the location of their base, we're going to deploy some of our men to keep an eye on them. Once we know their operating patterns well enough, we'll begin harassing them. If we hurt them enough, they may start thinking there are better places to be than here in Glimmer Vale."

Constable Malory did not look impressed. "No offense, but your last plan didn't work out very well. Why should this one turn out any differently?"

"Because this is not their plan, Mr. Malory, it is mine," Melanie said in her best, most condescending tone. Annoying as it was to be on the receiving end of that tone of voice, Julian had to admit it was effective.

The Constable blinked, looking defensive all of a sudden. "I appreciate that, Mistress Klemins, but -"

"Do you have a better idea, Constable?" asked Raedrick.

Malory thought about it for a moment, then shook his head with a shrug.

"In that case, we'd like your help.'

"Anything we can do."

<hr>

Malory stomped his feet and hugged his arms tightly across his chest, rubbing his upper arms vigorously. It was bloody freezing. When he said anything we can do, he thought Baletier would ask him to help prepare defenses around town or something. *Not* sit out in the middle of nowhere all night and freeze his tail off.

He and one of Baletier's fishing men, Gilroy, were camped on a hilltop near a great crack in the hillside. Baletier and his friend called it a chasm, but that was a misnomer if ever Malory heard one. It was more a chimney than a chasm. But then, Baletier did not strike him as much of an outdoors man. Probably never tried his hand at climbing mountains, or he would have known the difference. There was no way that thirty to forty men were encamped in that little crack, so what in the hell was he doing here? He would bet two to one this was just some scheme to get him out of town so those two and their little trollop could do gods knew what-all without interference.

"This is a waste of time," he grumped.

Gilroy shook his head, looking at Malory with a mocking grin. "You didn't have to come, Constable."

Malory scowled. He didn't have to take that from a fishing man. He opened his mouth to retort, but stopped. "What are you doing, Gilroy?"

"Filling in a hole."

"I see that. Why? That's the second hole you've dug in the last ten minutes."

Gilroy spread his hands in an 'no idea' kind of way. "Just doin' what the lady told me."

"How's that?"

Gilroy stood and picked up a small bag that was sitting on the ground next to him. Fishing inside it, he pulled out a small object and held it out to Malory.

"She said to take these and bury them in a ring around our campsite. Wouldn't say why."

Malory accepted the object and turned it over in his fingers. It was just a small piece of rock, mica from the look of it, with a small engraving of a person crouched beneath a shelter of some kind on one side.

"What is this?"

"Don't know. She just said to bury them with the carving facing outward and we would be safe through the night."

Great. Superstitious nonsense. That was all he needed. It was bad enough the Mayor insisted on shackling him with that pair, but now they brought a bloody-minded woman into it with a bunch of silly notions. He shook his head vigorously.

"I'll have none of that foolishness. Rocks to keep us safe?" He snorted and tossed the rock off into the grass. "Safe from what?"

Gilroy gasped as Malory threw the rock away. "Sir, she said it was very important," he said, and he bounded off in search of it. How he thought to find it in the quickly fading light was beyond Malory.

"Get back here, Gilroy, you fool."

Gilroy hesitated. He looked back and forth between the grass and Malory, indecision on his face. Malory scowled and waved vigorously for him to come back. "Now, Gilroy!"

The fishing man looked one last time at the grass where the rock fell then nodded and walked back to camp, his eyes downcast. "She was very specific, Constable."

He snorted again. "Specifically foolish." Malory turned and stomped over to the edge of the hill. The last of the light was just about gone, but he could just make out the valley below, and the bottom of the chimney. Nothing moved down there. Nothing would all night either.

To hell with it. Damned it he was going to stay up all night for nothing. He threw himself down onto the ground and pulled a blanket over himself. "You've got the first watch," he growled to Gilroy, then he rolled over to go to sleep.

Gilroy ran. Despite the burning in his lungs from breathing the cold night air. Despite the crushing pain in his side and the wetness running down his hip and thigh. Despite the fatigue that made his legs feel like rubber. Despite every part of his body screaming at him to stop, to rest.

He ran because to not run was to die.

He couldn't hear his pursuers any more, but he knew they were back there, somewhere in the darkness. They had been on his tail for hours, it felt like. To think they had decided to stop chasing him now after all that time was foolhardy at best.

So he kept on running.

They came just after midnight, as he was turning over the watch to the Constable. It had taken forever to wake him up, and then he had done nothing but grumble before finally getting up to take the watch. But then Gilroy figured that's why he had become Constable in the first place. He would have been kicked off even the slackest boat on the lake inside of a week. Until recently, there was not much for the Constable to do in the Vale except tell himself how important he was; Malory was custom-made for that sort of job.

Gilroy lay down and wished again that Raedrick and Julian had not forbidden fires. It was going to take forever to get to sleep in the cold, especially with Malory stomping around. Eventually, he managed to set aside his general discomfort and doze off.

The sound of a twig snapping startled him to wakefulness. Sitting upright, he ignored the rush of cold as his blanket fell off his body and looked around. Malory stood off to the side, closer to the edge of the chimney, looking down into the valley.

"Did you hear that?" Gilroy whispered as urgently as he dared.

Malory turned his head toward Gilroy and sniffed. "Go back to bed or I will."

"No really. I heard something."

Gilroy stood up. As he did, he heard a soft whistling, then something slammed into his side and sent him tumbling back to the ground.

For a heartbeat there was no pain, only the shock of impact and an unusual feeling of pressure. Then that all gave way to agony.

He heard himself cry out before he realized he was doing it. Anxiously grasping at his side, his hand came to rest on a long, thin piece of wood.

An arrow.

On the other side of the camp, Malory shouted an oath. Gilroy looked toward him and saw several dark shapes emerging from the undergrowth around the camp.

They advanced on the Constable. He drew his sword and made an attempt at fighting back, but it was obvious he was not going to last long before they brought him down beneath the weight of their numbers.

In a panic, Gilroy clawed at the dirt, crawling away from the Constable and his attackers. He had to get away!

He felt a flash of shame but forced it down. There was nothing he could do for Malory; he had to take his own life into consideration now.

Gilroy reached a small tree near the edge of the camp and, grabbing hold of the trunk, pulled himself to his feet. He almost collapsed again; every movement sent a new rush of pain from his wound. But he managed to keep his feet.

Leaning against the tree for a moment, he looked back and saw Malory pinned to the ground beneath a great bear of a man. Three others stood nearby, one of them grasping at his arm as though wounded. That was something at least.

"Tie him up," ordered the wounded one in an unexpectedly high tenor. "Where is the other one?"

"He went down over there..."

One of the others turned to point toward where Gilory had fallen and breathed a curse when he saw that Gilroy was no longer there.

"Find him, you fool," barked the leader.

Gilroy did not need any more encouragement. He turned and ran as fast as he could.

Which, admittedly, was not very fast. Every step was new agony as the arrow wrenched in his wound. He became light-headed from the pain and exertion and from the knowledge that they would catch up to him any moment.

Yet somehow they did not, and he found himself still running, though in honesty it was more a slow, hunched jog than a run.

At some point, he could hardly remember when, he had snapped the arrow off in the wound. It hurt enough that he actually passed out for a moment, but he managed to make better time without the shaft impeding the movement of his arms.

Gilroy managed to smile in spite of it all. There ahead of him, as the western sky began to lighten from the pre-dawn glow, he could just make out the Eastflow. He was almost home.

❧ 22 ☙

REPERCUSSIONS

"**T**his is a disaster. A total disaster."

Julian looked over at Fendig and felt a surge of contempt. Ever since they received the news of what happened, he had been less than useless. He fidgeted, whined, and paced, but didn't actually contribute anything of use. It was clear why he was the Deputy and Malory the man in charge.

"Calm down, man," he said. "It's not as bad as all that. At least Gilroy made it back so we know what happened."

Fendig sniffed and turned away, clearly not encouraged at all. Julian just rolled his eyes.

"The real question is what to do now."

The Mayor did not look any more pleased than Fendig. And truth be told, Julian was upset as well, though he suspected not for the same reason they were. They cared about Malory, and that was fine. In Julian's mind the greater cause to be upset, angry even, was that the whole thing was preventable. If they had just set up the ring like Melanie told them to...

"Now you do your Mayor thing and keep everyone calm," Raedrick said, "We'll continue fortifying the town."

"That's it?"

Raedrick nodded. "That's it for now."

"What about the Constable?" Fendig demanded. "Those thugs have him. Who knows what they'll do?"

"What they'll do is question him vigorously," Julian began.

"You mean torture."

"Most likely. Then when they have learned all they think they can, they'll either kill him or send us a demand for ransom."

Fendig paled and he licked his lips. "K-kill him?"

"It's possible," Raedrick replied, looking askance at Julian. "But not likely. Isen-holf knows Lydelton values him, so he is worth more alive than dead. I'd expect a ransom demand." Looking at the Mayor, he put on an apologetic expression. "Looks like the payment due next week just got a bit bigger."

The Mayor sighed and slumped into his chair. "I suppose so." He barked out a half-laugh and shook his head. "Not that it matters. We don't have the funds to pay the original demand as it is."

"Leave that to us, remember?"

Mayor Brimly nodded.

———

"The Mayor's right, you know," Raedrick said as he and Julian left the Town Hall.

"About what?"

"We need to do something else besides fortify."

Julian shrugged. "Hiram and Rolf are good shots. The others are becoming decent. Why don't we just attack? We were going to in a few days anyway."

Raedrick shook his head. "They'd kill Malory for sure."

"And that will be his own damn fault. Bloody fool."

They turned into the stable yard of The Oarlock. The midday customers were beginning to roll in, from the look of things. Pleasant odors wafted from the open windows to the kitchen, reminding Julian that it had been a long time since breakfast. He picked up the pace toward the taproom door, but froze as Raedrick grabbed his arm. Julian turned around to tell him to let go, but his friend suddenly wore a deadly serious expression.

Moving a little bit closer, Raedrick spoke in a low tone of voice. "Maybe not. He and Gilroy had the first shift, and they lit no fire. Even with Melanie's concealment circle incomplete, don't you think it was awfully convenient that Isenholf's men showed up right then?"

Julian frowned. "He's not a fool. He probably has his men do sweeps every so often."

"Yes, but to find them so quickly? They could have been stationed on any one of a dozen hilltops nearby."

Julian saw where he was going, and did not like it one bit. "You think he's getting information from someone."

Raedrick nodded. "It's the only explanation that makes sense. Someone told him where to look for our scouts, and when."

"There's only a few people who knew the plan."

"I know."

🦋   23   🦋

TO CATCH A RAT

Fendig left the Constable's Office shortly before noon. That was not out of character, from what Julian had seen. But instead of turning right toward Main Street and the tavern where he normally took his lunch, he turned left toward the makeshift archery range at the edge of town.

"He knows there's a fight coming. Maybe he just wants some practice."

Julian snorted. "Fat chance. He could have joined us there every day for the last week."

Raedrick chuckled softly. "True. But give the man benefit of the doubt."

Benefit of the doubt was one thing, but that was not their purpose this afternoon. They were out to catch a rat.

Julian and Raedrick were not making use of Melanie's concealing spell this time, just good old fashioned cover and concealment. They wanted to be able to confront Fendig if their suspicions proved true, after all. So they crouched behind the door in the back of a shop that stood adjacent to the Constable's Office. As Fendig walked out of their field of view, they crept out and darted around the next building, then the next, to keep him in sight.

Sure enough, he did not turn into the archery range. Instead, he continued on into the grasslands east of town.

Cover became more difficult as they left town, so Raedrick and Julian let Fendig get further ahead of them. Fortunately, there were a few hillocks, bushes, and trees scattered here and there they could use for cover. A good thing, too, since Fendig occasionally looked backwards, clearly checking to see if he was being followed.

"Being awful cautious, isn't he? That says it all right there."

"Not necessarily," Julian replied. "He could be meeting his mistress or something."

Raedrick gave him a look that practically screamed, 'Are you serious?'

Julian just shrugged and smirked. "Hey, you never know."

Fendig continued on for a couple miles until a large copse of trees came into view on a hilltop off to the southeast. He veered to the right, directly toward the copse, and picked up his pace. From time to time, he looked skyward at the position of the sun, but he no longer looked behind. Either he was convinced he was in the clear or he was pressed for time. Or both.

After a brief conversation, the two friends decided to risk being seen by closing the distance between themselves and Fendig. They set off at a jog, circling off to the side and following the rise and fall of the terrain toward the hilltop in question, being careful to keep the rise of a hill between Fendig and themselves as long as they could, to avoid being seen. But eventually, they came to a point where there was no more cover between the copse and them, and they were forced to wait until Fendig entered the trees before sprinting to the copse themselves.

For a moment, Julian thought he had given them the slip. The copse was larger than it had appeared from the distance. It would not be difficult for him to slip out while they were looking for him within the trees. But then the sound of a branch breaking, followed by a loud thud and a muffled curse, issued from the undergrowth ahead.

Julian bit back a chuckle and exchanged a sardonic look with Raedrick, who looked just as amused, and relieved, as Julian felt.

Raedrick indicated, using hand signals, that they should separate and circle around Fendig. Julian nodded and moved slowly around to the left, being careful to disturb as little of the underbrush as possible. It would not do to give away his presence.

In reality, he need not have worried. Fendig shoved his way through the copse without bothering to try to be quiet. Julian shook his head in amusement. Fendig would never make it as a...

"Took you long enough."

Julian froze. The speaker's voice was deep and gravelly, and came from the area ahead of him and to the right, right around where Fendig was. Moving slowly, Julian tried to see who it was, but even without more than the buds of leaves on the plants' branches, there was too much undergrowth between him and them to make anything out.

"Sorry. It took longer than I thought to get away." That was Fendig. He sounded nervous, but not surprised, to be meeting the other man here.

It looked like Julian's suspicions were correct. Raedrick would owe him a drink after this. Smiling thinly, Julian cautiously moved forward until he reached a place where he could see what was going on.

Fendig stood facing three rough-looking men in a small clearing. They could only have been Isenholf's men. They wore the same leather and steel armor the others of his band wore and they had the shifty look of men who prey off others. No wonder Fendig looked about ready to jump out of his skin from nerves.

"So what do you have for us?" The man in the middle was the speaker. A few years older than the others, he had several visible scars on his head, neck, and arms. No doubt who the leader was here.

Fendig swallowed and looked around the area quickly, almost as though he was afraid to speak. Finally, he replied, "What did you do with the Constable?"

The brigand snorted. "What do you care? He's out of the picture, and now you're no longer the Deputy. That was what you wanted, isn't it?"

"Yes, but..." Fendig wrung his hands anxiously, then tried again. "I thought maybe you'd scare him off, discredit him. Not... you know."

All three men burst out in mocking laughter which lasted for almost a full minute. Wiping his eyes as he got himself under control, the leader shook his head. "Don't worry, little Constable. He's not dead." His grin turned positively vicious. "Not yet."

Fendig shrank back, his eyes growing wide.

The leader rolled his eyes and said, "What did you think was going to happen? Did you think we were going to just let them spy on us? Should we have just asked please, with sugar on top, stop doing that, and, by the way, please send us the Constable so our pal Fendig won't have to live with his condescension anymore?"

Fendig's gaze fell to the ground, and he shook his head. Clearly he was out of his depth. Scared, ashamed, guilt-ridden. Julian almost felt sorry for him. Almost.

Then the brigand leader pulled a small pouch off his belt and shook it. It jingled loudly; from the sound of things, it was full of coins. "Maybe this will help you feel better," the leader said.

He tossed the pouch to Fendig, who caught it with a half-smile. The smile became a full-faced grin of avarice when Fendig looked inside the pouch at the coins.

Whatever temptation Julian had to feel sorry for him evaporated completely.

"What do you have for us today, Constable?" The brigand leader put special emphasis on the title, and Fendig's grin expanded a little bit.

"They're focusing on building defenses around the town," Fendig said. "I think the incident with their scouts has them a bit spooked."

"Is that right," said the brigand leader. It was not a question.

Fendig nodded quickly.

"Anything else?"

Fendig frowned and stood in silence for a time. Thumbing at his lip, he appeared uncertain as he pondered things. Then his eyes widened.

"Yes! There is one more thing. There is a woman working with them now."

"A woman?" The brigand leader looked surprised.

Fendig nodded. "The lone survivor of your attack on a merchant caravan in the pass, two weeks ago. For whatever reason, she is involved now. Though what she does, I could not say."

The brigand leader frowned, but did not say anything.

Fendig apparently took his silence for disapproval and swallowed hard. "I...I know she gave instructions to the scouts. The survivor said..."

"Survivor?"

Fendig blinked. "Yes. You took the Constable, but the other man made it back to town."

The brigand leader's grimace made Fendig go pale until he gestured for Fendig to continue.

"He...he said she told him to bury things to protect the campsite, but didn't say how they would. I'm not sure what that means. But she seems to have some authority with the two men the Mayor hired; they do what she says."

Julian had to stop himself from snorting. They did *not* take orders from Melanie!

The brigand leader had a different reaction entirely. His eyes grew wide when

Fendig mentioned burying the stones. He glanced at his fellows, who had similar reactions, then returned his attention to Fendig.

"You need to get more information about this woman. Who is she? Where did she come from? Who does she spend time with? Every detail. Do you understand?"

Fending looked confused, but he nodded acquiescence.

"Good. Meet back here in three days. And you better have something useful to tell us."

Fendig swallowed. He looked as though he was going to say something more, but instead he just nodded and backed away until he was out of reach. Then he turned and hurried back the way he came, snapped twigs and branches with every step.

"That's bad news, Yosef," said the man to the brigand leader's right. after Fendig was out of earshot.

The leader, Yosef apparently, nodded, though he looked uncertain. "Possibly."

The other brigand snorted. "Bollox. Just superstition from a woman who don't know no better."

"And the two heroes?" Yosef spat the last word in disgust.

He snorted again. "The same. Only reason we know the difference is we've seen the real thing."

The leader shrugged as though conceding his comrade's point. "Regardless, Farzal will want to learn of this. Let's get back to base."

As they turned to leave, a branch moving on the far side of the clearing caught Julian's attention. Looking there more carefully, he saw Raedrick through the branches. He had a deadly serious expression on his face. Pointing at the three brigands, he made a quick cutting gesture in the air.

Julian nodded in reply. He agreed completely; those three did not need to return to give that report to Isenholf.

Fendig's expression when Julian and Raedrick pushed the leader of the three brigands ahead of them into the Constable's Office was priceless. Surprise morphed into recognition combined with irritation, which then changed into shock, followed by dread and, no doubt, the recognition that he had been caught. Fendig's eyes danced between them and their captive wildly and his jaw worked as though he was struggling to find words to say.

"Look what we found, Fendig," Julian said with a jolly grin. "Care to open up a cell for us?"

Fendig nodded quickly and pulled out the cell door keys, then led them back into the cell block.

"We caught this fellow and his two friends about four miles east of town. They attacked us on sight. Between that and their attire, they're Isenholf's men for sure."

Fendig nodded quickly. His hands trembled as he turned the key in the lock of the third cell door on the right. "Where are the others?" he asked, a noticeable tremble in his voice.

"Still out there." Raedrick made a vague gesture toward the east. "Scavengers need to eat, too."

Fendig paled. Gulping, he swung the cell door open and waited while Julian shoved the brigand inside. Then he moved quickly to slam the door shut and lock it. As he turned the key in the lock, Fendig avoided looking at the brigand, who was slowly collecting himself. Rubbing at his wrists where Julian had bound him, the brigand almost looked grateful to be in the cell and untied. Except for venomous look he directed at Julian and Raedrick, and the look of contempt he reserved for Fendig.

"Let me out of here, Constable, or you'll be sorry," the brigand growled.

Fendig blanched and turned away.

"Now, that sounds familiar, doesn't it, Rae?" Julian said.

Raedrick nodded and fixed Fendig with a piercing gaze. "The first thug we brought in said almost the same thing to you, Fendig."

"Well why shouldn't he? Until you guys came here, they pretty much had free rein. I expect he thought Malory and the Mayor would be too intimidated to keep him."

"He thought wrong."

The brigand barked out a mocking laugh. "Wrong? They released him with apologies, didn't they?"

Raedrick favored him with a smirk. "Because we told them too, so we could follow him back to your hideout."

The brigand's eyes widened momentarily, his mocking grin slipping a bit. He glanced from Raedrick to Fendig and back and ran his tongue over his lips as though suddenly uncertain of himself. Julian couldn't help but chuckle.

Turning back to Fendig, Raedrick's smirk faded, replaced by a grim expression. "Of course, both he," he jerked his thumb toward the locked-up brigand, "and the first guy asked *you*, not Malory. Almost seemed like he knew you."

Fendig spluttered. "Preposterous! I introduced myself when you came in. And this guy knows they have Malory captive, so he can't be Constable anymore." His tone was affronted, but his expression was frightened. The little weasel knew he was caught but was trying to feed them a line anyway? He had more nerve than Julian thought.

Raedrick nodded slowly and pursed his lips in the way he did while considering something carefully. After a moment, he looked at Julian and gave a little shrug.

"Relax, Fendig," Julian said and he stepped forward to clap the deputy on the shoulder. "It's just that we've been thinking Isenholf must have a mole here in town. So we followed you this afternoon."

Fendig's eyes went wide and he tried to pull away.

Too late, little man.

Julian took a firm grip on the former Deputy's forearm and used his own momentum to twist the arm behind his back, slamming him into the bars of the cell next to the brigand's.

"How long have you been feeding them information, you slimy little worm?" Julian growled into his ear.

Fendig cried out in a mixture of pain and despair. Tears welled up in his eyes, but he did not say anything. Next to him, the brigand's eyes grew even wider, then narrowed in chagrin. There would be no release for him. Not unless Isenholf emerged victorious. That had to look like long odds from where he was sitting.

Julian snatched the cell keys from Fendig's hand and tossed them back to Raedrick, who proceeded to open the cell across the hall from the brigand.

As he pulled Fendig away from the bars and shoved him into his new cell, Julian quipped, "Enjoy your stay."

24

THE SIGNAL

A column of smoke rising from the south; that's what he was watching for, and there it was. Hiram knew it would be coming, but dreaded it. They had trained for nearly two weeks straight, and though he felt comfortable with his own marksmanship, he was far less confident in that of some of his fellows. As for the sword...he just hoped it wouldn't come down to that.

He sat on a rooftop near the edge of town. The Mayor, at Raedrick and Julian's behest, had convinced the house's owners, and the owners of the house across Main Street from his perch, to erect a platform up there, to facilitate keeping watch. And to aid in the defense of the town, if it came down to it.

Which it looked like it was about to. Fortunately for Hiram, the plan called for as many archers as possible to man the rooftop platforms, then pull up the ladders behind them. He should be relatively safe from having to use his sword up there. Hopefully.

Hiram picked up the horn resting on the platform next to his water barrel and lifted it to his lips. Blowing into it, he blanched when all that came out was a little squeak. He hated the damn things. Wetting his lips, he took a deep breath and tried again.

The horn's call rang out strong and true.

Down on the street below, every eye turned toward his position. The people stood motionless for a long moment. Hiram could practically see the thoughts churning in everyone's head. Is it for real? Is this another drill?

Then a second horn sounded, from the platform across the street.

The people on the streets scattered, running as quickly as they could to the boats or to designated mustering points. It was pandemonium for a few minutes, then the streets became eerily silent, empty.

That would change.

Hiram looked back to the south and his heart sank. The smoke column stopped abruptly. The smoke that was already in the air continued to rise, but no more rose to follow it. It was almost as if someone had taken a blanket and smothered the fire in an instant. He was not sure how that could be done, and he preferred not to think about it.

He just hoped the sentries at the Eastflow had managed to get away after lighting the signal. He was not intimate with the two men on duty this day; they were from different boats than he. But he had gotten to know them a bit over the last couple weeks. They were good men, and it would be a shame to lose them.

A group came running from the center of town toward Hiram's position. He recognized Raedrick and Julian at the head of the group. Selam was close behind, along with half a dozen of his fellow fishing men, bows in hand. Strangely, that Klemins woman was with the group as well. Now *that* was a good looking woman. A bit uppity for Hiram's taste, but good looking regardless. Why was she there? A fight was no place for a lady like her, whether she was close with Raedrick and Julian or not.

Hiram was not sure what to make of those two. He and the others who had been with them to confront Farzal in front of Town Hall had heard the revelation about their background. They had not discussed it much, but Gilroy and Rolf did not care either way, and Selam...well, those two seemed to go up in Selam's estimation after that. But then, he had always been a strange fellow. But Hiram's father had raised him to value honor and to always do his duty. The thought of a man running out on his oaths by deserting the Army revolted him.

And yet...

And yet, Raedrick and Julian were stand-up guys. They did not have to stay here to help with the town's problems. Yet here they were, putting their butts on the line. It was hard not to respect that.

The group came to a halt on the street below Hiram's post and Raedrick shouted up to him, "Hiram, what do you see?"

"Smoke from the south, but it stopped all of a sudden."

Raedrick nodded with a frown and turned to the group. Speaking quickly, he issued orders that Hiram could not make out. Not that he needed to, since they all knew the drill.

Four of the bowmen split off from the group; two headed to Hiram's platform and two to the one across the street. Meanwhile, Julian, Selam, and the other two bowmen jogged to the end of Main Street, where workers had erected a makeshift barricade. To one side, an empty cart stood ready. The four men pushed it into the narrow opening in the barricade, then, working together, tipped the cart up on its side, effectively blocking passage.

Hiram's two additional bowmen reached the top of his platform. Hiram turned to greet them and was surprised to see that Mistress Klemins had climbed up as well.

"My lady, what are you..."

"Doing?" she finished for him. "Nothing you would understand. Get back to keeping lookout and don't worry yourself about things that don't concern you."

Well she did not need to be rude about it. Feeling more than a little affronted, Hiram was tempted to snipe back.

Unfortunately, she was right. He had more important things to do than get into an argument with her. Instead, he re-verified the storage bins were full of arrows and then looked out to the southeast, where Farzal's men would most likely come from.

There was not much to see, though. And it was hard to maintain concentration with her chanting behind him. What was she doing? At one point, she even sprinkled him with dust of some sort. Him, and the other two men with him. And then the platform, too! He opened his mouth to protest, but the expression on her face made him bite his tongue.

Mistress Klemins finally stopped her chanting and climbed down the ladder. "Thank the Gods," Hiram breathed. That chanting was driving him crazy.

Then he realized there was a bit of a commotion in the street and the other platform. Men in both places were talking excitedly to each other, some of them with expressions of shock or fear. And they were pointing at him and his platform.

"What are they going on about?" he asked, receiving shrugs from the two men with him.

Then Mistress Klemins mounted the other platform and performed her chant there as well, and he got his answer. No sooner did she stop chanting than the platform, and all the men on it, disappeared! His jaw dropped. Impossible! Rubbing his eyes did not help; they were gone.

Except he could still hear them. What the...

It came to him, and he looked down at Mistress Klemins in amazement. She was a mage! That was the only explanation for it.

"Nah. Women can't be mages," said one of his companions on the platform, as though responding to Hiram's thoughts.

"Apparently this one can," Hiram replied. He realized he was grinning, and the anxiety he had felt just moments ago was significantly lessened. With a mage on their side, they might just make it through this with their skins intact.

Raedrick nodded approval as the second archery platform vanished from sight. Or whatever it was that Melanie's spell did to make it appear to vanish. "That trick of hers never gets old, does it?" he quipped.

Julian grinned in response. "Yeah, she's right nice to have around."

Raedrick almost choked at that. Really? Julian must really be smitten. Raedrick did not think he would ever use the word nice to describe Melanie, however good to look at she might be. Although truth to tell, he preferred Lani in that way, too.

Funny how that worked out. He had not thought about the fact that she would still be here when he decided to take the route through Glimmer Vale. He had only thought to get a good rate on a room for the night from Molli. And now he could not bear the thought of leaving Lani when this was all over.

But that was a thought for another time.

Raedrick spent the next several minutes looking over the barricade carefully. He was far from satisfied. It was ramshackle, obviously put together in a hurry, but that was to be expected. The best he could hope for was that it would delay Isenholf's men enough for the archers to drive them off. If not...

"I hope she has something with a little more firepower up her sleeve," he said as he turned back to face Julian.

And found himself facing Melanie as well. That was fast.

"I have a few other tricks, Raedrick. Fear not."

He nodded. "Fair enough. Hold off until I give the word, if you can. I'd like to keep you as a surprise for as long as possible."

She frowned, but nodded. "It will likely not be long. Once the archers begin to fire, their mage will put two and two together and take steps to find and counter them."

Raedrick did not want to think about what would happen when that started. "Can you handle him?"

Melanie looked at him like he was daft. "Do you have some information that I do not, Raedrick?"

"No. What -"

"Then you have just as much an idea how to answer that question as I do."

"Ah." He had no idea, and apparently she did not either. Wonderful.

"Riders approaching!" The shout came from above. It sounded like Hiram.

Raedrick looked up and nodded, then did a double-take, as he was able to see Hiram's platform clearly. For a moment, anxiety welled up, far more than the normal pre-battle jitters Raedrick always felt. But then he moved his eyes slightly, and Hiram's platform faded from view again. It must be what Melanie said the first time: he knew it was there, so he could see it. If he worked at it, or surprised himself.

"Time to roll the dice."

Raedrick looked over his shoulder at Selam and nodded. The swarthy swordsman had a way with words, sometimes. Then he stepped up onto the small walkway that was constructed on the back of the barricade and looked out at the oncoming riders.

It was time to roll the dice indeed.

※ 25 ※

FIRE AND BLOOD

I t was worse than he hoped for, but about what he expected. Julian counted thirty riders approaching. That meant that Isenholf had almost his entire force with him on this excursion, assuming he was not so stupid as to leave his base completely unmanned. And he was not.

Isenholf was taking this seriously, at least. His expression as he slowed his horse to a slow walk and approached the barricade was not the same mocking, amused smirk that he had worn before. Now his face was a mask of focus and malevolent intent.

Isenholf reined in, halting his horse about twenty feet from the barricade. He took a moment to look it over and made no effort to hide his disapproval.

Behind him, his men arrayed themselves in a loose pack. All were armored as before. About half carried spears in addition to the swords on their hips. The rest carried bows.

Except for one man at Isenholf's right. He wore armor but carried no weapon that Julian could see. Instead, a number of bulging pouches hung from every place possible and he carried a thick leather tome balanced in front of him on his saddle. Unless Julian missed his guess, that would be the mage.

Isenholf completed his survey and turned his gaze on Raedrick and Julian. He nodded in greeting, a politeness that did not carry over to his expression or his tone.

"Baletier. Hinderbrook. You are becoming a true nuisance, do you know that?"

"That's why we're here," Julian replied, affecting a good-humored tone.

Isenholf's eyes narrowed a bit, but he did not acknowledge Julian's words. Instead addressing Raedrick, he said, "I have been more than patient. I gave you a chance, yet you continue to provoke me. Why?"

Raedrick shrugged and replied, "That's why we're here." He leaned forward and rested his forearms against the top of the barricade. "This town is closed to you,

Theobald. You'll not get the money you want, so why don't you just go somewhere else? Somewhere with duller teeth?"

Isenholf snarled, showing his teeth. "Sharp teeth? Is that what you think you have with five men to defend your little wall?" Shaking his head, he went on, "No, I like it here. For the same reason you do: no authorities to come and check on things. A man can live on his own terms in a place like this. I think I'll stay."

"It appears we are at an impasse."

"Not at all. You can ride away right now, and I'll not chase you down." Isenholf paused for a moment, then added, "Last chance."

"Funny, I was just about to say the same thing to you."

Isenholf shook his head with a smirk, then turned away and rode back to his men.

"Any second now," Julian said.

They would just take a minute to get organized and then they would come. The barricade would not hold against their rush, and they knew it. He and Raedrick traded glances. His friend grinned and clasped hands with him.

"Ready?"

Julian nodded. "Let's do it."

Isneholf turned his horse around. His men gathered their reins. Those with bows nocked arrows. He opened his mouth to order the charge, but Raedrick beat him to it, simply thrusting a fist in the air and shouting, "LOOSE!"

Eight bowstrings snapped in unison: the six hidden on the platforms and the two behind the barricade. Six of Isenholf's men screamed and clutched at arrows that were suddenly lodged in their bodies; four fell to the ground, but the others stayed on their horses. Julian was actually impressed at the archers' accuracy.

Stunned surprise showed on every face in Isenholf's group. They froze for a crucial heartbeat, which allowed the archers to launch another volley before they scattered. Only three were struck this time, though it was not because of poor marksmanship. Two separate arrows flew toward the mage; both rebounded before striking him, as though they had struck a solid object.

A third of Isenholf's force was down or wounded. The rest darted for cover haphazardly. For a moment, Julian thought Lydelton might have an easy victory.

That hope was short-lived.

Isenholf shouted, "Open it up," and the mage - the man had not moved a muscle despite the chaos around him - chanted a series of strange words at the top of his lungs and cast an object that he was holding toward the barricade.

Julian could not make out what it was, but when it struck the overturned carriage, a tremendous sound, like a clap of thunder, rang out and the carriage launched backward as though kicked by a giant. It actually rose into the air for a time before falling onto the street and shattering about thirty feet behind the barricade.

Julian was stunned, as much by the noise as by the display of power. He had seen mages work their art before, on the front lines. But never from this close. It was impressive!

The others on the Lydelton side were apparently just as stunned as he, because no further arrows were launched for several seconds, allowing the brigands to surge forward toward the gap in the barricade.

Four men with spears led the charge, riding two by two through the gap. The two men in front threw their spears as they rode through, forcing the two bowmen on the barricade to duck to avoid being skewered. Then they were through, and there was no one to stop them from riding straight on to the center of town.

Except Melanie. She stood in the center of the street, her face the picture of calm, and regarded them with the contempt she would show a bug in her tea.

The brigands in the lead grinned viciously and drew their swords, then spurred their horses forward.

In spite of his knowledge of her abilities, Julian felt a surge of panicked protectiveness. He hopped down from the barricade platform and drew his sword from his baldric. But even as he charged, he knew he would not make it in time to help her.

He needn't have bothered. Melanie tossed her head, sending her hair flailing around dramatically, and chanted three words while pushing toward the charging horsemen with outstretched hands. Something in her hands flashed into flame, but for a heartbeat that was all that happened.

Julian thought sure whatever she had tried failed, and she was about to be ridden down. Then abruptly the four horses screamed and reared, throwing off their riders, then fell to the ground themselves. The men hit the ground and screamed as well. Man and beast alike writhed in agony as bit, bridle, horseshoes, swords, breastplates, helms, belt buckles - everything made of metal - began to glow as though just removed from the forge. Flesh, clothing, and hair began to burn where it touched the white-hot metal pieces, and the air began to fill with the sickening smell of burning flesh. Within seconds, the charging quartet and their mounts were fully ablaze.

Two more brigands, who had followed the first quartet through the gap, pulled up short of their burning comrades, stunned horror on their faces. Arrows from the hidden archers slammed home, knocking them both from their saddles.

Reminding himself never to make Melanie truly angry, Julian turned away from the still screaming bonfire and hurried toward the gap in the barricade. More men would be coming through, and he needed to stop them.

Raedrick and Selam were already in the gap, each bracing a spear against the paving stones of the street; they no doubt retrieved the spears from where the brigands had thrown and missed. Another two horsemen tried to make it through, but were brought up short as the horses impaled themselves on the spears.

But throwing spears are not designed to hold up against the weight and momentum of a charging horse. The shafts cracked and then split completely, forcing Raedrick and Selam to dive aside to avoid being trampled. Julian heard Raedrick cry out in pain, but could not see what happened to him in the tussle of arms, legs, and bodies as the horses fell forward, sending their riders sprawling.

Julian rushed forward, cutting one of the fallen brigands down before he could extricate himself. The other was more nimble and met Julian with an attack of his own. Julian retreated, knocking the brigand's sword away as he gave himself more room to maneuver.

A sudden concussion from above drew his attention. The archery platform on the right side of the street blew apart. The men stationed there fell, grasping desperately at the shingles of the roof where the platform rested as they tried to slow or arrest their descent. One succeeded; Julian thought it was Hiram.

But he did not have time to find out for sure as his foe rushed forward, thrusting the tip of his sword toward Julian's gut.

A sloppy attack. Even the fishing men, novices to the blade as they were, would not have tried it, but Julian supposed the brigand counted on his being distracted by the events on the roof to make it successful.

Unfortunately for him, Julian sidestepped the thrust with ease and brought his blade down onto the back of the hapless man's neck. As the brigand's head went bouncing down the street, Julian thought he saw his last expression: a look of almost comic surprise.

❧ 26 ☙

MELEE

Melanie noted with satisfaction Julian's expression, shocked and intimidated, as he turned away from her and rejoined the fray. He was charming enough, and certainly nice to look at, but it never hurt to keep a man off-balance. Besides, he, and Raedrick as well for that matter, seemed to forget sometimes that she was no delicate flower that needed protection.

Julian disappeared into the fray, and Melanie turned her attention elsewhere. The gap in the barricade was temporarily stopped by the corpses of a couple horses. Some of Farzal's men were climbing over on foot, though. Selam stood alone, sword in hand, to meet them.

He could handle himself, from what she had been told.

The two archers on the barricade were having a rougher time of it. Three arrows flew over the wall for every pair they sent over. In retrospect, they probably should have stationed those two in the platforms...

The concussion of the right side platform's destruction drew her attention. She had been a bit surprised the other mage had not taken a greater hand in things yet, but apparently that was done. If he had seen through that platform's concealment, he would likely find the second one also.

Unless she could defend that platform, their biggest advantage in this fight would be gone.

Drawing a deep breath, she opened her book. She had tabbed several pages, for quick reference. The third one dealt with incantations to repel hostile spells. She was familiar with them, and had practiced them many times over the last week, but it was vital to be precise, so she took a few seconds to glance through the text.

It never hurt to check her memory one last time.

Satisfied, she pulled the necessary components from one of the pockets in her cloak and began the chant of protection. Silently, she prayed that she would not mess it up.

117

The first of the thieves climbed over the dead horses. Selam moved back a step to allow the man proper footing and give him a chance to ready himself. Honor dictated no less, and while these men may have tossed honor to the wind, Selam was not willing to debase himself that way.

Incomprehensibly, the thief looked surprised at Selam's gesture. How could a man fall so far as to not even realize what the dictates of propriety were?

Grinning in what Selam presumed the thief intended to be an intimidating manner, he whipped his sword, a cheap-looking thing with too wide a blade to be practical, around in the air a few times. The fool should have just come for him instead of revealing how inept he was. He could not even flourish his blade properly!

Their encounter was over before the thief made his move. Selam could have taken him in his sleep; he had already shifted his focus to the next two coming across the horses when the thief made his completely predictable attempt at an attack and wound up skewered on Selam's sword instead.

Selam stepped forward and heard the thief stagger to his knees behind him, then fall over completely.

The two approaching thieves saw their ally's death and paused in their advance. They looked to each other for a moment then, reassured in each others' presence, moved toward Selam. They need not have been reassured; from the way they walked, their skills were no more impressive than their fellow.

All the same, the two of them together were not to be dismissed as easily.

Selam stepped back again, out of politeness, and awaited their approach.

Beads of sweat budded on Melanie's brow and ran down her face. The strain of maintaining her concentration on the protective spell was getting worse. The other mage was strong. Very strong. She was not sure how much longer she could keep his attacks at bay.

Another attack came, stronger than the last several had been, and she staggered backwards. She almost lost her footing and her concentration.

Ahead of her, she noticed Selam squaring off against two of the brigands.

Where were Julian and Raedrick? She had not seen them in some time. For that matter, the two archers from the barricade were gone as well. A chill went down her spine and she had to suppress a surge of panic.

Was it just down to her and Selam, and the three men she was struggling to protect up on the platform?

The first of the pair of thieves fell beneath Selam's sword. He never stopped moving, dancing beneath the other's too-high cut and ending him as well with an upward slice of his blade.

Selam spun back to face the gap in the barricade before the second thief hit the ground.

The area within the barricade was clear, for now.

"Selam."

The voice came from ahead, near the gap.

Selam frowned and moved ahead cautiously. There, behind one of the dead horses. A hand was waving. Sprinting forward, low to make a poor target for an arrow or thrown spear, he reached the barricade and looked down.

And saw Raedrick lying beside him, his legs pinned beneath a horse. He managed to grin. "Took you long enough."

"Are you hurt?"

"Not badly, yet."

Selam grabbed Raedrick by the armpits and pulled him free. It was easier than he expected, making him surprised that Raedrick had not been able to free himself. But the angle was awkward; it would be more difficult for him alone.

Raedrick had just regained his feet when a great concussion from overhead announced the destruction of the second archery platform.

Julian parried an overhead blow from his foe and countered with a kick to the man's groin. His eyes bulged as Julian's boot made contact and he staggered backward. To his credit, he remained upright and kept his hands on the hilt of his sword instead of grasping at himself. But he was slow to react as Julian followed up the kick with his sword, and he fell in a heap at Julian's feet.

Four more of his comrades, and Isenholf himself, were drawing nearer. This was definitely not one of Julian's smartest moves ever.

He had felled his opponent and rushed to the barricade, ignoring the ache in his thigh which grew stronger with every passing moment. The wound had not yet fully healed, but sometimes you don't get to choose when you fight, so he had gritted his teeth and continued. At the barricade he met up with Willem and Gregor, the two archers. They were pinned down, but they saw one of their own, Tomi, who had fallen from the right-hand platform. Tomi had landed outside the barricade, but he was alive. For the moment. The brigands had not paid him any mind, but that could not last forever.

So naturally Julian came up with the idea to hop over the barricade with those two and rescue Tomi.

Like he thought as the five brigands approached, murder in their eyes: not his smartest move. Willem had an arrow through his upper arm and could not shoot. Gregor was as yet unharmed, but encumbered as he was dragging Tomi away, there was no way he could help. It was up to Julian alone, with support from the last archers in the platform, to hold the five off long enough for them to get Tomi to safety. Wonderful.

Then the other platform blew up, and whatever small hope Julian had blew up with it.

"Get him out of here," he shouted, and he backpedalled as quickly as he could.

The first of Isenholf's men got within sword length and attacked, but Julian avoided the cut easily. Then the second arrived, and he had to throw himself to the side to avoid being run through.

Rolling to his feet, Julian spun around in time to catch another cut, from the first man again, with the flat of his blade. He pulled back again, dragging his blade down and to the side along the brigand's. He smiled as he felt the slight tug on his weapon caused by the tip of his sword cutting the brigand's right forearm.

The smile was short-lived, though, as the second and third men reached him again, flanking him on either side. No way to avoid this one. He gritted his teeth and prepared for the pain he knew was coming.

And was amazed when the brigand on his right stiffened and a sword tip exited the front of his chest.

Raedrick's face appeared behind the man's shoulder. He winked at Julian and quipped, "Don't say I never did anything for you." Then he withdrew his saber and the man collapsed.

Needing no encouragement, Julian spun to his left and engaged the brigand standing there. His face, triumphal just a second before, now was a mask of dread as he fended off Julian's first cut. He countered, but Julian continued forward, not even bothering to block as he stepped within the circle of the brigand's swing. The hilt of his sword struck Julian's shoulder painfully, but more painful still was the stab wound that Julian's sword made as it entered the brigand's belly where the ribs met. The man coughed, spasmed, and slumped over, falling to the ground as he slowly slid off Julian's blade.

Julian turned back around to find the other brigands down. Raedrick and Selam stood nearby, their curved blades red with the blood of many foes. Before them, only Isenholf stood. His pale face was streaked with blood from a cut over his left temple. It made a nice counterpoint to his other scar, really. He no longer wore his mocking expression. In fact, his eyes danced from Raedrick to Selam to Julian nervously. But he did not back down or lower his sword.

"The offer still stands, Theobald," Raedrick said across the intervening distance between them. "Ride away now, and we will not follow. You've lost a lot of men today, but you don't have to die as well."

Isenholf chuckled. "I have not yet played all my cards, Baletier." He cocked his head to the side and shouted, "Lorent!"

From off to the side, a deep, raspy voice replied, "Here, Farzal."

Julian turned his head and saw the new speaker. He instantly recognized him: the mage.

The mage stepped from behind a jutting balcony that would have hidden him from the archers' lines of fire. With him were three more brigands. Two of them were dragging a man with a bag over his head between them.

The small group walked over to Isenholf's position and took up station just behind him. He smirked again and said, "Lower your arms. Or he dies.'

The brigand with his hands free reached out and pulled the bag from atop the prisoner's head.

Julian already knew who it was, but all the same his heart sank to see Constable Malory in that condition. He had obviously been beaten repeatedly. His nose was broken in more than one place. Both his eyes were black, his cheeks were swollen and he was bruised all over. It took a moment to recognize him, in truth.

But his eyes...

His eyes were fearful, tight with pain. Yet Julian saw a hint of iron within them that he never thought to see. An unwillingness to yield. From the look in his eyes, Malory seemed a totally different man than the Constable Julian had known. Stronger somehow. Which was exactly the opposite of what Julian would have expected, considering the torture he had endured at Isenholf's hand.

Looking back at Raedrick, Julian could tell that his friend was wavering, and he fully understood. Killing in battle or for justice was one thing. But for all his faults, Malory was a good man and did not deserve this. Julian could hear the thoughts going through Raedrick's head, because they were going through his as well. *How could I live with myself if I caused his death?*

But it all came down to numbers. Sometimes you did not risk those twenty men to save the one who was most likely dead already. And sometimes you don't sacrifice the wellbeing of hundreds in a town for one you happen to know personally. Julian opened his mouth to tell Raedrick this, but was surprised when Malory beat him to it.

"Don't do it," Malory called. "He'll kill me anyway, and then all of you -" His words ended in a pained grunt and a fit of coughing as the brigand who had removed the bag punched him in the belly.

"What's it going to be, Baletier?" Isenholf saw Raedrick's hesitation, and that mocking smile returned to his face.

Raedrick looked at Julian. He could see the conflict in his friends eyes. Slowly, Raedrick lowered his saber to his side and bent his knees. He was going to do it.

"NO!" shouted Malory, who had regained his breath. With a sudden jerk, he pulled his left arm free of the brigand on that side, then elbowed the man in the face. The brigand stumbled backwards, his hands grasping at his jaw where Malory's elbow impacted.

The Constable followed up with a roundhouse punch that caught the brigand who held his right arm in the nose. Even from where he stood, Julian heard the snap of breaking bone as that man also stumbled away. Malory righted himself...

And buckled over as the third brigand struck him again, this time in the chest. But unlike the last blow, he used a knife, not his fist. Malory coughed and a spray of blood flew from his mouth. His expression was one of disbelief as he fell to the ground, clutching at the wound that Julian knew would kill him in moments.

Raedrick halted midway to the ground. His eyes grew wide in outrage and, as Malory fell to the ground, a guttural roar issued from his lips. He heaved himself upwards and forward toward Isenholf, a murderous grimace on his face.

<hr>

Melanie stepped through the gap in the barricade in time to see Constable Malory fall from the blow to his chest. She felt the sting of his wound as though it was her own; it made no difference that she hardly knew the man and thought him an incompetent fool.

As Raedrick, Julian, and Selam surged into action, the mage on Farzal's side began chanting a spell that Melanie recognized. It could freeze their muscles in place if he got the spell off, leaving them wide open to their foes. Without stopping to check her spellbook, Melanie immediately began the chant that she had used to protect the archery platform. The fact that she had not been successful in her attempt at protection never entered her mind.

Selam leapt to the side to avoid the thief's thrust. This was the first of the bunch who actually knew what he was doing. He and Selam had made two passes against each other, and each bore cuts as remembrances of the exchange.

He landed square on his feet and spun to face his foe. The thief was slightly off balance, the thrust having taken him farther than he probably expected when it did not meet Selam's flesh. He was wide open for the kill, but Selam stepped back a pace out of courtesy.

Such a skilled foe should not be done in by a blow to the back.

To his right, Julian cut down another of the thieves, but received a cut to the meat of his shoulder from a second before he could spin out of the way.

Further over, Raedrick and the lead thief faced off. Raedrick's dance was a beauty to behold. His foe was his equal in grace, if not in cunning, but the lead thief's greater strength seemed to be making up the difference. Had he the leisure, theirs was a duel that Selam would very much have enjoyed watching.

But his foe had regained his equilibrium and demanded his attention. The thief stepped to his right, circling cautiously as his eyes locked onto Selam's intently. Selam circled in the opposite direction, his easy movement on the balls of his feet keeping pace with the thief without difficulty.

It felt as though they circled each other for a long time, though Selam knew it had only been a few heartbeats. He was in no hurry to assume the offensive, though. He had taken the initiative on the first pass and nearly taken a mortal blow because of his miscalculation.

He would not make that same mistake again, not against this man.

The pain of the cut to his shoulder flared counterpoint to the ever increasing ache in Julian's thigh. He backpedalled, evading a sweeping cut from his opponent by sheer speed of motion, and settled into a ready stance. He tried to flourish his sword, but could not do it properly with the wound to his shoulder.

So as his foe advanced again, Julian switched his sword to a left-handed grip and advanced to meet him with a cut from left to right. His left was not his preferred hand, but he had practiced fighting with it for just such an occasion.

The brigand's eyes widened in surprise as Julian's cut came from the opposite angle he was expecting, and it was his turn to backpedal.

But he was not as quick as Julian; he escaped the attack, but his studded leather breastplate was cut clean through from nipple to nipple. The brigand staggered back a half-step, and Julian was gratified to see a slow seep of blood begin to ooze through the cut to the breastplate.

Julian grinned and flourished his blade, easing back into a stylized stance with his weight entirely on his right foot, his left only touching the ground with its toe, his sword parallel to the ground pointing at the brigand's throat, and his right hand above his head.

The brigand swallowed and recovered himself, his movements a bit more ginger as he no doubt began to feel the stinging from his chest.

Julian winked at him.

At first Melanie was amused by the expression of shock on the other mage's face when his spell encountered her protective charm and he looked around to find her the only person not engaged in hand-to-hand combat. The notion that a *woman* had been the one to thwart him all this time was no doubt doubly infuriating.

But his shock quickly turned to fury and he turned his full attention to her. Chanting an incantation that would stop her heart in her chest, he flung his hands out wide, casting a quantity of sulphur in her direction.

Desperation lent her swiftness as she shifted the focus of her protective chant from the men to herself. All the same, her chest constricted and she literally felt her heart skip a beat before the charm took effect. It was as though the weight of a dozen horses had been lifted from her chest. She breathed inward, feeling like it was the first breath she had ever taken.

But there was no time to rest. The other mage snarled and began chanting again. This chant was more complex, but she managed to beat him to the punch with a quick incantation of force which knocked him onto his backside. He yelped, his incantation ruined, and clambered to his feet.

His face was a mask of fury as he began chanting again.

Selam felt satisfaction tinged with a shade of regret as his sword rose above his opponent's defenses and lifted his head from his shoulders. The thief's torso stumbled forward, completing the half-step he had begun before his death, then tumbled to the ground, spewing a small geyser of blood from the wound.

Selam stepped back, avoiding the body's fall, and bowed his head for a moment. He said a silent prayer for the dead thief's soul; he may not have been a man of honor, but his skill deserved a mention to the Gods. Maybe they would lessen his punishment in recognition of his ability. It was a small thing to hope for, but the notion of an artist like him languishing in never-ending torment caused Selam heartache for a moment.

The moment passed in the time it took for him to raise his head again and survey the field.

He saw Julian's foe fall beneath his blade, but Julian looked worn, battered. He limped toward Selam, and he was bleeding profusely from his shoulder. He would not be useful in battle for much longer, but his eyes were alight with the heat of bloodlust. He would drive himself to his death if he was not careful.

And no wonder. Selam turned to follow Julian's gaze and was once again entranced by the duel between Raedrick and Farzal. The two danced as smoothly as if they were a couple on the ballroom floor. Each thrust, cut, and parry was met by precisely the exact counter from the other as neither was able to make any headway.

Julian reached Selam's side and moved as though he intended to come to his friend's assistance. Selam reached out and grabbed Julian's arm, arresting his movement.

The young swordsman turned to look at Selam in confusion and anger. "Let go of me, Selam," he said in a low, dangerous tone.

Selam shook his head. "This contest is for Raedrick to win or lose on his own. You will dishonor him if you interfere now."

One of Julian's eyebrows rose in confusion and he pulled away from Selam's grasp. He took a step forward, then stopped as he truly saw the duel for what it was. He slowly nodded and stood still to watch the drama unfold as the Gods intended.

28

SHOWDOWN

There was no way Julian was going to be able to assist Raedrick against Isenholf, not without putting himself or his friend in greater danger. The two of them were too closely entwined, the duel too dynamic. He could step in and stab at Isenholf only to find Raedrick in the way of his sword before the blow fell.

So he stayed out of it, as Selam advised.

He had always been impressed with Raedrick's skill with the blade, but he had never seen Isenholf duel before. Silently thanking the Gods that it was not himself having to face their former comrade, Julian had to admit the other reason he did not step in to help. He knew just from watching that he was no match for Isenholf; he would fall before him within a single pass.

A concussion to the left drew his attention away. He felt as though he had been poleaxed when he saw what was happening over there.

Melanie and the mage stood about twenty feet apart, both chanting and executing the hand and body gestures of their art as rapidly as possible, to impressive effect. The source of the concussion that drew his attention was unclear, but a large plume of smoke rose from the ground not far from Melanie's feet. Her eyes were wide, with relief he thought, but she chanted on resolutely.

He glanced aside at Selam and saw that he was looking at the mages' duel now as well.

"You don't object to helping her do you?" Julian asked, with no intention of not helping whatever Selam said.

As he finished the question, Melanie completed her chant, and a ball of fire streaked across the distance between her and the brigand mage. It exploded upon reaching him, and for a moment Julian thought maybe she did not need help after all. But very quickly it became clear that while the fireball had engulfed the area around him, the mage himself was untouched.

Sneering, the mage finished his own chant and made a flicking gesture of his own. The grass between him and Melanie bent over, blown by a fierce gust of wind. Her eyes went even wider as the gust struck her, and she flew back against the wall of the building nearby. The wind left her lungs in a loud grunt of pain, and she slumped to the ground.

"I do not object," Selam said as the swarthy swordsman set off running toward the brigand mage.

Julian ran as hard as he could, slowly passing Selam toward the Mage as he willed his aching thigh to cooperate for just a few minutes more.

The magic-wielding thief stalked toward Mistress Klemins, a fiendishly delighted look in his eyes as he beheld her prone form.

Selam did not hold much with the magical arts, by and large. They were a diversion for men who lacked the strength, skill, and courage to face other men without prejudicial advantage. He recognized that magic had its occasional useful qualities; today's gambit with the archery platforms was one such bit of brilliance. Perhaps not completely honorable, but then neither was archery itself. But when faced with overwhelming odds, there is no dishonor in trying to level the playing field. All the same, useful things are not always things to be treasured, or held close. So it was with magic users, by and large.

But then there was Mistress Klemins herself. Beneath the cold and detached veneer she wore, Selam believed her to be among the most virtuous women he had met. It would not do to have the likes of her despoiled by a man such as this.

Melanie lay on the ground aching all over, and struggled to regain her breath. She knew the brigand mage would take advantage of her helplessness and tried to will herself to her feet. But her limbs would not respond for a long moment.

Finally, she managed to draw a deep breath and force herself to her knees. Looking up, her heart sank.

The brigand mage stood a few paces away, looking down at her with contempt. "You dare to challenge me, girl?" He spat the last word almost as a curse, his tone conveying all of the contempt for her gender that had been brewing within the Magestirium for centuries.

He flicked his fingers, and Melanie felt a force grasp her by the throat, force her to her feet, and pin her against the wall. Grinning sadistically, he closed his hand slightly and she felt the force tighten around her neck, constricting her airway. She could hardly breathe!

The brigand's expression became more amused as he watched her struggle. "Where did you get -"

A body crashed into the brigand, knocking him to the ground in a tangle of arms and legs. Shocked, Melanie recognized Julian's profile and for a moment she felt relief. Then Julian cried out in surprise and pain, and he launched up into the air. For a second, he seemed to hang there, about ten feet up, then he crashed back down to the ground and lay still.

No!

She tried to force herself away from the wall, but the force held her fast. Its grip had lessened when the brigand fell, but not enough to break free. She managed to draw a deep breath though, and began chanting, desperately hoping she remembered the words to the counterspell incantation correctly.

The magic-wielding thief stood up and brushed himself off. He looked a bit disheveled but otherwise none the worse for wear from Julian's uncoordinated attack.

Selam shook his head in chagrin at the man's foolishness. Stab or cut, do not tackle! The moment of surprise was lost, and Selam was sure the magic-user would not be caught unawares again.

Sure enough, the thief stopped abruptly, his eyes narrowing as he beheld Selam, who stopped in his tracks.

For a moment, the two men stared each other in the eye. The thief looked tired, and though he put on an air of confidence, he was afraid. Men always had a certain shadow in their eyes when fear had a grip on their souls. When that happened, dishonorable men could easily be induced to flee. There were many ways to accomplish that with a swordsman.

But Selam had never tried to spook a magic-user before.

Melanie watched as Selam advanced slowly toward the brigand mage. For a moment, she ceased her struggling against the force that held her fast, the sheer grace and economy of movement in his combat stride drawing her whole attention.

He was not much to look at normally, but in this circumstance... He was in his natural element here on the battlefield, with his sword in his hands. That was obvious in the way he moved. Despite herself, in that moment Melanie couldn't help but think he was beautiful.

But that might just be because he was coming to her aid.

She shook herself, and was surprised and relieved to find she had continued the counterspell chant while her mind wandered. Timon's hard discipline while he taught her was paying off, it seemed.

The chant was nearing its climax, and she would need the components soon: an ounce of wolfsbane and a sprinkle of copper powder. Blessing Timon's instruction to always have a hidden backup silently in her mind as she continued the chant, she shook her left arm vigorously - or as vigorously as she could in her constrained state - and a pouch that had been tucked up within her sleeve dropped into her hand. That pouch contained the components she needed; she had put it there on Timon's advice, given so many months ago.

She managed a smile as she continued chanting.

The magic-using thief backed away as Selam advanced. Fear showed more plainly in his expression; he was almost ready to break.

Then the thief surprised him. He made a raising gesture with his hands and from the ground around him several arrows and a pair of spears lifted up into the air. Stopping at waist level, the missiles all turned to point at Selam.

The thief smiled, a sadistic grin of triumph. Then, with a flick of his fingers, the first of the missiles hurtled forward.

Melanie's heart sank. Though she chanted as quickly as she could, there was too much of the counterspell incantation remaining for her to stop the brigand mage. His incantation was complete, and so long as he maintained his concentration, he would be able to do as he willed with force. She was actually halfway surprised he didn't just bind Selam as he had done her. He must be nearing his limit. Not that it mattered; arrows and spears would be more than enough.

Selam was doomed.

The arrow streaked toward him and Melanie cringed inwardly. Then she nearly lost her place in the incantation from shock as Selam, with a seemingly minuscule flick of his sword, knocked the arrow off course. It passed him harmlessly by and he continued to advance.

How did he do that? She had never heard of such a thing. A glance at the other mage showed he was just as shocked as she.

The brigand mage backed away a half-step and, with a flicking gesture of his hand, launched another arrow toward Selam. But he spun away at the last second with only a tear in his sleeve to show for it.

Another arrow. Then another. And another. Selam avoided them all, receiving only minor scrapes and cuts. Melanie had never seen such grace! Still he advanced, and still the mage retreated and circled to his left to keep as much distance from Selam as he could.

The last of the arrows spent, the mage flung his first spear at Selam at the same moment Melanie completed her incantation. Clenching her fist in time with the final word, she felt the wolfsbane and copper grind together as the final syllable left her lips. A puff of smoke announced the components' destruction and Melanie stumbled forward as the force that had been pinning her to the wall abruptly disappeared.

She immediately began a new incantation, reaching into to her cloak for components.

The brigand mage recoiled as though smacked and the spear that had been heading toward Selam veered off course, sailing far away from the swordsman. Eyes wide in sudden fright, the mage screamed, "BITCH!" and made a pushing gesture with both hands.

The second spear, which had been hanging in the air pointing at Selam, turned and streaked toward Melanie.

Her incantation forgotten as her throat clenched, she found herself frozen in place, unable to move as she watched death approach. She could not even manage a scream.

An unexpected blow from the side sent her tumbling to the ground, a heavy weight upon her.

Selam grunted at the impact as well, his eyes going wide for a moment. Then he rolled off her. She gasped as she saw the spear protruding from his side. His breath came in short, rasping pants and he clutched at the shaft of the spear.

Melanie had no chance to assist him though. A great force took hold of her by the throat again and lifted her to her feet. The mage! She tried to begin her incantation again, but when she opened her mouth, the force pinned her arms to her sides and forced her jaws apart.

Sparing only the briefest of glances at Selam, the brigand mage stalked toward her. "No one left to save you now, girl," he said.

Looking over his shoulder, Melanie saw Julian stirring. Though she was relieved to see him alive, he was obviously not going to be useful any time soon.

Over to the right, Raedrick and Farzal remained locked in their duel. Both men now bled from wounds: Raedrick on his left upper arm, Farzal on his right hip. But neither seemed to notice what was happening with her.

Melanie looked around frantically. Where was everyone else? Surely one of the archers, or some of the other townsfolk, would come.

But there was no one else. The mage was right. She was on her own, and helpless.

"You will tell me who betrayed our secrets to you," said the mage. Standing directly in front of her, his breath was hot on her face and unpleasant. She instinctively tried to recoil, but was held fast by the force of his spell. "Tell me sooner, and you will suffer less. Delay?" His lips twisted into a sneer and he looked her up and down. Then he licked his lips, and Melanie had no doubt what he intended to do to her.

The mage traced the edge of her jaw with his index finger. Helpless to move away, Melanie cringed inwardly and tried to think of a way to escape. If she could only move her arms, the knife she kept up her right sleeve could...

Unexpectedly, the force holding her jaws apart disappeared. Shutting her mouth quickly, she moved her jaw from side to side, feeling grateful in spite of herself at the relief.

"Talk, girl. Let's end this quickly."

Melanie swallowed the saliva that had been pooling in her mouth and cleared her throat. "He's dead," she replied. It was the simple truth, but she knew it would get her nowhere.

The mage sniffed. "Don't take me for a fool."

Melanie glanced over his shoulder and her spirits buoyed to see Farzal fall, hamstrung by a low cut from Raedrick's saber. "Your boss is about to die."

The mage's eyes widened and he looked back at the dueling men. Raedrick stepped toward the fallen Farzal and raised his saber for the killing blow. The mage cursed and extended a grasping hand toward him, and Raedrick froze in place.

Raedrick's eyes widened in surprise and he glanced around. Seeing the mage and Melanie, his face dropped in recognition of what was happening. On the ground before him, Farzal went from cringing in anticipation of Raedrick's blow to grinning in victory.

Melanie's spirits, so recently buoyed, sank like a stone. A sob welled up, and though she tried to suppress it she nevertheless felt tears stream down her cheeks. It was not until she wiped the tears away that she realized that her arms were free.

The brigand mage must have decided she was incapable of doing him harm; as close as he was, he could stop any incantation she tried well before it could be completed. The fool disregarded what she could do with her hands when he used the energy he needed to trap her arms to trap Raedrick instead.

Knowing with certainty that he never would have disregarded a man so, Melanie felt more than a little satisfaction as she shook her knife from its sheath in her sleeve and into her right hand, then plunged it into the side of the mage's neck.

29

PAYING TRIBUTE

Isenholf rose to a sitting position. He clutched at his wounded leg with his left hand, but grabbed his sword from the ground with his right. Looking up at Raedrick with a cruelly triumphant grin, he said, "You should have taken my offer."

Raedrick strained against the force holding him fast. They had come so close! He had long since stopped believing in fairness, but all the same the injustice of losing this way was too much to take.

Isenholf pushed himself across the ground using his good foot and drew his sword back. "Time to die," he said as he thrust upward with his blade.

All at once, the force holding Raedrick vanished, and he brought his saber down. The two blades met in the air before his belly, but not before Isenholf's sword tip struck home. For a heartbeat, he felt his mail straining and he knew it was going to fail. Then he twisted his hips and leaned backward. The sword cut a trail upward from his navel up to the lower ribs on his left side before the impact of his saber forced it aside. The pain of the wound told him his mail had failed at least partially. But it was not the crushing agony of a death blow, so he counted his blessings.

Isenholf's eyes went wide with shock at Raedrick's sudden movement. He lost his grip on his sword as Raedrick's saber struck it, and he collapsed back onto the ground. "How?" he said weakly.

Raedrick glanced over to the side and saw the mage lying on the ground, blood spurting from a wound in his neck, and Melanie helping Julian to his feet. "You chose your friends poorly," he said. Turning back to Isenholf, he moved the edge of his saber to the side of the brigand's neck.

"Do it," Isenholf said through gritted teeth.

He almost did. But looking down at the brigand, helpless on the ground, he recalled the screams of the villagers that day, the day he decided to follow Isenholf's earlier lead and desert. A very different reason, but the same path. If he killed Isenholf now, while he was helpless, how would he be better than what he had run from?

Raedrick shook his head and stepped back a pace. "No."

Isenholf looked at him with unbelieving eyes. He opened his mouth, but Raedrick cut him off with a boot to the nose. He fell back onto the ground, knocked senseless.

"See you at your trial."

With that, Raedrick turned away from the defeated brigand and hurried over to Melanie and Julian.

Julian was on his feet and standing next to Melanie by the time Raedrick got to them. But while she stared at Selam as though stricken, he looked over the battlefield.

Several of Isenholf's surviving men had already fled, those who were able to ride quickly outdistancing the others. There were not that many of them, maybe a dozen total. He had to hand it to Raedrick, the gambit with the archers worked beautifully.

Truth to tell, he was amazed they were still alive. Although from the look of things Selam would not be able to claim that for much longer.

Raedrick nodded to Julian in the same businesslike manner he always affected after a battle then squeezed Melanie's shoulder briefly before squatting down next to Selam.

"Did we...?" Selam said weakly.

Raedrick nodded. "Victory is ours."

Selam smiled. His cheeks were very pale and his breath came in shallow rattles. He reached with a trembling hand for his sword, lying off to the side just out of reach. Raedrick stretched out and moved the sword closer, placing the grip into the palm of Selam's hand. The dying man inhaled deeply and pressed the sword hilt to the center of his chest, over his heart.

"I have..." A sudden fit of coughing interrupted Selam's speech. "I have no sons," he said finally. "No one to pass it on to." He inhaled quickly and pressed the sword handle up to Raedrick's hands. "Use it with honor."

Raedrick's eyes widened and he shook his head. Pushing the sword back down to Selam, he replied, "Selam, I can't take -"

"Do not dishonor me." Another fit of coughing racked the stricken swordsman. His strength was fading quickly, but he managed to push the sword back up to Raedrick.

Julian's friend hesitated, then nodded slowly. His hands closed over Selam's on the hilt of his sword, and for a moment the two men looked at each other in silence. Then Selam smiled again and he let out a long rasping breath. His eyes glazed over and he did not breathe again.

Standing next to Julian, Melanie sobbed softly.

The funerals took place the next day.

By tradition of the Vale, family and close friends of the fallen cleaned the bodies and dressed them in their Holiday best. Then, at first light, they carried the bodies down to the docks and laid them in dinghies made for just such an occasion. For the rest of the morning, acquaintances would come by to pay their respects and offer gifts for the fallen to use in the next life.

Constable Malory drew a visit from just about every person in town. Selam, much fewer. Perhaps it was because he was a transplant and liked to keep to himself. Regardless, as Julian stood next to the dinghies all morning and watched the relative paucity of visitors who came for Selam, irritation grew within him, eventually turning to anger. Friendly or not, Selam had given his life for the people of the Vale. He deserved more recognition than this.

By the time Melanie limped down to pay her respects, Julian was about ready to hit someone. But for some reason, seeing her there, even as bruised and battered as she was, made him feel better. She waited in line to offer flowers to Constable Malory and say a short prayer, but she did not linger. Until she came to Selam's dinghy.

Melanie nodded a greeting to Julian and moved quickly to the dinghy. She crouched down next to it and dropped something inside. When she did not rise after a few minutes, Julian became concerned and stepped over next to her. Crouching down as well, he saw that she was weeping.

They crouched there in silence for several minutes; Julian because he did not know what to say and did not want to intrude on her thoughts, Melanie for her own reasons. It was she who broke the silence.

"I only spoke with him once, and I was a condescending ass."

Julian was tempted to inquire how that was different from any other conversation she had, but thought better of it. That would have been perhaps a bit too harsh under the circumstances. Instead, he reached out and gave her shoulder a gentle squeeze.

"I didn't know him well, but he was a man of honor. Protecting you was his duty, so he did the right thing."

She nodded. "I know. That's what makes it so hard."

Julian drew a deep breath. "I've been fuming all morning about how many more people have been paying respects to Malory than him. Why was he so less deserving than Malory, you know? He deserves just as much a tribute from these people, and they're snubbing him. But now I think maybe that's ok. The fact that you're alive and able to carry on, that's a better tribute than some trinkets thrown into a boat."

Melanie nodded slowly, but didn't say anything. She just reached up, laid her hand atop his, and squeezed it gently.

At noon, the official funeral procession, consisting of the Mayor, Lydelton's High Priest, and the deceased's families, followed by musicians playing a memorial dirge on pipes and harps, walked from the Temple down to the docks.

The usual funeral ingredients came next: selected stories from the person's life, words of encouragement for the mourning, reminders to hope in the gods and look forward to righteousness' rewards in the next life. Julian listened impassively, paying little heed to those words, meaningless as they were. Melanie and Raedrick stood at his side. She wept again. He stood at attention as though he were still in the Army, which Julian supposed was appropriate.

After all the words had been said, men hoisted sails on the dinghies, untied the boats from the dock, and pushed them out into the lake. The light breeze filled the dinghies' sails, carrying them further from shore. When they were about fifty yards out, Hiram and Rolf, carrying bows, limped to the end of the dock along with Gilroy, who carried a lit torch. The bowmen nocked and held their arrow tips into the torch's flame. Tips afire, the men drew back and sighted in carefully.

The loosed arrows rose in a graceful arc then descended, landing squarely in the center of each dinghy. Flammable materials had been strategically placed in each, and when the arrows struck the flames quickly spread until both dinghies were aflame from bow to stern.

The crowd gradually filtered away until only the deceased's closest family and friends remained. Julian, Raedrick, and Melanie remained even after they had departed, only leaving when the last remnants of the dinghies had sunk beneath the water of the lake.

❦ 30 ❦

HOME BY THE LAKE

The next morning, a knock on their door took Julian and Raedrick by surprise.

"You weren't expecting any visitors, were you?" asked Raedrick.

Julian shook his head with a shrug, then walked over to the door and pulled it open. Mayor Brimly stood outside in the hallway.

"I hope I am not interrupting, gentlemen. May I come in?"

"Please," replied Julian as he opened the door fully and stepped out of Mayor Brimly's way.

Mayor Brimly walked across the room to the window. Looking outside, he spoke as though talking to the town outside.

"You gentlemen did the people of this town a great service." Turning back to face them, he smiled apologetically. "I know our agreement was that I would not act on my knowledge of your desertion from the Army if you helped us. That I would let you go about your lives as you see fit."

Where was he going with this? Julian began to get a twinge of apprehension in the pit of his stomach.

Mayor Brimly continued, "But I have a better idea."

Raedrick replied in a tight, angry tone. "If you're thinking of reneging on the deal..."

The Mayor raised his hands in a placating manner. "Not at all. Not at all. I just thought maybe you would prefer an alternative."

"What alternative?"

"Malory is dead. Fendig..." The Mayor scowled and muttered a curse under his breath. Then, giving them a direct, serious look, he went on. "This town could use a couple good men to take their places. Frankly, I can't think of anyone more quali-fied than the two of you."

That was not what Julian expected to hear. He and Raedrick? Constables? The

137

thought was so ludicrous that he almost burst out laughing. Only the Mayor's serious tone and demeanor stopped him.

"How are you going to explain to the kingdom your putting two deserters on the town payroll as law enforcement?" he asked, in lieu of laughter. "Because they *will* ask, you know."

Raedrick nodded in agreement. "We appreciate the offer, but it's too much of a risk -"

The Mayor snorted loudly. "The blasted kingdom's near enough forgotten us up here. Most all the major trade goes through the southern passes these days, so we're hardly worth noticing most times. We haven't even seen a tax collector in five years." He chuckled in amusement and shook his head. "That's got some in town asking why I bother collecting the taxes at all. They say I should just give the money back."

"Why don't you?"

The Mayor looked at Julian like he was daft. "I'm not a fool, am I? Some day the kingdom will remember to send a tax collector, and he'll want every penny. Better to have the money set aside."

"You make our point for us," Raedrick said. "They will return, and you'll have to answer questions."

The Mayor made a dismissive gesture. "The gods alone know how long it will be before that happens. And we can deal with it then if it does. In the meantime, you could have a good life here. And you'd be doing us a service, too. Who knows, when the kingdom does think to come calling, could be your serving here would be grounds enough to forgive your other offenses." He raised one eyebrow. "Can't hurt, that's for sure. Think you'll get a better deal somewhere else?"

Julian had to admit, Brimly made a good argument. And truth be told, their plan had always been a bit nebulous beyond putting as much distance as possible between themselves and the war zone. And it was true that they were much more likely to be caught and hanged near a large city than in a fly-speck of a town in the middle of nowhere.

He half-smiled at those words, which both he and Melanie used not so long ago to describe this place. He had to admit, it had begun grown on him.

"What do you think?" Julian turned to see Raedrick looking thoughtfully at him. From the expression on his face, Julian could tell he was mostly sold on the concept.

"I guess it wouldn't be too horrible to stay here for a while longer." He grinned and clapped Raedrick on the shoulder. "You get to be the Deputy, though."

Raedrick rolled his eyes but returned Julian's grin. Turning back to the Mayor, he held out his hand. "It looks like you have a deal, Mr. Mayor."

The Mayor took Raedrick's hand and shook it, then shook Julian's as well. "I'm glad to hear it. Welcome home, gentlemen."

Welcome home. Julian liked the sound of that.

Julian knocked on Melanie's door with his usual staccato rhythm. She took her time in answering.

Naturally.

When the door finally swung open, she wore a severe expression, as though she was prepared to lash whomever it was that had disturbed her up one side and down the other. Seeing him, her scowl faded, replaced by something that almost, but not quite, resembled a smile.

"Good afternoon, Melanie," Julian said with a jaunty grin.

She sniffed and turned away, retreating into her sitting room. She left the door open, though, so he took it upon himself to follow her inside.

"How are you holding up?"

Melanie shrugged and settled down on her couch. Sitting on the coffee table was a small figurine of a woman carved from a black substance of some sort. Julian thought it might be coal, but it reflected the light from her window slightly. What was it?

Noting his gaze, Melanie touched the figurine with her index finger. "I found this among Farzal's mage's belongings," she said. "Have you ever seen obsidian?"

He shook his head.

"It is made when the molten rock from a volcano cools." She looked back at him and rolled her eyes in consternation as she saw the confusion on his face. "Don't tell me you've never heard of a volcano."

He shook his head again.

"A mountain that releases smoke and spews out fire?"

Well why did she not say that in the first place? He said as much, and she chuckled.

"Julian, you amaze me sometimes." She patted the figurine again. "Anyway, I believe this is the object that controls the trans-planar rift in the hills. I have no idea how it works, though."

"I'm sure you'll figure it out in time." He paused for a moment before adding, "I have some news."

"Oh?"

Julian grinned and reached into his pocket. As he withdrew his new badge of office, the silver fist holding the dangling scales of justice, Melanie's eyes widened.

"You've got to be joking. Raedrick as well?"

He nodded.

She shook her head and stood up, then made a little curtsy in his direction. "It seems these yokels truly *are* desperate. Congratulations. I think."

Julian smirked in amusement. Leave it to her to ensure even a compliment held a little barb. Strangely enough, he found he did not mind. "Raedrick and I were hoping you would remain here as well."

Melanie snorted. "Why on earth would I want to do that? This place is..."

"Not nearly as bad as you've been saying, and you know it."

She was silent for a long moment while she sat back down again. Finally she nodded. "Fine, I'll admit there is a certain rustic charm here. That doesn't answer why I should stay."

"Did you have a destination in mind when you signed on with that caravan or were you just putting miles behind you?"

Melanie stiffened, looking at him through narrowed eyes.

"I don't know what you left behind, and it really doesn't matter. You could work your craft here and no one will get in your way. Hell," he gestured toward the window, "most folks think you're even more of a hero than me."

"That's not particularly hard to believe."

At least she grinned slightly when she said that. Julian could not help but chuckle and nod in response. "Well think about it at least. I don't doubt we'll need to contract for your help from time to time, and I've already heard a number of people talking about how useful it will be to have a professional mage in town." He stood up. "Isenholf was right about one thing. If a person needs to hide, there are far worse places than here, but few better."

With that, he walked over to the door.

"Julian."

He stopped and looked back at her over his shoulder.

"It has been a long time since I've been made to feel welcome anywhere," she said, "or since I've had anyone I can call a friend." She drew in a long breath and looked at him. He was shocked to see that she wore an expression of gratitude. "Thank you. I will seriously consider your offer."

Julian nodded and left. She was going to stay, he could see it in her eyes.

As he descended the stairs toward the Taproom, he passed one of the inn's cleaning maids, who stopped and made a quick curtsy.

"Constable," she said respectfully, by way of greeting.

Julian blinked, surprised for a heartbeat. Then he smiled and replied, "Good afternoon," before continuing on his way.

He could feel her eyes on his back as he walked away, as well as the respect, awe almost, contained in her gaze. The reality of his new position hit him, and he shook his head in wonder. He was a respected public figure. Who would have thought?

GLIMMER VALE CHRONICLES #2

OUT-DWELLER

MICHAEL KINGSWOOD

OUT-DWELLER

A series of brutal murders puts constables Raedrick Baletier and Julian Hinderbrook on the trail of a killer.

With Lydelton's populace growing increasingly uneasy and few leads to follow, they must move quickly to find the culprit and bring his reign of terror to an end.

But they are not the only ones who are hunting, and some foes require more than just skill at arms to defeat.

❈ I ❈

FRESH KILL

aelin unstrung his bow and shoved it over his right shoulder, under the strap of his backpack, then crouched down and gathered the spoils of the day's hunt. It had taken a while to dress out the buck and he would lose the light soon; it was well past time to get back home. Ilsa would begin to worry if he tarried too much longer, to say nothing of the scolding she would unleash if he caused dinner to grow cold.

He smiled at the contradiction in her possible reactions - and he had seen them both before. But then that was the essence of woman was it not? Contradiction.

The buck was heavier than it looked, and it took a moment to get it settled over his left shoulder and balanced well. Baelin adjusted his brown hunting cloak a bit so that it settled better over himself; summer was coming to a close, and the evening's chill had grown bitter over the last week. Then he set off down the hill toward town.

The northern slopes of the mountains surrounding Glimmer Vale were covered in dense evergreens and he had to weave his way through a seeming maze of tree trunks as he made his way back toward Lake Glimmermere and Lydelton. Many a man with limited experience had gotten lost in these woods, called the Glamorwood by the locals. Some of the more gullible townsfolk told tall tales of spirits living amongst the trees. So with the exception of logging expeditions that never went in further than the edges of the forest and outdoorsmen like Baelin, most people from Lydelton and the town's surrounds did not venture here.

Which suited Baelin just fine. Most people were not worth dealing with, and the fewer who came here the more likely he was to be able to enjoy the woods in peace.

And it made venison more rare in town, which meant he could charge more for his take.

Baelin's smile grew a bit more broad at that thought.

The shadows were growing long now as the sun made its way to its resting place in the east, below the ridges of the Saddleback Mountains. Off to the right, a Night Thrush called out, breaking the silence with its ululating chirp. Baelin quirked an eyebrow; it was a bit early to hear that particular breed up and about, but the early bird gets the worm, or something.

He descended further, moving carefully to avoid tripping in the elongating shadows. After about a quarter of an hour he stopped for a moment. The buck was heavy. That was good, made for more meat. But it was growing uncomfortable carrying it as he was; the muscles in his left shoulder were beginning to shout in protest and he felt a cramp coming on.

Grumbling to himself, Baelin rolled his right shoulder and shoved the bow further down. Then with a huff he shifted the buck over to his right and rebalanced himself before heading off again.

A few paces later, a snort from off to his left stopped Baelin in his tracks. What was that?

He turned his head, peering around carefully and trying to ignore the sudden whisper of alarm that began to take shape within him. He had never heard a sound like that out here before, and he had tracked or hunted just about everything that lived in these woods at one time or another.

The snort came again, a bit louder this time. With it came a strange odor that seeped into the normal scent of fallen pine needles like a bit of dye dropped into a cup of water. He almost had not noticed it was there at all, subtle as the new scent was. Sharp and tangy, with an unpleasant undertone, like something rotten.

Baelin scowled, that whisper becoming more like a person speaking in a normal tone of voice now. He shivered from a surge of adrenalin. Something was not right here.

He stood there for a long several moments, his free left hand resting on the grip of his long hunting knife, where it was sheathed on his hip. His left was not his best hand, but he was not completely inept with it. And right then the feel of the weapon in hand was all that mattered.

The odor grew stronger, and a branch snapped somewhere behind him. Baelin turned quickly. The buck slid off his shoulder and landed on the ground with a muffled thud, but he paid it no mind.

He squinted, trying to see what was out there, but the light was going fast, and here beneath the canopy of the trees it was already getting on toward twilight.

He saw nothing, but that was no comfort. *Something* was out there. Something foul.

Calm down. You're not some tenderfoot, out in the woods for the first time and scared of his own shadow. It's just a hog.

The thought was logical, but Baelin's instincts rejected it out of hand. No hog ever smelled like this.

He looked around for another minute or so, the strange odor growing steadily stronger the entire while, but still saw nothing. Neither was there any other sound besides the tree limbs stirring in the breeze and the pounding of his own heart.

It was nothing. He just stumbled a bit too close to the remains of some predator's kill.

And speaking of which, he had his own kill to take care of, and it was well past too late to be out in these woods.

Baelin crouched back down and maneuvered the buck back onto his shoulder; his left this time. Straightening, he turned back toward town.

And came face to face with something right out of his nightmares.

His scream, loud and terrified, echoed through the woods for a long several seconds before it abruptly cut off in a strangled gurgle.

Then all was silent.

❧ 2 ☙

BREAKING FAST

J ulian spat the last of his teeth-cleaning solution into his little washbowl, then straightened and smirked at himself in the mirror. He had almost become civilized.

He took a moment to lace up his boots—brown leather, weathered and comfortable, that came almost to his knees—then he pinned his badge of office, a silver fist grasping a set of scales, onto the breast of his dark green tunic and strapped on his sword belt. A moment later he was out the door, ready to face another day as the hammer of justice.

Or, more likely, the solver of middling disputes.

As he pulled the door to his small flat shut behind him and locked up, Julian reflected that life as Constable of Lydelton was not quite what he thought it would be. Hardly surprising, considering how he and Raedrick came into the job. But still, he had expected a bit more excitement, more challenge.

In retrospect, he should have known better. Lydelton, though prosperous, was not a large town. When the merchant caravans were not in town—and they were few these days—only a few hundred people, maybe a thousand tops, lived in the town proper. That did not make for much in the way of crime, at least among the locals. The rest of the Vale held probably double that number, but they were spread around enough that Julian hardly ever interacted with them; for the most part they took care of matters that needed taking care of themselves, and resented having their business butted into.

So Julian's days mostly consisted of sitting in the Constable's Office and making sure the place was kept up, making a stroll or two around town and checking in on the various businesses and residents, and preparing the weekly report to Mayor Brimly.

Hardly the epitome of excitement. But then again, it could be worse. A lot worse. Julian had seen more than his fair share of action and, for lack of a better term, excitement in the Army, on the front lines. Though it was more like moments

149

of sheer terror between weeks of absolute boredom and frivolous make-work. The quiet life here in Lydelton was quite an improvement from that.

A narrow set of stairs led from his flat's doorway to the ground floor below. Julian took them two at a time and emerged a moment later onto the street outside.

His flat rested on the second floor of a small building on Cannery Street, two blocks from both Main Street to his right and Lake Glimmermere, with its multitude of fishing docks, to his left. The first floor of his building was dominated by his landlord's canvas shop, which supplied sails and other gear to the fishermen on their boats. Master Feldmyn did a steady business from what Julian could see, which explained why he lived in a good-sized house on the west side of town instead of in the flat above his shop. And why the rent on the flat was so reasonable.

Or it could have been Julian's status as a genuine local hero that lowered the rate, but he doubted it.

Julian turned right toward Main Street, but took the first right and walked several blocks down until The Oarlock came into view. Two stories tall and impeccably kept up, the Inn had quickly become Julian's favorite supplier of drink, food, and company.

He wasted no time, but strode quickly up to the main entrance and stepped inside.

As always, it took a moment for his eyes to adjust to the relative gloom of The Oarlock's taproom. The windows were few, and draped, letting only a small amount of sunlight within. Instead, oil lamps on sconces around the room lent a dim, flickering glow to the place. When it got colder, they would be augmented by fires from the twin fireplaces in the corners to his right and left, but for now the fireplaces were empty, barren.

A long bar stretched along the length of the wall to his right. The remainder of the room was filled with tables, most of them unoccupied at this early hour. A staircase in the rear corner led up to the rooms on the second level, mostly unrented at this point unless Julian missed his guess; it had been some time since a caravan, or any travelers, had come through the Vale. A set of swinging double-doors at the rear led into the kitchens, and off in the rear right lay a less obtrusive doorway that led out to the lower level privy.

It almost felt like coming home.

Julian sidled up to the middle of the bar, where a woman of late middle years, dressed in a simple brown dress and a white apron, was wiping down the taps with a pristine white rag. He had never seen Molli ever use a dirty rag for that job; he supposed the dust was likely too scared to come anywhere near her bar, as much a neat nick as she was.

Molli flashed a warm smile at Julian as he settled down onto one of the stools lining the bar. "You're late," she said.

Julian snorted. "It's not yet 8 o'clock." He glanced aside, toward the mantel overtop the fireplace on the right, where a large wooden clock ticked away the day's hours. The Gods alone knew where Molli acquired the gold to afford something like that; she sure was not telling.

Molli shook her head in response, then pulled a plate that was covered by an off-white cloth napkin out from where it had been resting below the bar. She slid it across the polished wooden surface toward him. "This has been growing cold for ten minutes," she said, and quirked an eyebrow at him. "You're late."

Julian could only spread his hands helplessly and give her an abashed smile. There really was no other response; she had him cold.

Molli looked gravely at him for a few seconds, then chuckled and turned away, toward where a pitcher that was beading with condensation sat next to the taps. She grabbed a goblet from a shelf above the bar and filled the goblet with dark fluid from the pitcher, then set it next to the plate, along with a fork and knife. "Eat up."

"Yes, ma'am," Julian said, inclining his head in supplication.

He whipped the napkin off and revealed his breakfast: lightly fried fish bits, fresh caught from the lake of course, alongside finely chopped and baked potatoes and a hard-fried egg. Combined with the cold-brewed tea in the goblet, it was everything his belly needed to be happy for a good long time.

Julian considered, for the hundredth time, that it would be better to eat slowly, savor every morsel. Somewhere in the back of his head, he heard his mother's voice saying that was more healthy. Or something. But in the end, the rumbling of his stomach won out, and in the space of just a few minutes half the food on his plate was gone. It was beyond delicious, as always. It pained him for a second that so little remained to eat. And then he set to again.

Molli spoke again at some point, but he missed what she said, so engrossed was he in the joy of breakfast well crafted.

"Eh?" Julian managed after swallowing.

Molli rolled her eyes. "I said, has Ilsa Rorickson come to see you?"

Julian raised an eyebrow and took a drink of tea to give himself time to think. Rorickson. Who was... Ah, the woodsman's wife. Her face came into Julian's mind: round, just past homely toward cute, not showing nearly the amount of care lines one would expect from a woman her age, with sharp green eyes and a narrow nose beneath light brown hair. He had only interacted with her and her husband a couple times in the months since he and Raedrick took over for the late Constable. They seemed decent enough, if a bit standoffish.

"Should she have?"

Molli pursed her lips slightly. "She was in here late last night, looking for Baelin. Caused a bit of a fuss."

Julian raised an eyebrow. "So?"

"Apparently he didn't come home last night. Ilsa all but accused Helena Winslow of helping her sister steal him away."

Oh brother. Another one of *those* problems. Julian sighed and dropped his fork onto his plate, the metallic clank making a fine counterpoint to the annoyance surging within him. "I'm not a bloody marriage counsellor," he muttered, scowling.

Molli smirked back at him. "Sure you are. Goes with that fancy pin you wear around." She gestured toward his badge of office.

Julian met her gaze levelly for a moment, then groaned and picked his fork back up. He went back to shoveling his breakfast into his mouth, the succulent flavors suddenly tasting a bit more bitter than normal.

It was going to be a bad day. He could see it already.

❦ 3 ❦

COMMUTE

The walk from The Oarlock to his and Raedrick's small Constabulary seemed to drag, though it was only a few blocks. Julian strongly suspected he would find Ilsa there, slinging accusations of her husband's infidelity, and he really did not want to deal with that. This was what passed for excitement these days, and for a moment Julian almost found himself wishing for some nice honest brigands to fight off.

He shoved that thought away, a half-remembered twinge of pain from his left thigh almost causing him to limp for a pace or two. They had been damn lucky, beating Isenholf's group of bandits. The fight could easily have gone the other way. And even though the town emerged victorious, several good men had paid with their lives, and many people's livelihoods had been harmed; some were only now beginning to recover from the episode, months later.

So no, the drudgery of playing wedding savior was much preferable to the alternative.

Julian emerged onto Main Street and smirked as his boots went from kicking up dust to clumping along on the well-laid flagstones of Lydelton's only paved street. Why they had not bothered with the other streets was beyond him, and Raedrick had never been able to properly explain it. Nor had anyone else in town, for that matter.

He turned right and strolled another block, nodding to a pair of men who were just starting up the day's business as they opened their leatherworking shop. A moment later, he paused as a gaggle of children burst out from another building. The group was ushered along by a pair of nearly identical older ladies, their grey hair done up in matching buns and their dresses matched to compliment each other's colors. That was on purpose, Julian was certain.

The group of youngsters giggled their way past him and the lady in the rear nodded her head politely to him. "Constable."

153

Julian grinned and made a little bow. "Good morning, Beverlee," he said brightly, earning a flash of a smile from her before she swept past.

Julian watched the procession maneuver down the street, then turn left toward the docks. Must be a lesson about the lake, or how boats work.

"Damn shame, that," a gruff voice said.

Julian turned toward the speaker, a short but powerfully built man in his early middle years. Grey flecked the black hair on his head, and he had a puckered scar over his left eyebrow. He wore a simple white shirt and brown pants, and carried a heavy leather apron slung over one shoulder that smelled of woodsmoke and metal. A blacksmith, evidently. Julian did not know him.

"What is?"

The smith nodded toward Beverlee, just before she disappeared around the corner. "Keep forgetting you're new around here. Them two were the loveliest lasses in town, once." He grunted. "Never married though; said they never wanted to. Just lived together and taught the kids, nothin' more."

Julian frowned. "Nothing wrong with teaching."

The smith snorted, casting a baleful look Julian's way. "'Course not. That's not the shame of it." He turned away, shaking his head, and stomped off down the street, continuing back on his way to work.

Julian watched him go. The man paused at the cross-street the ladies and children turned down. Julian could have sworn he looked down the street with longing in his eyes for a moment before moving on himself.

<hr>

Julian stopped in front of his destination and paused, contemplating whether he really wanted to go in or not.

The building he shared with Raedrick was small, one story tall and constructed of pale-stained wood. A pair of hitching posts flanked the stairs leading up to the front porch, which ran the length of the building. The hitching posts were empty; hardly unusual, considering how few of the townfolk rode horses as part of their daily routine. Overall, the building had an official look to it that went beyond the simple sign reading "Constable" above the front door. Maybe it was the iron bars over the windows.

Might as well get to it. With a small sigh, Julian strode up the stairs and stepped inside.

The front room stretched the length of the building. A pair of desks faced each other on either side of the room; his on the left, Raedrick's on the right. A shelf with a number of books—city ordnances, the laws of the kingdom, local histories, that sort of thing—stood against the far wall, near the steel-barred door that led back into the cell block. A chest-high cabinet with a multitude of small drawers containing case files and the like stood on the other side of the cell block door. Behind Raedrick's desk was a rack of swords, behind Julian's a rack of bows and his favorite feature of their office: a small but very well constructed fireplace.

Raedrick was already at work, sitting behind his desk and reviewing some paperwork, when Julian walked in. As always, his friend wore his black hair tied into a short pony tail at the nape of his neck and was dressed well, in a dark blue shirt that was open at the collar.

Raedrick looked up as Julian entered and grinned. "You're late."

Julian rolled his eyes. "Everyone's been saying that today." He stomped over to his desk, unhooked his scabbard from his belt and leaned it against the wall, then sat down and kicked his feet up. "Hear about the fuss over at The Oarlock last night?"

Raedrick quirked up one eyebrow. "In gruesome detail."

Julian chuckled. No doubt Lani had left no detail out. She was Molli's daughter and worked the inn as well. She was also Raedrick's "friend", though Julian wondered how long they were going to keep up that charade rather than just come out and admit what everyone in town knew: they were sweet on each other. Disgustingly so.

"Wonder how long it'll take before she shows up here," Julian quipped, trying to sound amused rather than resigned about the situation.

Raedrick did not respond to Julian's attempt at frivolity. Leaning back in his chair, he ran one finger absently along the edge of his desk for a few seconds, frowning. Finally, he said, "From what I hear, it's not like Baelin to not return home as planned."

Julian gave him a level look. "All sorts of reasons why a man might have to spend the night out in the woods." Or, for that matter... "Or not in the woods."

Raedrick nodded, still frowning, but did not reply.

It took a lot longer for them to get company than Julian thought it would, but it was not Ilsa who came to see them.

Shortly after noon, the door to their office opened to admit a tall, lean man who was well along in years but still walked with the posture and vigor of youth despite the deep canyons lining his face. His hair was fully grey, with only a few wisps of its original black still showing, and hung loosely past his shoulders. He boasted a full beard of similar color that reached nearly to the collar of the leather jacket he wore in spite of the lingering late-summer heat. Like him, the jacket showed signs of great age. Also like him, that age did not seem to do anything except make the jacket better. It hung down to the man's thighs, covering up a patched set of clothes that looked made to blend in with the forest. He bore an unstrung bow in his left hand, and a quiver hung over his shoulder. A long hunting knife and knee-high boots that looked to be ridiculously comfortable completed an ensemble that screamed "woodsman" louder than a company of men shouting in unison.

The old man squinted at them from just inside the entranceway for a moment, then snorted. "You two're the lawmen 'round here." Julian was not sure whether it was a statement or a question.

Raedrick answered first. "We are. I'm Raedrick Baletier and that's Julian Hinderbrook." He stood from his desk and walked around it, extending his hand for a shake. "How can we help you?"

The old woodsman looked at Raedrick's extended hand as though uncertain what his intentions with it were, then shrugged and gestured toward the door. "Got something you want to take a look at, in the hills above town."

Julian and Raedrick exchanged glances. "What sort of something, Master..." Julian left the sentence die away into a question.

The old man grunted. "Man got himself torn up. Ain't never seen nothing like it." He grimaced, as though talking about it was bringing up an unpleasant vision. For a moment, it almost looked like the man was going to be sick right there.

This was not good at all.

❧ 4 ❧

GLAMORWOOD

It was not until they were almost out of town, following Main Street northwest toward the forest-covered hills beyond, that the old woodsman finally revealed his name. It took Raedrick finally straight-out asking, instead of the polite half-question Julian had tried in the office.

The old man squinted at Raedrick as though surprised for a heartbeat or two, then shrugged. "Name's Dewey." He left it at that, focusing his attention on the road ahead.

Julian exchanged glances with his friend, who shrugged and smiled slightly, clearly amused. Julian was inclined to agree. The old man was eccentric, for sure. But, looking at the signs of more decades than most men ever saw on Dewey's face, Julian figured he had earned the right.

They passed the last buildings on Main Street, and with them the road's paving stones. Just like that, Lydelton lay behind them and they were strolling through rolling grasslands that stretched on as far as Julian could see off to east. To the north and west, though, evergreen trees loomed a mile or so away. Even at the outskirts of the Glamorwood, the trees were tall and proud. Julian knew men went into the woods from time to time to harvest lumber, but they were either very careful about it or the forest grew back very efficiently; he could see no sign of logging's impact on the woods. Maybe they simply were not close enough to notice.

But as they drew nearer, the pristine look of the forest remained, and Julian was forced to conclude the logging men simply went elsewhere. It was a large forest, after all.

The road ended at the edge of the forest in front of a low building. Constructed of carefully placed stones that were held together with mortar, with a thatch roof that looked freshly changed-out, it looked as though it had stood in that place since the mountains had first come to be. A small sign hung next to the narrow wooden door that was set in the middle of the building's front wall. It read, "Ranger Station".

Julian blinked, surprised. "There are Rangers stationed here?" An icy shiver of concern raced down his spine as he waited for Dewey's reply. The Rangers were officials from the Kingdom. They would certainly have heard of Julian and Raedrick's status in town, and of their past. And they would certainly have reported it.

Perhaps this place was not to be home after all.

Glancing to his left, Julian saw a similar concern on his friend's face, though Raedrick hid it well enough that only someone who knew him as well as Julian did would be likely to notice.

Dewey snorted again and shook his head quickly before spitting onto the ground in front of the door. "Ain't been a Ranger here in thirty years," he said, "and we don't need none, either. They all left, reassigned some place down south, but no replacements ever came in. Town still maintains their station though." He paused, then turned away from the building and gestured for Raedrick and Julian to follow him into the woods. "Good riddance. Come on."

The tension went out of Julian's body in a rush, and he found himself drawing in a deep breath. Had he been holding his breath there for a minute? He was not sure.

Beside him, Raedrick's grin returned, this time far more warm and comfortable than Julian would been able to manage right then. Their eyes met.

"Surely we would have heard of their presence before now," Raedrick said in the oh-so-calm voice he used back when he was the Squad Leader.

That voice really irked Julian sometimes. He snorted. "You got worried too," he said, then turned to follow Dewey into the woods.

The bright afternoon sunlight became muted by the Glamorwood's canopy, leaving only the occasional beam of brightness streaming down to the earth below. Between the slender trunks of the evergreens, the ground lay covered in a loose layer of fallen pine needles, lending a faintly sweet aroma to the woods and muffling the trio's footsteps as they proceeded inward, and upward.

The hills that would soon become the mountains that marked Glimmer Vale's northern boundary began as just simple rolls in the terrain, but soon enough they became more steep. Before long, Julian found himself covered in sweat and breathing heavily at the effort of following Dewey higher.

And the old bastard did not seem to notice, or struggle with, the climb at all.

"Not much farther now," Dewey said over his shoulder, his tone level and his breathing slow and measured, as though he were taking a leisurely stroll along the lake.

Julian had to force himself not to grind his teeth. That would take more energy than he could afford to use, right then.

Beside him, Raedrick grunted. He looked just as wiped as Julian felt; a small comfort, that. But at Dewey's words, the weariness seemed to drain from his features, replaced by the sharp focus he always got when he was preparing for action. Julian took a deep breath and tried to follow his lead. It would not do for the Constable to be anything but professional while on the job, after all.

They topped a particularly steep rise and stepped into a small clearing where a jagged boulder lay half-buried In the turf, surrounded by a small cluster of bushes. As he rounded the boulder, a new odor assaulted Julian's nostrils. Metallic, sickly-sweet, rancid. A mixture of the smells from a latrine and a battlefield, and beneath something else. Something...unwholesome, sickly.

He stopped, coughing as the odor seemed to hit him like a physical blow.

"Gah," Raedrick said, giving voice to Julian's thoughts.

Dewey nodded gravely. "Don't often encounter a smell like that, less'n something big's died and rotted. I figgered it was a predator's kill, but..." He gestured for them to continue onward, and pushed his way past the bushes on the other side of the boulder. Julian followed, and quickly wished he had not.

Julian was no stranger to death. He had seen it, and dealt it out, on a dozen or more battlefields. Had knelt with the dying as they gasped out their final breaths, patched up the wounded in the mud. Horror had almost become commonplace during his time in the Army, so he thought he was prepared to handle whatever Dewey had to show them. But this...

Blood was everywhere, coating the ground, the bushes, the trunks of the closest trees even though they were nearly twenty feet away. The body, if it could be called that, lay in bits and pieces, strew around as though it had been somehow ground up and then spread like manure on a farmer's field. At first glance, only the presence of torn clothing, one impossibly intact boot, and broken but recognizable hunting equipment would have even told Julian this had once been a man.

"Gods be merciful," he breathed.

Dewey shook his head. "They sure weren't to this fellow."

"Was it a bear?" Raedrick's voice was hushed, almost reverent.

The old man shook his head again. "A bear don't attack a man, not less'n he's mad or injured. An' if he did, he wouldn't leave it like this."

"Mountain lion?"

Dewey just snorted and shot Raedrick a look like he was daft. "Lions don't leave meat untouched." He gestured over to the side, past the blood splatter, where a deer carcass lay, intact and untouched except for where the hunter had evidently dressed it out before he had been killed.

Julian frowned. That made no sense. Scavengers should have made off with that carcass, or at least bitten off parts of it, by now. And Dewey was right: why would whatever killed the hunter have left the deer untouched? "What, then?" he asked.

Dewey shrugged. "Told you, ain't never seen nothing like this." He looked down at the bloodied remains and pursed his lips. "Poor bastard."

"Where's his head?" Raedrick asked.

Julian stiffened and looked around the clearing quickly. Raedrick was right. Pieces of the body were everywhere, but none of the pieces could have been the man's head. Where was it?"

Dewey scowled and pointed over Raedrick's head.

Julian turned and looked where Dewey pointed. In a little nook near the top of the boulder, higher than he could have reached if he were standing on his tip toes, lay the man's head. He was not young, but not old either; probably approaching forty. His hair was long and wavy, dark brown and pulled back from his face by a leather headband. His mouth was locked into a soundless scream, his face frozen in a rictus of pain and utmost horror, his dark eyes wide and locked forward.

The dead man's expression made Julian's blood turn to ice water, and all the more because he recognized him from an occasional night at The Oarlock.

"Baelin," Julian breathed.

Dewey grunted agreement.

❧ *5* ❧

UNEXPECTED VISITOR

"**A**ny idea what did it?"

Julian swallowed a gulp of Molli's ale and lowered his mug back to the bar before he shrugged. "Animal of some kind," he replied.

His companion was an older man with dark grey hair and a matching beard who wore a cloak that was almost the same color as his hair overtop the loose-fitting garments that the fishermen of Lydelton tended to favor. He sniffed and considered that for a half minute before taking a swig himself. "Bad way to go," Horace said.

Julian nodded agreement.

The Oarlock was full to overflowing, unusual considering it was the middle of the work week. But having to go about their tasks tomorrow had not stopped people from coming out to Baelin's funeral, and afterwords to the various taverns to lift a mug in the dead man's honor.

How many even knew who he was, Julian wondered. Not many; he had kept to himself while in town, and was more often to be found out in the woods than anywhere else. The only reason Julian knew him was because they happened to both like The Oarlock.

More people knew Ilsa, of course. And a good thing, too. With Baelin gone, she would need help with their three children. Julian did not envy her the workload she had to bear.

Horace drained the last of his drink and stood up from his stool. "I'd best be off," he said. "Got a meeting with management in the morning." His lips twisted in distaste for a moment, then he grinned wryly. "Got to look respectable for them, or somesuch."

Julian snorted. "You don't have that kind of time."

Horace put on a look of feigned injury, then grinned even wider and clasped hands with Julian before turning to leave. Julian watched the old fisherman weave his way through the taproom and shook his head, amused.

161

His amusement faded as Horace passed a table near the door, and its occupant. The man was small, slight, easy to dismiss. He wore a black shirt, or maybe extremely dark blue, that was open at the collar and had loop earrings in both ears. His skin was past swarthy toward dark, like the men from the southern shores of the great sea, and he wore his black hair cut short around his ears and neck but longer on his crown, so that it hung to his ears almost like vines dangling over the side of a cliff.

The man's appearance was unusual enough; few people in Lydelton even approached his skin tone. But what truly drew Raedrick's eye was the staff that lay propped against the empty chair to the man's right. Long, probably longer than the man was tall, it was sanded smooth and varnished until it glinted in the light from the fireplace a few tables away.

Julian frowned. He had seen men with staves like that before, in the Army. Unless he missed his guess, the fellow was a mage, and a high-ranking one at that.

"Son of a bitch," Julian muttered.

He turned back to the bar and waved Molli over. She took a minute to fill a couple of tall tankards and set them down on one of her servers' trays before coming over with a friendly grin. "Need a refill?"

Julian was about to shake his head, but he glanced down and saw that his mug was just about empty. "Sure, why not." He swallowed the last gulp and pushed the mug over to her.

Molli grabbed it up and retreated to the taps. A moment later she returned, foam very nearly overflowing from the top of Julian's mug. "Here you go."

Julian grinned his thanks and set a silver coin down on the bar.

Molli's eyebrow twitched upward. "Starting a tab?"

Julian nodded over toward the apparent mage's table. "When did that fellow check in?"

Molli's eyes tracked over to the newcomer's table and her grin faded slightly. "This morning, a little before noon. Why?"

Julian did not answer immediately. He took a drink while considering. The man was probably just passing through; it was not unheard-of for individuals to travel the mountain passes alone in the summertime, though it was not common. If he did not linger, it would probably not be a problem, but all the same... "Did he say how long he's staying?"

Molli's grin faded completely, becoming a concerned frown as she regarded Julian. "No, but he paid enough for a week." She added a bit more force to her words. "Why?"

Julian sighed and stood up, taking his mug with him. "He's a mage," he said. Molli's eyebrow quirked upward, but he could see she did not understand the issue. "Send over another of whatever he's drinking, will you?"

She nodded, and Julian turned away. As he walked over to the stranger, he felt almost as though he was getting ready for battle.

He weaved past several intervening tables, watching the mage carefully as he went. The man appeared to be taking his ease, munching on a plate of Molli's signature fishcakes and watching the goings on around him with an expression of mild amusement. And why not? People watching could be entertaining, especially when they had some drink on. But as he got closer, Julian noted that the amusement on the mage's face did not translate over to his eyes, which were sharp, watchful. Piercing.

The mage noted Julian's approach and turned to regard him, his eyes tracing up and down Julian's body in a quick once-over that lingered on the badge of office he wore. Something in the mage's demeanor shifted upon seeing the badge, becoming more stiff in a subtle way that Julian probably would not have noticed had he not been watching.

"Constable," the mage said by way of greeting, and inclined his head politely.

Well, the badge was good for something at least. "Good evening," Julian said, and gestured toward the other empty seat at the mage's table. Not the one holding his staff upright. "Mind if I join you for a moment?" He smiled, to show he meant no imposition.

"Of course," replied the mage. "Always happy to make the acquaintance of a public servant."

Julian smirked as he sat. "Don't know I'd call myself that." He set his mug down and held out his hand to the mage. "Julian Hinderbrook."

The mage looked at his hand for a second before clasping it. "Loran Haversted."

"We don't get many members of the Magestirium coming through," Julian said, still grinning. "Just figured I'd welcome you to town."

Loran's eyebrows lifted, in surprise, Julian was sure. "Not many people in places like this would know a member of the Magestirium by sight." The question, unstated, hung in the air for a moment.

Julian shrugged and took a sip from his mug. "Haven't always lived here."

"Ah."

A serving girl came around to the table, carrying a glass that was halfway filled with an amber fluid on her tray. She made a shallow curtsy and set the glass down in front of Loran, then turned away to continue her rounds.

"Miss, I - "

"It's on me," Julian interjected.

Loran looked at Julian through narrowed eyes for a moment, then inclined his head in a seated half-bow. "Thank you," he said blandly.

"My pleasure. So," Julian took another sip before continuing, "I'm sure the Mayor would love to meet you, give his regards to your order, that sort of thing. Will you be in town long?"

A slight shrug of his shoulders preceded Loran's reply. "Just long enough to see my business through, then I will be off."

"And what business is that?"

Loran's eyes hardened. "None of yours, Constable, I assure you."

That was plain enough. Fine, if that was how he wanted to play it... "I don't mean to pry," Julian said, redoubling his efforts at grinning. "The Mayor's a busy man, as you know. I wouldn't want him to miss the opportunity to say hello."

The drink Julian bought lay on the table between them, untouched. Loran never looked at it, just at Julian, his gaze intent, probing. Julian made a point of not meeting his eyes directly. Rumor had it that a mage could read your thoughts if he looked into your eyes for too long, and that would not do at all, if the rumor was true. He would have to ask Melanie about that when he saw her...

Damnit. Don't go there.

Finally Loran smiled again, ever so slightly. "I expect I will be in town for two or three days, maybe a short while longer. I trust that will give the Mayor sufficient time to clear his schedule?"

Julian nodded. "Almost certainly. I'll have the Mayor's office leave word with Mistress Millens as to the best time. If that will suffice?"

Loran nodded, more a gesture of concession to an inferior than an agreement between equals. Julian had to stop himself from scowling in annoyance at the sheer arrogance of it.

"Well then, I'll leave you to your entertainment." Julian stood and made a half-bow to the mage, his grin still plastered to his face.

"Thank you, Constable. I look forward to our next meeting." Not really, Loran's eyes said.

Julian turned away and walked back to the bar. There, he drained the rest of his mug in a long, smooth swallow, then he set it down and turned to leave the Inn. It was not until the front door swung shut behind him that he realized he had just left Molli and her girls one hell of a tip.

Oh well. He had more pressing matters to attend to. He just hoped Melanie would be sensible about this.

❀   *6*   ❀

THE DOWN LOW

Raedrick knocked once, then pushed open the door to Melanie's Mystical Crafts and stepped inside. Julian followed on his heels, a sense of urgency competing with profound reluctance for dominance in his head. How Melanie would react to Loran's presence was hard to say, but in her place Julian would probably be packing to leave town fairly quickly. The Magestirium did not deal kindly with outsiders who practiced their craft, and Melanie, as a woman, was an outsider by definition.

Julian was not sure what irked him more: the stupidity of that policy or the thought of Melanie leaving.

They had become good friends over the last several months. Well, friends anyway. Or maybe trusted acquaintances and colleagues. Or something. Regardless, it would be hard to see Melanie go, even if it was necessary for her own protection.

And she had done so well for herself here.

Her shop lay at the northeastern edge of town, away from the Lake and from casual attention from non-locals. The small building had once been an old spinster's house, but it had fallen vacant when the poor woman passed on, in late Spring. There had been a small squabble among her surviving relatives—two brothers with enough wrinkles between them to make a prune appear smooth—over who would get the house afterwords. Melanie had solved that by plopping down enough coin to satisfy them both, and that was that. She had to have paid more than the place was worth, though she denied it. Although Julian supposed maybe the two brothers were secretly relieved to put the silly conflict behind them. Regardless, it was a quick transaction, and within a few weeks Melanie opened up her shop.

The door swung shut behind Julian and he paused for a moment, taking in the ambience. Symbols and words of power, or at least of spiritual significance, decorated the walls, up high near where they joined with the ceiling. Bottles containing remedies and the like rested upon a shelf off to the right. Directly across from the door, pendants and other trinkets, all bearing pentagrams or other symbols of power, were on display. A small bookshelf sat in the middle of the shop, partially full with tomes that were decorated with strange texts and symbols. The heavy odor of incense lay over it all, from the burner which sat behind the counter to the left, on top of a strongbox that Melanie claimed held her most rare, powerful, and valuable, items.

Julian had to hand it to Melanie; she did not play around. She aimed for mystical, and went well past it to almost weird. Not that he would ever tell her that straight out. The memory of a quartet of mounted men and their horses suddenly erupting into flame with the flick of her wrist sprang to mind. Best not to make her really angry.

Julian snorted to himself; that was just silly. They were friends, after all.

Nevertheless, he could not help but remember the strength and power that lay beneath Melanie's decidedly appealing exterior. Her feminine wiles concealed a deadly and cunning opponent, if one was unfortunate enough to get on her bad side.

"Where is -"

No sooner had the words left Raedrick's lips than Melanie stepped into the shop from a small doorway in the left rear corner, behind the counter, that was enclosed by hanging beads.

Tall and lush, Melanie was, as always, dressed impeccably. Today she wore a flowing dark-blue gown that was cut tight at her waist and flared below her hips. The collar was ruffled in a lighter shape of blue, almost white, and cut low enough to reveal a hint of her impressive cleavage. A simple black leather belt with a silver clasp, from which hung a small knife that rested over her left hip, set off the dress and further accentuated her curves. A silver necklace and earrings completed her ensemble. Wavy dark-brown hair hung just past her shoulders, and her eyes, just slightly lighter in color than her dress, shone with intellect and confidence.

"Well, well," Melanie said in her melodious alto, "my two favorite law men." She smiled warmly, an eyebrow quirking upward to accentuate the teasing tone she took. "To what do I owe this pleasure?"

Raedrick shared a glance with Julian, then cleared his throat. "Not sure it's a pleasure this time."

Melanie's smile faded slightly, but she remained silent, her eyes questioning.

"A mage from the Magestirium is in town. Checked into The Oarlock yesterday, and he looks to stay for a while."

The smile left Melanie's face completely and she looked from Raedrick to Julian, the questioning look more intense, if anything. He nodded in confirmation. And now for the panic.

He should have known better.

Melanie looked gravely at the two of them for a moment, then said, "Who?"

Raedrick blinked and looked at Julian meaningfully for a moment, then nodded. As though he was not going to tell her.

"Loran Haversted," Julian said levelly.

Melanie nodded and looked away. She licked her lips as she thought for a moment.

Then she burst out laughing.

Julian traded another look with Raedrick. The former squad leader scrunched up his eyes the way he always did when he got confused. Julian could not say he blamed him. The Magestirium was famously protective of its secrets. No one, especially a woman, would be allowed to walk free once learning them. Loran was a clear and present danger to Melanie's wellbeing. And yet, she laughed.

And kept on laughing for a full minute. Finally, she stopped and wiped the beginnings of tears from her eyes. Tears of mirth, of course. Then, shaking her head, she said, "Honestly, boys, do you think I've never been in the same town as a member of the Magestirium before?"

"Well," Raedrick began.

"We just thought," Julian said at the same time.

Melanie rolled her eyes in annoyance. "Don't worry about him. I'll be fine."

She was capable, that was for sure. But this was a serious problem. She must not have understood. "You don't understand. This guy - "

Melanie's eyes flashed to anger in an instant, and she fixed Julian with a glare that stopped his words in his throat. "No, *you* don't understand. Those...men..." she said the word like a pejorative "see only what they wish to see. Women cannot be mages, so they are not. All a woman must do is surround herself with the superstitious trappings of a cottage wise woman, or whatever they call them in whatever shanty town they happen to be in, and the Magestirium will just see a peddler of nonsense and think nothing more of it."

Julian chewed on that for a moment, and looked back around the shop again. Come to think of it, most of the products Melanie had up on display strongly resembled others he had seen in any number of home remedy shops, fortune tellers' parlors, and the like. He found himself pursing his lips in appreciation as he really saw the place for what it was: a quite convincing front.

Except...

"People in town know you're more than just some woman selling herbs in water that don't do anything," Raedrick said. "They've seen you work."

Melanie sniffed and waved a dismissive hand. "This isn't a grand metropolis, Raedrick." Her eyes flicked toward Julian and some of her smile reappeared. "You acknowledged that when you asked me to stay. No better place to hide than in a small town, isn't that what you said?"

Julian swallowed, the concern still heavy in his chest. "Yes, but I didn't mean - "

"Ask yourself this. How likely do you think the people in this town are to sell out someone who they know is responsible for saving their homes and families from depredation, and who they know can exact terrible vengeance upon them if they do?"

Another good point. If anything, the people of Lydelton looked at Melanie with even more awe than they did Raedrick and Julian, and that was saying something. And they were good, honest, hardworking folk, for the most part. Julian found himself nodding in understanding, and agreement.

"They would not. Not if they could help it."

Melanie returned the nod, her smile growing ever so slightly. "I have been discrete in the aid I've lent since the battle. No one has borne witness save the people I've helped, and the things I've done were personal enough that they won't come forward to tell about them, I assure you."

Raedrick looked abashed, probably no less than Julian did. He felt like enough of an ass, anyway. Of course Melanie would know how to hide in plain sight. She had been doing it for... Come to think of it, Julian had no idea how long she had been on the run before she settled here in Lydelton. It was probably just as well.

"Alright," Raedrick said, trying to regain some authority, or at least dignity, with his tone. "Just wanted you to know he was here, so you can take steps." He gave her a rather lame-looking smile.

Melanie rolled her eyes again, but her smile became more warm. "I appreciate your concern." She glanced at Julian and her smile widened a hair. "Both of you. But I'm a big girl. I can take care of myself."

There was not much else to say in response, so Julian did not bother to try. Neither did Raedrick. A few moments later, they hit the streets again. By his expression, Raedrick felt just as silly as Julian did. Some heroes they were.

———

Melanie pushed the door shut behind Raedrick and Julian. The click of the latch seemed to echo through the small front room of her shop, conveying a sense of finality.

Of doom.

She sagged against the door and her head fell limply against its surface. Fear, anger, despair, and a red-hot desire for vengeance all battled within her for a long moment. Unbidden, tears left her eyes and ran down her cheeks, then dropped and fell to the floor with inaudible splats that seemed to echo through her consciousness.

Loran was here.

Melanie drew a deep breath, trying to get control of herself. She was better than this. Timon had taught her better. But try though she might, the only things she could think of were the last time she saw Timon, bound and gagged, his eyes tight with agony as the Magestirium's questioners began their work on him, and the look on the Vigilant's face: beatific, full of a righteous ecstasy that only the most fanatical, most hateful of people could attain.

She wanted to kill him.

She needed to flee from him.

Melanie let her breath out, and, unbidden, a loud sob escaped her lips. Before she knew it, she was weeping. Weeping for her lost love, who had risked and, in the end, given everything so that her curiosity could be sated. And weeping for herself. She had dared to hope that here she could find refuge. Here she could find peace, and maybe happiness. And perhaps even love.

But no longer.

The man who killed Timon was here, and he would find her. And then he would kill her, brutally and without mercy. Of that, Melanie had no doubt.

The notion of flight crossed her mind, and she shrugged it away. Fleeing never helped those the Magestirium set out to destroy, not once the Inquisitors had their scent. It was only a matter of when and where. The only reason she had lived long enough to get here was because Timon had kept quiet about her. He must have; of that she had no doubt.

But they would be looking for a woman who practiced Magery, and word must have gotten out from somewhere that there was such a woman here in Lydelton. She was caught. Well and truly caught; the noose just had not tightened yet.

Unless she could turn the tables.

Melanie blinked away the tears and lifted her head off of the wooden planks that made up her shop's door. She had not considered that. Perhaps Vigilant Haversted had not yet fully discerned her location. If that were the case, he may not yet be ready to strike.

He would be unprepared. Vulnerable.

Melanie's lips turned slightly upwards as the thought lifted some of her despair. She may yet be able to salvage the situation. But she would have to move quickly.

❧ 7 ❧

DEATH'S DOOR

"**C**onstable!"

A woman's high-pitched scream stopped Julian in his tracks. He was walking down Water Street, one of the three imaginatively named main roads that led down to the docks from Main Street, heading toward the Covington Brothers' warehouse in his normal mid-morning round of the various businesses in town. Julian had just been thinking it was well past time Raedrick took a turn at this particular check—the warehouse was...fragrant...from the multitudes of fish that had been processed there over the years—but for one reason or another he always begged off on it. And so it was not without a certain sense of relief that Julian turned around to face the woman calling for him.

The relief faded as soon as he saw the woman sprinting down the road toward him. She wore a plain yellow dress, with a white sash around her waist that was embroidered with yellow, blue, and pink flowers, and simple white shoes, almost slippers. Her graying hair was done up in a bun atop her head, and she wore no makeup. Julian recognized her at once: Helena, Beverlee the teacher's sister.

She was old for his taste, but Julian had to admit she had kept herself up well through the years. Like her sister, she was a spinster and there were all sorts of rumors around town about her. About both of them. The sorts of rumors that were primarily spoken by women in half-whispers where they imagined men could not hear them. Of course, the rumors got around anyway. Julian did his best to pay them no heed, but he still caught himself wondering sometimes.

This was not one of those times. The look on Helena's face—horrified beyond reason, desperately hopeful and yet also full of despair—would have sent any such frivolous thoughts from his mind even if her tone had not.

Helena slid to a stop in front of him, gasping for air for a moment. Julian put a hand on her shoulder to steady her. "What's wrong?"

"Beverlee," Helena gasped. "She's..." She gasped again, then clapped her hand to her mouth as though suddenly realizing what she was about to say. The desperation and fear on her face gave way to grief and loss so profound that it looked as though it shattered everything else in her, and she let out a little wail.

Her knees buckled, and Julian had to move quickly to catch her before she hit the ground. The little wail become a long and guttural scream of denial, loss, bitterness. Pain. She clung to him like a drowning man clinging to a scrap of wood and shivered, her chest heaving as her scream gave way to sobs, then full on weeping that seemed as though it would never end.

Julian's heart sank to the ground at his feet. He did not need to ask what had happened; it was obvious. Helena's sister was dead. He held her close, letting her cry.

Two deaths in less than a week. This was not good.

Beverlee and Helena lived in a small flat atop a house near the eastern edge of town. Not too far from the final battle between Lydelton and Isenholf's band of brigands, earlier this year. The building was far enough into town that Julian and Raedrick had not imposed on the landlord to erect scaffolding for archers, or to erect a barricade alongside his house. But the landlord nonetheless tried, once or twice, to boast of his proximity to the fight over a pint or two of ale.

But only once or twice. The glares of the men who had actually been there, and the names of the men who had fallen, spoken by his neighbors, silenced his words better than any threat could have.

The house was stoutly built and not overly pretty. But then, it did not have to be. The stairs up to the flat were sturdy, though uncovered, so the sisters had to endure the elements on their way up and down from their home, even in the depths of winter, which in Glimmer Vale could be bitter indeed.

As Julian tramped up the stairs, he glanced behind at Helena, who waited on the street below with haunted, sunken eyes that were red from tears. His heart went out to her, and not just for her loss. A woman alone in the world faced a challenging life. It would have been difficult enough with her sister by her side. But now...

He shook his head. "It's just not right," he murmured.

Raedrick, leading the way up the stairs, nodded concurrence. "Is it ever?"

Julian had no answer to that.

The stairs doubled back upon themselves and ended at a simple wooden doorway that jutted out form the peaked roof of the building as though daring the winter's snow to cause it trouble. A foul odor permeated the landing, the smell of rotting meat and corruption.

It took a moment for Raedrick to get the key to work in the lock; the landlord had apparently not seen to any maintenance on the lock in some time. Although, if there were any things that required attention, the lock becoming more difficult to open would likely rate near the last on the list. Finally, Raedrick got the door open, and the stench hit them even like a jab from a pugilist. It was bad enough with the door closed. Now that it was open... Julian almost gagged at the smell.

This was going to be bad.

Raedrick looked no more eager that Julian felt. They shared a resigned look, then stepped inside.

The flat was more spacious than Julian expected from looking at the building from the outside. A good-sized living area, with a serviceable kitchen nook off to the left, greeted them as they entered. A pair of closed doors, nearly identical in their dark-stained wood, stood opposite the entrance, no doubt leading to the sisters' bedrooms. The living area was simply furnished with a stout wooden table in the middle and a pair of chairs toward the front of the house, where a broad window, framed by drapes that were embroidered with cheery forest scenes involving horses and other small animals strutting through the trees, let in a greater than average amount of light from the outside. A small bookshelf stood along the far wall, about two-thirds of the way filled with tomes of various sorts, and the kitchen was well stocked with utensils and foodstuffs. It was warmly decorated with rugs on the floors and paintings, many obviously from children's' hands, all over the walls. The sisters loved children, and it showed. Strange that neither chose to have any of her own.

It was a good home. Neat, warm, with all the charm and appeal of a well-lived-in place that oozed good feelings and simple contentment.

As long as you did not look at what was on the table.

Beverlee had not been dead for very long, but already the day's heat had crept up into the flat and things had begun to go rancid. Not to mention the things that happen to a body soon after its death. Julian had seen it on a dozen or more battle-fields, the body's muscles letting go once its spirit had left, letting its filth fall where it may.

There was never dignity in death, but some people should not be degraded like that. Beverlee was one of those; she had given her whole life to the children of Lydelton.

If the normal after-death loosening of the bowels was all that had befallen her, it would have been bad enough. But this...

"Gods above," Raedrick breathed, his face ashen and his tone matching it, if a man's tone could be said to have a color. "It's just like with Baelin."

Julian nodded his head mutely, struggling to take it all in.

The table was strewn with body parts. Little bits and pieces here and there, some recognizable as a hand or part of a leg, but many of them too savaged to tell. But just like with the woodsman, the head was clearly gone, missing from the rest entirely.

It rested upon the curved outlet of the small wood-fired stove that dominated the kitchen area, nestled onto a bend in the pipe not far from where it ran out through the building's roof. Beverlee wore almost exactly the same expression Baelin had: eyes locked wide open in a horrified stare, her mouth wide as though trying to scream, and her expression past terror to a fear so primal that it defied immediate description.

"Bugger me," Julian managed, finally.

Raedrick did not respond. His initial shock had faded, and he was beginning to look around with more of his normal manner, his face set in a stern mask.

This was bad. Julian had thought that already, but it was more true than he figured he knew. And one thing was certain.

"This was not the work of an animal."

Raedrick had taken the words right out of his mouth. Julian nodded agreement. "Animal that could do this would not have made it into town without anyone noticing." He took a deep breath, through his mouth so as to avoid as much of the stench as he could. "Which means..."

Raedrick finished the though. "Whoever did this also killed Baelin." He turned and looked gravely at Julian, his blue eyes seeming two or three shades darker than normal in the grisly room. "We're looking for a man."

Julian nodded agreement. Though he could not imagine the kind of man who would do something like this.

※ 8 ※

FORMALITIES

Mayor Brimly's scowl seemed to take up his entire face.

He sat behind his massive wooden desk in his office on the upper floor of City Hall—though city was perhaps a bit of a stretch—and looked at Julian and Raedrick through narrowed eyes that gleamed with concern. So did the sweat that ran down his brow and along the line of his chin to pool at its tip before dropping with a silent splat onto the blotter that lay atop his desk.

The mayor was somewhat more than plump. As usual, he wore his badge of office, a golden fish jumping out of the water, prominently on the left breast of his summer jacket. Today, the jacket was off-white, just the slightest shade of yellow, with a collared white shirt beneath. Julian had not seen his leggings yet, but no doubt his attire was perfectly matched. His wife always saw to that.

Julian had no desire for a wife like that. He would not dream of dictating a lady's choice of attire, as long as it lay within the bounds of decency. Why should a lady make such demands of him, or any man?

Stupid question, right there.

"Are you sure it's the same thing as Baelin?"

Raedrick kept his face smooth, neutral and respectful, but Julian knew it was only with difficulty. The Mayor could be...trying...at the best of times. But when things got stressful, he was not the most steady of individuals.

"Completely," Raedrick replied. "The bodies were arranged almost identically."

Mayor Brimly blew out a long exhalation and turned in his chair—it was set on a pivot, a nicely made contraption—to look out the window behind his desk, scowling. "People are not going to take this well."

Of course not. Though not universally well-respected—women who seemed to spurn even the idea of marriage stood out and were not well regarded by some—Beverlee was at least appreciated for the services she provided to the town's children. Or at least that portion of the town's children that she had the time to take under her wing. And whose parents were able to meet her price.

175

Come to think of it, there were likely some people in town, more than a few, who may have held a grudge against poor Beverlee and her sister, for just that reason.

But that was not what the mayor was getting at.

He looked back at the two of them. "I want this kept quiet."

Julian blinked and traded a glance with Raedrick.

"That will be...difficult," Raedrick said. "Plenty of people know Beverlee is dead already."

Mayor Brimly snorted softly and waved a dismissive hand. "I don't mean the fact that she's dead." He leaned forward, his face grim. "I mean how she died. And how it compares with Baelin. If people start putting two and two together, we'll have neighbor suspicious of neighbor. Before you know it, folks will start accusing each other for all to hear. Then there'll be fighting." He shook his head. "We need to avoid that."

"I doubt it'll come to that," Julian said.

Mayor Brimly snorted more loudly and scowled at him. "You've not been here that long. Trust me, this place will go up like a haystack if we let it."

Julian frowned. He was not so sure about Mayor Brimly's appraisal there. The people of Lydelton could have broken, fractured, when Isenholf's brigands put the pressure on. But instead, men went against their employers' wishes to fight alongside he and Raedrick, the populace at large hunkered down and helped out as best they could, and the town in general pulled together.

But that was against an external existential threat. How well would they stick together if it had been one of their own working against the rest of them?

Suddenly the Mayor's concern did not seem quite so far fetched. Damnit.

Raedrick frowned as well, and Julian could tell he was thinking along the same lines. Slowly, he nodded to the Mayor, conceding the point. "I'll talk with the people who have seen the body so far. It was only Helena, their landlord, and the priest's assistants. I think I can convince them to keep quiet."

Mayor Brimly nodded, his expression still grave. "I hope so."

A knock on the door to the Mayor's office interrupted the rest of his words. Mayor Brimly cocked his head at the door for a second, as though considering whether to answer. Then his eyes flickered over to the clock that rested on a shelf between two windows on the wall facing Main Street and he blanched.

"Come."

The door swung halfway open and the Mayor's secretary, a slight woman in her early middle years who wore her red-blond hair short, barely clearing her ears in back, stuck her head in. "Magester Haversted here to see you, Master Mayor."

Mayor Brimly grunted and shoved himself to his feet. "Send him in, Frieda," he said as he rose.

Julian and Raedrick stood with him. Julian could not help but watch as the door swung open fully and Loran strode confidently into the room. He was dressed more formally this day, in flowing robes that reached his feet and were a blue so dark they could almost be mistaken for black. A golden medallion hung around his neck, supporting the symbol of the Magestirium on his chest. It seemed to glow with an internal light. Neat trick.

Loran ignored the two law men as he entered, his gaze instead fixed completely on the Mayor. He strode to the front of Mayor Brimly's desk with a smooth, confident gait that seemed more fitting for a ballroom than a small office, and never mind the staff in his right hand, then inclined his head in greeting. "Master Mayor, it is a pleasure," he said in a formal, courtly tone.

Mayor Brimly perked up at Loran's demeanor. By the time the mage had finished greeting him, the Mayor's chest puffed out and he almost seemed to preen. He always was one to be impressed with a good show.

"The pleasure is mine, Magester Haversted," Mayor Brimly replied as he made a half-bow from his waist in response to Loran's greeting. "Lydelton is honored to welcome an esteemed member of the Magestirium to our midst."

Loran merely smiled, the kind of smile that said he was accepting a just supplication from one inferior to himself. It set Julian's teeth on edge.

"I believe you have met our Constables already," Mayor Brimly said, gesturing to Julian, then to Raedrick.

Loran cast only the briefest of glances at Julian, and he thought he saw the mage's lips twist in the tiniest of smirks there for a second, before turning his attention upon Raedrick. He, Loran studied intently for a brief moment, and Julian got the impression he had taken Raedrick's measure completely before Loran smiled and made the slightest of nods toward him.

"I have already met Constable Hinderbrook," he said, "but I am pleased to make your acquaintance." One eyebrow quirked upward, questioningly.

"Raedrick Baletier."

Raedrick held his hand out, and for a second Julian thought Loran was not going to take it. Then he clasped hands with Raedrick in the way a soldier greets a man he has fought beside. Raedrick's eyebrows quirked upward in surprise, but he returned the shake in a like manner.

"A pleasure, Constable Baletier," Loran said. His eyes flickered downward quickly. "It is most unusual for a man of your heritage to carry a Tyrashi blade."

Julian blinked in surprise and his gaze shifted unconsciously to the sword that hung from Raedrick's left hip. Slightly curved, with a hand-and-a-half hilt, it was a far cry from the saber he used to wield. Longer, heavier, and far more elegant, at least to Julian's eyes. It had belonged to Selam, a citizen of Lydelton who like them had come here from elsewhere. Selam died protecting the town from Isenholf's brigands, and had bequeathed the blade to Raedrick. It was some sort of family heirloom, but Raedrick had never explained its significance fully and Julian had not pushed. Raedrick and Selam had fought together, forged a sort-of friendship together, and that was not something that Julian felt comfortable shoving his nose into.

That said, he had never heard Selam say where he came from. If he was Tyrashi...

Come to think of it, Julian still had no idea where Tyrash was. He never had gone back to Melanie to find out.

Raedrick cleared his throat, his left hand coming to rest on the hilt of his sword almost unconsciously. "A gift from a friend," he said, simply.

Loran's eyebrows lifted high onto his forehead for a second. "A very generous gift." His eyes never left the sword. His tongue flicked across his teeth as though tasting something sweet, and Julian got a distinct sense of avarice from the man. "Unless my guess, that is Farelio's workmanship."

Raedrick blinked, confused, but Julian beat him to the question.

"Who?"

The mage looked back at him and truly did smirk this time. "Tell me you've not heard of Farelio? He was one of the greatest swordsmiths of the last half-millenium." He shook his head slightly, then turned back to Raedrick. "May I see the blade?"

Raedrick hesitated, his expression doubtful.

"Come now. I only wish to see if his mark is upon it." His tone and expression shouted that Raedrick would be beyond silly to refuse the request.

Raedrick glanced from Loran to Julian, who shrugged; what could it hurt? Then, with the soft sound of metal dragging against hardened leather, Raedrick pulled the sword out and held it upright between himself and Loran, turned so the mage could see the flat of the blade.

Julian had seen the sword many times, but its elegance and beauty never ceased to amaze him. The blade was curved and honed to a razor-edge on the entire convex side, as well as on the last third of the concave so its wielder could cut with a backswing almost as easily as with a front. That was not so terribly unusual; Julian had seen one or two blades of similar design. What set Selam's—Raedrick's —sword apart were the intricate engravings on the flat of the blade. Running the entire length of the blade, except along the cutting surfaces, they interlocked in a construct of artistry that rivaled anything Julian had ever seen.

The sword's effect on Loran was impressive, well beyond what Julian would have expected. The mage's eyes widened and his breath caught in his throat. He stood speechless for a full minute as his eyes traced the engravings on the blade, his expression clearly that of a man who cannot believe what he is seeing. He reached out as if to touch it.

Raedrick, frowning slightly, pulled the sword away and said, "Careful, Magester. It's very sharp." Then he re-sheathed it with a single smoothly-practiced movement.

Loran blinked, then flashed a rueful smile and chuckled softly. "Of course." He drew a deep breath and inclined his head toward Raedrick, a bit more deeply this time. "That is a princely gift, Constable Baletier. I would be sure to keep a close eye on it, were I you." He quirked an eyebrow upward slightly, then turned to face Mayor Brimly fully, who stood looking more than a little confused.

"Now then, Master Mayor, I believe we have business to discuss."

Mayor Brimly nodded, wiping the confusion from his face with practiced ease and replacing it with an ingratiating smile. "Yes, of course." He glanced at Raedrick, then Julian. "Thank you, gentlemen."

The dismissal was plain. Raedrick inclined his head to the Mayor. "Master Mayor," he said, then nodded to Loran again. "Magester."

The Mage returned the nod peremptorily, though his eyes flicked back to Raedrick's sword again, ever so briefly.

Julian said his farewells quickly then followed his friend from the office and pulled the Mayor's heavy wooden door shut behind them. "Well," he said, "that was interesting."

Raedrick smirked slightly and made a little shrug, but Julian could see the wheels turning behind his eyes. Loran knew something about his newly acquired sword. Something Raedrick did not, and it was going to eat away at him until he figured it out.

✤ *9* ✤

SAYING GOODBYE

They wasted no time on Beverlee's funeral, same as with Baelin.

No sense in putting it off any longer than necessary, especially with the bodies in the state they were. And so that very evening, Helena led a long procession—almost as long as the procession for the men who died fighting Isen-holf—down to the docks, where her sister's body lay wrapped in clean cloths that covered her from head to toe in a small boat.

The cloths were a necessity because of the state her body was in. But they were not unheard-of in any case. Some families preferred to look on their dead one last time, but many did not. And sometimes there was enough of a delay before the ceremony that decay began to set in, and it would not do for the guests to see the deceased in that state. So no comments were made at Beverlee being made up that way.

At least not openly. But Julian saw the looks between individuals in the crowd, the furtive whispers, the speculative expressions. Everyone was wondering about the similarity with Baelin's funeral, just a couple days before. It did not take a mental heavyweight to wonder whether she had been murdered in the same way he had, and if that were the case it was not an animal that did him, was it?

He could practically see the rumors that Mayor Brimly warned he and Raedrick about beginning to take form.

The ceremony was quick, as Helena apparently wanted it. Mayor Brimly said a few words, which was appropriate for a woman who had contributed to the youth of the town for so long, and then men hoisted the boat's sail and cast it off from the dock.

The breeze caught the sail, pushing the boat further from shore. When it got about a hundred feet out, a man knocked an arrow and dipped the head into a torch, setting it alight. Then he aimed and shot, and the arrow tracked across the sky to the boat, where the carefully prepared wood caught fire quickly. It burned for several minutes before the boat sank beneath the still waters of Lake Glim-mermere.

Then the crowd began to break up, and before long the only people remaining on the dock were Helena, Raedrick, and Julian. She just watched the patch of water where her sister sank down to her final rest in silence. They did not intrude upon her grief.

🦋 10 🦋

QUESTIONS AND QUESTIONS

"There has to be some connection between Baelin and Beverlee."

Julian sipped at his drink and frowned as he turned Raedrick's words over in his head. After a moment, he shrugged. "Does there?"

Raedrick gave him a long-suffering look, the kind that made people feel stupid.

"Don't look at me like that," Julian said. "Could be there's nothing in common between them, and this is all just..."

"Random?" Raedrick finished for him. He picked up the knife lying next to his plate and cut off a piece of his fish, then began chewing rapidly. He swallowed and made a jabbing motion with the knife, toward Julian. "You don't really believe that, do you?"

Julian sighed and leaned back in his seat. He turned his head to look out over the taproom at The Oarlock, where they were taking their lunch. It was a good-sized crowd today, the day after Beverlee's funeral. Cobblers, smiths, workmen of all sorts, and a few ladies who worked the trades as well, were sitting in small groups of twos or threes at tables scattered around the room. A good crowd, but the boisterous conversation that normally filled the taproom was muted. There was a tension in the air, an unspoken worry that seemed to have lowered everyone's spirits.

Two people were dead, and despite his and Raedrick's efforts to stem rumors over the last day since their meeting with the Mayor, enough people had begun to put two and two together that Beverlee had been murdered. Folks were beginning to worry that there might be another incident. And if so, who would be next? Why?

The mood was not contained within The Oarlock's walls either. Julian had sensed it, more diluted but still there, in the people as he made his rounds this morning. People were worried, afraid. He had not seen the town worked up like this since Isenholf.

Julian looked back at his plate and jammed a cut of fish into his mouth and forced himself to chew it, not even noticing the spicy deliciousness that was Molli's signature recipe. In truth, he hoped the two murders were related somehow. It would be much more difficult to figure out who was responsible if there were no link between the two victims.

All the same, though, Baelin? And Beverlee? He could not imagine how they would have crossed paths, except in passing.

"Rae, Baelin did not have the money to have anyone but Ilsa teach his children, and Beverlee never really had anything to do with the men in town except for business. What connection could there be?"

"I don't know. But there has to be something. Maybe Ilsa and Beverlee..."

Julian shook his head. "I asked Helena. They were passing acquaintances, nothing more."

"Well that just..." Raedrick dropped his knife and threw his hands up, helplessly. "Yeah."

They sat in silence. Julian was certain he looked as puzzled, frustrated, and worried as Raedrick did. He certainly felt it.

The serving girl, a slight little brunette named Sophie who wore the standard blue dress and apron that Molli made all her girls wear at work, came by a minute or so later. She paused, looking suddenly uncertain, as she saw their faces. For a second, Julian thought she was going to turn and leave, but instead she visibly collected herself and coughed slightly.

"Can I get you anything else, Constables?"

Raedrick gave a little jerk as though startled. He truly had been lost in his thoughts, if he had not noticed her arrival. He flushed slightly under Julians gaze, then smiled abashedly and shook his head to the girl. "I'm fine, thank you."

The serving girl looked at Julian, and he shook his head also. She paused, biting her lip for a moment, then glanced around furtively before asking in a low voice, "Do you know who did it yet?"

Julian blinked. That was unexpected. Though perhaps it should not have been. He traded glances with Raedrick, then cleared his throat before answering, "Can't really talk about that, Sophie."

"In other words, no."

She was no dummy. But then, Julian had seen Sophie befuddle many a man in this taproom. Granted, most times those men were more than a little tipsy, but she had always been quick of wit. He sighed. "We're working on it," he began.

Sophie nodded slowly. "I hope so. Beverlee and her sister taught me when I was younger. What happened to her was so... What kind of beast would do such a thing?" Her voice broke and she looked down at the floor, her face pale, sorrowful. Fearful.

Son of a bitch. Julian looked over at Raedrick, scowling. It looked like their attempts at rumor control had failed worse than they thought.

"It'll be all right, miss," Raedrick said, in that comforting tone that he did so much better than Julian. "You'll see."

Sophie put on a brave smile, but her eyes said she doubted it. She bobbed a little curtsy and went on about her rounds. Julian followed her with his gaze, and not just because of the wonderful way her hips swayed when she walked.

"So what's the plan?"

Raedrick said, darkly, "I'm working on it."

Back in Beverlee and Helena's flat.

It still stank, though the odor had lost much of its punch. The landlord had left the windows fully open through the night; Helena had stayed with friends. Small wonder why. There was no way Julian could have been convinced to stay there another minute, were he in her shoes.

He looked around the flat's interior and found himself shying away from the table where Beverlee's corpse had lain. He told himself to grow a spine, not shy away. But he found he almost expected to see her lying there when he looked, and worse, lying there staring at him with accusation in her eyes.

I am dead and I should not be. What kind of law man are you, to let this happen?

Julian blanched and looked further away from the table toward the chairs on either side of a small window that looked down at the street in front of the house. He almost did not realize he was avoiding looking until Raedrick cleared his throat.

Julian looked at his friend and noted the quirked eyebrow, the knowing stare for a moment before he shrugged, ever so slightly. "I'll look over here."

Raedrick smirked and for a moment Julian thought he was going to sling a verbal barb his way, but then he just nodded and stepped over to the little kitchenette. He began opening cupboard doors, looking in containers, intent on his search.

Julian's search of the living area took only a few minutes. As far as he could tell there was nothing out of place, or unusual to be found. A small stack of books between the chairs, mostly for learning but a few that had obviously come from one of the more recent caravans; no one in these parts penned stories about fainting damsels and unbelievably handsome and gallant princes.

Julian snorted. A gallant prince. That would be the day.

He turned to find Raedrick with his arms crossed and a frown on his lips. His right index finger tapped absently on the meat of his left forearm. "Anything?"

Julian shook his head and turned toward Helena's bedroom door. He hated to intrude on her privacy. Again. They had not found anything during their search yesterday afternoon. But maybe they had overlooked something. There had to be *something* pointing to why she had been killed.

He was just pushing the door open when a tentative knock at the flat's front door brought him up cold.

Julian spun around and blinked when he found his sword hand on the grip of his blade. He did not really expect trouble *here*? Did he?

A tall, plump man stood in the entrance doorway, his hand still raised against the open door where he had just finished knocking. He was an elderly man, old really, with thin wisps of silver hair that struggled mightily to cover the gleaming pate that was the majority of his head. His clothing was the kind of modest quality that bespoke a moderately successful tradesman who was careful to not step above his station by out-dressing his betters. He had grey-green eyes that twinkled with intelligence but were wide with alarm as he looked at Julian, and more in particular his weapon and his readiness to use it.

Julian flinched as he recognized the building's landlord and took his hand away from his sword, clearing his throat in embarrassment.

At the other end of the room, Raedrick also had turned to face the entrance, but he stood calmly, his face passive and his arms still crossed over his chest. Bloody man and his unflappable nerve. It was sometimes quite annoying, though in all honesty Julian could remember a number of times when he had seen Raedrick unnerved.

"Master Lepolo," Raedrick said gravely, and inclined his head in greeting. His eyes flickered Julian's way and Julian thought he saw a little rebuke in his gaze.

The old man cleared his throat and returned Raedrick's nod with one of his own, though he kept a wary eye on Julian. "Constables. Just wanted to check who was up here, after..." He cleared his throat again, suddenly looking uncertain about something.

Raedrick frowned. "After what?"

Lepolo looked over his shoulder, down the stairs leading to the street below, and chewed on his lip for a second, as though considering how to answer. "Fellow came by here early this morning, asking to take a look at the event, as he called it. I told 'im to get the hell out, and he went. But when I saw the door open, I thought maybe he came back."

Julian felt his eyebrows climbing high onto his head. The only people who would have had any reason to come in here, besides Beverlee and Lepolo, were he and Raedrick. It was no one else's business, or at least the people in town new better - and were in general not inclined - than to butt in.

"Who was it?"

Lepolo shook his head. "Can't rightly say. Never seen 'im before today. Small fellow. Wiry. Black hair, dressed all fancy. Young. Carried a big ol' staff, which I thunk was odd 'cause he didn't have any trouble walking around." He gave a little shiver. "Seemed polite enough, but there was something about 'im..." He trailed off.

Julian met Raedrick's eyes and found that his friend's eyebrows were also riding high, though he had a grim expression on his face. Julian couldn't blame him. He knew who the landlord's visitor was, just as Julian did.

Julian sighed. Mages were such a hassle.

HOT PURSUIT

Tracking Loran down was harder than Julian thought it would be. He was not at The Oarlock. When asked, Molli shrugged and replied that he had gone to City Hall. But there was no sign of him there either. In fact, the clerks on duty had not seen him since his meeting with Mayor Brimly, the previous day.

That put Julian's hackles up. There seemed no reason to lie about where he was going. Not to his innkeeper, at least. What was Loran up to?

"He did say he was in town on Magestirium business," Raedrick said as they departed City Hall. "I know Melanie said not to worry, but..." He left the rest unsaid.

Julian could not stop the little icy ball of fear from forming in his belly.

He did not need to ask; neither of them did. With unspoken resolve, they turned left toward the outskirts of town, and Melanie's shop.

And found it locked up, closed for the day.

Julian stared at the shop door, and the little CLOSED sign hanging in the window, and that little ball of ice grew larger. He glanced up at the sun, about halfway down toward its resting place in the east. It was still relatively early in the afternoon, far to early to have ended business for the day, and Melanie was meticulous about her business. Where was she?

"I don't like this."

Raedrick nodded agreement.

"You don't think he's taken her?" Julian paused. "What does the Magestirium do when they catch..." He let the thought go.

"You know as much about their procedures as I do, Julian." Raedrick's tone was solemn, in that way he got when he was trying a little too hard to be comforting.

"So nothing, in other words." Julian turned on his heel and strode back toward Main Street. After a few strides, he realized he was more stalking than walking and forced himself to slow to a more normal pace, but it was tough. He felt as though he was about to jump out of his skin, anxious as he was becoming.

"I'm sure she's fine." Raedrick had to hurry to catch up, despite having the advantage of longer legs. "She's more than capable of - "

"You think I don't know that?" Julian winced inwardly at his own tone. He did not need to be snapping like that.

Raedrick did not reply, but walked at his side, his expression serious, focused.

They turned right onto Main Street and passed several crossing streets before Julian began to think about where he was leading them. Where would a Mage go who had captured an enemy of the Magestirium? Maybe to the local Constabulary? No, he would not trust them with this, or even the local judge. This was an internal Magestirium matter, and the Magestirium answered to the King but few others. Loran would bundle up his prisoner and get her out of sight, or just leave town immediately.

He had not departed yet, though. Julian was certain he would not leave his Inn bill unpaid. So there was still time to rescue Melanie. Maybe.

They passed City Hall and continued down Main Street. All around, the people went about their business with an air of wariness. Furtive glances down each side street and between buildings. People walking in clusters more than singly. Children who normally would have been allowed to roam freely kept within arm's reach of their mothers.

The town was on-edge, even more so than it had been this morning. In his own nervousness about Melanie, Julian had failed to notice it, but a patina of fear lay over everyone. The rumors must have spread, and in spreading multiplied as rumors do.

"And we don't have a clue, still," Julian muttered under his breath. He came to a halt. Raedrick stopped next to him, a questioning eyebrow quirked upward.

Julian sighed. "This isn't accomplishing anything," he said. "If he's taken her, we won't be able to get her back from him." It was like a knife in the gut, admitting that, but it was true. The only reason they had managed to overcome Isenholf's Mage ally was Melanie had lent her own skills to the fight. Without some form of magical backup, Loran would wipe the floor with them. "Maybe we should..."

He stopped speaking as a figure caught his eye down the street. Slender and small, in loose-fitting dark clothing that was almost a robe, the figure had dark skin and black hair, and bore a staff in his right hand. Loran. He was walking toward them from the edge of town, where Main Street became the dirt road leading to the old Rangers Station.

"Maybe we should go say hello," Raedrick said, not quite finishing Julian's original thought.

Julian nodded agreement. "Let's."

They met on the south side of Main Street, in front of a seamstress shop that was owned by a friend of Molli's, a pleasant, plump woman of advancing age who still had a mind as sharp as a tack, and a wit to match. Julian had more than once been moved to near tears over one of Poleen's stories, funny as they were. As he and Raedrick stopped in front of her shop, he could see her through the window, leaning over one of her apprentices as the younger girl worked. Correcting her stitching, no doubt.

Loran stopped a few paces in front of them, a vaguely amused smirk on his face. "Pleasant day, Constables," he said by way of greeting. It was, in fact, stifling. And humid. The back of Julian's shirt felt like it was going to be permanently stuck to his back by sweat, and he could really use a drink or six. Loran, however, looked as though he was not sweating at all. "To what do I owe the pleasure this time?"

"Why did you try to enter our crime scene this morning?" Raedrick asked without preamble.

Loran blinked twice, cocking his head to the side almost like a bird. For a second he almost looked surprised by the question. But that surely was not the case. He had to know Lepolo would have told them about his visit. Finally, he rolled his shoulders in a relaxed shrug and answered. "Mere curiosity. I've seen a number of murder scenes in the past, but only rarely one so gruesome as that."

Raedrick's eyes narrowed. "You went inside, after Master Lepolo told you to leave?" There was more than a hint of steel in his voice. He was clearly irritated.

Julian was right there with him.

Loran waved his free hand dismissively. "Hardly. But the events in that flat are the talk of the town. Or hadn't you heard?" A single eyebrow quirked upwards, mockingly. "Remarkably similar to how you found the man in the woods, hmm?"

Raedrick rested the palm of his left hand on his sword's pommel. "What are you about here, Magester Haversted?"

"As I said, just idle curiosity." Loran looked away from the two law men, his expression relaxed, almost bored. "If you will excuse me." Then he stepped to the side and around Raedrick and commenced to resume his walk down the street.

Raedrick turned with the Mage and watched him walk away, his expression stony.

"He's up to something," Julian said, "and I'll wager it's not good."

Raedrick frowned ever so slightly. "Perhaps." Then he straightened his shoulders and drew in a quick breath. Turning toward Julian, he grinned quickly. "At least we know he doesn't have Melanie. That's something."

Julian nodded, but could not quite return the grin. It *was* something. Not much, but something.

❧ 12 ❧

AN OATH BETRAYED

Baelin and Ilsa owned a small cottage on the west side of town off Cannery Street, not far from Julian's own flat as it turned out. Down a small intersecting street that more fit the term alley—as far as Julian knew it had no official name, it was just "That Alley Over There" to the locals—that ran between a pair of large boarding houses where the younger fishing men tended to live, the cottage, though small by any standards, had a certain charm to it. It was obvious that Baelin cared for their dwelling; the roof and shutters were in good repair and while the sides did not exactly gleam, they clearly had a fresh coating of paint done this summer. A well-ordered garden lay off to the cottage's left side, planted with all manner of vegetables and a couple of small trees - fruit bearing, Julian was sure. All told, the cottage was a home, well and true.

It seemed a shame to bring more trouble to this family's door.

Raedrick knocked on the front door, his expression stolid; he did not like being here either. But there were questions that needed answering.

The door cracked open a short moment later and a young boy looked out at them. Maybe seven years old, with dirty-blond hair and eyes that were red as though he had been crying—and why not?—he wore a rumpled off-white shirt and baggy brown pants, and no shoes.

"Deven," Raedrick said, recognizing the boy from Baelin's funeral, "is your mother home?"

Deven bit his lip and nodded quickly, then disappeared from view, leaving the door ajar. The sound of low conversation followed briefly, and then the door opened fully.

Ilsa was small and lean, with short-cut hair that was blond but these days going more to silver. She wore a simple light-blue dress with little white flowers at the hem and collar, and a white sash about her waist. She wiped her hands on a stained piece of cloth and looked that them with the expression of a person who had just sucked on a lemon.

"What do you want?" Her voice was strained, weary, to go along with her sunken eyes. She had not been getting much sleep these last few days, from the look of her.

"We don't mean to intrude - "

"Well you are." Ilsa began to push the door closed.

Raedrick stepped forward raising his hands in a mollifying gesture. "Please, Ilsa. We need to ask you some questions, in light of what's happened."

She scowled. "You weren't so keen on questions when it was just my Baelin. But now that that hussy died too, *now* you want to talk with me?" She snorted, then slammed the door in Raedrick's face.

Raedrick took a step back from the door, open confusion on his face. He looked at Julian and spread his hands helplessly. "What was that?"

Julian just shook his head, as stunned as Raedrick looked. He had never heard anyone in town say anything bad about Beverlee. At least not openly. There were the rumors, spoken in whispers behind her back, but they mostly dealt with speculation about why she seemed to have no interest in men at all. There was never any hint of implication that she was of low character.

"I don't know," Julian said. "It's almost like..." He trailed off as a thought struck him.

It was out of the question. Completely. And yet...

"What if..." He stopped, cleared his throat, then started again. "Molli told me that on the night Baelin died, Ilsa accused Helena of helping her sister fool around with him." He leaned a little closer to Raedrick and said, more softly, "What if that was more than just insecurity speaking?"

Raedrick's eyebrows climbed high on his head and his mouth dropped open for a second. Julian could see the wheel turning, though, and shortly he was all business again, his lips compressing into a grim scowl. "If Beverlee *were* seeing anyone, Helena would know."

Julian nodded. "She's holding out on us."

The sun was just half its own width above the mountains to Lydelton's east when Raedrick and Julian got to the little storefront that Helena and Beverlee had converted into their classroom. One building down from a leatherworking shop and across from a carpenter, it was not exactly the location Julian would necessarily have picked for a school. He would have thought of someplace more quiet, pristine. But then, the sisters' business was thriving, and had been for years, so they were doing something right. Who was Julian to criticize?

Helena was just closing up when they arrived, the children having long since gone back to their parents for the evening. As they approached, Julian watched her locking up the front door to their school with a mixture of admiration and confusion. He did not think he could have brought himself to do anything the day after his twin and best friend had been buried, let alone try to teach a bunch of demanding children.

Hell, he was surprised the parents sent them at all this day. But then, looking at the determined set of her face as Helena turned away from the door—it almost concealed the pain in her eyes. Almost—he would have given good odds she stalked over to each house herself to collect the kids for their lessons. That took some gumption.

Helena saw him and Raedrick approaching and offered them a quick, tired smile that almost, but not quite, reached her eyes. "Constables."

Julian returned her smile with one of his own. "Good evening, Helena," he said, as gently as he could.

Raedrick merely nodded politely in greeting.

They stood there in silence for a short while, just looking at each other. For his part, Julian was not sure how to bring it up all of a sudden. How do you ask a grieving woman if her twin had been engaging in adultery? He cleared his throat. "We need to ask you a...delicate...question."

Helena drew back slightly, her expression becoming guarded. Her eyes flicked between Julian and Raedrick, questioningly.

Julian drew a quick breath, then found he could not figure out how to say it -

"Was Beverlee in a relationship with Baelin?"

Julian recoiled almost as much as Helena did, the way Raedrick just threw it out there. He glanced aside at his friend. Raedrick wore the smallest of scowls, his brow furrowing in focused disapproval. Julian was a bit shocked; Raedrick was normally more politic than this.

Helena swallowed and wiped her hands along the front of her dress, black today, to reflect her grieving status. For that matter, why was Ilsa not dressed for mourning? Helena opened her mouth to speak, then shut it and lowered her eyes. Then, almost imperceptibly, she nodded.

"Tell us," Raedrick said.

Helena did not look up. If anything, she seemed to shrink back even further. "It started six months ago. Baelin helped her with a problem parent who had been harassing her. She..." Helena bit back a sob. "She had not been interested in men at all, not for years. Not since Ferdrik."

She wiped her nose on the back of her hand, like a little kid, and glanced up at them quickly. If she expected them to recognize the name, or see some significance in it, Julian did not know what it was.

After a moment, she began again. "Baelin must have heard about the harassment from one of the other men. He..." She shrugged. "Well, whatever he did, word got back to Beverlee, and she wanted to thank him. One thing led to another, and..." She trailed off, lowering her eyes back to the ground. "They met once or twice a week in his hideaway, somewhere out in the Glamorwood."

She was clearly conflicted. On the one hand, she had to be happy that her sister had found joy, if not love, in her life.

Not to mention sex.

On the other hand, Beverlee's actions were shameful, in the extreme. Julian was not sure how he would have reacted, if his brother had done the same.

Strange that he had not thought about his brother until just then. It had been how many months now, since he and Raedrick fled their unit in the Army? And how many months—hell, years—before that since he last saw Jered? He must be a full-grown man by now, laying waste to entire platoons of maidens, judging by the way the school girls used to swoon over his every smile.

Julian almost found himself chuckling over his brother's imagined antics, until he remembered where he was, who he was speaking to, and the circumstances. And even though he was more than halfway expecting it, the outright admission made Julian's stomach sink a bit. There was the answer, to both questions. Ilsa was not keeping with the normal mourning rituals because she was not truly mourning.

Ilsa was their killer.

COMPARING NOTES

"That doesn't make any sense." Raedrick snapped the words off quickly, but it sounded almost like he was trying to work himself through the notion more than he was trying to refute it. "How would Ilsa be able to do...that...to Beverlee, let alone to Baelin? She's not a big woman. I doubt she could lift an axe big enough to chop a body apart like that, let alone wield it effectively."

Julian had to admit, he had a point. Ilsa was the prime suspect, from circumstance and motive if for no other reason. But the method of the killings... That was troublesome. "Maybe she hired someone. Or she learned a little magic somewhere."

"What, like Melanie?" Raedrick shook his head and rested his palms on the top of his desk.

They were back in their office. After leaving Helena, they had walked back to the Constabulary, for lack of any better place to go as much as for the need to sit and think it through, and settled down into their respective seats. The brainstorming had gone downhill almost from the start.

"I truly doubt more than one Melanie will happen in any generation," Raedrick said, to complete his thought.

"Well, I should hope not."

Julian leapt out of his chair at the completely unexpected voice, which seemed to emanate from the air itself. Without thinking about it, he pulled his longsword from its scabbard and vaulted over his desk, landing on the balls of his feet in a ready stance.

Across the room from him, Raedrick had done similarly, except that he stood with most of his weight on his rear foot and he held his Tyrashi blade in both hands, with the sharp side of the blade pointing toward the ceiling and the hilt even with his right shoulder.

Julian had never seen such a ready stance before; where had Raedrick learned it?

Then he looked more closely at his friend and saw that his feet were positioned awkwardly, far enough apart that it would be difficult for him to move quickly, and his shoulders were very tense. It was almost like he was trying to force the stance, to merge himself into some form that he thought he should be taking. To match the sword?

From sparring him, Julian knew that Raedrick, despite months of training with his new blade, still was not comfortable with it. He still wanted to revert to the movements and forms he knew, and executed so well, from his old saber. His moves, though improved, were awkward, like he was fighting himself.

Before he accepted Selam's blade, Julian knew he would not have lasted a single pass in a duel with Raedrick. Now... Now, Raedrick was a shadow of his former self, at best Julian's equal, but by no means the master he once had been.

Raedrick flexed his fingers on the grip of his sword, his eyes glancing around the room nervously. How much of that nervousness came from his uncertainty with his weapon?

Julian looked around the room and scowled. There was no one else here, so where did...

Deep laughter emanated from out of nowhere, a vibrant chord that Julian recognized after a second or so. He should have known immediately who it was, but the shock of hearing that voice stopped his brain from working. He lowered his sword sheepishly and rose from his ready crouch.

"Dammit, Melanie!"

Her laughter only intensified as, off to Julian's left, in front of the cell block door, Melanie suddenly appeared in his view. She stood with her arms crossed over her breasts, shaking her head with a look of mocking amusement on her face. As always, she was dressed impeccably. Tonight, it was a deep burgundy dress and what Julian assumed was the same belt as before.

She smirked at the pair of them. "Honestly, boys, you are *far* too easy."

Julian sheathed his sword. He put an extra little zip into the process at the end; the steel of his blade's hilt struck the metal mouth of his scabbard with a fair-sounding CLACK, and all the while he just glared at Melanie. She returned the glare with a sardonic look of her own.

"What do you think you're doing?" Raedrick said sternly. He had also replaced his sword. He regarded her with his hands on his hips, looking for all the world like he was about ready to chew her a new one.

Melanie shrugged slightly and said, calmly, "Do calm down." She swayed over to one of the chairs that sat along the wall near the front door and settled down, taking a moment to smooth her skirts. "I thought we could compare notes."

Julian and Raedrick shared a look. The stern expression remained, but Raedrick looked puzzled now.

"I don't think so," Julian said. "We're still in the middle of our investigation and you're not..."

"Involved?" Melanie quirked an eyebrow archly. "You seemed to think I would become involved, the other day."

Julian rolled his eyes.

"Have you learned something that might help us find the killer?" Raedrick cut straight to the point, at least.

Melanie shrugged. "Maybe, but I doubt it." She crossed her legs and leaned back in the chair. "Not unless Loran turns out to be the guilty party. I've been following his movements."

Raedrick lost his stern expression, his mouth instead falling open in surprise. Julian felt poleaxed, though of course thinking about it he really should not have been. Melanie had taken their warning and turned it on its head, taken the initiative to ferret out how much she needed to be concerned. That was laudable.

But still...

"That's a big risk," Julian said. "If he caught you..." He shook his head. "Better to just stay clear of him."

Melanie blew out a forceful snort that somehow managed to not seem at all un-ladylike. "So he can ambush me at a time and place of his choosing?" She shook her head with vigor. "I am quite capable of discretion, if you recall. Unless he were actively taking precautions against my techniques—and I assure you he did not—he would not notice if I were standing two feet from him."

Julian frowned as he thought that over. Melanie's concealment spells were potent, he knew that for true. They were perhaps *the* primary reason the town won out over Isenholf's brigands. But Loran was a mage as well, and from what hints Melanie had dropped probably much more skilled than she. Somehow Julian was not so certain he was as oblivious as she claimed, or hoped.

All the same, Loran had been acting strangely. Julian glanced over at Raedrick and shrugged his shoulders. The die was cast; might as well make use of the result.

Raedrick sighed again and nodded, then he settled back down into his desk chair. "Tell us."

"He has crisscrossed the town over the last couple days, and performed a number of detection rituals." She held up a forestalling hand at Julian, no doubt seeing the sudden flash of alarm that shot through him. "Not the sort that would have detected my spell. Something else." She frowned slightly, shaking her head. "I did not recognize the specifics of the ritual, just enough to know that it was meant to find something or someone. Who or why, I can only speculate upon. However," she leaned forward and looked meaningfully at both of them, "he went by Beverlee and Helena's house this morning, and was in the midst of setting up another ritual when their landlord chased him away."

Loran's presence at their flat was hardly surprising. The fact that he was preparing a spell, though...

"And then what?"

"Then," Melanie said. "Then, he walked into the woods past the Ranger Station to a clearing with a large boulder. The place you found Baelin, yes?"

Julian and Raedrick both nodded, soundlessly. Melanie returned the nod with a look of satisfaction.

"He performed his ritual again. This time he seemed quite a bit more excited, as though his results were different than at the other locations. Whatever he is looking for, I would wager it has something to do with your killings."

"We knew he went to Beverlee and Helena's. We bumped into him on the street, and he said it was just idle curiosity."

Melanie smirked at Julian's words and gave a little shake of her head. "Loran Haversted does not engage in idle curiosity. There is a purpose to his every action."

Raedrick looked levelly at Melanie for a moment before speaking slowly, his tone chilly. "You didn't tell us you knew him."

"You did not ask, did you?"

Raedrick just looked at her, accusation in his eyes. Finally, after what seemed a much longer moment than it probably was, she rolled her eyes and raised her hands in supplication.

"Fine. Fine, I know him. Or rather, I know *of* him, and I am very glad that he does not know me." Her expression darkened, something like pain or...fear?...flashing across her face before she schooled herself to calm. "You recall the hypothetical mage we discussed when we first met?"

How could they forget? It had not taken long for Julian to puzzle out that Melanie was a mage, and bugger the restrictions against women studying at the Magestirium. One five-minute conversation, really. And when it became clear how overmatched the town was against Isenholf's brigands, he and Raedrick had sought her out for support. She had alluded to the possibility of a hypothetical mage and a hypothetical woman falling in love and him sharing the Magestirium's secrets with her, but she had not elaborated.

"I remember. Timon, you said his name was," Julian said, with no small amount of apprehension. For some reason he was not sure he wanted to hear this part of her story.

Melanie nodded and flashed the barest hint of an approving smile before replying. "Loran is a Vigilant—one of the Magestirium's Inquisitors."

"Inquisitors? I haven't heard of them before," Raedrick said, one eyebrow quirking upward.

"And you would not have. They are the Magestirium's internal police force, and rarely interact with the uninitiated on official business." That little smile faded into a scowl. "Vigilant Haversted was the one who led the investigation into Timon's...impropriety." She shuddered visibly and looked away from them, off into space. "I do not know how long they tortured him before the end, but I do know he did not betray his secrets, at least not the ones he kept closest to his heart."

"How do you know that?"

Melanie gave Julian a direct look, one filled with suppressed pain that was eclipsed by a deep and abiding anger. "Because I am still alive." Her lips compressed for a moment and then, with the brush of her hand through her hair, the deep emotions were gone, replaced by her normal slightly sardonic half-smile. "So." She clasped her hands together and leaned forward slightly. "Ilsa?" She shook her head. "She's not the murdering type."

Julian had to do a double-take, quick as her demeanor changed. Glancing over at Raedrick, he got a cocked eyebrow in return, followed by a quick shrug of the shoulders before Raedrick answered.

"You knew her well?"

Melanie shook her head again. "Not really. She came into the shop once or twice, looking for home remedies. Although," she frowned slightly and tapped the tip of her index finger against her lips as she paused, considering her words for a moment, "a couple weeks ago she alluded to having a more difficult problem she might need help with, but it never went any further than that."

"An unfaithful husband *is* a difficult problem," Julian said.

Melanie shrugged slightly. "Don't know what she would have expected me to do about that. No, more likely it was one of the children. Runny bowels for an excessive duration, or something."

Julian coughed into his hand; that was not the direction he wanted the conversation to turn. Melanie shot him an amused glance.

"So Baelin was cheating and she killed him for it. And Beverlee as well?" She shook her head again, her face doubtful. "I don't see it."

"We know he was unfaithful," Raedrick said.

"Do you?"

He exchanged a semi-confused look with Julian. "Helena said so, and Ilsa more than implied it."

Melanie spread her hands as though to say, "If you say so," but she still looked doubtful. Either about the infidelity or the murder plot.

Or both.

And Julian had to admit she had a point. All they had was implication from the wife and hearsay from the sister. Though why would Beverlee lie to Helena about that? But that would not be enough to bring before the judge. If they had some proof...

"Helena said Baelin had some sort of hideaway out in the woods, and that's where they met." Julian looked over at Raedrick and leaned forward. "Maybe there's something there that can shed some more light on what was going on."

Raedrick frowned, chewing at his lip for a moment, then he nodded. "True. But do you have the first idea where to look for it?"

"No." Before heading out to the site of Baelin's murder, Julian had never set foot in the Glamorwood. He would not have a clue where anyone... But then, he did not have to. "But I think I know who would."

❧ 14 ❧

BOOZE AND BLOOD

Julian expected Melanie to make more of a fuss, so he was surprised when her only response to his suggestion that she not accompany he and Raedrick was to arch an eyebrow at him and say, "Of course."

He just stared at her in silence for a moment. He had carefully prepared arguments ready to use about how it would be best if she were not visibly associated with this case, since Loran was apparently so interested in it. And maybe she should keep up the disappearing trick she pulled the last couple days, just in case. But with her ready agreement, the arguments all fell out from the bottom of his brain.

Melanie stood and walked toward the door, shaking her head slightly. "It's better if I not stick my neck out. Loran does not appear to be looking for me after all, but that doesn't mean I should bring attention to myself."

And then she left their office.

As the door swung shut behind her, Raedrick said, "Well. That was easy." He sounded as surprised as Julian felt.

"Yeah."

Raedrick stood up. "Where are we going then?"

"I figure if anyone knows where Baelin's hideout is, Dewey does." Julian took a moment to adjust his swordbelt, then set out for the door. "I heard him saying he was going for a drink at Holb's Tavern after Baelin's funeral. Could be they'll know where to find him there."

Raedrick blanched visibly.

Holb's Tavern was similar to The Oarlock in that they both served ale. Aside from that, though...

While The Oarlock was really an Inn with a spacious taproom and well-run kitchens, Holb's was almost literally a hole in a wall. The building it resided in was at one point in time an armory, or so some of the oldsters in Lydelton told Julian. Sitting on the western edge of town, a block and a half from the last of the finger-piers that jutted into Lake Glimmermere, the building was squat, long, and narrow, painted a deep red that was nearly black, and steadily falling past ill-kept toward dilapidated. Down near the end of the building farthest from the center of town, a twenty foot section of the outer wall had been removed and a wide awning installed that extended a good thirty feet out from the side of the building. The bar took up the entire length of the building where the wall used to be, and the serving area was a paved expanse beneath the awning. That awning served as the tavern's main shelter from the elements. Julian would have thought Holb would close up shop when it got cold because of that, but apparently he had canvas sides that laced in place around the awning. Those combined with braziers inside made the tavern pleasantly warm. Supposedly.

"I can't believe so many people frequent this place," Raedrick said as the two of them came to a halt in front of the old armory.

Indeed, a fair-sized crowd was already gathered, in spite of the relatively early hour; it was just getting toward dinner time, and Holb's did not serve food, only drink. About two dozen men, and a few women as well, mostly fishing men and laborers of other stripes from the look of them, drank and laughed in the serving area. Though their laughter was a bit less raucous than usual and several of the faces in the crowd had a strained look that even the flush of drink could not mellow.

Even here, there was fear.

Julian smirked at Raedrick's remark. "It can be an entertaining place."

Raedrick just snorted, a look of distaste on his face. Apparently he still felt the sting from his last visit.

Julian led the way into the serving area, slipping past a group of men who were crowded around a table where a pair of particularly burly fellows were engaged in an arm-wrestling contest. They were quite enthusiastic in cheering on their favored contestant, and from the way the men's arms were shaking it looked like they had been at it for a while. Julian chuckled and turned away. A moment later, groans of chagrin mixed with cheers of triumph as the contest ended.

Julian strode up to the bar and smacked his hand down flat on it.

The bar was not polished or stained. It was bare wood, pine he presumed though he could not tell from looking at it, and sanded to a smooth texture. Stains from multiple mugs and glasses and crude—and rude—drawings and writings of all sorts marred its surface, giving it a strangely homey look.

The man behind the bar was anything but.

Tall, with shoulders that dwarfed those of the bulkiest man in the tavern, he had a square face that seemed locked into a sour expression behind a thick black beard. Julian supposed his hair would have matched his beard, if he had any. But his head was completely bald, as though he shaved it regularly instead of his face. He had dark brown eyes that twinkled with intelligence, and irritation, and wore a stained white apron over a light blue, almost grey, shirt and black pants. A puckered scar crossed his forehead from just over his left eyebrow to his left ear, and that ear had a little notch cut out of it.

Julian had never heard how Holb got that scar. The one time he asked Holb about it, he received only a sour grunt in response, and no more drink that evening.

Holb scowled a greeting at Julian, but when his eyes moved from Julian to Raedrick the scowl became a near-feral growl, complete with baring of teeth.

"Whoa. Take it easy, Holb," Julian said, quickly. "We come in peace." He looked back at Raedrick, who was returning the hostile look in kind, and amended, "He comes in peace." He looked back at Holb and put on a winning grin, raising his hands in a gesture that he hoped was placating. "Just have a couple questions."

For a few seconds, Holb just stared daggers at Raedrick. The area became hushed, as the patrons around them sensed the tension between the two men. The silence grew quickly until it encompassed the entire serving area. Everyone — Julian did not stop to look but he was absolutely certain everyone in the area—was staring at them in hushed anticipation.

The last time Raedrick came here, he had somehow managed to insult Holb's wife. Julian had no idea how; he had never seen Raedrick behave except chivalrously. But somehow he managed it, and Holb had personally come over the bar and thrown Raedrick out of his place. Julian had not seen it, but rumors were Holb did it with embarrassing ease. Whatever the truth of the incident was, and he never spoke of it, Raedrick had moved rather stiffly for the next few days, and he had never returned to Holb's Tavern.

Julian fervently hoped there was not going to be a repeat this evening.

Finally, Holb nodded, ever so slightly. He snorted Raedrick's way then turned his full attention on Julian.

Softly, almost imperceptibly, it seemed the entire population of customers and serving girls let out a breath they had all been holding. Julian found that he did the same.

He cleared his throat and put his smile back on. "Two pints of ale please, Holb." Holb's scowl intensified again. "Ok, just one." He waited until the barkeep brought his drink, then plunked down payment and took a swig before speaking again. "Have you seen Dewey around?"

Holb cocked his head to one side and his bushy eyebrows rose slightly. "What ya want wit him?"

Julian took another drink and paused, looking down at the mug. It was good. Damn good. "You using a new formula?"

Holb shrugged ever so slightly and grunted in reply. Julian could not be sure, but it almost looked like he might have slightly smiled for a second. "Just 'xperimenting."

"Well that's pretty damn tasty."

Holb's head dipped ever so slightly in acknowledgement. His brow furrowed a bit. Get to the point, Constable.

"Right." Julian took another sip. "We need to ask Dewey a few questions about Baelin. Part of the investigation."

Holb's brow furrowed even more and his scowl deepened.

"He's not in trouble or anything. We thought he could help us out, is all."

The big barkeep glowered for a long, silent moment. Then he shrugged and turned away. He walked over to where one of his serving girls waited, then proceeded to fill several mugs from one of the kegs behind the bar. He placed them on her tray, and she departed.

Julian could not help but follow her with his eyes. Holb's girls always wore the most appealing outfits. Tight in just the right areas, but not so much as to do more than tease. It made for a good sight.

Holb's big beefy hand slapped down on the bar next to Julian, and he jumped ever so slightly as he turned to look back at the big bartender. "Bigsbe's," said Holb.

Julian nodded. "Thanks."

Holb just grunted.

Bigsbe's Boarding House lay on the north side of town, only two blocks away from Julian and Raedrick's office. Two stories tall, it boasted twelve small rooms on the upper level, a small common area on the ground floor that held a couple bookshelves, a quartet of chairs, and a small writing desk, and a common bath house and privy in the rear. Julian had visited the place on two previous occasions, to mediate minor squabbles between a few of the tenants, and found it relatively clean and well-cared-for, as boarding houses went.

Madaleen Bigsbe, the proprietress, held court from a small office near the front of the common area. But when Julian and Raedrick walked in the stout wooden double-doors at the front of the building, she was nowhere to be seen. Small wonder, concerning the hour. She had family to attend to, after all.

"Isn't there a night attendant?"

Julian sniffed in amusement at Raedrick's words and almost voiced a bitingly sarcastic riposte, but looking at him, he was still perturbed from their interaction with Holb. So Julian let it lie. Mostly. "It's not an Inn, Rae."

"I know that. But if she's going to leave the place unlocked, someone ought to keep an eye out. Keep thieves from making off with her books, if nothing else."

Fair point. Julian shrugged and poked his head into the little office. It was just large enough to contain a stout wooden desk and chair, a trio of narrow cabinets that Madaleen used for storing files, and a strongbox. The chair was pulled back from the desk as though someone had gotten up from it quickly. Adding to that impression, a cup of dark fluid, tea probably, sat on the blotter. Steam was still rising from the cup, and some of the tea had splashed out onto the blotter.

Julian frowned. "Looks like they left in a hurry." He looked back at Raedrick.

His friend returned his frown and loosened his sword in its sheath. "Something's not right here. Look sharp."

They separated by a few paces and advanced through the common room to the passageway leading toward the bath house. Just outside the common room, on the left, a narrow set of stairs led up to the level above. Raedrick took the stairs two at a time, and Julian followed, a gnawing sense of dread in his gut that got more pronounced by the second.

The stairs ended at a small landing, then bent back on themselves before reaching the doorway to the second floor. They had just reached the landing when the soft sound, like a groan, reached Julian's ears.

He froze, drawing his sword and waiting, listening, for another sign. After a dozen or so seconds of silence, he glanced at Raedrick, who wore a mask of grim focus. Then another sound: breaking glass. Their eyes met, and Julian saw the same resolve, and dread, as he felt himself.

Not again.

The two men burst into the second floor corridor and looked quickly left and right. The stairs lay in the center of the building; in either direction were three pairs of doors, across the corridor from each other. Small oil lamps in wall sconces provided illumination that was just a bit better than twilight. But that was enough to see a figure lying prone near the farthest pair of doors to the left.

"Son of a bitch," Julian said as he sprinted down the corridor to the downed figure, Raedrick at his side.

They pulled up short and saw immediately that the prostrate person was dead. Her—and it was a she, a once very-pretty she too—head was twisted completely around so her glazed, lifeless eyes looked up at the ceiling despite the fact that her body lay on its belly.

"Son of a bitch," Julian repeated, more loudly, and squatted down next to the dead girl.

"Julian."

He looked up at Raedrick, and his friend nodded at the right-hand side door. It lay a couple inches ajar, and a cold breeze wafted into the hallway, carrying an unmistakable and recognizable stench. Julian's blood, already cold from finding the body, went like icy water, and that sense of dread returned threefold.

The scene inside the room was every bit as bad as Julian feared. And every bit the same as before.

The room was maybe ten feet square, with room for a bed and a desk and a small cabinet. The entire room was covered in blood, from the floor to the ceiling. Body parts were strewn everywhere, but mostly lay on the bed. As before, it was difficult to tell which part was which. Except for the head, resting atop the cabinet and staring at the scene in abject horror. Julian recognized Dewey's face immediately.

The room's lone window was shattered, only a few shards of glass still remaining in its pane. The drapes wafted in the chilly nighttime breeze lazily. For a moment Julian found himself focusing on that motion to the exception of everything else; a single point of normalcy in the insanity of the scene.

And then Raedrick was past him and peering about through the window. He hissed.

Julian hurried over and looked down. It took a short while to make out anything in the darkness.

"There."

Julian followed his friend's outstretched finger and squinted. There was nothing...

Wait. In the shadows between two adjacent buildings, something was moving. Hurrying away from Bigsbe's, but not running; that would draw attention. The figure kept to the shadows, moving furtively, until it reached the street.

It turned left and vanished from sight, but just before that happened, the light from a streetlamp cast details on the figure. Short, with dark hair and wearing dark robes. And carrying a large staff.

Julian felt his eyes growing wide.

UNDER ARREST

They ran to The Oarlock.

Raedrick had longer legs, and Julian had to push hard to match his pace, By the time they reached the Inn, he was out of breath and his legs felt rubbery. He did not normally run so far so quickly.

He derived some comfort from the fact that Raedrick was also breathing heavily. Some.

They burst into the taproom and veered straight toward the bar, where Molli held court. Julian hardly noticed the patrons except to think mildly that it was nice how they all got out of their way.

Respect.

No, wait. That wasn't it. They all looked startled, frightened. One serving girl squeaked as they rushed past and dropped her tray, and its contents, to the floor.

Molli watched this and scowled, planting her hands on her hips. "Stop right there!" Her voice cut through the air like a horn, bringing Julian up short, and Readrick with him. He had not heard someone shout like that, since...

All at once, he realized he still had his sword brandished. And...

He looked down at himself. His clothing was bloodstained in many places, from the scene in Dewey's room. Raedrick was in a similar state, and wore an murderous expression to go with it.

No wonder people had cleared out of their way. He and Raedrick must have scared the hell out of them.

Stupid.

"What do you think you're doing, charging in here like this?" Julian had seen Molli irritated before, but never truly angry. Until now. Her brow furrowed, her face flushed deep red, and her eyes glittered dangerously. "You get yourselves - "

Her tirade vanished beneath Raedrick's shouted, "Quiet!" His tone was the same whip-crack of command that he used during the heat of battle to order his squad to change tactics. He must have practiced it for weeks, because it was unerringly able to pierce the din of battle or, in this case, Molli's speech. Raedrick fixed a deadly serious stare on her, and she shrank back. "Loran Haversted," Raedrick continued in that same tone of command. "Where is he?"

All around, patrons looked at each other, Raedrick's words having easily reached their ears. Already he could see the wheels turning, the seeds of new rumors beginning to flourish.

Molli blinked, taken aback but obviously still angry. "His room, I think. What is this about? You have no right - "

"Which room?" Raedrick waited a half-second, then demanded again, more loudly. "Which room?"

"Room Seven. What - ?"

"The key."

Molli drew herself up and shook her head. "Now see here. You can't just barge into one of my guests' rooms. I've got a - "

"The key, or I break down the door."

Silence followed for several seconds and Molli and Raedrick locked eyes, her seething anger mixed with no little confusion against his rock-solid resolve. Slowly, Molli's expression changed, moving away from anger toward nervousness and then fear. She swallowed.

"He's not the one who..." She trailed off, her words lowering to a whisper as the import of what was happening sunk in.

"Just give us the key, Molli, so we can handle it."

Molli nodded shakily and reached into one of the pockets in her apron. She pulled out a medium-sized key ring and took a moment to fumble through them until she found the one she needed. She had to try twice to get it off the ring, and then she held it out to Raedrick.

"Thank you," he said, and snatched it out of her grasp. Then he turned toward the staircase at the rear of the taproom, glancing at Julian as he went. "Let's go."

Raedrick led the way up the stairs, with Julian right behind him.

It had been some time since he had last been on the Oarlock's upper level, and as they burst onto the upstairs landing, memories swept back over Julian. Good times, and bad. Mostly stressful, to be honest; they lived here during the conflict with Isenholf, and that was as stomach-clenching a situation as Julian had seen. Up until now, anyway.

He shoved the memories aside and followed his friend down the hall and around the corner to Room Seven. It was conveniently located adjacent to the baths and privy, but Julian was surprised that Loran had not opted for Molli's more luxurious suite. He certainly had the coin for it. Not that it mattered now.

They reached the door and paused for only the briefest of moments. Then Raedrick jabbed the key into the lock and shoved the door open.

The room was small, smaller than the room at Bigsbe's, but well furnished. It differed from the room Julian and Raedrick had stayed in in that there was only one bed, but aside from that it was identical.

Except that this room had a short mage with one leg out of the window, looking like he was just returning from some bit of malfeasance or another.

"Well," Julian said, "that answers that."

"How dare you?" Loran snapped, wrenching his leg over the window sill even as he reached for his staff, which lay on the floor, where he had dropped it while climbing in. "What is the meaning of this?"

Raedrick wasted no time in answering. Moving with all the speed at his disposal, and he had quite a lot, he bounded across the room and struck Loran with a left cross.

The mage did not even try to block it, so surprised he was. Raedrick's fist struck him in the cheek, and his head snapped backwards and to his left. He staggered backwards and struck the wall, then fell forward onto his knees as his hands flew to his face.

Raedrick grabbed him by the back of the neck and flung him to the ground, then straddled him as he took hold of his wrists and forced his hands behind his back. Then Raedrick looked up at Julian and quirked an eyebrow at him. Julian smirked and reached into the belt pouch where he kept his manacles, then handed them to him.

"Loran Haversted," Raedrick said in his most professionally cold tone while he locked the manacles around the mage's wrists. "You are under arrest for the murders of Baelin Rorickson, Beverlee Winslow, Cora Frederlan, and Dewey the woodsman."

"Preposterous," Loran said. "I demand you release me at once!"

Raedrick just snorted in his ear then, with Julian's help, hauled him to this feet.

Loran's right cheek was already beginning to swell. It was going to be one hell of a bruise. He was lucky Raedrick had not struck him lower, or he would have lost several teeth. All the same, his eyes were defiant, furious. "You are making a grave mistake, Constables." His voice was cold, venomous, promising swift retribution against them.

The problem was, Julian was not sure that he could not deal out that retribution, even from a jail cell. From the look in his eyes, Loran believed he could do just that.

Julian just hoped they were right about this.

The journey from The Oarlock to the Constabulary was normally fairly quick, but this night it seemed to take forever. Halfway there, Loran seemed to come out of a daze and began to struggle surprisingly vigorously for a man his size, especially one who presumably did not get much in the way of exercise—after all, what need does a Mage have for physical force? It took both Julian's and Raedrick's full effort to keep him in line and going the right direction.

By the time they reached their office and got the cell block door open, though, it seemed to get through Loran's head that he was stuck and they were not going to let up. He ceased his struggles and complied with Raedrick's commands without complaint, even walking himself into his cell.

When they closed and locked the cell door, he wore a mocking little grin on his face that never translated to his eyes. They burned with simmering anger. Julian had been stared down by many men before, but he could not recall anyone off-hand who had done it as effectively as this Mage.

He hurried out of the cell block as quickly as he could once the cell was secured. He thought he heard Loran chuckle mockingly as he went.

❧ 16 ❧

A NOT-SO-FRIENDLY CHAT

The two of them divided their efforts. After getting Loran secured in his cell, Raedrick went back to Bigsbe's to more thoroughly investigate the scene, while Julian went back to The Oarlock to look through Loran's effects. Julian did not envy Raedrick his half of the night's investigation. Not one bit. But after an hour and a half in Loran's room with nothing of pertinence to show for it, he almost could have considered swapping.

Almost.

Finally, he decided to call it quits, and went back to the office.

Word had spread quickly about the arrest, or so it seemed. The streets were more crowded than normal for the hour—it was approaching four bells, bedtime for most—especially on a work night. But tonight groups of men turned to watch him pass at every street corner. A few shouted inquiries at him. Had they truly caught the killer? Was it safe for their wives to go out again? What about the children?

When was the hanging?

That came the most often, making Julian swallow nervously as he answered with only a shake of his head. If people got it into their heads that a hanging was in order, they might not be satisfied with anything short of that very thing. And if that became the case and they decided to take things into their own collective hands...

That could get ugly real quick.

Julian picked up his pace, hurrying his pace, but not enough to make it seem he was doing anything but walking. It was almost with a feeling of relief that he turned the last corner and caught sight of the Constabulary.

The feeling passed quickly as he beheld the scene there.

Mayor Brimly stood with Raedrick on the front porch outside of Julian and Raedrick's office. The Mayor was barely dressed. His leggings were clearly pajama pants that had been tucked hurriedly into his boots, and Julian could swear beneath his formal coat was only a pajama top. He wore his mayoral badge prominently though, and despite his disheveled appearance he did a fairly decent approximation of a man with power who was Lording over his subordinates.

Too bad Julian had seen him cower in the face of danger, not so very long ago, or he might have believed the act.

Mayor Brimly wrung his hands anxiously as Julian stepped up onto the porch, but the look he directed at Raedrick was made of steel. "What do you think you're doing?"

Raedrick was far more politic than Julian would have been. "Master Mayor, we caught him red handed, sneaking through the window of The Oarlock after we observed him fleeing the scene of tonight's murder. There can be no doubt."

Mayor Brimly began chewing on his lip for a moment, still wringing his hands while he pondered. Then, finally, he sighed, his shoulders slumping. "Do you have any idea what the Magestirium will do when they hear of this? It simply is not done, accosting a high-ranking member of their order like this."

"How many high-ranking members of their order engage in capital crimes, Master Mayor?" Julian could not keep the scorn from his voice. And why not? Any group that would blindly defend their own even when in the wrong was deserving of such.

Mayor Brimly glanced over at Julian and his scowl grew more dark. Then after a minute he nodded, conceding the point. "I still don't like it. We'll pay for this, mark me."

"But you agree we may proceed?"

Mayor Brimly inhaled and for a moment Julian thought sure he was going to say no. But then he let his breath out in a long sigh and nodded.

Raedrick returned the nod and pulled the Constabulary doors open, then disappeared within. Julian paused to make a quick half-bow, as befitted the Mayor's rank and position, then followed his friend.

Julian followed Raedrick into the cell block and tried not to shrink back from nerves. Mages were dangerous. Yes, they had taken away Loran's staff and anything that looked like it could be used as a component in some spell, but that did not mean Loran could not have other tricks up his sleeve.

The Mage was ensconced in the last cell on the left, as far from the barred doorway into the front office as possible. Very little light from the cell block's two lamps made it back into the cell, and for a moment it almost looked as though Loran was not there at all. Then a soft rustling issued from the cell and the shadows in the rear of the cell moved as Loran sat up from where he was lying on his little cot.

"I trust you have not come to set me free."

Julian snorted loudly and crossed his arms over his chest.

"Why did you kill them?" Raedrick's voice was cold, his expression sharp and focused, the way it got before a fight.

Julian's eyes had adjusted better to the dimness. He could just make out the outlines of Loran's face as he shook his head. "I have killed no one. Here."

"So it was just a coincidence that you were at the scene of tonight's murder." Raedrick sniffed slightly.

"Only the simplest of minds believes in such a thing as coincidence." Loran added an extra emphasis, and bit of derision to the last word.

Julian and Raedrick shared glances. That was not a denial. It also was not an admission.

"Alright," Raedrick said, "Why were you there, if you didn't do it?"

"Why were *you*, Constable?"

This was getting nowhere. "We're asking the questions here," Julian said, irritation lending extra heat to his tone that he had not intended. "If you don't want to never see the outside of a jail cell again, you'll - "

Loran chuckled, a soft sound that carried easily to Julian's ears and contained entire levels of disdain. "I do not answer to a man who lowers himself to the use of double negatives. And I will remain in this cell only as long as I deign to allow it. And not one second more." The shadow of his head shook and his body shifted, lying back down onto his cot. "Now leave me."

Julian ground his teeth to stop himself from lashing out with all manner of curses against the mage's lineage, particularly his mother. He had no idea what Loran was talking about, but he could deal with that. What really got under his skin was the superior attitude, the condescension, especially now while he was locked up. Did he not understand the situation, or was he arrogant enough to truly think little things like the law did not apply to him?

Probably the latter, if truth be told. The Magestirium had a nearly free hand in most things, answering only to the King. Only a couple of ignorant bumpkins would dare lay hands on one of their Order, let alone a member with the rank Loran apparently held.

Lord, but he hated being called bumpkin. Even when it was he who was doing the calling.

"You didn't answer the question, Loran," Raedrick said softly. His eyes seemed to burn, reflecting the dim lamp light as though the lamp's fire was their own.

"But I have, Constable. You simply refuse to hear it." The shadow that was Loran moved slightly, making a mockingly dismissive gesture at them unless Julian missed his guess.

Then he lay still.

A moment later, soft snoring issued from the cell. How in the hell had he gotten to sleep that quickly, and with the pair of them standing right there, no less?

Julian shook his head and stalked toward the front office. He looked back as he stepped through the doorway. Raedrick was still there, staring daggers into the cell. He remained for almost a full minute before turning away and moving to join Julian.

Yes, this was not going well at all.

Raedrick closed the door to the cell block and locked it, then replaced the key on its ring near his desk. "What do you make of that?" he said.

"Arrogant cuss."

Raedrick snorted out a half-chuckle. "Did you expect anything else?" He flopped down into his desk chair and leaned back, chewing on his lip in thought.

"We could always yank off a fingernail or two," Julian offered as he took his own seat. "That'll help ease his tongue." He meant it as a bad joke, but the look Raedrick shot him stopped Julian cold. He raised his hands at the simmering anger in his friend's eyes. "Joke, Rae."

Raedrick scowled. "It's not funny."

"Yeah I can see that." So much for a little levity. "Well let's review. We've got him dead to rights at the scene, but we need more before he goes to the Judge." Julian held up a finger. "No blood on him. No sign he's been in a fight. Ever. No - "

"Only a mage could have killed those men the way they were, and a mage could easily clean himself up."

Julian nodded. "Yes, but do you think that will satisfy the judge? Did you find anything more definitive at the scene tonight"

Raedrick sighed and looked down at his desk. The simmering anger was gone, replaced by frustrated acceptance as he shook his head.

"I don't think so either."

"Any ideas?" Raedrick did not sound particularly hopeful.

Julian could not blame him. Maybe things would look better in the morning.

❧ 17 ❧

MISCALCULATION

They did not.

Julian and Raedrick met at their office just before dawn, with the intent to get back to questioning Loran again as soon as he woke. Maybe the initial disorientation of waking would shake loose some of the obstinance and get him to reveal something more.

Should have known better.

After a fruitless half hour, during which the only thing they managed to accomplish was establishing that the jail rations were not up to Loran's exacting standards, they left the cell block with no more answers than they had to begin with.

"Maybe we're - " Julian began.

Raedrick raised a finger to his lips and nodded toward the cell block door. Julian shut his mouth; his words would carry to Loran's ears easily through the bars. He followed Raedrick out to the front porch and closed the door, then began again.

"Maybe we're going about this wrong."

Raedrick quirked an eyebrow at him. "You think he's innocent?"

Julian shrugged. "Didn't say that."

"But you have doubts."

Julian spread his hands helplessly.

Raedrick nodded. "Me too." He sighed and looked away, toward the intersection with Main Street. "Dammit. We acted too soon, didn't we?"

"Hardly a surprise."

Melanie's voice, so unexpected right then, made Julian jump. He spun around and found her sitting on one of the paired chairs at the far end of the porch. He had not noticed her there when they came out.

Raedrick was similarly surprised. He spluttered for a half-second. "Melanie! What - " He stopped and glanced toward the office door, as though checking to make sure it was still closed. "What are you doing here?" he finished, in a more quiet tone.

She smiled slightly and ran her hands down her legs, smoothing her dress. It was dark green today, laced in yellow-gold near the hems. "Checking up on you, of course. When I heard what happened last night..." Her smiled grew more broad. "I would have loved to have been there to see you hit him."

Julian did not have to work hard to keep from smiling in return. "You know something, don't you? Why don't you just spit it out?"

Melanie's smile faded a bit. She pushed a lock of her hair back over her ear and shrugged. "I know a lot of things. But as to Loran's guilt for the murders..." She shrugged. "I'd like to think he's guilty so he can get his just deserts. But I don't see *why* he would have done it. What's the gain?"

"Some people don't need to see any gain to kill someone. The killing *is* the gain to them."

Melanie frowned slightly, then inclined her head, conceding Julian's point.

"But he is too smart for that," Raedrick said. "If he were the bloodthirsty type, he would at least do it in a manner that he wouldn't be caught. Killing in a way that only a mage could... It's too simple to pin it on him."

Julian was forced to concede that. "That tracks."

"So why do you have him locked up in your cell block?" Melanie threw her hands up and rose from her chair, shaking her head with a mixture of bemusement and exasperation. She strode past them and descended the stairs to the street, still shaking her head.

"Honestly, you two," she looked over her shoulder at them and did not even try to keep the snark from her voice. She would have fit in nicely in the Magestirium, if only they allowed women. "You truly are incredible." She did not make that sound good at all.

She strode away in that half-sashay she used when she walked that made her hips sway oh so enticingly. Julian could not help but watch until she disappeared from view around the corner to Main Street.

"She's right, you know."

Julian nodded. "We've stepped in it this time. Mayor's going to have our heads. Assuming Loran leaves anything left for him."

Raedrick sighed. He ran his hand through his hair and just looked out at the street, almost empty of traffic at this still early hour. Finally, he said, "Let's set him loose."

🐝 18 🐝

TRADING SECRETS

Loran sat in front of Raedrick's desk and looked at him with coldly contemptuous eyes. The dark scowl on his lips made grim counterpoint to the swollen bruise that dominated his right cheek. That must have pained him something fierce, but he had made no complaint and it did not seem to phase him at all as he spoke.

"Well?"

Julian, standing to Raedrick's right, looked away from the mage, toward the front door of their office, and for a moment almost hoped that someone would come in. Like the Mayor maybe.

Now that was a stupid thought.

"I...apologize," Raedrick said, "for how we behaved toward you, Magester Haversted." He cleared his throat and lowered his eyes toward the top of his desk for a moment. Then he took a deep breath and forced himself to meet the Mage's gaze once more. "We jumped to conclusions. I have no excuse."

Loran kept his eyes locked on Raedrick's for several seconds. Then he sniffed and looked toward Julian. As his eyes met the Mage's, Julian felt his blood run cold. There was deadly menace there. The promise of retribution to come that no force in the world could prevent. He tried to swallow, but his mouth had suddenly gone dry.

"And you?"

Julian inclined his head, the way a man did when conceding defeat in the sparring ring. "Sincere apologies, Magester."

Loran waited for a half-minute, then gave the quickest of nods. "I accept your apology." He flashed a smile that oozed condescension. "You are dealing with forces beyond your understanding and comprehension. You can be forgiven for being...abrupt."

Julian ground his teeth to keep himself from voicing a retort in keeping with the

215

Mage's condescension. Fun as that would have been, it really would not do, not after he and Raedrick had put their feet into it so deeply with him.

Silence loomed for another half-minute. Then Loran stood and pulled his shirt - it was more a tunic than a shirt, truth be told - straight. He picked up his staff, which lay propped against the office wall, and the satchel which contained his other goods. "Good day, gentlemen," he said, and turned toward the door.

"Wait."

Loran stopped, looking back at Raedrick with a quirked eyebrow.

"You know something, Magester," Raedrick said. "Something about what's been going on here. The murders."

A smirk was the Mage's only response.

Raedrick rolled his eyes. "Dammit, people are dying. *Our* people, and we are the ones who are supposed to keep them safe. And the only thing we can tell is they were killed with magic. If you know something, tell us." He paused, then drew a deep breath and added, "Please."

That had to hurt. It made Julian's stomach lurch just hearing his friend all but beg from this man. But Raedrick was right. It had to be a Mage committing these murders. And if it was not Loran, and it certainly was not Melanie, that left the two of them without a clue as to the culprit. If Loran could offer any help at all, it would be better than what they had to this point.

Loran's smirk faded and he regarded first Raedrick and then Julian with unblinking, probing eyes for a relative eternity.

Finally, he let out his breath in an annoyed sigh and nodded, very slightly. "Very well."

He leaned his staff back against the wall and settled down into the chair he had just vacated. Leaning back in the chair, he teepled his fingers together in front of his chest and fixed the two of them with a look so severe, so commanding, that Julian found himself unable to look away.

"I am here on Magestirium business."

Not this again. "You said that before - " Julian's jaw snapped shut, cutting off his words as Loran's gaze became something deathly hard.

"I did. And you would have been wise to pay heed to my words. Were it not for your meddling, I may have brought the recent misfortune to an end days ago."

Julian squirmed on his feet, trying in vain to look away.

Loran remained silent for a time, his scowl returning in spades as he watched Julian. Then, finally, he shook his head. "I suppose you cannot be blamed for your ignorance. I sometimes forget how little the uninitiated understand of the real world." That evoked a slight grin from the Mage. Somehow that was even more disconcerting than the scowl.

Loran broke the stare with Julian and put his attention fully back onto Raedrick. "I came here in pursuit of a fugitive, one I have been tracking for some time. He passed through Mangin City a few weeks ago. There were only a very few places he could have gone from there, and I had tracers set up in all of them." His eyebrow quirked upward again. "Except here."

"And you did not inform us." Raedrick's words came out coldly, laced with entire layers of accusation.

"Of course not. He is a member of the Magestirium, not some chattel subject to your laws. And anyway, you could not wield power over such as he even if you had the right to make the attempt."

Raedrick had no response to that, apparently. He just scowled. He did not like the fact that Loran was right about the limits of their jurisdiction any more than Julian did. Far less actually, Julian was willing to bet.

"What did he do?" Julian asked. It had to be something big.

Loran's lips twisted into an expression of distaste. "You are familiar with the theorem of parallel universes."

Julian blinked his eyes. The what of the what? Raedrick looked as clueless as Julian felt.

The expression of distaste on Loran's face became one of disgust. He rolled his eyes. "The alternate planes of existence?"

Oh. That. "Why didn't you say so?"

Julian only thought Loran looked disgusted before. The look the Mage shot him was... Well, Julian had seen his General look at a new recruit who had just been convicted of cowardice before the enemy once. The General had more respect in his eyes than Loran did just then.

The Mage inhaled deeply and closed his eyes for a moment as though trying to will himself to calm. Then, very slowly, he said, "There are beings who live on other planes of existence than the world we know. Some of them are the entities we call the Gods, though that is far from an accurate description and gives most of them more credit than they are due."

"Don't let the temple priests here you say that," Raedrick said wryly.

Loran shrugged. "The ignorant always apply supernatural properties or divinity to the things they do not understand." He sniffed and made a dismissive gesture. "They count for nothing. The important thing is that these beings exist, and with skill and care, can be contacted. Some are benign. Others..." He trailed off and lifted an eyebrow meaningfully.

Julian swallowed. He had a bad feeling he knew where this was going.

"The fugitive made a practice of communicating with the Out-dwellers, as we call them. This is not unusual amongst the more skilled of our order. But he..." Loran shook his head. "He became obsessed. At some point, he began to believe he had a special bond with one being in particular, that he was this being's ambassador to the material world. Or maybe his Avatar. It is difficult to know the ravings of a broken mind. Regardless, he resisted all attempts to dissuade him from his studies until finally, we were forced to bar him from entrance to the facilities where trans-planar contact can be performed."

"I imagine he did not react well to that."

Loran nodded at Raedrick's words. "Though we did not know how poorly for some time. He disappeared into relative obscurity, and we presumed that, unable to continue that path, he found other avenues of study to occupy himself." He sighed. "That presumption ended up being...unwise. Corpses began appearing in the city. Thieves, whores, drunks. A few here and there, horribly mutilated. But at first no one paid them much mind, because who really cares if the dregs of society turn up dead? Better for all concerned, no?"

"No." Raedrick's voice was hard.

Loran's eyebrow quirked upward, but his expression remained smooth. "But then a member of the Magestirium turned up dead, in his quarters. I do not need to describe how his body was arranged; you have seen it. His name was Mattios, and he led the commission that sat in judgment on our fugitive. An investigation revealed a startling truth: he had been killed by non-human magical means."

"Non-human?" Julian said. "That doesn't..."

"Make any sense?" Loran made a soft tsking sound. "We thought the same. It was only after two more of our brothers turned up dead that we realized the truth. The fugitive had somehow designed a way to bring his familiar Out-dweller into our world. He set the Out-dweller against those he considered immoral, and it was happy to oblige, to sate its hunger for pain and terror. Then, once he was sure of their alliance, he turned the Out-dweller on the members of our order he believed had betrayed him.

"We attempted to take him into custody, but he managed to evade us. Four of our inquisitors were killed in the process. He fled into the country, and we've been looking for him ever since. He left signs of his passage: corpses, mostly. Always mutilated in the same way, always people on the fringe of society or morally corrupt in some way. It has been speculated that he targets them out of some deluded notion that he is doing good, but more likely the Out-dweller prefers the taste of such dregs."

Julian rocked back on his heels, stunned by the mage's account. He had never heard of anything that even came close to matching this. Ever. He glanced at Raedrick and saw that his friend was similarly taken aback, though he hid it well behind an implacable mask.

"Does this fugitive have a name?" Raedrick asked.

"Of course. But I will not speak it. He knows he is being hunted, and it is perfectly within his capability to enact tracer spells that will let him know when his name is spoken, where, and by whom."

"So?" Julian said incredulously. "He has to know you're in town, if he's here. You've not exactly been keeping out of sight."

"There is a good chance he may not. He tends to keep out of public places, preferring hidey-holes and the like. But even if he has seen me, he cannot know I am hunting him specifically."

That was a big assumption. Not one Julian would have been comfortable making, were he in Loran's shoes. But whatever; what the mage did with his skin was his own business.

"If this man is as dangerous as you say," Raedrick said, "dangerous enough to kill four of your order during his escape, how is it you are here alone?"

Julian nodded. "Yeah, I would want backup if I were you."

"Then it is a very good thing you are not me, Constable," Loran replied. He leaned back in his chair and regarded the pair of them for a moment, then smirked. "I am quite capable of dealing with him. He was my student, before he went awry. He was never my equal, and that remains true to this day."

Hubris, thy name is Loran. But again, it was his skin to risk. Just so long as he stayed away from -

"Alright. So how can we help?"

Julian looked incredulously at Raedrick. Was he nuts? Defending the townsfolk was one thing, but they had neither the expertise nor the equipment to deal with this rogue mage and his pet whatever-Loran-called-it. Better to let Loran handle it, if he was so certain he could. Julian opened his mouth to say that very thing, but he was silenced by the determined look in Raedrick's eyes.

Julian suppressed an inward groan. There would be no getting through to him; when Raedrick had that expression he was as stubborn as a mule.

Loran snorted. "Just stay out of my way."

Raedrick quirked an eyebrow at the mage. "You were here for quite a while before we," he flashed an apologetic smile, "picked you up, but you were not able to find him. Seems to me having local assistance can only be helpful."

The mage shook his head. "He is using concealing magic, but there are ways to see past that sort of thing, or to track the magical residue left by its use. His trail was fresh. I would have found him rather quickly, except..." He stopped talking, frowning as though unsure whether to proceed or not.

"Except what?" Julian said. He did not get to play the mysterious mage anymore, not now.

Loran looked at him and for a second Julian thought the mage was going to rip his head off. But then, instead, Loran sighed and nodded as though coming to a decision. "Except he has found an ally here."

Julian's jaw dropped open and he felt like he had been hit by a tone of bricks.

"What?" Raedrick sounded more angry than shocked.

"He has an ally. At least one. At first I was only able to detect one person's concealment spell. But then, about a day after I arrived, a second individual began using concealing magic here."

"Wait. You can tell when different people cast different spells?"

Loran smirked. "Of course. Every practitioner is different, has his own unique temperament and focus when he casts a spell. That uniqueness passes on into his spells, and if one is knowledgable and skilled enough, one can pick out those unique elements."

"I had no idea," Raedrick said, turning eyes that were suddenly troubled toward Julian for a heartbeat before looking back at Loran and carefully schooling his face back to calm.

Julian swallowed, suddenly feeling faint with tension as his heart leapt into his throat. That second residue could only come from one person.

"It is not an easy talent to master," Loran said, looking amused at their reactions, "but it is quite useful. There is something familiar about the accomplice's residue. I can't quite put my finger on it, but..." He shrugged. "No matter. I will located them both, and they will answer for their crimes, not just against the Magestirium but against your people as well, I assure you. It is only a matter of time."

Loran smiled at them confidently and his dark eyes twinkled with cold anticipation. Just then, he looked like a predator getting ready to leap upon an unwary prey.

THE GUILTY PARTY

"Melanie! Open up!"

Julian pounded on the door to Melanie's shop, heedless of the CLOSED sign hanging in the window. He had to find her before... He put that thought out of his mind. He did not want to consider what would happen if—no, when—Loran caught up to her. She had convinced herself that he was not looking for her, and he was not. But now she had unwittingly placed herself in his sights. The situation was precarious, and she did not even know it.

Of course there was no answer. She had not opened her store in days. Julian would not have put it past her to have stayed beneath one of her concealments spells more or less continuously since they let her know of Loran's presence in town. A great idea, but now it was one that would get her caught.

Julian backed away from the door and had to hold back a snarl borne of frustration and worry. He peered up to the shop's second story, where Melanie made her residence. The windows were dark, the curtains drawn. There was no indication she was upstairs at all, and surely she would have come down when she heard his knock. Where could she be?

"Dammit," he muttered.

This was taking too long. He glanced up at the sun; just past noon. He was due to meet back up with Raedrick soon. He had gone to fill the Mayor in on the developments with Loran. Ordinarily Julian would have gone with him, but Melanie needed to be warned. Raedrick had not objected to Julian taking the task of finding her, and the Gods knew Julian was more than happy to avoid that meeting with the Mayor. So he bowed out. It almost made him feel a tiny bit guilty.

Almost.

The lack of Melanie was a problem, though. Julian considered leaving a note, but shelved that idea as being too risky. And besides, he did not have any paper with him. So, with a sigh, he turned away from Melanie's shop. She would just have to take care of herself, for the time being at least.

Raedrick was just emerging from City Hall when Julian got there. He looked his normal self: well-tailored clothes and boots that, despite being common in cut, still somehow managed to give him a swashbuckling look. His expression was calm. Only a tightness about his eyes revealed how wound up he was.

"That bad?"

Raedrick shrugged, but winced slightly before he was able to school his face to smoothness. "About as expected."

Julian nodded. "That bad."

Raedrick coughed out a half-chuckle and flashed a grin that almost made it to his eyes. "Any luck?"

Julian shook his head.

"Damn." He drew in a breath and held it for a few seconds before exhaling slowly and smoothly. It was a calming exercise that Raedrick had picked up somewhere. He tried to teach it to the squad, back in the Army, but as far as Julian was concerned it never seemed to work any better than anything else. It looked like it worked ok for Raedrick today, at least. "Well, we'll just have to keep an eye out for her and hope she doesn't cross paths with Loran. In the meantime, though, we have an appointment."

Julian quirked a questioning eyebrow at him.

Raedrick saw the expression. "Remember what Loran said? His fugitive and his pet Out-dweller only killed people who were morally compromised."

Julian nodded.

"How do you supposed this fellow decided that Baelin and Beverlee fit the bill? I never heard a whisper that there was anything going on between them. Did you?"

That was for certain. It had been a bit of a shock learning of their affair, and not just because Beverlee never seemed interested in any man. Baelin was not exactly well-known in town, as much time as he spent off in the woods, but everyone regarded him as a fine family man who put his wife and children first above all things.

Well, apparently not above all things, after all.

Julian shook his head, his brain making the logical leap before Raedrick could voice it for him. "Only Isla and Helena knew, and of the two of them..."

"Only Ilsa had reason to wish them ill," Raedrick finished.

So they were back to Ilsa being the culprit once again. Just in a different manner than they initially thought.

This was going to be one hell of an interesting appointment.

Ilsa answered the door herself when Julian knocked.

She looked horrid. Her eyes were sunken, with dark circles beneath them that scream she had not been sleeping. Little strands of hair stood up in wisps atop her head, having pulled free from the bun she wore. How long had it been since she last did her hair up? For that matter, her dress was rumpled. Had she slept—or rather not slept—in it?

Ilsa's eyes flicked between him and Raedrick and Julian saw fright competing with resignation for a moment. "I said before I've got nothing else to say to you."

"We know who killed Baelin, Ilsa," Raedrick said. "And Beverlee."

She blinked and fell back a half-step, letting the door swing open an additional foot before she caught herself. "What?" Her voice quavered a bit. From her expression, she had to work hard to keep it from doing more. "Who?"

"Did anyone else other than you know about Baelin and Beverlee's affair?" Julian said.

Ilsa swallowed and opened her mouth as if to speak, but no words came out. After several seconds, she sighed and lowered his eyes. Then she stepped back and let the door swing open fully.

"You'd better come inside." Her voice as she spoke was defeated, seemingly devoid of hope. She did not wait for them to respond, but turned her back and walked further into her house, She quickly disappeared around a corner.

Julian exchanged a quick glance with Raedrick, then followed her in.

They found her in a small sitting room at the end of the cottage, adjacent to the home's small cooking area. It was sparsely appointed, but what furniture there was was well-crafted, by Baelin's own hand Julian wagered. Several small drawings were stuck on the walls, the children's handiwork from the look of them, and a faint, pleasant aroma permeated the room. It was from some manner of spices that Julian could not put his finger on, but the scent leant the final touch to make the room feel warm and welcoming.

Or at least it would have under different circumstances.

Isla sat in a rocking chair in the far corner of the room, gazing at the floor and wearing the most pained expression Julian had seen on her during this whole episode. She had not looked that mournful at Baelin's funeral.

"Where are the children?" Raedrick asked as he came to a halt in the center of the room.

"School," Ilsa said in a monotone

Julian blinked in surprise. As far as he knew, Ilsa did all the schooling for her children herself. "Come again?"

She snorted out a half-laugh. "Helena came by yesterday. Said she felt horrible for everything that had happened. 'Bout time she felt bad." Her lips twisted into a snarl for a moment, but then just as quickly fell back into their earlier defeated frown. It was like Ilsa's face did not have the energy to support her being angry. She continued in that same monotone. "I was about to kick her off my land when she offered to teach them free of charge." Another snorted laugh. "Can you believe it?"

Raedrick sounded incredulous as he said, "And you accepted?"

Ilsa shrugged. "I wanted to tell her to shove her teaching up..." She stopped speaking, flushing a bit for a moment before she cleared her throat and continued. "But I thought about what it could mean to them to get properly schooled." Another shrug. "I don't care if it makes the hussy feel better about things, but if it does my children some good... I can pretend."

Julian cleared his throat. "You told Melanie Klemins that you had a serious problem you needed to discuss, but you never told her what. You meant Baelin and Beverlee, didn't you?"

Ilsa merely nodded.

He exchanged another look with Raedrick. His friend looked resolved, but also pained, as though dreading to hear this. Julian could relate.

Julian waited for a moment, hoping Raedrick would pick up the line of questioning. And so silence loomed for a long moment.

"I couldn't go to her," Ilsa said before Julian could give voice to the next question. "It'd be all over town, and then..." Her voice broke and for a second or two it looked as though she was going to dissolve into a fit of weeping. But then she surprised Julian. She straightened her back and raised her eyes from the floor for the first time since they walked in. "If she could not help, no one could, so I decided to drink instead."

"Uh..." Julian began.

Ilsa quirked an eyebrow at him. "I went to Holb's, and was having a merry time of it. Until *he* showed up." Her expression darkened, then reverted back to its earlier hopeless and defeated mask, and she lowered her eyes once again.

"He?" Julian said, and was surprised at how hesitant, how uncertain, he sounded.

Ilsa nodded. "The one you're looking for."

Raedrick perked up, his entire body seeming to spring forward in a rush even though all he did was take a half-step toward the woman, and a slow half-step at that. "Who is he?"

Ilsa shrugged. "Never got his name. Never saw him before that night, either. I was sitting at the end of the bar, and he sat down on a stool next to me. I remember thinking it had been a long time since a nice looking man had tried to approach me socially, and he had this look in his eye..." She shivered visibly. "It made me remember."

"Ah," Julian began, "That's..."

Ilsa cut him off. Though in reality she did not seem to have heard him, or at least she did not seem to care that he was speaking. She just kept right on talking as though he did not exist. "He said he could see that my heart was troubled, that I had been done wrong." She drew a quick breath and held it. When she finally exhaled, it was like a sigh of regret, tinged with longing. "He said a woman as lovely as I am should never be heartsick like I was." Tears welled up in Ilsa's eyes and began to run down her cheeks. "How could he have known how I was feeling so clearly? How desolate my heart was?" She sobbed softly and pressed her hand to her mouth in a vain attempt to hold her emotion back.

Julian looked away, embarrassed for her despite their suspicions about her culpability in her husband's death. A man did not intrude on a lady's grief unless invited, after all. From the corner of his eye, he saw Raedrick doing the same.

After a pause that seemed to take forever, Ilsa sniffed and wiped the tears away. Then her voice gained a little bit of strength. "I told the man about my suspicions about Baelin and Beverlee. I knew Baelin had a little hideaway in the woods somewhere. I didn't know where, but I was certain they met there for their little trysts."

Raedrick's voice was quiet, but hard as steel. "And what did this man do?"

"Nothing. At least nothing right then. He patted my hand, bought me a drink, and said that if my husband had truly betrayed me in that way, he would get what was coming to him." She shuddered. "When he touched me, it was like nothing I had ever felt before. It sent a shiver up my arm and to my brain. But it was a good shiver. It made me feel like everything was going to be alright, that he would make all my troubles go away."

"What happened then?" Julian asked.

Ilsa did not move her head, but her eyes lifted to look at them. "I do not remember anything after that except waking in my bedroom here. Alone." She shivered again and wrapped her arms around herself as though to ward off the winter's chill. "Later the next day, you found Baelin dead."

It was not entirely unexpected, but the flat way she said it made Julian's blood run cold. "You think this man killed him." It was not a question.

Ilsa hesitated, then nodded.

"Why did you not come to us before?"

She sniffed back another round of tears. Or at least it looked like another round was due any moment, anyway. "What would I have told you? That I met some strange man in a bar and he whispered in my ear all night, and I couldn't remember anything after that? What would you have thought of me?"

Julian opened his mouth to retort, then shut it as the reality of her words sank in. What *would* he have thought? That she was running around on her husband and had remorse after the fact, that's what. Slowly, reluctantly, he nodded, acknowledging her point.

"It was not until Beverlee was killed also that I began to suspect. And by then..." She broke off and turned her head away again, raising a clenched fist to her mouth as she fought to hold back another sob.

She did not need to say it. By then, if she had come forward then, with a story as full of holes as this, she would have been high on the list of suspects, if not the only one.

Then again, she was high on the suspect list anyway, so a lot of good her silence did for her.

"What did this man look like?" Raedrick asked, softly, in the tone he reserved for the most delicate situations.

Ilsa shook her head. "I can't remember. The only thing I can remember is his voice. It was so soft." She drew a shuddering breath. "So soft..."

Raedrick and Julian exchanged glances. She was acting like a woman who was not entirely in her right mind. But then, Julian supposed that made sense, if the man she encountered was the fugitive Loran described. Who knew what a mage who was demented enough to kill - or have his other-worldly minion kill - in the way he had would, or could, do to an unwitting victim's mind?

Raedrick, as usual, had an easier time keeping his investigative wits about it. "Do you think you could recognize his voice if you heard it again?"

Ilsa nodded emphatically, but said not a word.

Raedrick returned the nod. "Thank you, Ilsa." He turned to leave.

Julian was about to turn to go when a thought struck him. "Where was Baelin's hideaway?" He almost smiled when he saw Raedrick stop abruptly, stiffening as he realized what he had missed.

Ilsa did not look at them. She just shrugged. "I don't know. Somewhere in the woods, above a big stone cliff." Her voice returned to its earlier, haunted monotone. "That's all he ever said about it."

Julian looked at her, and despite everything felt his heart going out for her. She had lost everything, and yes she may have borne some of the blame for what happened, but only a little. How could she have known who - what - she was talking to? He saw clearly the grief in her eyes, almost buried beneath mountains of confusion and guilt, and he knew there was nothing he could say to make it better.

But there might be something he could *do*.

He turned and brushed past Raedrick on his way out of the cottage. That renegade mage was going to *pay*.

$$\text{\Large 20}$$

SUSPECT

"**J**ulian," Raedrick said, his tone concerned but also stern in that way that he got when he was talking with a subordinate who had done something stupid. He should know better than that. He was not Julian's superior officer, not any more. They were friends, partners. Equals.

"I've had about enough of this," Julian growled, not slowing his pace. In fact, he sped up. He glanced up at the sun and did a quick computation in his head. About an hour after noon. Holb ought to be getting ready to open up.

"So have I," Raedrick said. "But what do you think you're going to accomplish running off in a fury like this?"

"Watch me."

Raedrick tried several times to speak with him over the intervening minutes that it took to reach Holb's Tavern, but he would have none of it. Their killer had been there, just a few nights ago. He had seduced Ilsa - maybe seduced was not the correct term, but how else to think about one person warping another's thoughts and perceptions to his will? - and someone must surely have taken note of him.

Holb was just rolling up the canvas tarp that blocked the bar off from the elements when Julian arrived, Raedrick on his heels. Funny how he had gotten quiet as soon as he saw their destination.

The large tavern-keeper eyed Julian with something between curiosity and annoyance as he approached, then he grunted. The grunt spoke volumes. What the hell did *he* want?

"The night before Baelin the woodsman died, a man approached his wife here, at your bar."

Holb grunted again, then turned back to the tarp and began tying it in place.

Julian ground his teeth. "I am certain that man is the one responsible for the murders."

Holb froze in place, his fingers in the middle of a knot that Julian had no doubt he would never be able to tie himself. Holb turned his head slightly and looked at them, his face implacable but one eyebrow twitching upward.

"Did you see him?"

Holb did not make a sound for several seconds. Then he rolled his eyes slightly and turned back to the knot. He finished it off with a swift tug of his wrists and turned around, wiping his hands on the apron he always wore behind the bar. For a moment, Julian wondered at the inanity of wearing that apron now, so far before his normal opening time. But only for a moment.

Holb cleared his throat and shrugged. "Saw a guy talking wit 'er," he said, his deep gravelly voice sounding thoroughly unconcerned. The glimmer of anger, and fear, in his eyes put the lie to his indifference. "Medium height, medium build. Light brown hair, tanned skin, like Selam." He frowned thoughtfully. "Aside from that, just looked sort of...average." He shrugged and turned back to the middle of the bar, where the next tie that held the tarp up dangled, ready to be fastened in place.

Raedrick finally broke his silence. "An average person. That's it. That's all you have."

Holb glanced back at him over his shoulder, and his frown turned into something that was more like a scowl. He held Raedrick's gaze for a second, then shook his head again and got back to tying the next knot.

"Have you seen him before, or since?"

Holb paused again, pondering, then shrugged as he pulled the knot tight. "Only saw him one other time. He was talkin' wit Dewey the other night."

"The same night Dewey was killed." It was not a question.

Holb froze still, then jerked out a nod. If Julian did not know him better, he would have sworn the big barkeep was spooked.

Julian looked over at Raedrick and saw his friend chewing on his lower lip, lost in thought. The wheels were turning quickly behind Raedrick's eyes, but Julian was fairly certain he knew where Raedrick was going. No one is average. No one. There is always *some* distinguishing characteristic about a person. Most people may not notice those characteristics, but they are there, and Julian was fairly certain Holb was not the type to miss those sorts of things. If *he* could only describe the guy as average, there was something else at work.

Magic.

There could be no doubt about it. They had finally found the trail of their killer. For a second Julian felt a surge of elation run up his spine. It quickly faded before reality. Sure they knew where the killer had been, and more or less what he was, assuming Loran had been truthful with his tale. But they still had no idea where the hell to even start looking for his lair.

Raedrick spoke up. "One more thing, Holb."

The bartender sent an icy gaze Raedrick's way and, if anything, scowled even more deeply.

Raedrick seemed not to notice. "Did Baelin ever come in here?"

Holb shrugged and gave a half-nod. The woodsman did not come by often, the nod said, but every now and then.

"Did you ever hear him talk about his hideaway in the woods? Where it was?"

Holb rolled his eyes slightly, then gave a quick shake of his head and turned away completely. It was obvious from the set of his shoulders that he did not intend to say another word to them.

Well, that had been better than nothing. *Far* better.

———

Raedrick looked more than a trifle reluctant as he raised his hand to knock on Loran's door, and Julian did not blame him. The mage had re-claimed his room at The Oarlock, but if Molli's extremely terse warning was any indication, he was in no mood for visitors.

Small wonder, that.

All in all, Julian considered that maybe going to him was not the best idea he had ever had. Hell, Raedrick as much as pointed that out, even though he was in agreement. They had uncovered an important lead, and Loran needed to learn about it, both because it might help him to finish his work and get out of town as soon as possible and because it would show they had some value to contribute. Ordinarily, Julian could not have cared less about what someone like him thought, but if he and Raedrick could convince Loran to let them on the team, they could work more efficiently towards capturing the rogue bastard.

And, maybe, keep Loran away from Melanie.

The door opened, and the mage looked out at the two of them with a quirked eyebrow. He was dressed in his formal robes, the same as he had worn to meet the Mayor, which seemed a bit odd.

"Constables. Have you come to escort me to the funeral?"

Julian blinked and traded a surprised look with Raedrick. "Ah...beg pardon?" he said.

Loran's eyebrow quirked up even higher. "The funeral for Master Dewey and that unfortunate young woman is this evening, is it not?"

Julian nodded, confused. As with Beverlee, the decision had been made to not delay any more than necessary. But Loran had not come to any of the funerals so far. Why would he care to come to this one?

Loran sniffed softly, dismissively. "If you're not to be my escorts, I would ask you to leave me in peace. I have preparations to make before I depart for the ceremony."

He began to push the door closed, but Raedrick pressed his palm against it, stopping its motion. "We need to talk."

"I think not. Last we talked, you were none too cordial or cooperative. As I said, leave me be. And maybe I will forget your transgressions when I make my report to the Magestirium." Loran smiled a nasty little smile that said his earlier forgiveness was not on the up and up. Not that Julian really expected it to be. "Or at least, I could lessen their severity."

Raedrick just gave him a level look. "We have information about the killer's identity."

Loran's smile slipped and he regarded first Raedrick and then Julian with a frank, appraising stare. Then, after a long moment he sighed softly and pulled the door fully open, waving for them to enter his room.

———

Loran frowned deeply when Raedrick finished telling what they had learned from Ilsa and Holb. He sat on the lone chair in the room, looking up at the two of them like a ruler receiving supplicants. Julian had to work hard to avoid letting his irritation with the man's demeanor show.

But then, he had to remind himself that they had put Loran out considerably over the last couple of days. A little smugness in payback was taking it rather light, to be honest.

Loran teepled his fingers in the air beneath his chin and did not speak for a good minute. When he finally replied, he spoke slowly, like a man tasting his thoughts before he let them pass his lips. Like a man reading a judge's sentence. "Thank you, Constables. This is most helpful."

Julian thought sure he was going to say something more, but after a couple seconds passed, he shrugged lamely.

Loran saw the gesture and smirked ever so slightly. "I mean it sincerely, Constable Hinderbrook. This information provides a great insight into the fugitive's next action."

"Ah... It does?"

"Indeed."

Silence loomed for another long several seconds. Loran looked at them expectantly the whole while. Finally, when it seemed the awkwardness of the moment could grow no larger, he rolled his eyes and spoke again. "Thank you gentlemen. That will be all."

"Magester Haversted," Raedrick said, "I really think..."

"I am well aware of what you are thinking, Constable." Loran tapped his right index finger against his temple, and Julian's blood ran cold. Gods above, he really could read their minds!

Raedrick snorted loudly. "Don't try that old trick. We're not a couple of bumpkins whose knowledge of the world goes no further than the edge of our village."

Julian glanced at his friend and swallowed. He was glad Raedrick, at least, was sure that particular rumor was untrue. For his part, Julian had never heard anything definitive either way - and hang it all, why had he never asked Melanie about it? But then, maybe as Squad Leader Raedrick received more detailed briefings, or met some of the Division's mages, or some such.

Loran looked at Raedrick for a couple seconds, then he smiled, a far more genuine smile than he had shown to either of them to date. He let out a soft chuckle and raised a hand in a mollifying gesture. "Say your peace, Constable."

Raedrick gave a quick nod, then continued. "We know he's been to Holb's twice, and that he picked his victims because of what he learned from Ilsa. We have information on where Baelin's hideaway is. I'll bet good money he went there a time or two, since Beverlee and Baelin met there. If..."

"Yes, yes," Loran said, waving dismissively. "I've seen this hideaway. A thoroughly unimpressive little shack. Unimportant."

Raedrick blinked. "What?"

"I'll tell you what *is* important, Constable." He leaned forward, peering intently at Raedrick. "You know why Baelin and Beverlee were killed: the affair. The young woman at the boarding house was almost certainly a case of being in the wrong place at the wrong time." He inhaled slowly, then spread his hands and asked, "But why was Dewey the woodsman killed as well?"

Raedrick opened his mouth to reply but paused. He looked perplexed after a second or so and closed his mouth again.

The question caught Julian off guard as well. If Loran's fugitive went after the morally depraved, Beverlee and Baelin were prime targets, because of their adultery. Dewey though... Julian did not know enough about Dewey to be able to say one way or the other what sort of man he really was. He had no idea about Dewey's habits except for the little he had observed during their tromp into the Glamorwood together, but Dewey did not have a bad reputation. So why would he...

It hit him all at once. He could not believe they had not seen it before. "Dewey knew about the affair and did not stop it," Julian said.

Loran turned his eyes on Julian and nodded, his expression almost approving. "Now. Did anyone else know this thing was going on?"

Julian's blood ran cold again. Frigid. "Helena." He had to forced the name out from between his lips.

"The dead harridan's sister, yes. She also did nothing to stop the affair," Loran said, "and so is equally guilty." He raised a forestalling hand as Raedrick opened his mouth to retort. "Or at least that argument could be made by someone who is less interested in truth than on wreaking vengeance. Someone like the fugitive to his Out-Dweller consort."

Raedrick's expression was beyond troubled. "You expect him to make a try for Helena. When?"

Loran shrugged. "If it were me, I would wait until after the funeral. More dramatic that way, more symbolic. He'll wait until later tonight, then he'll hunt her down and..." He left the rest unsaid.

"Bugger me," Julian breathed. "Well, at least we know where he's going to strike next."

Loran looked between Raedrick and Julian for another long couple of seconds, then sighed and shook his head. "I see that it is useless to tell you to remain clear of this." He stood up and smoothed out his robes. "Very well. Since you insist of butting in, you may assist."

"Assist with what?" Julian said, though he had a feeling he already knew the answer.

Sure enough, Loran grinned, a hunter's grin that showed his teeth. His canines seemed to gleam in the afternoon sunlight that streamed in through his window. "We are going to set a trap for this killer, this very night."

21

PREDATOR AND PREY

Julian shivered and pulled his cloak more tightly against his body. It was a chilly night, and dark with only a faint sliver of moon in the sky, and the mail he had donned earlier certainly did not help matters. But it was not solely the temperature that made Julian shiver. This was dangerous business they were on, and he was not entirely certain they were ready for it.

Oh sure, Loran put on a good show of confidence, circling around Beverlee and Helena's house with his staff dragging on the ground while he chanted in a low tone and in words - if they even *were* words - from no language Julian ever heard before. He was certainly casting a spell of some sort, but Julian only knew enough about magecraft to be able to tell when a man is casting a spell. He had no idea as to what that spell may do.

Julian glanced up at the stairs leading up the side of the house toward Helena and Beverlee's flat. Helena had moved back in just yesterday. Far sooner than he would have expected, but the men the town hired to clean up the mess had been thorough and she could not have much money stashed away to cover her rent and a room at an Inn or boarding house.

Strange that she did not have some friends who would let her stay with them, but she and Beverlee had kept to themselves, except with the children. And, apparently, with other women's husbands.

It almost made Julian wonder what Helena did in her private time. Like sister, like sister, perhaps?

He pushed that thought away. Even if it were true, it had no bearing on the night's mission: to save her life. Assuming Loran was correct, that was.

Just then, the mage finished his incantations and stopped, leaning on his staff for a good half minute. Julian blinked to see him breathing heavily, as after a hard bit of effort. But all he had done was walk a circle and chant. Strange, that.

Loran straightened and turned toward where Julian and Raedrick stood, at the front corner of the sisters' building. He favored them with the briefest of nods, then said, "It is done."

"What, exactly?" Raedrick voiced Julian's words just as plainly as he would have.

"A warding of sorts. It will alert me when the Out-Dweller crosses within, and take certain steps to reduce its power while it remains. Even the two of you could take it, if it came down to it, as long as it remained within the warding."

Julian whistled softly, the mage's barb ignored in the face of his explanation. From what the mage had said, this Out-Dweller thing was no slouch. If the warding was as good as he claimed, it was no wonder it had tired him out, casting it.

Loran smirked and glanced at Julian. "Best you not test that theory, though. I will take it. *Your* job," he added in a pointed, commanding tone, "is to ensure no surprises creep up on me while I do it. Understand?"

Julian glowered, but Raedrick nodded immediately so he followed suit. No sense griping, he supposed, but it still irked him, how Loran talked down at them sometimes. Most times.

The mage smirked again, then turned and walked up the stairs to the door leading into the sisters' flat. There, he retreated in the shadows of the entrance and effectively vanished from sight.

"I hope this works," Julian said, his gaze lingering on where Loran waited. "I don't like the notion of using Helena as bait."

"Me neither." Raedrick's frown spoke volumes that his tone did not. "But he's probably right. If she *is* the target they - it - will follow her wherever she is."

Julian nodded reluctantly. "I still don't like it."

Raedrick clapped him on the shoulder and they shared a grim smile before retreating to their positions. Julian settled into the deeper shadows beneath the eaves of the house to the sisters' left, Raedrick to a small alcove in the building to the right.

And then they settled down to wait.

Melanie stood in the doorway of a butcher's shop across the way from Beverlee and Helena's building, behind the veil of her concealment spell, and watched Loran complete his circle of enchantment. She frowned, recognizing parts of the incantation, or at least the movements Loran used, enough to figure out that he was setting up a warding of some sort, but she had never seen one quite like what he just made.

She only managed to catch fractions of the conversation between the three men as she followed them from The Oarlock, where she had been waiting for Loran to make an appearance, but she did not like the sound of the situation at all. "Out-Dweller" was not a title to make anyone learned about such things feel comfortable.

Truth be told, she had to force herself to keep her feet in place, lest she flee to a place of safety. If only half the things Timon told her about them were true, Julian and Raedrick were in far more danger than they knew.

And Loran as well.

She sniffed softly, ignoring that part of her mind. She did not care one whit if Loran put himself in danger or not. If he were butchered alive or not. He had...

Memories, pushed aside for so long, flooded back. Timon's smile, kind and warm. The feel of his arms around her. The joy, the *wonder*, of their time together. The heart-wrenching sound of his agonized screams when they took him. And the decision to flee, to save herself, that left her heart broken and bleeding on the stones behind her as she went, never to be whole again.

They had spoken of it. Of the danger they both faced from his teaching her, and he had made her promise to do just that, if they were discovered: to run. But that did not make it any easier, or lessen her guilt over abandoning him.

Melanie shuddered and drew in a deep breath to get herself under control. She swiped at the little tears that had fallen part-way down her cheeks, her returned grief changing to anger, a towering fury. She would not wallow in her tears again. Especially not now, not when she had the opportunity to strike at the source of all her pain.

She reached into the pouch that hung from her belt opposite her dagger and fingered through its contents. She knew each by touch, components that would help bring her spells to life. Oh, the things she could do, the pain she could weave onto the Inquisitor's form before he perished!

The men exchanged a few words, then Loran retreated up the stairs and Julian and Raedrick took up their positions. Their trap, and it surely could be nothing else, was set.

Just as she had hoped.

A battle with an Out-Dweller would be taxing, even with the warding, whatever it did. Loran would be exhausted once it was done. And then she...

A subtle sound, so low in pitch that it almost did not register with her ears, interrupted Melanie's train of thought.

She looked around, frowning, unable to tell the sound's source. A shiver went up her spine, and she found herself trembling. There was something about that noise. Something...unclean. Ominous.

The sound increased in volume and she began to make out a rhythm to it. A steady beat that made her heart race as it grew louder. It took a full minute for her to recognize the sound for that it was: footsteps.

Melanie panned around, seeking the source of the footsteps, but it was in vain. All was darkness and shadow except for the suddenly very tiny-seeming nimbuses of light around the street lamps scattered at irregular intervals. This section of Lydelton was not as well-lit as Main Street by any means, and even there the Lamp-lighters were sparing with their services.

Nothing moved, and yet something did. It crept - no, not crept, stalked - closer. Melanie could feel its presence, a palpable weight in her mind, and felt the first stir-rings of panic. This was the thing nightmares were made of.

Fitting that it comes now, in the dead of night. For it is death on the hunt. Come for you.

Where had that thought come from? Melanie shook her head to clear it, but the mental weight only got worse.

She smelled it. Faint on the night breeze at first, but growing steadily stronger as the thing advanced. Sickly-sweet, like fruit that had been left out too long and went rancid. It left her twisting uncomfortably, as if all the other stimuli were not enough.

Again she looked about. Still nothing, but it could not be long now. She glanced back at the shadowy areas where her friends - and her nemesis - waited. They must be feeling the Out-Dweller's approach, as she did. In her mind's eye, she saw Julian and Raedrick draw their weapons, bolstering their courage against this sudden terror with the reassuring feel of cold steel, useless though that steel would be against this foe.

The slightest shifting of a shadow off to the left drew her eyes, and for a second all Melanie could see was darkness. Then the darkness itself seemed to move, to slither through the intervening space between one building and the next, and the hairs on Melanie's neck stood up straight. Even beneath the crushing pressure she felt in her mind, she knew.

It had come. The Out-Dweller.

May the Gods help them.

22

THE OUT-DWELLER

The Out-Dweller moved quickly, more quickly than the pace of its footsteps would have suggested. In the darkness, Melanie almost could not follow its progress toward the sisters' building. She realized she was more than trembling; she was shaking from head to toe, the Out-Dweller's presence had affected her so. Part of her mind recoiled at her reaction, shouting defiance at the fear and demanding she get ahold of herself and Do. Something.

The more sensible part of herself replied that the best thing to do was keep back, out of sight, and pray the beast did not notice her.

It did not seem to. It kept to its course, a darker shadow that made the other shadows recoil in terror as it sped toward its target.

And then it stopped cold, and for an instant Melanie beheld it, in all its perversion.

Shadows wrapped the creature from head to toe, standing out against the backdrop of a lonely street lamp like a bird before the sun. Darkness swirled and swayed, obscuring the being beneath so that only portions could be seen in any particular instant. Short legs that ended in cloven hooves. A mammoth, hulking torso that was covered in spikes and barbs. Long arms that reached past its knees and ended in long, curved talons. A small round head. Or was it large, capped by horns? Or twin heads, laughing insanely at the world around them? The cloak of darkness made it difficult to see anything for certain there except for two pairs of eyes that glowed red like the depths of a smith's forge.

A new sound reached Melanie's ears. Higher pitched, guttural and scraping, like metal against stone: the Out-Dweller's breathing.

Melanie shrank back against the wall and found she could not breathe. Could not think, at least not of anything but flight. This was not a thing she could face and live. It would rip her very soul from her corpse and feed on it for all eternity.

Run, you stupid ninny. Run!

Somehow, she did not. Some part of her was certain that if she did, if she moved at all from that spot, the beast would detect her, chase her down, and then... She would have shuddered except she could not bring herself to move even that much.

The Out-Dweller growled, a deep basso that carried entire volumes of rage and hatred, then took another step forward.

And stumbled.

In a flash, Melanie realized why it had stopped in the first place. It was standing on the edge of Loran's warding. Had in fact pushed itself past the warding, and been hampered by it.

The Inquisitor went up quite a bit in her estimation. She knew beyond a doubt there was nothing she could have done to make such a being pause, let alone lose its feet.

Brilliant white light, more bright than the sun at noon, lanced out from the top of the stairs alongside the sisters' building and struck the Out-Dweller in the chest. The world exploded in a rainbow of light and the Out-Dweller's scream was only eclipsed by Melanie's own as she cowered back from the sudden assault.

More bellows and screams, and deeper sounds that more resembled the groans of a building about to give way than those of a living creature followed, and that was all Melanie could sense for a long moment. After-images of Loran's attack dominated her vision, leaving only a purple-white blob in front of her for what seemed an eternity.

The smell of smoke and burning flesh filled the air and the Out-Dweller stomped a foot down, or at least that was what it sounded like. A man's voice cried out. She could not make out who.

Melanie blinked her eyes quickly and turned her head away, trying to clear her vision.

Another bellow, this one from the beast again. Then the concussion of a detonation - from a fireball, by the sound of it.

Something struck her chest and Melanie was knocked back against the wall for a small eternity. The force constricted her and she could not breathe. Could not move. Could not see, though that was hardly anything new.

Then, all at once, the force was gone and she collapsed to the ground on her belly, gasping.

Still the battle went on, and from the sound of things it was not going well. Booms, growls, shouts, grunts, little explosions... Enough that it seemed she had been on the ground for hours.

But when she managed to push herself up to her hands and knees and raise her head to look, it was plain that only a few seconds had passed. Loran was advancing down the stairs, his staff clasped in both hands, one end of the staff shining like a little star. He wore an expression of grim determination despite the cut on his forehead and his disheveled hair. Raedrick lay on his back to the right, where he had apparently been thrown by the force that had knocked Melanie down, and was just now raising himself up onto his elbows. Julian was nowhere in sight.

The Out-Dweller reared up to its full height, easily ten feet if not a couple more, and the shadows ringing it whipped and whirled like tentacles. Tentacles that ended in scythes. Loran ducked beneath one, and it cut cleanly through the stairs above and behind him, sending them falling to the ground with a clatter.

The Inquisitor yelled a battle-cry in a tongue Melanie did not recognize - and she knew many - and leapt off the stairs to his right, dropping the dozen feet or so to land on the ground in the alley between the sisters' building and its neighbor. As he landed, a series of starlets, smaller versions of the brilliant beam that was his initial attack, shot from the end of his staff and flew at the Out-Dweller.

The beast growled again and moved its right arm. Tendrils of blackness whipped around in front of it and intercepted the starlets, one by one.

Loran snarled and took a step forward, barking out another incantation. A second series of starlets flew forth, more numerous this time.

Again whirling black tendrils reached out to intercept them, but this time the starlets were too many, and two struck home.

The Out-Dweller hissed and stumbled backward a half-step, looking for a moment as though it would fall completely. But instead it found its footing and rose upright once more, bounding forward toward the Inquisitor.

Loran's lips compressed and he thrust his staff out before himself.

A hemisphere of translucent blue energy appeared in front of the Out-Dweller, stopping it in its advance. The beast howled and pressed its arms forward against the barrier, rage at the minuscule rodent that was trying to thwart it evident from the way its eyes flashed.

Loran leaned forward against his staff as though it was a physical wall, and he cried out an incantation of force. Melanie recognized the spell at once: it had been among the first spells Timon taught her. For a second, she was surprised Loran would use that one; it was elementary. But then, the earliest teachings are often those learned the best, and against an onslaught like the one the Out-Dweller was bringing he would need something he knew instinctively and was very, *very* good at.

The Out-Dweller reeled backward as Loran's spell hit it, and again it looked as though it was going to go over onto its back. But as before it righted itself, and it pushed back.

Hard.

Loran was leaning against his staff like a man bracing a wall that was about to fall over. His feet were planted firmly against the dirt of the alley and, as the Out-Dweller came forward, he again shouted out the force incantation at the top of his lungs.

He may as well have tried to hold back the tide.

The Inquisitor moved backwards. Slowly at first, then more quickly as the Out-Dweller gained momentum. Loran's feet dug furrows into the dirt of the alley and he grimaced against the beast's onslaught.

Then the Out-Dweller bellowed, far louder than anything it had voiced to this point, and gave a great shove forward.

Loran flew bodily backwards through the air, losing his grip on his staff as he flew, and landed on his back ten feet from where he stood a second before. He hit the ground hard and did not move.

The Out-Dweller raised its head and howled in victory to the midnight sky above, then, slowly, implacably, it began to advance.

Melanie forced herself to her feet and reached into her belt pouch, watching the beast's advance through narrowed eyes.

And also watching Loran.

The Inquisitor stirred, moving sluggishly, like a man dazed - and small wonder - as he tried to push himself up to a seated position.

This was her chance for revenge. If she let the Out-Dweller do it, she would never have the satisfaction. She reached down into the belt pouch and pulled out the components for Timon's favorite offensive spell. The one she had to pay all manner of carnal prices to get him to teach. Prices that she was all too happy to pay, but prices nonetheless.

From off to the left, a figure emerged out of the shadows and raced forward. Lamplight and moonlight joined together to reflect off Julian's sword as he cut at the beast's quarter.

The Out-Dweller flicked its left hand contemptuously, like a man swatting at a midge, and a tendril of darkness whipped around and knocked Julian on his left temple. He fell in a heap.

Red-hot rage, and the shock of feared loss, threatened to intrude on the cold calm that Melanie had surrounded herself with. Her nemesis lay on the ground, helpless. She might never get this chance again.

But you couldn't take this thing on your own if you tried, and it's responsible for the murders.

She growled at herself and forced the little voice in her head away.

It will kill again and it will be all your fault.

So what? Timon, the love of her life, was dead. Dead in the most horrific way possible, and the man responsible was lying vulnerable at her feet, just waiting for her vengeance.

On the ground in front of her, Julian rolled over and raised his head. For a moment, their eyes met and she saw his lips moving. He shook his head in denial.

Melanie began her incantation and Julian's face became obscured behind the flames that flared up around her outstretched hands.

23

THROWING DOWN

The Out-Dweller advanced toward Loran, who was lying helpless on the ground.

Julian screamed at himself to move, to take action in this fight which could determine the future for his town, but found he could not.

Ever since the Out-Dweller appeared, he had been in a near panic. Nothing he had ever faced could have prepared him for this. The Out-Dweller's physical presence was enough to cow him. But more than that, he felt a weight on his mind, a crushing force that strove to drive him to his knees, and it took every ounce of energy he had to stop himself from doing just that.

He watched, immobile, as Loran attacked and Raedrick rushed to support the mage, but was repelled without even half a thought.

He wanted to help. He wanted to desperately. But he could. Not. Make. Himself. Move.

Little Stars flashed across his vision from the left, and a couple of them struck the Out-Dweller.

That just seemed to make it mad.

The beast came on, and pushed Loran's force-shield—or whatever it was—aside like it was so much rubbish. The mage went flying, and Julian hung his head.

It was over.

They had failed.

Then, off to his right, he saw movement. He glanced that way and stopped, staring, as Melanie pushed herself to her feet. Where had she come from? Wherever it was, she looked ready for a fight. A fierce fire lit up her eyes.

Julian looked at that raging fire and drew strength from it. This was the thing that had been accosting his people these many days. It had taken good people from their families, for its own foul amusement.

He looked back at the Out-Dweller as it stalked toward Loran's collapsed form and let the rage he saw in Melanie's eyes flow through him. He would not let this foul thing win.

He. Would. Not.

Crying out, Julian ripped his sword from its scabbard and bounded forward.

The small of the Out-Dweller's back was right in front of him. An easy target, one that would put the thing on its knees where the mages could take it down without any more trouble.

Something hit him on the side of the head, something that felt like six war hammers bundled together, and sent him reeling.

He hit the ground and all he could see for a long moment were flashing spots in front of his eyes. All he could smell was the Out-Dweller's rotten stink. All he could taste was the mud of the side street. Not that anything in Lydelton was *not* a side street, but still.

After a moment, he raised his head, and saw Melanie.

She was on her feet, a righteous fury in her eyes and a look on her face that he had seen a hundred times in a dozen battles. The look of someone ready to kill, without remorse.

The elation of impending victory leapt into him, but then he turned his head to follow her gaze. She was not looking at the Out-Dweller. She was looking at Loran.

By the Gods, she had chosen *now* to get her vengeance? She was going to kill them all!

"No!" he screamed, as loud as he could, looking back at Melanie in desperation.

Melanie's eyes locked onto his for a second and he thought she understood, then she looked away and began waving her arms around as she began a spell incantation. Flames sprouted out around both her hands, as though from nowhere, then she raised both hands.

A column of flame, as thick around as Julian's thigh, lanced out from Melanie's hands.

And struck the Out-Dweller in the center of its back.

The Out-Dweller bellowed in obvious pain as the fire billowed around its torso and engulfed it in a ball of living flame that encased it and burned its flesh from all sides. The beast spun a full circle and howled in agony, raising its head to the sky as it gave voice to its pain.

To Julian's left, Loran raised himself to his elbows, his eyebrows climbing high onto his forehead in surprise as the Out-Dweller was stymied. The mage wasted no time though. He rolled to his right, gathering up his staff mid-roll, and came up on one knee, the end of his staff pointing toward the stricken beast.

Miniature stars, the same things that had before harried the Out-Dweller, raced from Loran's staff and impacted the beast in its arms, legs, head...everywhere that was not covered by Melanie's fire.

The Out-Dweller screamed again, then turned away from Loran and ran. It fled past Julian, and he had to flatten himself beneath the heat of Melanie's flames as much as from the frenzied flailing of the Out-Dweller's shadow-tentacles, or whatever they were.

Melanie threw her hands up as the beast fled past her, and the flames winked out of existence, but the Out-Dweller continued running, its howls louder than the loudest thunder as it fled Lydelton.

All around, windows began lighting up as townsfolk, roused from their sleep by the sound of the battle, lit lamps. Chagrined shouts began echoing down the street as people threw up their sashes and inquired of their neighbors as to what was going on. Others began pouring out of their houses, looking around for the source of the disturbance.

Julian ignored them, pushing himself to his feet and walking over toward Melanie.

She stood with her arms limp at her sides, her eyes dazed as though she could not believe what had just happened. Julian could not blame her.

"Melanie?" he said. "Are you al..."

Loran's shout, filled with righteous indignation, interrupted his thought. "You!"

Julian turn to see the mage on his feet, advancing toward Melanie with his staff lowered, the end that had just shot starlets at the Out-Dweller pointed right at her.

"I should have known it was you!" Loran stalked closer, his snarl fitting a lion about to strike. "I always suspected..." He trailed off into a furious growl, and the end of his staff crackled with little bits of lightning.

Julian fell back a half-step and raised his hands defensively. "Whoa!" he said. "Loran, wait..."

Again he was cut off, this time by Melanie. Looking aside at her, she stood erect, facing Loran. Her eyes flashed with that same rage Julian saw earlier, and she had raised her hands before herself again in a defensive posture. The fact that her hands were again wreathed in flame lent entire volumes to the weight that posture gave.

"I *always* knew," Melanie said, her tone as withering as the flames she had just shot from her hands. "You killed Timon, and you loved doing it."

Her eyes widened even more and the flames around her hands grew until they almost eclipsed her face.

Aw hell. They were going to throw down right here.

Before he realized what he was doing, Julian leapt between the two of them, his hands raised, one palm facing each of them. "Whoa there," he said. "Stop!"

Loran's staff blazed with barely-contained energy, matching Melanie's flames in its incandescence. All of a sudden, Julian realized he had just done an incredibly stupid thing.

"Get out of the way, Julian," Melanie said from his left, through clenched teeth.

From his right, Loran added, "Yes, Constable, do move. It would be unfortunate if I harmed you while taking this abomination to ground."

Julian blinked, unable to believe what he had just heard Loran say. Suddenly Melanie's hands were not the only things burning with sudden fury. He turned on Loran. "Abomination?" he said, more like shouted. "This abomination," he pointed back at Melanie, "Just saved your sorry ass from that thing. Or hadn't you noticed?"

Loran's scowl only deepened. He did not reply, but the energy around his staff grew more bright.

Julian wanted to cringe, to duck, anything to avoid being turned into a charcoal briquette by the two mages. But he could not do any of those things. Not without sacrificing his dignity, and at the same time giving them leave to throw down on each other.

They stood there, tension so thick you could eat it with a spoon, for an eternity.

Then Raedrick, standing behind Loran and to his left, cleared his throat. "Might want to take a look around you, Magester," Julian's friend said.

Loran turned his head slightly to look at Raedrick, then his eyes widened and he panned his head around, taking in the scene.

Julian did the same.

All around, townsfolk stood, knives, shovels, and the occasional sword or bow - retrieved from the attic, no doubt - in hand. They stood in a loose circle around the two mages, weapons, makeshift or not, at the ready.

"You might want to rethink things, Loran," Raedrick said. "See, Melanie here saved this town and everyone in it. These people would much rather have her around than the likes of you."

A few men raised cudgels and smacked them into their palms in strident counterpoint to Raedrick's statement.

Loran's brow furrowed, and for a moment Julian thought he was going to rain down holy hell on the lot of them, and to blazes with the consequences.

Then, slowly, the mage nodded. He lowered his staff, and the crackling energy that had been gathering at its end dissipated and went out.

"I suppose a bit of negotiation is in order," Loran said.

That was the understatement of the year.

❧ 24 ☙

UNLIKELY ALLIES

"**W**e don't have much time."

Julian found it hard to argue with Loran's statement, but all the same his words, and more in particular his tone, made Julian want to punch him.

"Speak for yourself," he said, glancing around at the ring of men surrounding them. "I have all the time in the world, Magester." He added a bit of contempt to the last word, just because.

Loran quirked an eyebrow at him, then turned his gaze toward Melanie. "The Out-Dweller gets further away by the moment, my lady." The "my lady" contained all manner of derision. "We can track it for a time, but that time is not indefinite."

Melanie looked confused.

Loran smirked every so slightly. "Oh, you cannot track it? I'm so sorry." He looked away from her, disdainfully, toward Raedrick. "Is this," he gestured toward Melanie, "half-trained and mostly ignorant harlot really worth risking your town for, Constable?"

Melanie's eyes grew wide and she drew herself up, inhaling deeply through her nose.

Raedrick raised a hand toward her, ordering calm from his demeanor and expression alone. For a moment, Julian thought Melanie would ignore him and go for Loran's throat anyway. But she surprised him and exhaled deeply, shaking her hands at her sides to let the frustration Julian knew she contained loose.

"Get to the point, Magester," Readrick said. His tone was bland, but from the wrinkles around his eyes, Julian could see he was about ready to rip Loran's throat out himself.

Loran snorted disdainfully. "I am willing to let your alliance with this...thing...go unreported, Constable." Loran clearly did not know who he was talking to. Or rather, he did not know Raedrick enough to recognize the warning signs. Julian was hardly surprised at all when he just kept on going, digging his own grave. "But you must understand I have an obligation to bring her back with me to face justice."

Raedrick's nostrils flared almost as much as Melanie's did. Julian had to lay a restraining hand on her arm to keep her in check. He was not able to do the same with his friend.

In a flash, Raedrick's sword was out of its scabbard. The mage tried to retreat, but Raedrick grabbed Loran's right shoulder with his left hand and held him close, pressing the edge of the blade into Loran's throat. The mage's skin wrinkled beneath the sword's steel; just a hair's breadth more pressure and it would draw blood.

And Loran knew it. His eyes widened in shock. In fear.

Raedrick spoke very softly, very firmly. "Melanie is not a thing," he said. "Not an abomination. She is my friend, and you will not have her. Ever." He drew a deep breath and seemed to calm himself a bit. "We need your help, Magester," he said, and released the mage, giving the slight man a little shove away from him. "And you need ours. We will track this Out-Dweller back to its master with you. You will get your fugitive. But then you leave us in peace." Raedrick's brow furrowed and his voice took on a dangerous tone. "And you will never tell your people about Melanie. Ever."

Loran looked spooked. It was the first time Julian had ever seen him that way. He raised his fingers to his throat and felt along the area Raedrick's sword had touched, then pulled them away and looked at them as though expecting blood. Seeing none, his shoulders slumped. But his eyes still burned with pride.

"You are in no position to dictate terms, Constable," he said, spitting out the title with all the contempt he could muster. "The Magestirium has authority over matters magical, not - "

"Not here," Raedrick finished. "Not with her."

Loran glowered and looked away from Raedrick toward Julian.

Julian put on his best scowl and let his sword-hand fall onto the hilt of his weapon.

The mage sniffed and scanned the faces of the men surrounding them. They were all as implacable as Julian felt, and as Raedrick looked. Finally, Loran nodded.

"Fine. She goes free," he said. Then, raising his index finger, he added, "For now. But if she puts her foot wrong with the Magestirium again, or sets foot outside of this Vale..." He left the rest unsaid.

Raedrick nodded. "Agreed. Melanie?" He looked at her, questioning.

Melanie shrugged. "Didn't intend to go anywhere else anyway."

"Then we have an accord," Loran said. He rolled his shoulders and turned away from Raedrick, in the direction the Out-Dweller fled. He took a step, but the circle of townsfolk did not give way. Loran looked back at Raedrick, an eyebrow quirking upward again. "Do you mind?"

Raedrick nodded at the townsfolk, and the circle opened, letting Loran pass.

The mage departed, hurrying down the street after the Out-Dweller.

Julian looked at Raedrick questioningly. "You believe him?"

Raedrick shrugged. "If he's lying, we can kill him later."

Chuckling, Julian joined his friend as he followed along behind Loran. The game was afoot, after all.

25

PURSUIT

It was a half-block before Julian realized that Melanie was jogging along with them. And then only because she caught up to them and threatened to pass him up.

"You sure you want to come with us?" he said between breaths.

She rolled her eyes. "You'll all die if you go up against that thing without me," she said. "And then I'll have to clean up your mess. Of course I'm coming."

Julian would have chuckled, but the pace precluded it. Instead he just grinned at her. She returned it in kind, but the smile did not reach her eyes, which looked haunted. Pained.

"Are you going to be ok?"

Melanie flinched slightly, but her stride did not alter. She nodded quickly, but said nothing more.

Julian left it at that.

They jogged along after Loran, who turned through the streets of Lydelton seemingly at random but presumably following the Out-Dweller's trail toward its, or rather its master's, hideout.

"I thought you said the warding would weaken it enough so Julian and I could take it alone," Raedrick said, a question in his tone.

Loran managed a little shrug as he jogged. "I had not realized how powerful it is. It appears to be a Lord of one of the dark planes. They are," he paused for a breath and, Julian thought, for emphasis, "Formidable."

They ran on.

"Why doesn't it just go back to where it came from?" Julian asked after the third turn. "Why run away like this?"

Melanie opened her mouth to reply but Loran cut her off.

"Because it was summoned," the mage said. "It can only enter or leave this world from the place it was summoned."

Loran did not look back at them as he answered. He had not looked back at all.

Julian would bet good money he did not know Melanie was with them. He was in for a shock. Julian could not help grinning at the thought.

"So if we kill it here, away from its place of summoning?" Raedrick asked.

"It dies. Forever." Loran's voice held a certain satisfaction as he answered.

Wow. That was something Julian did not know. Although if he was honest with himself, the things he did not know could fill an entire library. All the same, he had always been taught that the denizens of the outer planes were immortal. Un-aging, undying. Even if you killed one of them, the legends said he would just regenerate and be ready to come after you again. But apparently that only applied on their home planes. If an Out-Dweller could truly die here, in the real world...

"No wonder they don't come here very often," Julian said aloud.

"Indeed," Loran replied. Then he turned right down a cross street.

"This street will take us out of town," Raedrick said.

Loran just shrugged and jogged on.

Sure enough, they passed the last houses of Lydelton proper, and shortly thereafter the street ended in the face of the tall grass that dominated most of Glimmer Vale during the warm months. Except that tonight, there was a path beaten through the grass. Half again as wide as the broadest man Julian had ever met, it led away from town to the north, toward the eastern-most edges of the Glamorwood and the hills and mountains beyond.

Loran pulled up short, panting heavily. He bent forward and rested his hands upon his knees, catching his breath. Part of Julian wanted to do the same, but he would not allow himself to mimic the mage's lack of conditioning, so instead he worked hard to keep himself upright. He took in long breaths and forcibly held them in to make it look as though he was not winded. That did not do much as far as getting his breath back, but it made him feel better.

For his part, Loran took several moments before he straightened. He looked back at Raedrick and Julian, then noticed Melanie and he scowled.

"I did not invite *you*, woman," he said, applying all manner of derision to the word woman as he spoke it.

"And yet here I am anyway, Vigilant Haversted," Melanie said calmly. She was not breathing heavily at all, curse her. "We both know you will need my help to prevail this night."

Loran scowled at her for a long moment. Then he looked away, saying nothing more.

"Enough," Raedrick said. He was not winded in the slightest, Julian noticed. He made a mental note to join Raedrick on his daily runs from then on. "Let's finish this."

Raedrick set off through the grass, his shoulders set in the determined manner Julian knew so well. It was kill or be killed now, until one side or the other prevailed.

"Right," Julian said. "Let's get to it." Then he followed his friend into the grass.

The trail was easy enough to follow, even in the dim light of the stars and the crescent moon, now low over the eastern hills as she got ready to lay down her burden for the day. Not that her burden was all that large at this time of year, but

Julian supposed her longer rest now made up for her greater burden at other times, when she had to shine the entire night through and some of the day as well.

As opposed to the Out-Dweller's course through town, the trail through the grass ran straight enough that Julian could have set his compass to it. Never once did the thing deviate from its track northward. It just continued on, and the mountains ahead of them slowly loomed closer, darker bits of darkness that slowly blotted out more stars as their little group drew nearer.

"Does this make sense to you?" Julian asked after a half-hour following the trail deeper into the wilderness. "Why would it run straight like this?" That question had been bugging him for the last quarter mile, and it just irked him more with every step.

"It presumes we lost its trail in the town," Loran said, again without looking back at Julian.

Julian stopped. "No way this thing is that stupid." Melanie stopped beside him.

Raedrick looked over at Julian and frowned, then slowed his steps and stopped as well.

Something was not right here.

Loran was not to be dissuaded, though. "It is injured, and needs to retreat to its home," he said, finally slowing to look back at them.

Just then, something reared out of the grass ahead of them and to the right, just past Loran's shoulder. A sickly sweet, rotten scent swept over them as it moved, a scent Julian recognized instantly.

The Out-Dweller.

"Get down," Julian and Raedrick yelled together, even as they both drew their blades and charged forward.

Melanie beat them both. They had not gone more than two steps before her hands again lit up with the fire. She raised both hands and fire lanced out over Julian's head - good thing he had decided to run at a crouch - toward the beast.

But the fire struck nothing. It just flew away into the night for several seconds before Melanie raised her hands and shut the flames off. Julian looked at her and noticed she was clenching her fists tightly; was that how she controlled it?

"It's still out there," Melanie said, cocking her head sideways, listening.

Julian did the same, and found that he could hear it too. Low, almost too low to register, but it was there. A rhythmic thumping. It was impossible to tell which direction it came from; it seemed to emanate from everywhere. He turned a complete circle, squinting out into the blackness, and flexed his fingers on the grip of his sword. Nothing.

"I don't like this," he said.

Raedrick grunted in reply, and that grunt carried entire levels of agreement.

The Out-Dweller's sound grew louder, as though it was getting closer. And then, abruptly, it stopped.

Silence reigned. Even the usual night insects were missing.

"I like this even less."

No sooner had the words left Julian's mouth than the silence was eclipsed by a roar that put the Silver Falls to shame. Waves of sound rolled over them, striking against them in a physical blow that sent Julian and his companions to their knees. He reflexively covered his ears with his hands as he went down, but it did no good.

The sound came on and on, hammering him again and again until he lay rolled in a ball on the ground.

He ached all over from the pummeling, his ears rang intensely, and he felt like he would never be able to move again.

Several seconds of lying like that before Julian realized that the onslaught of noise had ceased.

Or had it?

He pushed himself up to a sitting position and tried to say something to Loran, who lay sprawled next to him. But again all he could hear was the ringing in his ears; he could not even hear himself speak, the ringing was so loud.

This was bad. Very bad.

He had dropped his sword somewhere. Frantically he looked around for it. All around, his companions were slowly beginning to come to their senses, but they were not doing it fast enough.

There. He snatched up his sword and forced himself to his feet.

Just in time to see two pairs of gleaming red orbs approaching from within a shadow deeper than the blackest night.

Bugger me, he tried to say, though deafened as he was he could not be sure how it came out.

The Out-Dweller was at most twenty feet away, moving quickly.

Julian kicked Loran with the back of his boot and then advanced. Every part of his sane mind screamed at him to run the other way; he could not win this one. But this time that part of him did not come close to taking control. It was one thing to take no action while others could. It was something else entirely to flee while leaving your friends helpless.

Ok, Loran did not count as a friend. But for this night, at least, he was an ally, and that amounted to the same thing.

He stumbled as he advanced, suddenly realizing he did not have his equilibrium fully.

The darkness around the Out-Dweller swirled forward like a whip aimed at Julian's head, but passed over him. Had he not stumbled right then, he had no doubt the thing would have taken his head clean off.

Another tendril of black came at him, visible only because it was darker than the night around it.

Julian threw himself forward into a roll, hoping against hope that he had guessed right about the thing's trajectory but bracing himself in case he had not.

Again a miss. Somehow.

He came out of the roll and up to his feet. Mostly. And had to fling himself back to the ground and shield his eyes as the sun - or rather suns, dozens of them - flew through the air past him and into the darkness of the Out-Dweller's body.

The beast drew back. Julian presumed it roared, but even that mighty noise could not penetrate the ringing in his ears. He looked over his shoulder and saw Loran up on his knees, his staff in his hands.

Then another burst of stars flew from the staff, and all Julian could see for several long seconds were purple after-images.

The ground shook. Once. Twice.

Something hot flashed briefly overtop him.

And then all was still. Not silent; his ears still rang loudly. But still.

Just raised his head and looked around.

Loran stood leaning against his staff. Melanie was on one knee a short distance away, her hands aglow with flame. Raedrick remained on the ground. Dread flowed through Julian to see that. He pushed himself to his feet and stumbled over to his friend.

Or tried to. He fell back to his knees before he could go more than a yard.

Damn it!

Julian called out Raedrick's name, futilely. The others were likely no better at hearing that he was at the moment. But that did not matter. Raedrick needed help.

Julian pushed himself back to his hands and knees and crawled over to where Raedrick lay. The other man was sprawled on his back, his left arm bent at an unnatural angle from its shoulder. He eyes were closed, and in the flickering light of Melanie's fire Julian could not tell if he was breathing or not.

Julian reached out and shook his friend's shoulder.

Raedrick's entire body stiffened and he jerked up to a sitting position, his mouth wide as though he were shouting. Again, nothing but ringing in Julian's ears, but that did not matter. Right then, he was so happy to see his friend moving he did not mind one bit.

Julian grinned broadly. Raedrick replied with a grimace, and a look that could kill at fifteen paces.

He probably should have shook the other shoulder.

❦ 26 ❦

FIRST AID

The immediate aftermath of the Out-Dweller's attack would have been pure chaos had there been more than four of them in the grass. As it was, it was confusion that Julian would have found tremendously amusing in any other circumstances. But being in the wide open, in the middle of the night, with a large and apparently very angry other-worldly beast stalking around was not the right time for humor.

None of them could hear anything; or at least Julian presumed the others were as deafened as he was from their hand gestures and annoyed faces. Thus, it took a while for everyone to agree on the priority of tasks. Namely, making more light - how could they have been stupid enough to go running through the grass without bringing some light with them? - and seeing to Raedrick's shoulder.

Loran accomplished the light easily enough. He grimaced, stood to his full height - not that that was saying much - and mumbled something that Julian was sure he would not have understood even if he were not still deafened, and thumped his staff against the ground. A small sphere, glowing blue-white and brighter than twenty lamps held together, rose from the top of his staff and came to hover about ten feet over his head.

That illuminated things quite nicely.

Raedrick's shoulder took a bit more doing. Julian had seen similar injuries before; the shoulder joint was...dislocated, he thought the medics called it. He had seen a pair of them fix a fellow who had been hurt similarly. It required one of them holding the man steady and the other giving his arm a great jerk to set it in place. It seemed to hurt the poor fellow a lot, but after a few minutes, he was swinging his arm around almost like new.

Julian tried, using only gestures, to pass along what they would have to do and received only a blank stare and raised eyebrow from Melanie. Raedrick nodded; he had seen it done as well. Loran...

Loran could not be bothered to help. He looked down at Julian, Raedrick, and Melanie and sniffed, then looked away, out into the night.

Anger surged through Julian for a moment, then faded just as quickly. The mage had a point. They could not all tend to Raedrick. *Someone* needed to keep an eye out in case the Out-Dweller came back. Better he did it than, say Julian. He would be more effective against the beast, and anyway, Julian doubted he had the muscle to do what needed doing.

It made sense. It was still more than irritating.

Slowly, very slowly, in the midst of all that, the ringing in Julian's ears faded. It did not vanish completely, but it reduced, little by little until he could finally hear the others' occasional grunt or murmured curse of annoyance - no doubt uttered because they believed no one else could hear. Julian did not realize it had happened until, after Loran refused to take a hand with getting Raedrick's shoulder in place, Melanie let loose a particularly colorful remark about his heritage.

He couldn't help it. Julian started to chuckle.

Melanie looked at him, crossly. "What are you laughing at..." She stopped abruptly, and her eyebrows rose high on her head as she smiled. In relief, if she felt at all like Julian did.

They exchanged grins, and Julian could not help but notice how the blue-white light from Loran's spell made her eyes seem to glow.

A long moment passed, in silence.

Raedrick cleared his throat. "A little help here?"

Melanie gave a little start. Julian felt his cheeks go warm and he coughed into his fist.

"Right," he said. "This is going to hurt..."

"I know that." Raedrick was already speaking through clenched teeth. It hurt already. Obviously.

Julian gave him an apologetic half-smile - the most he could muster right then - which Raedrick returned with a roll of his eyes and an impatient grunt.

Melanie placed her hands on Raedrick's good shoulder and the meat of his neck on the injured side, being careful to keep clear of the shoulder joint itself.

"Ok," Julian said. He took hold of Raedrick's arm just above the elbow and placed his other hand on his shoulder. His fingers touched Melanie's, and for the briefest of moments his thoughts lingered on the softness of her skin.

Enough of that.

He took a deep breath and looked Raedrick in the eye. "Ready?"

Raedrick nodded.

"One."

Julian tightened his grip on his friend's arm.

"Two"

Raedrick drew a deep breath.

"Three."

Julian pushed Raedrick's arm upwards into its shoulder socket with all the force he could muster.

Raedrick cried out. Loudly. Very loudly. For a second, Julian wondered that his ears did not start ringing the way they had after the Out-Dweller attacked with sound, as loudly as he screamed.

And then, a moment later, it was over.

Julian released his friend and backed away. Melanie did the same.

Very slowly, Raedrick rolled his shoulder, wincing the whole way. "That..." he said, breathlessly, "was horrible."

"But did it work?" Melanie was all business in her tone, though her eyes showed her concern as she looked at him.

Raedrick gave his shoulder another couple rolls, then moved his arm back and forth a couple times. He nodded. "Think so. For the time being, anyway."

Relief flooded through Julian and he grinned from ear to ear. He stood and offered Raedrick a hand up. "Better have the healing house take a look at it when we get back, anyway," he said. "Just in case."

Raedrick accept the hand up - he used his sword hand, which was uninjured. "Oh, I will." He got to his feet then took a moment to retrieve his sword and re-sheathe it. Then he turned his gaze, all business again, toward Loran. "Well Magester? Do you know where it went?"

Loran was peering off to the northeast, into the grass away from the Out-Dweller's trail. He did not turn his head when Raedrick addressed him. He just looked at Julian's friend from the corner of his eye, and nodded. "It has moved away again."

"You can still track it?"

Loran nodded again. "The trail is fresh."

"Then let's get to it."

ON THE TRAIL

There was a brief debate over what to do with Loran's sphere of light, but in the end they opted to keep it lit. The Out-Dweller already knew they were there, and presumably its master, the fugitive, would find out as soon as it communicated with him again. Given that, thoughts of stealth lost out over the necessity of seeing their surroundings, the better to not be ambushed again.

They set off.

Almost immediately, the Out-Dweller's trail left the beaten path through the grass, veering more northeast than north. Julian presumed they would encounter another beaten path at some point, but after a quarter hour or so, by his best reckoning, it appeared that was not to be the case.

"It really was quite clever," Melanie said, from where she walked to Julian's left.

"Huh?"

She rolled her eyes and gave him a look of reproach. "That other path. The Out-Dweller must have laid it as a lure, a ploy to get us to go where it wanted."

He had not thought of that, but it made sense. He should have seen it before. He shook his head and let out a disgusted snort. "And we fell for it, like fools."

Ahead of them, Loran glanced back over his shoulder. "Never presume that an Out-Dweller is not cunning. Even some of the highest-ranking members of the Magestirium have been fooled by such as them." He paused, then added. "From time to time."

He went back to focusing on the way ahead, and Melanie...stuck her tongue out at his back.

Julian gaped at her, shock over her action rendering him speechless for a long moment.

Melanie looked sidelong at him. "What?" she said, in a low tone of voice that was meant for Julian's ears alone. "He was taken in just like the rest of us." She lowered her voice in a mocking imitation of Loran's voice. "Even members of the Magestirium have been fooled." She snorted. "Arrogant twit."

Julian laughed, more loudly than he meant to. Raedrick shot him a withering look from ahead, next to Loran, and made a shushing gesture.

Julian clamped his mouth shut, but still found himself chortling for a good several minutes, try though he might to stop.

It ended up not being an issue. In the darkness ahead, the mountains loomed higher and higher, blotting out more of the stars. Gradually, Julian realized that the gently rolling terrain of the grassland had changed, becoming more steep and varied.

They had entered the hills at the foot of the mountains.

Loran brought them to a halt atop a rise, the steepest one they had yet traversed, and Julian was struck by a memory from when he and Raedrick first arrived in Lydelton. They had tried to track one of Isenholf's brigands back to their base, at night. That had not worked out very well, he recalled.

Of course, they were not following a magical trail, or scent, or whatever it was that Loran was able to detect from the Out-Dweller.

"Still on top of it?" Julian asked.

The mage nodded curtly, then raised his staff and pointed directly north. "The beast passed by here not twenty minutes ago."

"We're gaining on it?" They had taken at least that long to recover their hearing, square away Raedrick's shoulder, and get moving again, by Julian's way of reckoning.

Loran made a noncommittal gesture with his free hand. "We've been keeping pace the last mile or two." He frowned. "It's as though the beast is not trying to lose us." He turned a concerned gaze on all of them. "Like it wants us to follow it to its lair."

Raedrick grunted. "That can't be good."

"No, I should think not." Loran gathered himself up and gave them a curt little nod. "Let's go."

The trail led down the hilltop where they stopped and then ran to the left, north-ward, in the small valley created by a trio of nearby hills. Again Julian was struck by the similarity with the brigand incident, and he found himself wondering whether the Out-Dweller and its master, or whatever their relationship was, were encamped in another one of those things the brigands had used. What was it Melanie called it? He could not recall.

Julian shook his head at his own foolishness. No way there were two of those things here in Glimmer Vale, not as rare as Melanie said they were. If so few mages could do it...

Wait a second.

"Melanie," he said. "I thought you said there were only a few men in the entire world who could make one of those plane things."

She quirked an eyebrow at him.

"You know, the between-plane-whatever-you-called it."

She smirked at him. "You mean a trans-planar rift?"

He nodded.

"They are exceedingly difficult to make. Only a very few have the skill."

"So this guy, this fugitive, is one of the most powerful mages in the world, if he can do that." Julian swallowed and looked around at the hills on either side of them, suddenly quite a bit more nervous. "How are we supposed to take someone like that down?"

Loran must have overheard because he broke in, his voice thick with disapproval. "You speak of what you do not know, Constable. We are not dealing with a rift, but a summoning." Loran shot a withering look at Melanie, the kind of look that said, "Why are you even talking about this with these ignorant louts, woman?"

Julian found that look a bit amusing, actually. She was already an outlaw in the Magestirium's eyes. Was she really supposed to keep all their secrets, despite that?

For her part, Melanie merely sniffed at the mage's look.

"What's the difference?" Raedrick asked.

Loran gave him a perturbed look, and for a moment Julian thought sure he was not going to answer. Normal people should not meddle in the affairs of Wizards, as some very pretentious mages - and that was saying something - who were stationed with the Army had taken to calling themselves around post.

But Loran surprised him. "A trans-planar rift is a connection between one plane and another. A boring through reality to create a passage. The energy requirements for that sort of work are tremendous, and the required control so fine, that one can easily study for a lifetime and still not develop the skill required to create one successfully."

He paused, quirking his head to one side for a moment. Then he nodded and changed course to the right, veering sidelong up one of the hills. "This way."

They turned to follow him. Loran grunted and stepped around a protruding rock before continuing. "A summoning is merely an invitation. The summoner calls out the creature's name and imbues it with power, usually using a summoning circle. The rite creates," he paused as though searching for the right word, "a thinning in the boundary to our plane. If the creature being summoned accepts the invitation, it then creates a temporary rift to that thinning."

Julian blinked. "It can refuse to come?"

Loran shrugged. "If the summoned creature is powerful enough, or the mage lacking in skill. For a man who is learned and practiced in these things, a summoning is closer to a command for any but the most powerful of beings. For beings like that, it is more...a negotiation."

"That means this particular Out-Dweller *wants* to be here," Raedrick mused.

Loran nodded. "Almost certainly." He smirked then, in a rather self-satisfied way. "Or at least, it *did*."

Don't throw your arm out of joint patting yourself on the back, Magester. Julian snorted.

"So how do we get rid of it?" Raedrick frowned as he asked the question. "Besides killing it, if we even can."

Loran shrugged. "Break the summoning circle. Kill the summoner. Perform a banishing ceremony at the place it was summoned. There are many ways." He drew a deep breath. "I am hoping," he said, "that I will be able to convince my former colleague to surrender, and break the summoning himself."

Yeah, like that was going to happen. "And when he doesn't?"

Loran looked at Julian, scowling. Then, after a brief moment, he relaxed his expression and sighed, looking resigned. "Then it becomes...more difficult."

Great.

They reached the crest of the hill and Loran slowed, looking left and right. Finally, he turned left and strode down the other side briskly, his gait businesslike and his shoulders squared like a man setting off for a long day of hard labor.

Julian looked up from the mage, toward the twinkling stars above. But before his eyes could reach them, another twinkling, faint but bright enough to draw his attention in the night's darkness, drew his attention. Yellow-orange, the light flickered fitfully and it took a short while for him to realize what he was looking at.

A campfire. Or if not a campfire, a fire of some sort. And either unshielded or large, to see it from this distance. Julian figured it to be a good four or five miles off, though it was hard to tell in the darkness.

In front of him, Raedrick took a step forward to follow Loran, but he stopped when Julian grabbed his arm. He looked back at Julian with questioning eyes. Julian nodded toward the distant fire. Raedrick turned his head to follow Julian's gaze, and frowned.

"Our destination," Raedrick said, certainty in his tone.

Julian nodded, swallowing despite the fact that his mouth had gone dry. He loosened his sword in its scabbard, for all the good it would do against a being like the Out-Dweller.

Raedrick gave a slow roll of his shoulders, and winced. His injured shoulder must still be paining him, and no wonder. "Well," he said, "let's get to it."

Then he followed Loran down the hill.

Julian glanced at Melanie, who still stood at his side. She wore a grim, determined expression. Their eyes met for a long moment, then she nodded at him, and her lips curled upward ever so slightly. He returned the nod.

Then, together, he and Melanie followed the others toward their destiny.

❦ 28 ❦

THE LAIR OF THE BEAST

At first glance, the camp, or base, or whatever, was nothing to look at. A lean-to lay propped up against a little spur of sheer rock that rose from the side of the hill, really the side of the mountain, as close they must have been to the true peaks of the Saddleback Range now, all twining branches with loose piles of fallen pine needles thrown atop it. It would barely keep a stiff breeze off its inhabitant, let alone a good rainfall or snowfall.

Not far from the lean-to, a bonfire burned. The same fire Julian saw from the hilltop an hour ago, though it was even larger than he would have thought, from so far away. The fire's creator had thought ahead, though. A circle of large rocks, almost knee-high, surrounded the fire, preventing it from growing beyond its intended girth.

Aside from that, there was not much else to the site. Just a makeshift wooden rack, from which dangled a couple small game animals, and a similarly rough stool that rested halfway between the fire and the lean-to.

But first glances were deceiving. All the more so in this site.

Off to the right, from Julian's perspective, and easy to miss in the immediate glare of the bonfire, the sloping ground leveled out into a flat area about the size of the front half of The Oarlock's taproom. A circle of candles, their flames flickering in the night breeze, ringed the area.

And moving around the circle, more like dancing around it, was, Julian presumed, the fugitive mage.

Julian and his companions crouched in a copse of trees, one of the final easternmost outgrowths of the Glamorwood, he presumed, about a hundred feet to the left and downhill from the camp. Summoning area. Whatever Loran wanted to call it. From that distance, it was easy to miss the comparatively dim glow of the candles, and it took Julian two tries to see the circle and its attendant after Loran pointed it out.

Julian pursed his lips as he studied the site. It was remarkably unfortified. They

261

would be able to simply march straight up there, and nothing would stop them. Except...

"Where is the Out-Dweller?" Raedrick asked, from his position off to Julian's right.

Loran crouched between them. He shrugged, but it was difficult to see his facial expression in the dim light; they had doused his floating sphere of light once they came within a half mile of the camp. His voice was level, apparently unconcerned as he replied. "I can still feel the power of its summoning. It is out there. Somewhere."

Melanie sniffed softly. Julian glanced to his left, toward her, and smirked in agreement, though he was all but certain she could not see it.

Raedrick breathed a soft curse. "It won't let us just walk up there and disrupt the spell." He paused for a second, then added, "Will it?"

Again Loran shrugged. "We dealt it no small amount of injury. It may prefer to retreat home where it can heal easily, then deal with us later."

The way he said "deal with us" sent a shiver - no, two shivers - down Julian's spine. Bad enough they might die tonight, but even if they lived, if the Out-Dweller escaped to its own plane, it would certainly seek vengeance against them. And it had the patience of an eternal lifespan to wait to achieve it.

Wonderful. Even if they won, there was a greater than zero chance that they would, in fact, lose.

"What's the plan?" Julian asked.

There was a long second or two of silence before Loran replied. "If at all possible, I need to bring the fugitive back with me alive."

"So, what, we just walk up there and extend him an invitation?" Julian could not have concealed his incredulity with that plan if he had wanted to.

Loran turned his head toward Julian, and he...nodded. "That's it exactly, Constable," he said.

And then Loran stood up from his crouch and set off, boldly and directly, toward the campsite.

"Aw hell," Julian muttered to himself.

Julian thought sure the Out-Dweller would pounce on them as they crossed the distance between their rally point in the copse and the campsite. But for whatever reason, it did not.

It was almost as though they were taking a nighttime stroll through pristine country, so easily did they reach the limit of the bonfire's light.

Julian thought to stop at the edge of that circle, to check the lay of the land before proceeding onward. But, as always, Loran had other ideas. He strode forward with that same bold, confident gait he always seemed to use, passing into the bonfire's circle of illumination apparently without care and veering directly toward the little candle circle, and the fugitive mage.

"Telurian!" Loran bellowed as he approached the circle.

The fugitive froze in mid-step, turning eyes that glinted feral in the firelight toward Loran as the Inquisitor approached him. Loran's steps did not slow, though Julian saw him flex his hands on his staff as Telurian's gaze settled on him.

"I am here," Loran said, somberly.

Julian followed a few steps behind Loran, Raedrick and Melanie at his side, all the while wondering if perhaps coming along was not the greatest idea in the world. And then he got a better look at Telurian.

The outlaw mage, seen up close, was pathetic. His clothing consisted of little more than tattered rags that might have been finery, a long, long time ago. His beard was scraggly, his light brown hair long and unkempt, with wisps sticking out every which way. He had to be younger than Loran, but his face was covered with so much soot and grime it was impossible to tell for sure.

But his eyes.

They were sharp, intelligent, lucid. And wild. They darted to and fro, as though he were afraid to leave his attention in any one spot for too long.

He looked haunted. Hunted.

"Master?" he croaked out, his voice raspy as though he had been shouting for a long while, or he was desperately dehydrated. In spite of that, he sounded almost relieved. Not what Julian would have expected from a fugitive.

Loran nodded, coming to a halt a half-dozen paces from Telurian.

The fugitive's eyes widened slightly, then he half laughed, half snarled. "You're too late," he said, the momentary relief leaving his voice completely. "It is done."

Julian glanced over at Melanie, hoping she had an inkling of what he meant, but she looked as confused as Julian felt. What is done?

"Nevertheless, I am here to bring you back. And you will come with me, Telurian, whether I must force you or no." Loran leaned forward, planting his staff on the ground firmly. "We both know I can do that."

Telurian shook his head, his eyes resuming their furtive dance around the area. "I cannot!" he said, sounding suddenly desperate.

"Send the beast back where it came from. Now."

Telurian recoiled beneath the power of Loran's command. It cut through the air like a whip, and for a moment the fugitive seemed stunned into stillness. Then he shook his head again and groaned. It was a sound of utmost despair, of someone who had witnessed horrors beyond belief and could not escape their memory.

"You don't understand," Telurian all but whispered, though his words carried through the air plainly. "I cannot control it."

He lowered his head, breaking contact with Loran's eyes.

At that exact moment, the earth just past the far side of the circle of candles burst open, and blackness incarnate swept over them all.

DANCING IN THE DARK

Julian should not have been surprised. He had been more than halfway expecting the Out-Dweller to attack them for most of the last hour or more. But regardless, when darkness flowed out of the ripped-open earth like a rolling wave, he stood rooted to the spot in shock.

And then the wave hit him, and he went reeling.

All light vanished.

All around, he heard his friends shouting, but they sounded a million miles away and he could not make out what they were saying.

Other sounds issued through the blackness, skittering sounds, like many-legged creatures crawling over stone, and he cringed.

There were...things...in the darkness, all around.

Julian drew his sword and turned a complete circle - or at least he thought it was a complete circle, but how to tell? - while listening carefully.

They were everywhere.

Off to his left, Loran's voice rose in a powerful chant that ended abruptly in a vicious-sounding word that Julian did not understand but sounded like something a judge might say to the executioner to order him to do the deed. A heartbeat later, a wave of heat swept over Julian, and he found himself driven back a couple steps.

His boot struck something momentarily, but then the thing was gone.

Uh-oh.

Julian slid away and cut downward with his sword toward whatever he had inadvertently kicked. The blade whistled through the air, meeting no resistance until the tip struck the ground in front of him. Nothing there.

Until there was.

Something struck the back of his left knee, and his leg buckled. He fell sideways, only months and months of training, honed by the stress of more battles than he wanted to remember, stopping him from landing, helpless, on his side. Instead, he tucked his shoulder and rolled, casting his sword aside as he went lest he skewer himself in the process.

A moment later, Julian was back on his feet, still just as blind as before and now feeling naked as well without nigh on three feet of sharpened steel to put between himself and...whatever that was. He settled for a little bit less than a foot, drawing his dagger from its sheath at the small of his back.

It did not offer much comfort.

The skittering noise came again, from the right this time, he thought. Julian turned to face it, part of him wondering what the point of that was, considering the thing could just move the other way to get behind him. He forced that part of him to shut up, best he could. It mostly worked.

A guttural roar, loud and full of fury - and pain? - assaulted Julian's ears. Again he stumbled a pace or so, and again his boot struck something. But this time it did not disappear as soon as he made contact. Suddenly Julian realized that the air behind him was hot. Very hot. The kind of hot that threatened to scorch him where he stood if he did not move.

The bonfire.

The skittering noise sounded again, more steadily this time, from in front of him and to his right.

It was growing louder; the thing was drawing near.

Then there was a hissing sound, almost like a man drawing a breath through a gap in teeth, and the skittering came again, more rapidly, then vanished.

The slightest gust of air against his face warned Julian of the danger, and he managed to drop to one knee before the thing, whatever it was, could hit him square in the chest. As it was, it struck the top of his left shoulder and stuck there. He almost reeled backward, into the flames, but he managed to brace himself. His nearly shouted grunt accompanied the movement of his muscles as he leaned forward, into the blow, then spun with it to the left instead of straight backwards, which undoubtedly had been the thing's plan.

Julian's left hand clamped down on the thing, whatever it was, and felt only a hard carapace, like on an beetle except so much larger it almost did not bear comparing the two. For a second, he paused, wondering about the creature that seemed to be embracing him.

And then the pain began.

When the dark wave rushed over her and she heard the skittering sounds in the darkness, Melanie had to fight back a surge of panic. Intellectually, she knew - or thought she knew - what was happening. The Out-Dweller had somehow summoned a few of its minions to this plane, to fight its battles for it. Its minions, at least the ones without the strength to resist its call - and it would not be a particularly strong call, coming from here and having to use Telurian's circle instead of one of its own - would be comparatively weak, and easy to dispatch.

Somehow, that knowledge was little comfort, there in the blackness.

She could not even see the flames that she knew flickered around her hands, the dark was so absolute. It was not just the absence of light; it was a dark the devoured any hint of radiance, a vacuum that removed all hope and joy.

They had brought a portion of their home into the material world with them.

Another skittering noise sounded, nearer than before, and the panic that had been threatening her psyche burst forth. It filled her, sending her heartbeat into a sprint so that for a few moments all she could hear was that pounding and, above it, the frantic sounds of her own breath.

They were doomed, here. She was doomed.

It was all she could do not to fall to her knees and weep in despair.

And then a voice, strong and assured, mighty, broke through the void and shattered the despair within her. She recognized the language it chanted in from Timon's earliest lessons, and for a moment she thought it was he, come back to save her.

The voice's timbre registered more fully and she recognized it. Her enemy.

Then a wave of heat struck her. And more than heat, light. A swift ribbon of flame washed over and past her, making her cringe backwards with the expectation that she had been badly burned. But when she looked down, her dress was intact and her exposed skin was untouched.

How?

She blinked, and it suddenly registered that she could see. She looked up and saw that she stood on the outer edge of a circle of light, not bright by any means but enough to see by, surrounded on all sides by blackness deeper than the darkest night. She could not tell the source of the light; it seemed to permeate the air itself within the circle. But the ring of darkness around her seemed to pulse against the light, surging inward all around as though probing for a way forward so that it could engulf her again. But it was repelled; the light prevailed, and she stood free to move and see the world around her.

But not alone.

Across the circle from her, Loran nodded with a certain satisfaction and glanced about. When his gaze fell on her, his lips turned upwards into something that almost, but not quite, more resembled a grin than a condescending sneer.

"I wondered whether you would be able to make it through," he said. "It seems you are not insignificant, after all."

Melanie just stared at him, confusion stealing her retort from her.

Loran read her lack of understanding from her expression and sneered all the deeper. "Or maybe not. Did your man Timon teach you nothing of this?"

She glanced around at the little space of light. It was still just her and Loran. She tried to put on an apathetic, or at least knowing, expression as she shrugged.

Mocking laughter was his only response at first. Finally, after several seconds, he brought himself under control and actually smiled at her. "The outside minions do not just bring darkness; they bring the essence of their plane itself. For as long as the summoning circle stands, this area is now, for all intents and purposes, part of their world, not ours."

Melanie swallowed. Hard. "So, you..."

"I brought forward a small area of our reality into their plane."

His words struck her like a sledgehammer. What he was describing... "That's not possible," she breathed. "A rift takes..."

Loran snorted with such derision she almost melted. "Did I say I created a rift, woman?" He looked at her incredulously and shook his head. Then he turned his back on her and raised his hands over his head, his staff held between them, parallel to the ground. He drew a deep breath and held it for a few seconds. When he let it out, he spoke again, and his tone was completely calm, completely cool and focused. "I have re-imposed our world onto the artificiality that these beings forced on it. There is no need for a rift; it is they who caused the disruption of our plane, not vice versa." He glanced back at her and crooked an eyebrow upwards. "The Out-Dweller will sense that imposition, and take it as a challenge. Any moment now."

Just then, right on cue, a guttural roar, so loud it felt as though it must overwhelm her and knock her senseless, issued forth from the surging blackness in front of Melanie and Loran. Then the roar ended, as quickly as it began.

Silence reigned for a few seconds, and even the dark ring seemed to grow still around them.

And then the darkness swelled upward and inward, toward them. The light in their little circle seemed to dim, and for a second Melanie thought it would go out altogether. And all at once, she understood why it just might.

The Out-Dweller approached.

❧ 30 ☙

HARD PRESSED

Melanie swallowed hard, trying to press down the sudden terror that surged within her. It was one thing to cast spells at the Out-Dweller from afar. But now it was coming, and only she and Loran stood before it.

She wiped a sudden sweat from her brow and was not surprised that her hand trembled as she did so. She hated to admit it, but the presence of Julian and Raedrick, and the steel of their blades, useless as it was against this foe, had offered her some comfort. Now, without them...

The darkness bulged inward like a blister, and right then a scream echoed from somewhere to Melanie's right. A man's scream, full of pain and fear. It only took a second for her to recognize Julian's voice.

The fear swelled within her, but so also did anger. Her dear friend was being tortured by this beast, or its minions.

It would pay.

"What should I do?" She hated to ask Loran for advice, but he was right. Timon had taught her next to nothing about dealing with the Out-Dwellers, just that they existed and the very basics of how a summoning worked. She could never achieve a summoning herself, and she was not foolish enough to try; if by some chance she gained the attention of one able to use a call as meager as hers to bring itself over...

Well, she had this night seen what such a creature would be like. She shuddered to think of trying to control it by herself.

Loran grunted, his eyes now fixed on the bulging blister of blackness. Any second now, the Out-Dweller would emerge, and he stood straight and tall to meet it. "I can banish it. Here." He paused, then added, "But I may need your help to hold it."

He said no more, and he would not see the gesture, but Melanie nodded. Hold it in place. She could do that.

She hoped.

"It comes." Loran could have been commenting on the return of a dog sent to fetch a downed pheasant, as much inflection as he put into his voice.

For Melanie's part, as the blister finally popped, it was all she could do not to retreat. Not that it made any great noise, or sent any force her way. But it concealed a thing of darkness, of powerful evil, and it would...

A figure fell to the earth as the blister of blackness burst and retreated back to the edge of their circle of light. Not particularly tall, though taller than Loran - who wasn't? - and thin, it was a man. He lay on his belly with his face in the dirt, but she knew immediately who he was.

Telurian.

Melanie blinked in surprise. "Is that supposed to..."

Loran shook his head. "No." He lowered his staff and frowned, then glanced back at her again. "No, that was supposed to be the Out-Dweller." He strode slowly forward, to Telurian's side, and squatted down. Pressing his fingers to the side of the fallen mage's throat, Loran paused for a few seconds, then nodded quickly. "He lives."

"Great." Melanie turned a quick circle, looking all around. It still was only she and Loran. "Now what?"

A second male voice cried out in pain from somewhere out in the blackness. Raedrick. Only then did Melanie to notice that Julian had ceased his cries. Gods, let him be alright. She was surprised to find how her heart ached over the notion that he may not be.

Not that she was any more worried about him than Raedrick. Of course not.

"Now," Loran said, returning to his full height and scowling out at the blackness that encircled them. He paused, then took a breath and continued. "Now, I begin a banishment ritual."

Melanie blinked in confusion. "Doesn't the Out-Dweller need to be present for that?"

Loran's scowl became a condescending sneer as he looked at her. "It *is* present, woman. This will take longer, and be more difficult, than if it were close enough for physical contact. But if it is within the boundaries of the summoning area, it cannot resist being expelled from our world, if the ritual is done correctly."

With that, he lowered his staff and turned a full circle, tracing a line in the dirt at his feet as he dragged the staff over the ground in time with his turn. His eyes met Melanie's, and she saw scorn - what else could she expect from the likes of him - but also resolve. But beneath that, fear.

Loran was afraid.

That made sense. Melanie was nearly beside herself with fear; she had never imagined a creature such as this Out-Dweller. It went well beyond the most stern warnings Timon had given her against trying her had at summoning, and those warnings had been energetic indeed. And she had taken them to heart; she certainly never thought to actually face a being such as this.

But Loran had been trained in summoning. As an Inquisitor of the Magestirium, he was intimately familiar with every school of magic, every incantation and ritual. If *he* was scared...

Melanie felt her bowels go to water, and it was all she could do not to flee right then and there. Of course, where would she run to? The darkness waited on all sides; there could be no escape for her, not without victory. So she gritted her teeth and inhaled deeply through her nose, then exhaled out of her mouth, keeping up a slow and steady rhythm despite her body screaming at her that she needed to pant, to get more air into her lungs more quickly NOW!

After a minute or so of forcibly slow, controlled breathing, she felt the panic fade. Only healthy fear remained, the kind of fear that could be acknowledged and controlled, but would not rule her.

Again her eyes met Loran's, and he gave her the slightest of nods.

Then he set to chanting.

31

RITUAL SACRIFICE

The words Loran used were in a tongue Melanie had never heard before. They were guttural, brutal, and harsh, the kinds of words that could never be sung but only screamed in fury. But Loran spoke them smoothly, in a perfectly controlled tone of voice that never raised or lowered, but continued as though he were speaking to a friend in a quiet sitting room.

But in spite of that, Loran's words cut through the dark of the night, and the deeper, unnatural blackness of the Out-Dweller and its minions, with apparent ease. His voice echoed around the area, and with each syllable, it seemed the blackness around he and Melanie retreated a bit.

He was doing it!

Hope slowly grew in Melanie's breast as the ring of blackness moved slowly but steadily away from them, and the circle of light in which she stood grew in time with the blackness' retreat. If that darkness truly consisted of elements from the Out-Dweller's home plane, and not of the mere absence of light in this world, its retreat could only mean that the Out-Dweller, mighty as it obviously was, could indeed be beaten.

The circle expanded a bit more, the darkness retreating at a more rapid pace. Melanie looked around, and saw the same thing occurring all around the circle. Until she saw the spot directly behind Loran.

There, the darkness, instead of retreating, pulled in on itself. It seemed to roil and swirl, like clouds during a thunderstorm. The circle of light pushed outward again, but there in that one place the blackness held firm, a bulging pustule of evil that held out against the light's advance.

Melanie fell back a half-step, swallowing hard. Hope, which had so suddenly surged within her, faded, turning to fear as that pustule of blackness pulsed, then swelled upward and outward, toward her.

Then the pustule burst.

Whipping tendrils of blackness shot forth, the same things the Out-Dweller had used against them before, and Melanie had no doubt the beast stood within that swirling blackness.

She heard herself crying out, chanting a quick incantation before she even realized she was doing it. Again fire blazed around her hands, and she sent out twin lances of flame to meet the advancing tendrils. The two forces met; fire against living blackness, and for a second Melanie thought she might be able to hold them back completely. But the blackness whipped and writhed, impossibly flexible. After the first resistance from her flames, they retreated, but then simply twisted around her spell, moving to her and Loran's flanks.

Then a third and a forth tendril joined the first two.

"Loran!" Melanie cried out in alarm.

But he paid no heed. He was deep into his incantation, his face a mask of concentration. Even if he had heard her through his focus, he could do nothing to help her. Locked into the banishing ritual as he was, he could not stop. To do so would be to invite disaster when the energy he had built up within the incantation sought release, in whatever random manner it could.

Melanie was on her own.

The tendrils, all four of them, squirmed closer. They lowered their speed for a moment, as though testing the area for threats, before proceeding onward. Her flames had taught them caution, at the least.

Part of her shouted with glee at that. Seldom had she had the opportunity to face off against another person, or being, who was magical in nature. Back when the opportunities were plentiful - and there never had been that many - she had given as good as she got more often than not. So Melanie knew she was no slouch. But it was one thing to face off against a fellow novice in the art and prevail, or at least break even. It was something else for a being as powerful as the Out-Dweller, from a plane as evil as the sun was hot, to recoil from her attacks.

This was the second time her fire had injured, or at the very least frightened, the beast.

But then, as the black tendrils began to pick up speed as the came for her - and Loran, though part of her scoffed that she did not care in the least if he were taken except that it would prevent her own revenge - the momentary injury she had apparently given the Out-Dweller at the sisters' house, and again out in the grass, mattered very little.

Fire was not the right tool to use. It had given the tendrils pause, but only momentarily. She needed something else.

Melanie sought through her mind, considering the various spells Timon had taught her and discarding them, one by one, as useless in this situation.

The tendrils swept closer, and she felt beads of sweat running down her brow, the growing panic within her threatening to break through.

There had to be something!

She glanced back at Loran again, but he was still wrapped up in his ritual chanting. How much longer would it take?

The first of the tendrils suddenly whipped forward at a speed she had never seen before. In an instant, cold so intense it burned wrapped around her legs just above the ankle and a force too strong to resist tugged her toward the pustule of darkness.

She fell, her back striking the earth unceremoniously. Caught up in the tendril as her legs were, she could not roll with the fall or do much of anything to reduce its force, and she lost her breath as the wind was knocked out of her.

She had to breathe!

But the air would not come. For several terrifying seconds, the only thing that registered in Melanie's mind was the lack of air, and she thought perhaps a tendril had wrapped around her body, constricting like a snake.

Then, at last, she managed to inhale, and it was like iced water on a sweltering day. She wanted nothing more than to lie there and exalt in the sheer joy of breathing, where just a moment ago she thought she might never do so again.

Then the force about her legs tugged again and she began to drag across the ground toward the bulging blackness, where the Out-Dweller waited. The relief that flooded through her with that first breath fled as quickly as it came and she had to hold back a whimper of despair.

It was so strong! She clawed at the ground, trying to arrest her motion, to no avail. If anything, her movement became more rapid.

She tried to kick her legs, to pull them free of the tendril, but they would not move. The thing was strong, but it was more than that. That burning cold, forgotten in her loss of breath, crept slowly up from where the thing was wrapped around her calves and had now reached her thighs. Where it passed was only numb, like her legs no longer existed; she was certain she could not have moved her legs below the knees even if the thing had let her go.

Fear surged higher, becoming almost panic.

She could not give in to it. That way led only to death.

Melanie looked back at the tendril and only then realized it was just that: a single tendril. But there had been four. Where were...

Loran!

She craned her neck, twisting as best she could to see him. Had he been taken as well?

Then he came into view, and the scene around the Inquisitor stopped her cold.

He stood there, looking for all the world as though nothing untoward was happening as he continued his ritual chant. As far as she could tell, he had not even looked up. The three tendrils of blackness hovered in the air all around him. They quivered with pent up energy as though eager to attack but hesitant, unsure as to what he was doing.

Melanie could relate. He was not a fool. Why would he leave himself so wide open?

All three tendrils struck at the same time, darting toward the mage at lightning speed. He could not hope to repel them all, not as quickly as they were moving.

He did not have to.

When the tendrils reached a distance of about three feet from Loran, they stopped completely. A glowing blue nimbus erupted where each stopped, bright like a campfire in the immediate vicinity of each tendril but growing quickly less luminous as the glow spread away from it. The light spread around, the three sources reinforcing each other enough to show the outline of a dome completely surrounding Loran, who still stood, chanting, apparently completely unconcerned about the attack his magic had just prevented.

That bastard!

He had set a defensive barrier up around himself, but spared not a thought for

Melanie, not even to inform her of that fact. And why not? She was just an abomination in his eyes, a beast to be put down. A beast he had to tolerate, for the moment, but if she were to fall in battle with the Out-Dweller, that would solve one of his problems for him, wouldn't it. Raedrick and Julian could not possibly fault him for her death in these circumstances.

She clenched her teeth, burning anger eclipsing her near-panic in a heartbeat. No, she would not give him that satisfaction.

The tendril about her calves yanked again, and Melanie was shocked to see she was almost to the barrier of blackness. Less than ten feet now, and that fiery cold now reached up to her hips.

It would drag her into the darkness in another few seconds. And once that happened...there would be no hope out there, beyond the light.

Down at the deepest register of her hearing, so low it came across as a vibration in her body as much as a sound impacting her ears, a rumble sounded. It only lasted for a second, but it twisted upward in pitch at the very end, making it sound almost sardonic.

Melanie realized what it was. The Out-Dweller's laughter.

And then the tendril pulled at her legs again, and the blackness swelled up to receive her.

32

THE WAITING BLACKNESS

There was no more time to think. There was barely time to react at all. As the blackness loomed closer, towering overhead like a wave about to crash down all around her, Melanie dipped her hand into the pouch that kept her spell components.

Her fingers quickly traced the shape of a carefully wrapped item and clenched around it, reacting to its familiar feel with the instinctive insight of hundreds of caresses, hundreds of incantations. She knew this thing without needing to think on it: the essence of the very first spell Timon had ever taught her.

The words of the incantation swept off her tongue without effort, so often had she given them voice in the past. Even had she the time to pull out her spell book, she would not have needed to consult it, so intimate was the spell. As she chanted and brought her hands together, crushing the cloth-wrapped seeds between them and twisting, she saw Timon's face, his dark green eyes sparkling with pride the way they had the first time she had successfully done this.

And then light, pure white light, erupted from her hands where the component was consumed, and spread outward.

She had put more into the illumination spell than she realized. It had never burned this brightly before. It out-shown a dozen lanterns, but somehow it was not painful to look at.

At least not for her.

The Out-Dweller, on the other hand...

It let out a shriek, from surprise as much as from pain, Melanie thought. But suddenly the tendril's grip on her legs eased and it seemed as though the blackness, which had been about to consume her a mere second before, was again drawing back, as it had from Loran's earlier spell. Except that this time it was like a rapid retreat more than a grudging withdrawal.

Understanding came all at once, and Melanie cursed herself, silently, for a fool.

The Out-Dweller dwelt in a world of darkness. Here on this plane, it had surrounded itself in darkness. In some ways, maybe it *was* darkness. Loran's attack, back at the sisters' house, had been one of light. Melanie's fire had been the deciding factor in driving it off. Maybe. But how much of that was because of the fire's heat and how much because of the light that came with it?

Melanie was beginning to think more of the latter than the former.

She shouted a secondary incantation and pushed upward with her hands, and the blazing light raised a few feet up into the air, then sat there, shining away. It would not last long, but maybe long enough.

She pulled another packet of seeds from her pouch and began the primary incantation again.

Almost immediately the tendril eased its grip further, as though anticipating the illumination to come. When it did come, the tendril shot backwards, away from her as it released its grip entirely.

With satisfaction, Melanie spat a curse at the thing. The satisfaction faded when she realized she still could not move her legs. Scowling, she again floated the ball of light then used her palms to push herself back away from the barrier of blackness as quickly as she could.

When she had put ten feet from herself and the Out-Dweller - somehow she knew it still lurked there, ahead of her - she pushed herself up to a seated position and again chanted the incantation of light. Again she crushed the seeds, and again her little glowing ball appeared.

Then she spoke the incantation again, and again the component was destroyed.

The ball of light grew larger, and far, far brighter.

Again. And again.

And then she placed her hand into her pouch and found no more of the care-fully-wrapped seeds.

It would have to do. And it looked like it was beginning to. All around, the blackness was pushing away from their circle again, and even the tendrils that were still attacking Loran pulled back, their aggression fading before the onslaught of illumination from Melanie's spell. She dared think that this one spell, multiplied onto itself as many times as it had been, might be enough to protect them completely for as long as Loran needed to finish the ritual.

Except that this time she did not intend to merely float it in place.

She drew her hand back, and the ball went with it. As she brought her hand forward again, she shouted out the secondary incantation, with a little added twist at the end, and the ball of brightness flew from her fingers. It flashed between its little siblings, hanging there in the air nonchalantly, and impacted the barrier of blackness.

It was like a stone dropping into a still pool of water.

The blackness boiled backward from the ball of light, flooding away from it in a wave that sped in both directions around the circle. Then the ball of light sunk deeper, and the blackness closed in behind it and it was gone.

Melanie blinked, drawing in a quick breath as the momentary elation she had felt over the spell's apparent success faded a bit.

Like the dirt kicked up by the stone impacting the bottom of the pool, light flared through the blackness in a hundred different places. Pinpricks and gaping beams of radiance swelled from the darkness, their number spreading outward from where the ball struck like a rash, but a rash of purity.

And then, with a brilliant flash, the darkness was ripped asunder. Little bits of blackness flew in all directions like dust before a great wind. Even as they flew, the bits of black seemed to shrivel and crumple apart until they disappeared entirely.

Melanie sat there, stunned at what had just happened. It took her a moment to take it all in, and to fully comprehend what she was now seeing.

Off to her right, a group of black, shiny....things...writhed around atop each other in a little pile. They scrambled as though fighting over something. A second pile lay off to the left, this one larger, made up of more of the beasts. Whatever they were, their sudden illumination made both piles stop their ceaseless motion. Then, a second later, the things began retreating, scampering back from the new light, toward the shadows of the tree line and between rocks on the mountain's flank. In ones and twos at first, then it greater numbers, and with greater speed, they went.

Melanie only noticed them in passing though. The Out-Dweller held all of her attention.

It had fallen onto its back, but it was slowly regaining its feet. In the replenished firelight and the illumination of her two floating lights, the beast was fully revealed; the smokey shadows that had obscured it before were gone, cast asunder by the force of the light she had used.

It was massive, more powerfully built than she had realized, and it had seemed barrel-chested enough before. Rippling muscles beneath scaly flesh that housed spikes and thorns of all sizes promised no end of pain when it took her. And the fire smoldering in its double-pair of eyes promised that no matter how she fought, how she resisted, it would take her, and bring her back to its home plane with it when it finally departed her world. And never grant her the release of death.

The promise of eternal punishment for her insolence bore down on her mind, the certainty of the Out-Dweller's victory casting all hope aside. She wanted to scream, to push herself away. To find a way, any way, to escape. To hide. To pull a mountain down atop herself, if only it would protect her from this beast's wrath. But she could not bring herself to look away from its fiery stare, and the agony it promised.

The Out-Dweller smiled, or made an expression that could she could only understand as a smile, hot in its gleeful malevolence, and took a step toward her. Then another.

Melanie's mind screamed to run, but her legs were still numb to the hip and did not respond. Or maybe she did not want them to respond. Suddenly she could not remember why she should.

Those eyes. They seemed to grow larger, opening wide to engulf her. Large as the Out-Dweller was, they made the rest of it seem tiny by comparison. She saw through them and gasped. Within lay fire, beautiful and terrible fire, that promise to caress even as it rent her soul asunder.

She shuddered. She screamed. She moaned.

But she could not move.

It was directly atop her now, the sickly sweet-sour stench of its body filling her nose, making her want to gag as the taste of it seemed to penetrate her tongue as well. It reached down with its huge talons, digits that would tear her flesh apart at the lightest grip. And still she sat still, fascinated by the play of fire within its eyes. It was so brilliant, so agonizing, so seductive.

A sudden new noise reached her ears. Coming from behind her somewhere, it seemed extremely loud, but for some reason she could barely register it. The noise was not worthy of her notice, not compared with the nearly-audible roar of the inferno within those eyes.

The Out-Dweller, though...

The noise seemed to strike it like a physical blow. The beast stopped midway toward grabbing her and fell back a half-step. Its head quirked upward, breaking contact with Melanie's gaze to stare at something behind her.

Reality came back to her in a rush. What had been happening in Lydelton these last several nights. The journey through the grass to this site. The battle against the darkness. Reality. And with it, all-consuming horror over what had almost just happened.

She did scream then, and fell backward onto the dirt, throwing up her hands defensively as though that alone could ward off the gargantuan beast that stood less than one of its paces away from her.

Again that new noise came, intruding on Melanie's sudden panic as she recognized it for what it was: Loran's voice.

He had spoken a single word, using the same guttural tongue he had been chanting in at the start of the ritual. That word must have held some measure of power, because again the Out-Dweller moved backwards.

Though not as far this time. It steeled itself visibly and managed to shrug off most of the effect of Loran's spell, whatever it was.

One of its great talon-hands moved behind its back, and when it emerged again, the talons were clasped around something long, black, and serpentine. Melanie cringed even more than she was already as she recognized it for what it was: a great whip. But not like any whip she had ever seen. This one cast about even though the Out-Dweller held its handle motionless.

Then it flicked in her direction and she scrambled backwards. It missed her, barely, but she got a better look at it as it did, and she screamed again at this latest horror.

The whip was alive. A living serpent, black and hooded around its head, like a cobra. Its eyes burned red like the Out-Dweller's, as did its fangs. Drops of some foul fluid dripped from its mouth, sizzling the earth where they fell at Melanie's side.

She kicked herself backwards again, but then stopped, surprised. Her legs worked!

A moment ago, they had been colder than deepest winter and completely immobile. Now, they at least obeyed her commands, even though they did not feel all that much warmer.

How...?

But there was no time the wonder about that right then. Loran shouted again, but this time the Out-Dweller did not move backward. Instead, it flicked the serpent-whip in his direction. It seemed to lengthen as it moved, stretching further than Melanie would have thought possible, and then even more; it would have no trouble crossing the distance between the Out-Dweller and the Inquisitor.

He could not possibly avoid the whip, as quickly as it came toward him, but he seemed unconcerned. He still had his shield, after all...

The serpent-whip struck Loran's shield, and again the blue-light flashed around him. Then the whip continued onward toward him.

Loran's eyes widened in surprise. In sudden fear. And then the serpent-whip struck him and he vanished beneath the serpent's coils.

✣ 33 ✣

ENFLAMED

Melanie cried out in denial as Loran was engulfed. It could not take him!

Let it.

The thought came unbidden, and with it a wave of self-loathing. What cared she if the Inquisitor was killed here this night? She had been ready to do it herself not so long ago. Only her realization that she - that they - needed Loran for this night's work, and her friends' intervention, had stopped her. He had been more than eager to profit from her death this night as well. What was good for the goose was good for the gander.

Hell, she ought to dance a jig and thank the Out-Dweller for saving her the trouble.

And you can take that thing yourself, can you?

She looked away from the squirming serpent coils, all that was visible where the Inquisitor was a moment ago, and toward the Out-Dweller. It wore a cruelly satisfied expression, or at least that is how Melanie interpreted the look on its face, as its whip did its work.

She swallowed and pushed herself to her feet. She wobbled for several heartbeats, but managed to retreat a step, both grateful that she was no longer the focus of the Out-Dweller's attention and ashamed by the truth she knew without a doubt.

Without Loran she could not prevail, and she would die here tonight. Or maybe not. The promise of being dragged to the beast's plane and tormented for its pleasure, forever, returned to its place at the front of her brain.

Melanie snarled, in anger at the horror that promise evoked within her and at the helplessness she had felt just moments ago, beneath the beast's gaze. And in frustration that she was going to have to come to Loran's aid. Again. It just was not fair. But there was no help for it.

She considered, and rejected, a number of components from within her pouch. All were for spells that she knew would be useless in this fight.

Light. She needed more light.

But she could not find any. No components for any illumination spell she knew remained within her pouch, and without them...

Her fingers closed on something soft, almost crumbly. Withdrawing the care-fully-wrapped object from the pouch, she brought it up to her nose and inhaled. She knew the sulfurous odor would be nearly enough to overpower her, knew what this material was for, but all the same she had to confirm it.

It had been months, more months than she wanted to think, since she had attempted this spell. It had been among the last Timon taught her, though truth be told she never had truly gotten the hang of it. She had forgotten she still had this component mixture at all; she must have grabbed it up by accident while she was packing her equipment for the night.

Fortunate that she had. If she could pull this spell off...

Loran cried out, more a shout of power and command than anything else, and for a moment the coiling snake-whip expanded as though being repulsed by some tremendous force. But then, just as quickly, the coils collapsed back down. Loran's next cry was one of anger and...fear? He did not have much time left, if he was letting that show.

Trying not to remind herself that she was about to save his sorry neck for the second time in one night, Melanie clapped her hands together, bursting the sulfur mixture's casing and smearing the concoction all over her palms. Then she turned so she could see the bonfire from the corner of her eye and raised her arms, one pointing at the bonfire and the other at the Out-Dweller.

Then she began her incantation

The pain lasted for an eternity, and just when it seemed it would never end, it got worse. It spread from his chest and shoulder to his arm to his belly to his leg to his other arm to both hands to his feet, and on and on until there was not a single part of his body that did not burn with agony. Any one of the points of pain would have been bearable. Any two or three, maybe. But dozens...

He vaguely recalled screaming, screaming until he had no more breath to scream with, despite the urge to scream all the more, all the louder. But it was all he could do to gasp in a what should have been a lung-full of air. But instead, all that came through was the barest of breezes, not nearly enough to satisfy his need. He tried again, somehow, but again it was not enough. Not enough to allow him to scream, and also not enough to quench his need for fresh air, though it was just enough to stop him from passing out

This new torment, the agony of being smothered without release, built upon his other pain until his entire world consisted of nothing else.

Had there ever *been* anything else?

He did not know; he could see nothing but blackness, hear nothing but that awful skittering sound and the last remnants of his scream, smell nothing but a rancid stink like rotting meat, think of nothing except for his torment, and the desperate need to escape it. But try though he might, he could not move to get away.

And so he lay there, a tiny part of his mind managing to wonder how long this could go on before he went well and truly mad.

There was no answer.

Time, if there was such a thing as time, slowed to a crawl, each moment an eternity of torment that was only eclipsed by the next. And then the next.

And then, all at once, something changed.

His foot ceased hurting. Then his lower leg. Slowly, but with a quickening pace, his other limbs and then his torso ceased their endless ache until, all at once, the last of the agony left him.

His lungs functioned again. He breathed in the largest gulp of air he ever had and cracked his eyes open.

A new agony assaulted him as light, light so bright it threatened to blind him, forced him to turn his head away and clench his eyes shut again.

A blessedly long moment devoid of pain passed, and he tried again. This time he could see without as much difficulty; the brilliant light had dimmed.

Regardless, he could make out details. A large fire burning off to his left. Trees at the edge of the darkness beyond it. And...things...black insectoid things scurrying away from him, or more correctly away from the source of that brilliant light and toward the shadows on all sides.

Revulsion filled him as he realized that those things had been all over him, that they were what had caused all his pain. He quickly felt all over himself, but could find no wounds, or any hint of one. So how...

A loud cry from the rear caused him to turn around.

A woman stood not far away. Dark-haired and lovely, wearing a dress that had once been fine but now was an irreconcilable mess and a frightened expression on her face. And to the left, a great mammoth beast that clutched some sort of whip in one hand.

The beast brought the whip down, and it coiled around a small man, who collapsed beneath the weight of the strange whip's coils.

It all came back to him in a rush. The Out-Dweller. Loran. The murders. Melanie.

Julian grunted and forced himself to stand, but only got as far as rolling over and pushing himself to his hands and knees when Melanie drew something from her belt pouch and rubbed it between her hands. Then she said a quick incantation, in a tone of voice he remembered from her so well: the tone that said she was trying not to show how frightened she was, and that fear made her angry.

Any sane man would stay away from a woman speaking in a tone like that.

She finished the incantation and waited. For a couple seconds, nothing happened. Then the heat from the bonfire at his back doubled, no tripled at least, and the entire area was bathed in a yellow-white glow that reminded Julian of a piece of metal that had just been withdrawn from a smith's forge.

The Out-Dweller recoiled from that burst of light, lifting its free hand to shield its eyes.

A heartbeat later, a horizontal column of white flame, as thick around as both of Julian's thighs put together, struck the beast in its chest. Strangely, it did not seem as though the flame was hurting it very much; no smoke rose from its chest, despite the scorching heat of the flame. All the same, the Out-Dweller stumbled backwards, raising its other hand to cover its eyes and letting the strange whip fall to the ground.

As soon as the whip's handle struck the ground, its coils exploded outward and

Loran rose from a crouch, his staff held in both hands in front of himself. He looked harried and he bled from his nose and the left side of his neck. But right then, the expression he wore was one of surprised amazement as he beheld the flame Melanie was directing against the Out-Dweller. His eyes flicked from the beast to the bonfire to Melanie, and he mouthed something soundlessly to himself.

Then, all at once, the great stream of fire winked out and the area was plunged back into comparative blackness.

Julian blinked, and for a moment could not make out anything at all while his eyes adjusted. Then, by the comparative dimness of the two floating globes of light, he saw the Out-Dweller beginning to recover itself, and his spirits sank. What happened to that fire?

He looked over his shoulder and saw that the bonfire, so large just a few minutes ago, had been reduced to little more than a softly-glowing pile of ash. A few larger coals smoldered in the center of the fire pit, but that was it. In a flash of insight, Julian realized what had happened. Melanie's spell had not created the fire, or lent it any extra power. It had merely sped up the rate it went through its fuel, consuming every scrap of it, and all the energy it contained, in a few moments, as opposed to the hours it would normally have taken to burn down.

Pretty impressive, but where did that leave them now? Right back where they started, from what Julian could tell.

The smart thing to do was run. Every fiber of his being told him to do that.

Across the way, Julian saw Raedrick stirring, pushing himself up. Melanie showed no signs of backing off, and annoyingly enough, Loran was stalking toward the Out-Dweller, his lips compressed into a determined scowl.

Muttering in annoyance about his lack of good sense, Julian boosted himself up onto his feet and grabbed up his dagger, which lay on the ground near his feet. Then, stumbling every other step and wishing again that he had his sword, he advanced.

❧ 34 ❧

THE CASTING OUT

Why had he bothered to grab his dagger? Julian did not fool himself: there was no way that small blade, well-constructed and finely-honed as it was, could do any real harm to the Out-Dweller. The beast was not of this world, and if Loran and Melanie's magics could do little more than stun it for a moment, the thought of his sword doing any better, let alone his dagger, was just laughable.

But laughable or not, Julian led with the tip of his blade as he charged. The Out-Dweller was not focused on him; the mages - Melanie was a mage, no matter what those asses in the Magestirium might say - received that honor. Maybe he could get that kidney strike in, after all.

On the opposite side of the brute, Raedrick had regained his feet, though he looked decidedly dazed. His scabbard was empty, his Tyrashi blade nowhere to be seen, but just that minute it looked like Raedrick had other concerns, namely not falling back down again.

It would be a while before he would be good for it. The fight would likely be over first. Too bad; it would have been nice to make a two-flank attack.

Oh well.

Julian's foot caught in a little hollow of earth and he stumbled, pinwheeling his arms and taking a quick hopping step to prevent landing on his face. As it was, he came to a halt about a dozen paces from the Out-Dweller, suddenly off his equilibrium.

It was then that he noticed one of the Out-Dweller's glowing red eyes, staring at him.

He was not sure how he knew it was watching him; the thing did not have pupils that Julian could see. But nonetheless, the thing had regained its balance and he was certain it was watching him with one eye, and the mages with the other three. Or really, two. It probably was keeping an eye on Raedrick as well.

The bottom fell out of Julian's stomach as he thought of how confusing it would be to interpret those disparate viewpoints. But apparently the Out-Dweller had none of the difficulty a human would, and that ruled out his being able to get in a surprise attack at the beast's flank.

A sound, almost like a crack of thunder but more short-lived and deeper, emanated from the Out-Dweller. Julian could have sworn it had snorted at his attempt. In...amusement?

And then the beast drew itself up to its full height and roared, baring the multitude of triangular, razor-sharp teeth that festooned its mouth. It was more like the impact from a shield-bash than a sound. It smacked into Julian's body and sent him stumbling backwards several steps, only quick backpedalling stopping him from falling over.

Raedrick, dazed as he still was, was not so quick, and he went over onto his backside. Melanie as well.

But when the roar reached Loran, a shimmering blue dome sprang to life all around him, glowing strongly for a half-second before fading into transparency once again.

The mage sniffed and looked at the Out-Dweller with a sneer. "Enough of this," he said in a smooth, calm voice. Whatever bumps and bruises he had taken so far tonight, they did not seem to have shaken his bravado. Then he spoke a single word that Julian did not understand and spun his staff over his head in a dizzying circular arc.

All around the flat area, candles, which had been lit when the group arrived before but had extinguished when the blackness rolled in, flickered to life, their little flames dim counterpoints to the two suspended balls of light. But somehow the candles' combined glow seemed stronger, more insistent, than those conjured balls.

The Out-Dweller blew out a hard breath through its nose - Julian had not noticed its nostrils before, two sets of vertical slits that lay between the pairs of eyes - and roared again. It was less loud this time, almost more tentative as though the beast were suddenly uncertain. Julian noticed one of its eyes tracking around toward the candles for a second.

And then it charged, straight toward Loran.

The Out-Dweller's hoofed feet tore great rivets in the ground as it rushed him, moving much faster than Julian would have thought a being of its bulk would be capable of. It closed the distance between itself and the mage in seconds and extended its arms, the great curved talons thrusting toward Loran. There was no way the mage could avoid being impaled, not as quickly as the beast had moved.

But somehow, when the Out-Dweller's talons reached him, Loran was no longer there. He vanished, reappearing six feet to his right, facing the Out-Dweller from its side.

Julian blinked in surprise, his jaw dropping open wide. What had Loran just done, and in the name of all that was holy, how?

This was no time to worry about it, however.

The Out-Dweller whirled toward Loran instantly. He was already within reach of the beast's great arms; again they lashed out toward him.

But Loran was the quicker. He spoke a hurried trio of words and thrust forward with his staff. What could only be called a hammer of light leapt from the end of his staff and struck at the beast even as it was bringing its arms down. Instead of tearing him to shreds, the Out-Dweller was lifted bodily off the ground and hurled backwards almost ten feet before it crashed to the ground on its back.

"Now, woman!" Loran barked.

Melanie had just regained her feet. She brushed her hair back from her face, clearing her vision, and cocked her head toward him, an eyebrow rising in an unspoken question.

Loran rolled his eyes disgustedly. "Hold it! Keep it on the ground!"

How in the hell was she supposed to do that?

Julian would have bet Melanie was wondering the same thing, but if she did she did not voice it. She merely nodded as though Loran had not just asked her to do the nigh-on impossible and stepped forward, one hand dipping into a pouch at her waist while the other pulled her notebook out and thumbed open a tabbed page.

Incredulity filled Julian. What was she going to do, read about it?

But he should have known better. She glanced at the page for the briefest of seconds, then began a quick, precise chant that took only slightly longer than the glance had been. The incantation culminated in her throwing a small object, the thing she had taken from her pouch Julian was sure, at the Out-Dweller, which was just beginning to get itself righted.

The object Melanie threw landed on the ground a pace away from the Out-Dweller, and for a second or two nothing happened.

The Out-Dweller got itself up onto its hands and knees and was beginning to push itself erect again. Julian's heart sank. Whatever the spell had been, it had not worked, or Melanie had missed.

Suddenly, the earth cracked open where the object Melanie threw landed. Great green shoots grew out of the crack, a half dozen of them, each twisting a different direction as it grew and each sprouting leaves as it went. The plant moved as though it were a sentient being, its shoots ensnaring the Out-Dweller in a dozen different ways between one breath and the next, and still it grew, its twining vines becoming more and more intricately interconnected until Julian could not tell where one of the shoots stopped and the next began.

Neither, apparently, could the Out-Dweller. It howled in fury, but Julian could also detect a note of frustration there as well, as the rapidly growing plant caught it in its embrace. The beast struggled, ripping at the plant with its talons and trying to pull away using sheer strength and mass.

At first, for all its thrashings, the Out-Dweller was well and truly caught. But the plant's growth slowed and then stopped, and within moments it became clear that the Out-Dweller would be the winner in the contest between the two of them.

But it would take time.

The Out-Dweller ripped a growth of vine off, but there were literally dozens more to remove before it would be free of the plant.

It was a brilliant spell. But was it brilliant enough? Julian looked away from the Out-Dweller toward the mages.

Melanie watched the Out-Dweller struggling to free itself, her face a mask of concentration, and Julian realized she still must be controlling the plant's actions in some way.

Loran, too, was deep in conversation, but he was also chanting, a deep, rhythmic incantation that rolled off his tongue barely any louder than if he were having a conversation over tea. And yet, those incantations fairly boomed with power. The candles all around them pulsed in time with his words, and the breeze began to pick up.

Slowly at first, but then faster and faster, the breeze became a gust and then a full-on wind that swirled all around the flattened area. The circle of candles flickered, their flames dancing in time with the wind's movements. Julian was sure they should have gone out, extinguished by the suddenly fierce blow, but instead the flames merely moved with the wind's motion. If anything, the little flames grew, becoming torches in their own right and bathing the entire area in a radiance that came to almost rival the morning just after sunrise.

The Out-Dweller bellowed and raised its arms almost reflexively against the suddenly more intense light all around it. For a second it lay stunned, but then it began thrashing all the more fiercely. It was as though the beast sensed that its time was short; it tore at the vines that trapped it in a fury, ripping them away two or three at a time, its monstrous talons and unmeasurable strength making the task appear easy all of a sudden.

And then it was free.

To his left, Melanie recoiled as though struck physically and stumbled backwards, landing awkwardly on her backside. She did not move, her expression stunned and her eyes unfocused.

The Out-Dweller bellowed again, in victory Julian thought this time, from its tone, and pushed itself to its feet. It spun, turning its quartet of burning eyes onto Loran.

The Inquisitor stood tall - well, as tall as he was capable of - and met the Out-Dweller stare for stare. And all the while he kept up his chant, his words coming forth in the same steady rhythm but increasing in volume and power with each breath.

The Out-Dweller stepped toward Loran, but its movement was far slower than it had been just a moment ago. It looked at him for a second, perplexed, then its gaze went skyward and its eyes widened.

Above the beast, the wind, which now was whipping past Julian to rival any storm he had ever seen had gathered up all of the loose dust and debris in the area. A funnel formed just above the Out-Dweller, sort of an inverted tornado. All around the Out-Dweller, bits of grass lifted up, struggling against their roots to join the vortex above. More dust and loose dirt flew upward all around the beast.

Then, in the middle of the funnel came a flash of light, like a single star giving birth, directly above the Out-Dweller.

The beast howled then, its earlier cry of victory becoming one of desperate denial.

The Out-Dweller fell forward, hitting the ground with a near deafening THUMP, and then dug into the earth with its talons. It roared again, as though trying to call on its reserves of strength.

All around the beast, debris, small at first and then larger, began rushing toward the flickering light at the vortex's center. Watching them go, faster and faster, Julian was surprised that he was not following with them. But strong as the wind was, he felt no greater force than he had before.

And yet now things that were clearly large, nearly as large as he, were being pulled into that light.

Every time one of them struck the light, it flashed a bit brighter and expanded, casting a pure white illumination on the area.

One of the objects flew past his shoulder and Julian saw a black carapace and multitudes of long, clutching legs and pinchers that tried to grab him before it, too, was consumed by the light. And he understood. Everything that was being drawn into the vortex was something the Out-Dweller had brought over into this plane with it.

And after they were gone, the Out-Dweller would be next.

The Out-Dweller knew this as well. It bellowed again and tried to dig its feet into the ground, but its hooves could not dig as well as its talons and they gained no purchase. Again crying in denial, it was helpless to prevent its feet from being drawn upward. Finally, it sat there like a gymnast Julian saw in a traveling show once, standing upright on just the palms of his hands. But this time, the Out-Dweller was working to hold itself in place, its talons dug in deeply, desperately.

But still the vortex pulled it upwards.

Slowly, inexorably, one of the Out-Dweller's hands pulled free from the earth. For a second, Julian thought that would be it, but the beast flailed around and its talons came to rest on something else that was lying on the ground nearby. Something limp and bony, dressed in the robes of a mage.

Telurian.

The Out-Dweller drew the hapless mage closer to itself and stared at him, its eyes filled with malevolent intent. Telurian jerked and then his eyes flew open, meeting the gaze of the Out-Dweller without any opportunity for defense.

Telurian's scream rang out, loud even above the howling tumult of the wind, the power of Loran's chant, and the rasping growl of the Out-Dweller's breathing. On and on the hapless mage screamed; though the Out-Dweller did nothing to him but hold him and look at him, it sounded as though he were being flayed alive, he screamed so. He began to spasm uncontrollably, his body flopping around like a puppet whose strings had been cut.

The Out-Dweller smiled slightly, a look of pure, evil enjoyment.

And then its other hand lost its grip on the earth, and the beast flew upwards into the vortex and the brilliant light at its center. The Out-Dweller struck the light, and it flared all the greater, lighting the area more intensely than the sun could have a noon.

And then the light was gone, and with it the storming wind and the struggling beast from the outer planes. Only Telurian remained. He seemed to hover in midair for several seconds, but then he fell to the ground.

The thud of his body landing seemed far louder than it should have in the absolute silence that followed.

❦ 35 ❦

FLOTSAM AND JETSAM

Julian stood there, speechless. What could he say? His mind struggled to wrap itself around what had just happened, but it could not get there. He swallowed and tried a different tack. The Out-Dweller was gone. That much seemed certain.

That reality crept into his psyche, and all of a sudden relief flooded through him like a river past a dam that had been breeched. When he charged that thing with only his little dagger for a weapon, he truly had not though he would see the next hour, let alone the next ten minutes. And yet, here he stood, and the Out-Dweller had, apparently, been vanquished.

He was on his knees. When that happened, Julian could not say. But right then, it did not seem inappropriate.

"It worked." Melanie sounded just as relieved as he did, but when Julian turned his head to look at her, she was still on her feet. Showoff.

"Of course it worked." Loran sniffed contemptuously as he replied, then strolled, apparently without care as though he had just finished his early afternoon tea, over toward where Telurian lay. He stopped when he reached the other mage and looked down at him, frowning for a long moment before squatting down next to him.

Melanie crossed her arms under her breasts and stared at him, not at all pleased by his response. "You're welcome," she said, finally, no small amount of scorn in her tone.

Loran glanced at her and shook his head slightly, but did not reply. Telurian had his entire attention. Loran felt alongside the other mage's neck for his pulse, then forced his eyelid open. He peered into Telurian's eye for a long while, then sighed. He released the fallen mage and stood, wiping his fingers on his cloak as though he had dragged them through mud, his expression deeply saddened.

"Is he alive?" Raedrick asked. He had regained his footing and his equilibrium, and he stood facing Loran with his best all-business expression on his face.

Loran shrugged. "After a fashion."

"Meaning what?"

Loran turned a cool gaze on Raedrick and was silent for several seconds. Then he sighed and lowered his eyes to again look at Telurian's prone form. "His body lives. And will, if history carries out, accept food and water when forced to. But his essence...his mind..." Loran shook his head and grimaced. "We do not know whether he still lurks somewhere within his body, insanely driven to hide away from the world, or whether the Out-Dweller drew him out and bore him back into the netherworld with it."

Julian shuddered at the thought of going to wherever the Out-Dweller came from. It could only be horrid, being there. He flashed back to the feeling of the Out-Dweller's cronies crawling all over him, hurting him everywhere and depriving him even of breath even as they blotted out any shred of light and beauty. Horrid would not even begin to describe what it would be like to live where those things dwelled.

He cleared his throat. "Sounds like this has happened before."

Loran glanced Julian's way and nodded. "There are some historical accounts, but none match what Telurian did. At least none within the last four centuries." He sighed. "I had thought...hoped...that he had only contacted a lesser being from the dark planes, and that he had bound the creature to his will, to do evil according to his whims."

"Didn't he?"

Loran shook his head in response to Raedrick's words. "Did you not see that creature? Did you not hear Telurian's words?" He gestured at the prone man, who was beginning to drool all over himself. "Telurian was far from the strongest man I ever taught, but even he could have dealt with one of the lesser Out-Dwellers. No," he shook his head again, "somehow he invited a Lord of the netherworld over, and very quickly *it* overwhelmed *him* and twisted him to its will." He lowered his eyes, sadly. "And now he has paid the price."

Loran was silent for a long moment. Then he drew in a deep breath, through his nostrils, and looked back up at Raedrick, then Julian. "I will need your help to get him back to town." His eyes held a question, nearly a pleading, and a deep sorrow that Julian would not have expected from a man who had been sent to hunt down a criminal.

Then Julian remembered that Loran said Telurian had studied beneath him at some point. Almost against his will, Julian found he could understand, even relate, to Loran's pain. He had helped train many young recruits who showed up to his unit, barely trained and completely unprepared for the realities of life along the battle lines. More of those young men - Julian refused to allow himself to admit that they were not really all that much younger than he was himself - died on the battlefield because he and his fellows did not have time to prepare them adequately than he liked to recall.

But he did recall the ache in his heart...in his soul...every time one of them passed, far too early and far too uselessly.

Julian nodded his assent. He would help carry Telurian's body - and it was just a body, little more than mobile flesh, if his mind truly had been sucked away by that beast - back to town. Much as he disliked Loran, he could not deny the bond the inquisitor felt for his former student, and Julian could not turn his back on that.

Melanie, however...

"What do you mean, he's paid the price?" Her tone was hot, the sort of hot that Julian had learned over the last several months of knowing her foretold that the person she was speaking to was treading on extremely - extremely- dangerous ground. "You're not going to just let him go on living, after what he did?"

Her words were met only be silence for a time. Julian thought about responding, to explain things, but found he did not have the words. He looked over at Raedrick and saw that his one-time squad leader was in a similar quandary; he understood the root of Loran's feelings, just as Julian did, and that emotion conflicted with his innate desire to see justice done.

And how could justice be done while Telurian breathed, when so many of his victims did not?

Finally, Loran answered. His tone was cold, and he looked at Melanie with the contempt one normally reserves for the lowliest of slaves. "I mean what I say, woman." He imparted the word "woman" with such scorn and derision that, for a moment, Julian thought he would perhaps vomit from having to voice such a word. Then he continued, in a more normal tone. Cold, but normal. "The torment he endures at the hands of the Out-Dweller far surpasses any that we mortals could inflict." He scowled slightly, then added, "But if perchance he somehow managed to escape that fate, and he comes back to his senses, he will stand trial and be punished according to the law."

With that, he turned his back on Melanie and once again squatted down next to Telurian.

"You believe he really was brought over with the beast." Raedrick was stating a fact, not asking a question.

Loran nodded, saying nothing more.

Raedrick returned the nod, his face solemn. The two men shared a long look. Then finally, Raedrick nodded again, and Loran inclined his head, his lips turning upwards into a slight smile of gratitude. Raedrick took a moment to locate his blade. He sheathed it and walked over to Telurian's body. Then he and Loran together lifted the fallen mage, and they began the long trek back to town.

Julian stayed behind with Melanie for a time. She had not budged from the spot where she stood, watching the Inquisitor and the Constable walking away with their burden. It took Julian a minute or two to realize she was crying. Or at least tears were dripping from her eyes.

"Are you alright?"

Melanie sniffed. "That man killed dozens, or more. And *he* lets him live." She drew herself up and inhaled quickly, steeling her expression into something that resembled a statue. "Timon was guilty only of teaching me what I wanted to learn, and they tortured him to death for it." She turned her head and looked at Julian, her eyes tight with suppressed pain and anger. "Do you call that justice, Julian?"

She did not wait for his answer, but went stalking after the two men, and their burden.

Julian lingered for a time, watching them go.

He had no good answer to her question.

✳ 36 ✳

FAREWELLS

The grooms lifted Telurian into his saddle. The mage went along limply, almost sliding off the horse altogether before the two young men got him properly situated. They lingered for a few moments, watching him warily as though expecting him to slump over and fall off any second.

And small wonder. The mage just sat there, staring blankly at the area in front of himself, his face expressionless and his mouth hanging slightly open. A drop of drool slowly began to accumulate at the corner of his mouth, but he did not lift a hand to stop it. In fact, his hands never left his saddle horn; he had not even taken hold of the horse's reins.

If it were not for the dark blue robes, almost black, that he wore, and the golden necklace around his neck that announced his status as a member of the Magesterium, no one would take him for such a lofty personage.

But not so lofty any more.

Loran regarded the young grooms with a disapproving frown and waved them away. One of them opened his mouth to object, no doubt still concerned that Telurian would fall, but the look on Loran's face stopped him. The groom bobbed his head in a quick half-bow, then hurried away after his comrade, who had fled as soon as Loran indicated he should.

Julian did not watch them go. He stood beside Raedrick, across The Oarlock's stableyard from where Loran and his erstwhile fugitive were, and watched the Inquisitor's actions closely.

They were there to make sure Loran and Telurian left town quickly, and caused no more trouble as they did. And to make sure they avoided one particular bit of trouble more than any other.

Loran scowled after the grooms, then flung his saddlebags over his own horse's back. He cinching up his own robes before mounting - he had worn his formal attire for departure, and not just because he had met with the Mayor earlier in the morning to bid farewell. And so the Mayor could try to do some damage control.

297

Small chance of that.

Loran grabbed the reins of Telurian's horse and wrapped them around his own saddle horn, then made a soft clucking noise that just barely carried to Julian's ear. His horse began walking forward at a slow walk, and Loran nudged it to the left, toward the open gateway leading out to the street. As he turned, his eyes alighted on Julian and Raedrick, and his expression grew a bit more dark than it had been before.

Loran pulled his horse to a halt when he was a few paces away from them and nodded quickly, the short nod of superior to subordinate, one meant to remind the subordinate of his place.

"Constables. Here to see me off, I presume."

Raedrick returned the nod with one that was deep enough to convey respect but shallow enough to discount the difference in stature between them. "Just making sure you have all that you need."

Loran sniffed, and was silent for a moment. His eyes moved slowly from Raedrick to Julian and back, but aside from that his expression did not change.

"You do not trust that I will do as we agreed and leave your...woman...alone." His tone was neutral, but his eyes flashed with anger, and scorn. He did not like this arrangement one bit. That was hardly surprising.

"I did not say that." Raedrick, too, kept his tone neutral.

Loran rolled his eyes quickly. "I am a man of my word." He nudged his horse, turning it away from Julian and Raedrick, toward the gate. Then he paused, looking back at them. "Were I you, I would reconsider my choice of friends. A woman driven to revenge, against people who have not wronged her, is not..."

Julian could not help it. He interrupted Loran's words, speaking hotly. "You killed her lover."

Loran shook his head. "I brought a man to justice who was guilty of crimes against the King and the Magestirium. That this Timon was her lover was unfortunate. For her. But there was no malice meant in it."

"How can you say that?"

Loran looked at Julian like he was daft. "This man you fought some months ago. Isenholf. Did you bear malice toward his family and friends when you sent him to the gallows?"

Julian felt the wind taken out of his sails by Loran's words, and he closed his mouth without replying. No, he did not think about Isenholf's family at all when he put him on the cart for Mangin City, where a Magistrate who was empowered to deal with Capital cases held court. He would have preferred to settle it all locally, but their judge was only commissioned to handle more mundane issues. Julian supposed the powers that be in the Kingdom decided towns as small as Lydelton would not have to deal with those offenses, or at least not often enough to warrant the extra cost of a higher Magistrate and his staff.

But that was neither here nor there. Loran was right. Julian had not thought at all about the people who would be sorry to see good old Theobald hanged. Although, he could not fathom there were that many who fit the bill. But there must have been *someone*.

Loran smiled, ever so slightly, seeing that he had scored a point. "You see? We are not as different as you would like to think, Constable Hinderbrook." He returned his gaze to Raedrick. "Of course, at the time we did not know the full extent of Timon's crimes, or of Mistress Klemins' participation in them. Had we..." He paused, meaningfully, then said, "Good health to you, Constables." Then he turned his back and nudged his horse's flanks with his heels.

The steed set off at a walk, and Telurian's horse followed suit. A moment later, the two men were gone from view.

"Do you really believe he won't tell his people about Melanie?" Julian said.

Raedrick frowned and shook his head, but said nothing. His eyes tracked toward where Loran must have been, had he followed the most efficient course toward Main Street and then out of town.

"Me neither."

Melanie's shop was open, for a wonder. It felt to Julian as though it had been closed for months, with all that had happened. Strange to think it had only been a few days.

He pushed the door open and stepped within, then paused for a moment, inhaling the odor of some exotic incense and smiling. Melanie always knew how to keep a welcoming feel about her place, but she had never burned this particular incense before. Or at least, Julian did not recognize it. It smelled expensive, though.

Melanie was seated on a stool behind her counter. She wore a simple but elegant green dress that was embroidered with flowers and birds around the ends of the sleeves and about her neck. She was reading a small book, but she looked up as the door swung closed behind Julian.

Upon seeing him, she quirked an eyebrow upwards and smiled, ever so slightly. "Julian."

"Feeling better?"

She shrugged, the smile leaving her face as quickly as it came. "Not particularly."

He walked over to the counter. There were a few nicknacks in a small bin at the counter's end, and he rummaged through them for a short while, trying to figure the right way to say this.

Melanie looked at him askance, but said nothing.

Finally, Julian decided to just put it out there. "Loran left town a couple hours ago."

He expected a reaction, but an almost un-caring shrug was not it. "So I heard."

Julian looked at her more closely. Her expression was nonchalant, but that indifference did not make it to her eyes. They were slightly bloodshot, and the bottom of her nose slightly reddened, as though she had the sniffles. Five to one odds she had cried herself to sleep the night before, and again on waking this morning.

He was not stupid enough to say that to her face, of course.

"I more than halfway expected you to make a try for him before he left. Wasn't that your plan?"

She frowned and looked away from Julian, toward the case of remedies in the center of her shop. "He knew I was coming, or he must have. He would have made preparations, and he is more than my match in a stand-up fight." She inhaled through her nose - that sounded suspiciously like a sniffle - then turned back to him and smiled more broadly. But again the smile did not reach her eyes. "The point was to get even, not to kill myself."

Julian nodded understanding. Melanie was no fool. He had overstated things a bit; he had been far from halfway expecting her to attack Loran. More like a third-way, or a quarter. All the same, though, she had been practically bursting at the seems a few times over the course of the night before last. And if...

But she had not. That was the important part. Well, *an* important part.

The other part was much more difficult.

He drew a deep breath. "Loran knows where you are now."

Melanie nodded, the smile fading again. Her eyes widened ever so slightly, and she suddenly looked nervous.

"I don't believe he'll hold that information back from the Magestirium and neither does Raedrick. Maybe it would be best if..."

Melanie held up a silencing hand, looking beyond nervous toward frightened. "Don't."

"Melanie, I..."

"Don't send me away, Julian."

Looking at her, he saw an openness, a...vulnerability...that he had never seen in her before. The facade of supreme confidence bordering on arrogance, the sense of quiet strength coupled with worldliness and knowledge that she normally projected was gone. All that remained was a woman suddenly afraid of losing... Losing what?

She sniffed again, and blinked to stop upwelling tears, but she was not success-ful. "I've finally made a home here. It's been so long since..." She wiped her eyes and coughed out a half-laugh that rang with self-directed disgust. She drew herself up, drawing a deep breath. "I'm not going anywhere. So don't try to suggest I do anything different."

And she was back, just like that. The stare she directed at Julian was challeng-ing, daring him to push the topic.

"They'll send someone for you. Maybe several someones. You know that."

She nodded.

"And us as well, for harboring you."

That made her flinch, but the challenging stare never wavered.

Julian looked her in the eye for a few seconds, and as usual could not stop admi-ration from welling up within him. And not just for her looks, which would normally be enough in and of themselves. He was not sure he could stay firm like this in the face of what she faced, especially having witnessed what the Mage-stirium was capable of with Timon.

No, he was certain he could not stand firm. He, and Raedrick as well, had fled the consequences of his actions in the Army, rather than stay and face the heads-man's axe.

That admiration just got larger.

"Just wanted to make sure we were all clear on that."

Melanie smiled again, ever so slightly, then nodded.

Julian returned the nod, then walked over to the the door. He reached for the latch, but paused and looked back at her. "See you at The Oarlock later?"

Melanie smiled at him, and for the first time since he walked in it seemed the smile was genuine. "Wouldn't miss it."

Julian returned the smile with a grin of his own, then he opened the door and went out. There was a town to see to, after all.

TOLLARD'S PEAK

MICHAEL KINGSWOOD

TOLLARD'S PEAK

A man from Raedrick Baletier and Julian Hinderbrook's past turns up on the outskirts of Lydelton, nearly dead from exposure and telling of an injured comrade on the flanks of Tollard's Peak, the tallest mountain in the region.

Despite the harsh winter conditions, the constables form a rescue party and set off to find the injured man.

But the elements are not the only danger that waits to strike down the unwary in the mountains surrounding Glimmer Vale.

FAMILY COUNSELING

Raedrick Baletier glared at the two men before him and shook his head. This was foolishness, and he expected better, even from them.

They stood, cowed and mostly staring at the floor in front of their feet, in the front room of the Constable's office, a small building that he and Julian Hinderbrook shared as their place of work. The two men were dressed similarly, in bedraggled tunics and breaches; the man on the left in predominately greys and browns, on the right in blue and white. Or at least those had likely been their colors originally. Now their material could better be called stained, it was so covered in grime. They wore matching beards, at least two weeks' worth, and had similar eyes of grey-blue. The rest of their appearances were equally identical: their height, their breadth of shoulder, their lack of a paunch despite their advancing years, their retreating hairlines…

Men such as they, with as many years behind them as they had, should have known better than to get into a brawl in a pub over a woman. Especially over a woman like Yleen Henery, who was young enough to be the daughter of either of the brothers who now looked so abashed in his office.

"Giorg," Raedrick said, and the man on the left gave a little start in recognition of his name. "Pedros." The other man jerked, in the same way that Giorg had a moment before. "What were you two thinking?"

The question sat there in the air between the three of them, unanswered but also somehow unable to depart. It lingered in the air, daring one of the brothers to challenge its primacy over this moment.

Neither did.

Raedrick sighed. "You know I could bring you both up before Judge Telmon."

The pair nodded, in unison.

"Well? Why should I not? You made a mess of Molli's tap room today."

For the first time since Julian, the other of Lydelton's Constables and Raedrick's long-time partner, bundled them into the building, the two brothers glanced at each other. Furtively, as though feeling each other out. But that was a start, at least.

Giorg cleared his throat. "See, it was like this, Constable."

Pedros interrupted. "I've been seeing Yleen for a week now, and he's jealous!" He stretched out a hand toward his brother, his index finger pointing accusingly. Just the way a three year-old would do.

Readrick rolled his eyes and exchanged looks with Julian. The lean man had close-cut brown hair and wore calf-high boots, tight light-brown leggings, a plain white shirt, open at the collar, and green coat that was lined with yellow thread about the cuffs and collar. He leaned against the side of his desk, which lay opposite Raedrick's, his arms crossed over his chest nonchalantly and his lips turned up in a sardonic grin. He winked, and Raedrick had to restrain himself from grinding his teeth in irritation.

He took his irritation out on the twins. Julian may have added the spark that set the tinder ablaze, but they were to blame for stacking the tinder in the first place, so Raedrick did not feel particularly guilty about it.

"I happen to know," he said, in the most biting tone he could muster right then, "that Yleen is all but promised to the young smith's apprentice who works with Fredlin on the east side."

The pair blanched, but said nothing.

Raedrick scowled all the deeper. "You want to tell me why she would be interested in either of you, when she could instead spend her time with him?" Fredlin was just about ready to send his apprentice off on his own. The young man was good-looking - more than good-looking, truth be told - and by all appearances highly skilled and motivated. Small wonder that he was well known as probably the most eligible bachelor in Lydelton.

The brothers traded glances. Silence reigned for a full minute. Then Giorg cleared his throat.

"It's like this, Constable. She smiled and gave me too much change back at lunch."

"She gave me an extra pour of whiskey two nights ago!" Pedros piped up, his tone affronted, almost challenging.

Giorg scowled and drew himself up.

Unbelievable. They were going to fight again, right here in the office. Raedrick glanced past them and saw Julian covering his mouth with his left hand, unsuccessfully trying to hide a broad grin as he clearly attempted to hold back guffaws over the two brothers' cluelessness.

Raedrick rubbed at the bridge of his nose with the thumb and index finger of his left hand, willing an impending headache to stop before he could actually feel it. A headache was the last thing he needed to deal with.

"Gentlemen," he said, using his best parade ground tone, the tone and volume that could cut through the varied sounds and distractions of the grounds to reach his men's ears without difficulty.

They two brothers stopped their glaring and clenching of fists and looked at him, a single eyebrow on each man's forehead rising so similarly that for a second Raedrick wondered whether he was just looking at one man, reflected in a mirror.

He shook his head, focusing in on Giorg, since he had been the instigator. "You do realize that, as a waitress, she had to be nice to her customers, so she can get a larger tip?" He turned his eyes toward Pedros, whose triumphant smile faded immediately when his eyes met Raedrick's. "Or that she might pour more into a customer's cup for the same reason?"

The brothers glowered for a moment, then shook their heads as one.

Raedrick sighed again. "Well, they do." He put on a forced smile and looked the brothers in the eye, one at a time. "Trust me, gentlemen. She is well and truly caught. You need to set your sights elsewhere."

"And if you must fight it out, take it outside," Julian added from behind them. He was still unsuccessful in hiding his disdain for the pair of men.

The brothers looked over their shoulders at Julian and nodded, their expressions rueful.

"Any questions?" Raedrick asked.

Giorg and Pedros looked back at him and shrugged, then shook their heads.

"Good. Now. You're going to pay Molli for the damage you did to her taproom. If I hear from her that you haven't..." He left the threat unstated.

The brothers' faces dropped even further than they had been before.

Raedrick paused for a moment, then continued, "Don't let this happen again or I really will throw you in front of the judge, just to see what he does with you."

The men's eyes widened, going from grudging respect to outright fear in a heartbeat. Poor fellows. They had been in the wrong place at the wrong time, and had gotten the short-end of the intellect stick for decades. But they were not bad people. Not really.

All the same, Raedrick could not have them starting fights in The Oarlock. Even if Molli had not been a friend, The Oarlock was a prominent local business, and it was the Constable's job to maintain the peace.

The twins each made a half-bow and turned away, hurrying out the door as though afraid Raedrick would follow through on his threat right then and there. They hardly glanced at Julian as they left, and his grin faded a bit.

"Well," Julian said, after the door swung shut behind the pair. "How long do you think until we have to deal with them again?" He shook his head and boosted himself off his desk, then sauntered over to the wood stove in the rear corner of the office. Flipping open the little door on its side, he grabbed a piece of seasoned wood from a small stack nearby and shoved it inside the stove. The fire within, which had been on the wane, flared to life again with the soothing popping that always comes from fresh fuel.

"A fortnight at most," Raedrick said. He leaned back in his chair and clasped his hands behind his head, looking up at the ceiling. "Some people have misfortune and trouble follow them, no matter what they try to do to avoid it."

Julian snorted and looked over his shoulder at Raedrick. "There's also people who seek it out, whether they realize it or not." He rubbed his hands in front of the stove for a couple seconds then nodded to himself and moved back over to his desk. He slumped into the chair and kicked one booted foot up. The boot was still soaked with water that a few minutes ago had been snow, and several drops fell onto the blotter that was the primary decoration on Julian's desk.

Readrick nodded. "Granted." He sighed and looked down at his own desk. It was only slightly more cluttered than Julian's. Truth told, their lives as co-Constables of Lydelton were not particularly busy, aside from the routine reports they owed to the Mayor's office. He had seen the offices of big city Constables; they were always covered with files of the cases they were working. Not so for him. His desk held just his blotter, a feather pen and an ink pot, and a small calendar. It was this last that drew Raedrick's attention. He looked at the date, and in particular the date for tomorrow, and sighed again, with more resignation.

"Getting to be that time again," Julian said, his normally cheerful voice growing more somber.

"It is."

Julian cleared his throat. "We don't have to do it, you know."

Raedrick looked askance at him, raising an eyebrow.

"We're in a good place now. There's no need…"

"You know better than that."

Julian frowned, and for a second Raedrick thought he was going to argue more. For what it was worth, Raedrick understood what he was saying, and part of him agreed. Or wanted to, anyway. But it was too soon to set their tradition aside, for many reasons.

Finally, Julian nodded. "All right." He stood and smoothed his tunic then headed toward the door leading to the street. "I'll see you dark and early then," he said. He paused to pull a heavy wool cloak from its peg by the door and settle the garment over his shoulders. Then he stomped his boots into a pair of crampons and flicked the cowl of his cloak up. He looked back at Raedrick, questioningly.

Raedrick returned the nod. "First light. At the end of dock one."

Julian flashed a grin that did not reach his eyes then pulled the door open.

Outside, a bitter wind was blowing, sweeping the snow that had collected along the sides of the street into long drifts and now into their office as well. Julian shivered and pulled his cloak tight around himself. Then, after a long moment, he stepped out into the dimming light of the late winter afternoon. He pulled the door to behind himself as he went, and it shut with the familiar click of the latch catching hold.

Raedrick sat still at his desk. His eyes drifted toward toward the wood stove, where the flickering fire within was just visible through narrow slits that allowed air to flow in. He watched the fire burn and let his thoughts wander. But they never were able to stray far from that horrible day, two years earlier. The day when his world had changed forever, and when he had walked away from any hope of ever having honor again.

Or so he had thought.

Weariness welled up, sparked by the enchanting light of the flames and stoked by his memories, until gradually his eyelids fell and he drifted off into sleep, and the memories of long ago.

❦ 2 ❦

BACK IN THE DAY

Hinderbrook reined in his horse next to Raedrick and made a quick salute, his working uniform stained and dirty over top his mail and his cloak, torn in several places, billowing in the chill wind. The salute was not needed now - in truth, it never had been; Raedrick was no officer - but old habits die hard. Raedrick did not correct him; he just returned the salute.

"What news?"

Hinderbrook rested his hands on his saddle horn and leaned toward him, his normally cheerful eyes somber, troubled. "I think we've lost them. There's been no sign since three days ago, and..."

"You can't know that for certain. They could be just over the next ridge, lying in wait." Tolburt piped up, interrupting the scout's report, and no matter the breach in etiquette. What did such things matter now?

Hinderbrook snorted at the younger man's statement - and Tolburt *was* young; only three months on the front with their unit, and before that he had enlisted at the earliest possible age - and cast a derisive eye his way. "Maybe when you get a little stubble on your chin, you'll figure out how stupid that sounds. I've -"

Raedrick held up a hand and snapped, "Enough."

Hinderbrook fell silent, and Tolburt shut his mouth before speaking the retort that had to have been building on his lips. Both men looked away from each other and focused on Raedrick. Everyone did. All around, the other half-dozen of what remained of Raedrick's squad looked at him intently. Fear, shame, grim determination, but no hope, competed for dominance on their faces.

No hope.

Why should they have any hope? They had done the unthinkable: abandoned their posts, deserted their unit, and in the process killed several of their former comrades. And at least one officer. They could never go back; that would mean the gallows or worse. They could not go home; that would mean the same. Go over to the enemy? That did not even bear consideration. Even if they wouldn't have been killed on sight, why would the enemy welcome them at all? They would certainly never trust them, or allow them to truly join their ranks.

So what could they do? Where could they go, now that they had cast their lot?

Already men had left Raedrick's band. He had not tried to stop them. What right had he to dictate any man's actions now, after what he had led them into? Frankly, he was amazed they all had not left. But men cling to what they know, and there was safety in numbers, especially for men such as they.

He drew a deep breath. "Peace, Tolburt. Let Hinderbrook finish his report."

Hinderbrook nodded quickly, then resumed, Tolburt apparently forgotten. For now. But Raedrick had no doubt Hinderbrook would rib the younger man mercilessly later on. It was all in good fun, of course.

Fun. There was another thing that once had been easy to find, but now seemed lost for all time.

"As I said, no sign. Could be they've called off the hunt."

"Small chance of that," said Kilfer, from Raedrick's right.

Raedrick shot Kilfer a hard look, and the sandy-haired man flashed an apologetic grin. He was right, though. The Army generally did not make it a policy to actively hunt deserters; they tended to show up sooner or later when they got in trouble again - those kinds of men always do - and then they could be taken into custody again easily.

Those kinds of men. His kind of men now.

Raedrick put that thought out of his head, focusing on the immediate problem. It was true that no pursuit was generally conducted, but never before had an entire unit deserted. Raedrick supposed that earned him - and his men - a bit more notoriety and thus more direct attention than the usual discontented riffraff or cowards who generally made up the ranks of deserters.

What he had done, he had done for a reason. A good reason.

It almost helped, telling himself that.

"How far back did you go?" Raedrick asked, turning his attention back to Hinderbrook.

Hinderbrook shrugged. "About a half-day's ride."

Raedrick frowned, considering.

"Maybe he's right." Shermyn murmured.

"Could be," Raedrick replied. He turned to Laremy. "Get the map."

Laremy nodded and opened his saddlebag. He rifled around in there for a few seconds, then pulled out a rolled up piece of parchment, which he brought over to Raedrick and unrolled onto a moderate-sized rock that protruded from the ground.

Raedrick squatted down, frowning at the map. It was no great piece of cartography; a squad leader does not rate those. Hand drawn, copied from the real maps kept by the general's staff, it only showed the major features of the area immediately around the current area of operations. In this case, it extended only as far east as Ysoldor, the Kingdom's western-most outpost, though it could hardly be said to reside within the Kingdom's borders at all. The next city worthy of the title that the Kingdom claimed, and that the Kingdom truly held dominion over, lay a good two months' ride further east.

The rest of the map's features were less familiar. The great sea to the south, the mountains to the north, and the enemy's strongholds and cities to the west and northeast. There were many places they could go, and a few that may offer the promise of refuge; they might be able to hire on to a ship at one of the ports along the sea and sail to some distant land where no one would know or care about what they had done.

All the same, Raedrick's eyes kept drifting back to Ysoldor and beyond, to the east. Toward home.

But going that direction was madness.

"I think you're right, Kilfer," Raedrick said, earning a quirked eyebrow in response. He managed a wry grin. "The ships are our best bet." He traced a line from the little X where Larmey had marked his best approximation of their current position to the nearest port city, a place called Qoramyr. "We ought to be able to make it in a week or less, if we ride hard."

Kilfer smiled, the first genuine smile Raedrick had seen on his face in more days than he wanted to count.

"Thought you'd never see the light."

Raedrick shrugged. "I wanted to be sure before..." He left the rest of the thought go unstated.

All around, his men nodded slowly, their faces solemn. Only Kilfer seemed to relish the notion of taking the ships. For the rest, taking that route would be as it was for Raedrick: a trip with no return, their homes forever lost to them. As long as they remained on the mainland, there was at least the slight hope that perhaps they could return someday. But if they left...

Raedrick sighed and stood from his crouch, pulling his vest down over his hips better. No sense dwelling on what could not be. They needed to get going if they had any hope of getting there without being caught.

"Saddle up,"

His men dispersed to their mounts. Within five minutes, they were gone, leaving no trace behind except tracks in the turf.

As they rode away, Raedrick looked back at the little hillock that had been his, and his men's, home for the last several days. Professional pride over his people's ability to remove all sign of their presence fell beneath a deep and abiding sadness. Would they ever again have a place to call home, where they could actually set down roots?

In the lands beyond the sea. If there was any hope at all, it lay there.

He straightened in his saddle and faced forward, then spurred his horse to greater speed, not daring to allow himself to believe in that hope, beckoning like a will o' the wisp in the dark.

Ten minutes later, even that tiny shred of hope withered and died.

Raedrick and his men rounded a fair-sized hill - they road around its base instead of riding over it, to avoid standing out to any spying eyes - and found themselves face to face with a platoon of the Kingdom's Elite Guards.

Fifty soldiers in mail and plate, their armor gleaming in the afternoon sunlight, their banners whipping gently in the breeze, sat mounted in a semicircle blocking the path ahead and avenues of escape to the sides.

Raedrick reined in, his heart in his throat, before the gruff voice of the Guards' commander could order it. This the worst of all possible things that could have happened. The Guards, lying in wait for them. How?

He jerked on his reins, to turn his horse and gallop back the way they came, but no sooner did he get the animal's head around than he saw a second platoon fanning out behind them, cutting off any retreat.

Laremy drew his sword. "We can cut through." He voice trembled slightly, the only hint of nervousness in his demeanor; coming from him, that indicated absolute terror.

Raedrick reached for his saber. It was hopeless, but better to go out fighting, as a free man, than to await the end in the prison at Divisional Headquarters.

Cold steel, honed to a razor's edge, came to rest upon his throat, stopping him. Raedrick turned his head, ever so slowly, to see his attacker, and all hope, all will to fight or even try any more, left him.

Tolburt swallowed, beads of sweat forming on his brow quickly, despite the afternoon's relative coolness. What he did terrified the young man, but he did not lower the blade, nor did it tremble at all in his hand.

"I'm sorry, Corporal," Tolburt said.

And then the Guards moved in.

MAKING THE ROUNDS

Raedrick jerked awake. For a moment, he was unsure where he was. Then his mind absorbed his surroundings: the long room with a plain desk opposite the one he sat behind. The rack of swords behind the other desk and the wood stove in the corner to its right. The cabinet of files next to a door made of steel bars that led further back into the building.

His office.

Embarrassment flooded through him. He had not realized he fell asleep. It must have been the late night last night, out with Molli and Lani, Molli's daughter and partner in the running of the Oarlock, and Raedrick's...he was not sure what to call their relationship. More than friendship certainly. But beyond that... He shook his head. The remaining fatigue from their fun combined with the fire and the memories coming back must have lulled him. And in the middle of the afternoon, as well. That simply would not do.

Raedrick glanced at the window.

Dim light still shown from outside; he must not have slept very long, thank goodness. There was still work to be done today, preparations for tomorrow morning. He could understand Julian's reluctance, his desire to move on, put the past aside. But Raedrick still felt the need to pay homage. Maybe someday it would be different, but not now.

He shook his head with a snort and pushed himself to his feet. That was enough grousing. He ought to make one last sweep of the town before it got dark.

Raedrick took a moment to buckle on his sword belt, strap on his crampons, and slip on his cloak, thick black wool that was lined in some sort of softer fabric that prevented the itching that he always hated about wool. Then he tugged on his gloves and slipped out the door.

The wind, if anything, was even worse than it had been before. He had to brace himself against its force to make headway toward Main Street, and his cloak constantly threatened to flap open, exposing him to winter's icy embrace. He hunched over, resigning himself to making slow progress and questioning the wisdom of going back outside again.

But he had a job to do.

Main Street's paving stones presented a different challenge than the dirt - well, dirt below the layers of snow and ice that had accumulated over the winter - of the side street that housed the Constable's office building. The fishing guild, and others whose normal jobs offered little in the way of employment during the winter months, did a better job of keeping the stones clear of snow than the dirt. But the stones also made for a more ready surface for ice to cling to. Thus, it was always a challenge walking anywhere. Very early in this, their first winter in Lydelton, Readrick and Julian had learned the value of strapping crampons onto their boots, even in town.

Raedrick turned east and began walking. The street was empty of people; everyone else had the sense to stay inside where it was warm.

Why don't you?

Raedrick smirked at his own foolishness, then pressed on to the edge of town, where Main Street ended and turned into the dirt road that stretched southeast from Lydelton along the shore of Lake Glimmermere to the Eastflow.

He always started on the east edge of town and moved west during his sweeps. No particular reason why, except maybe that was the direction Isenholf's band of brigands had come from, all those months ago when Raedrick and Julian had helped defend the town from them.

He wondered how Isenholf had met his end. When he went to the gallows in Mangan City, had he taken it with pride and dignity, or had he begged and pleaded? Theobald had never been the bravest of men in battle; Raedrick could not recall any instance during their time in the Army together that he had led the van. But he was skilled - very skilled - and seemed to relish a fight when it was one-on-one. The ghost of remembered pain in Raedrick's leg recalled the wound he had taken during the final fight with Isenholf, and he grimaced for a moment before bringing his thoughts back to the present.

A sound carried over the howling wind, making Raedrick stop in his tracks. It was a person's voice, raised in a shout, but he could not make out the words. He turned a circle where he stood, peering out into the storm.

From the west, a man was laboring through the blowing snow, hurrying in Raedrick's direction. The figure shouted, and Raedrick could just make out the word this time.

"Constable!"

Raedrick hurried toward the approaching man, his mind whirling through the possibilities that could bring this man chasing after him in these conditions. None of them were good. He met the man a minute or so later, and he saw it was Tom, one of the fishing men who worked for the town during the winter months.

Tom was older, well past his prime. On the boats, he was the master navigator. His joints would not let him haul in the nets the way he used to, but he still had a fine eye and he knew the shoals and hazards of the Lake better than anyone, or so Horace, the head of the local fishing guild, had told Raedrick. Raedrick did not know Tom all that well; the thing that stood out most was the older man had scraggly gray hair that shot out in all directions when his head was uncovered. Now, he was bundled up for the cold in a heavy coat, gloves, hat, and boots. Only his face, and his long, bulbous nose, was exposed to the elements. Right then, Raedrick considered that Tom was quite a bit smarter than he was.

"What is it, Tom?"

The older man leaned forward, placing his hands on his knees and panting for a few moments before answering. "They need you at the Healers Circle," he said after he had regained his breath.

Uh-oh. "Did they say what the problem is?"

Tom shook his head. "Just to come get you."

That really did not sound good.

"Alright, I'm on my way. Please find Julian, and ask him to join me. He's probably at The Oarlock."

Tom's face lit up at the mention of the Inn's name. No doubt he was looking forward to getting indoors and having a pint or two. For that matter, Raedrick could use some of that as well.

"Can do, Constable," Tom said. Then he turned and shambled off through the snow.

The Healers Circle in Lydelton occupied a small building on the north side of town, one block north of Main Street and two blocks west of Raedrick's and Julian's office building. Like all Healers Circles across the Kingdom, it was of simple construction, sturdy and functional, with no excesses to speak of. The front of the building was dominated, as most buildings in Lydelton were, by a porch that ran the building's width, complete with hitching post. A simple sign announcing the Healers Circle's ownership of the building hung over the double-doors leading within, and was the only nod to the need for advertisement at all.

Not that there really was any need for the Healers Circle to advertise. Their guild was known far and wide: men and women who willingly gave aid to whomever needed it, regardless of circumstance and of the patient's ability to pay. For the Guildsmen of the Healers Circle, treating illness and injury was all, everything else was secondary.

Or at least that's what they told the world. Raedrick had often wondered how they got the funding to go about their mission without charging anything beyond a request for whatever donation a person felt reasonable and responsible to give. He had donated to them a number of times himself, though he had never had occasion to require more than simple services. But the little he gave could not have stretched far. He could not fathom how the guild stayed afloat if that was the only way they gained income.

Which was neither here nor there for this afternoon's purposes.

Raedrick rapped firmly on the entrance doors, then stepped back to wait. One did not burst into the Healers Circle, after all; there was an etiquette to it that had to be obeyed, if one wished to remain in their good favor. Of course, they would still treat you, even if you fell out of favor with them, so a cynical man might wonder what was the point? Raedrick prided himself on not being cynical.

Several minutes passed, and the cold, held at bay before by the energy he used to walk here, quickly soaked through his heavy cloak and into his flesh. By the time the door latch clicked open, he had begun to shiver. Quite a bit. This was not shaping up as a good evening to be out and about.

The door opened and an elderly man of average height - though he once had been tall, judging by the stoop of his shoulders - dressed in the white and yellow robes of the Healers Circle guildsmen looked him up and down for a second.

"Ah, Constable," said the man, as he flashed a warm smile Raedrick's way. "Good of you to come." He pulled the door open fully and waved for Raedrick to enter.

Moving quickly, and grateful to get into the warmth, Raedrick stepped inside and cleared the way so the guildsman could shut the door behind him. "My pleasure, Master Sebastini." Raedrick glanced around the familiar entryway and did not see anything awry. The armchairs lining the far wall, where people with conditions that were non-emergency in nature could sit while awaiting the guildsmen, were as they always had been. The tapestries depicting guildsmen treating patients in all manner of settings still hung, intact, on the walls. The usual subtle scent of cleanness lingered in the air. No, nothing appeared out of the ordinary at all. "What seems to be the trouble?"

Sebastini pursed his lips and gestured for Raedrick to follow, then set off through the narrow doorway leading back into the treatment rooms and guild spaces in the rear of the building. "Not trouble, as such. But I thought you ought to know we have a new patient."

That was hardly unusual. "Oh?"

Sebastini nodded, not looking back at him. "One of Horace's men found him curled up on the ice of the lake, beside one of the docks. They brought him here not a half hour ago."

Raedrick blinked. "He was on the ice?"

It was hardly unusual for people to go out on the lake in the wintertime. The ice was, by now, more than thick enough to support them, and they found all manner of amusements on its frozen surface. Raedrick almost killed himself the first time Lani introduced him to those things she called skates, and he had not attempted it a second time. But there were many in Lydelton who reveled in them. And some of Horace's fishing men would actually cut holes in the ice to fish through. It did not make for a large catch by any measure, but they seemed to enjoy it.

But no one would go out on the lake in conditions like existed today. That was just asking for trouble at best, tragedy at worst.

The old man stopped in front of a closed door and gave Raedrick a wry look. "He is not a local or I would chalk it up to a young man behaving foolishly on a stormy day." He drew himself up and seemed to undergo a transformation. The stooped, kindly man suddenly took on an air of calm professionalism, and for a second it was like Raedrick was looking at a different man. "We are keeping the room quite warm, to ease the chill from his bones." He lifted an eyebrow.

Raedrick nodded acknowledgment, and Sebastini unlatched the door and led in him side.

Quite warm was not the word for it. The room was very nearly stifling, like a hayloft on a hot summer day. But then, Raedrick had to admit that a spring afternoon would likely feel stifling to him right that moment, having come so quickly out of the bitterly cold evening.

The room within was not large, and it was nearly filled with furniture and the accoutrements of the guildsmen's trade. The heat came from a brazier full of hot coals in the far corner. Light smoke wafted from the brazier, bringing the scent of some exotic incense Raedrick did not recognize. Shelves full of jars containing medicines of some sort or other lined the wall to Raedrick's right and a bureau rested against the wall to his left. A narrow bed stood in the center of the room. A thin, tall man with scraggly black hair and a matching beard lay sprawled unconscious on the bed, covered head to toe in blankets.

Beside him, on a small wooden stool, sat a younger man in guildsmen's robes. Dark skinned, with black hair that reached to his shoulders and eyes that were closer to yellow than brown, Sebastini's apprentice - or whatever the guildsmen called their underlings - nodded and flashed a quick smile of greeting. "Constable."

"How goes our patient, Willam?" Sebastini said, closing the door behind them.

Willam shrugged, then bent over to where a bucket lay on the ground. He reached into the bucket and pulled out a water-logged rag. Wringing out the majority of the water, he dabbed at the unconscious man's forehead gently before replying. "Better, Master," he said. "He mumbled something a few minutes ago, but I could not make it out."

Sebastini nodded. "That is a good sign."

Raedrick stepped to the bedside, peering down at the sick man. He was pale, extremely pale, and his cheekbones protruded from his skin as though he had not had a good meal in a while.

Willam dabbed at the man's forehead again, and he wriggled slightly, turning his head away from the apprentice's ministrations. The man's profile stood out for a moment in the glow from the brazier, and Raedrick frowned. There was something familiar about him.

"What is his temperature now?" Sebastini asked.

Willam frowned and consulted a small notepad. "Twenty-six, as of five minutes ago."

Sebastini gave a satisfied nod and pulled a small bottle down from one of the shelves. "It should be safe to try to wake him now," he took a dropper out and, unscrewing the bottle, withdrew a small small amount of green-blue fluid. Then he replaced the bottle's top and returned it to the shelf, and came over to stand next to Raedrick, "so the Constable can do his job."

"Is that a good..."

The patient let out a little groan and turned his head again. His eyes cracked open slightly.

Sebastini chuckled and glanced at Raedrick with a little shrug of his shoulders. "No need after all, hmm?"

The patient squirmed weakly beneath the covers and blinked his eyes several times. He tried to say something, but all that came out was a croak.

"Easy, son," Sebastini said. "You've had a hard afternoon." He looked up at his apprentice. "Water."

Willam already had things in hand. He held a small cup to the man's lips. He drank, sparingly at first but then with greater gusto, grabbing the cup with both hands. He finished with a sigh and held the cup out to Willam, who went to refill it from a decanter on the shelf nearby.

"Who are you?" Raedrick said, leaning a bit closer.

The man turned bleary gray-green eyes toward him, and Raedrick took a half-step backwards in shock. He knew those eyes.

The patient's eyes widened and his expression changed from confusion to shock to hope to fear to resignation in under a second. He spoke, barely loudly enough to hear, his voice trembling. "Corporal... Is it really you?"

The voice made the patient's identity a certainty, though Raedrick had never thought to see him alive again.

It was Tolburt.

$\mathbf{\mathscr{X}}$ 4 $\mathbf{\mathscr{X}}$

STRANDED

"Throw him out into the snow."

At first, Raedrick thought certain Julian was not being serious. Then he saw the fire in his friend's eyes, the scowl that spoke of an anger beyond rage, and he realized Julian would do exactly that, if Raedrick let him.

They stood in the entrance hall of the Healers Circle, where Raedrick and Master Sebastini had retreated after Tolburt drifted off to sleep again. He had not said much more, being only awake for a few moments, and left Raedrick with more questions than answers about what he was doing there. Julian had arrived only a few minutes later and Raedrick briefed him on the situation.

Sebastini moved before Raedrick could respond to Julian's reaction, interposing himself between Julian and the doorway leading back to the patient rooms and placing his hands on his hips in a manner that managed to look imposing, despite his stoop. "You will do no such thing, Constable. He is our patient, and under the protection of the guild. If you think you can force it..." He shook his head, giving Julian a level look that spoke of a willingness to use whatever force necessary.

Julian looked incredulously at Sebastini for a moment. Their eyes met, and Julian's widened ever so slightly. Then he turned away, muttering softly to himself. Raedrick could not make out the words, but his disgusted tone was plain enough.

"I understand how you feel, Julian," Raedrick said, "but..."

Julian whirled on him, jabbing a finger into the air between them. "Damn right you understand. He sold us out. And now we're offering him aid." He snorted. Loudly.

Raedrick could only nod in agreement. What else was there to say?

"*You* are not, young man," Sebatini said. "We are." He glanced between Julian and Raedrick for a second, clearly curious about their history with Tolburt. Then he shrugged slightly. "If you will excuse me." He did not wait for them to respond, but turned and departed the entrance hall.

No doubt he was going back to help Willam. And Tolburt.

Silence reigned for a full minute, Julian, from all appearances fuming quietly to himself while Raedrick tried not to follow suit.

Finally, Julian broke the silence. "What the hell is he doing here?"

Raedrick shook his head. "No idea. He only woke up for those couple of minutes."

"Well there has to be…"

He broke off as Willam walked into the room. The young apprentice nodded to them politely by way of greeting. "He is awake again, and asking for you."

Raedrick shared a brief look with Julian. He looked strangely reluctant; Raedrick suddenly felt similarly. But whatever his feelings about the return of their erstwhile comrade…betrayer…whatever, he had a job to do. So he squared his shoulders and followed Willam back into the treatment room.

<hr>

Tolburt was fully awake when they returned to the room, and halfway sitting up supported by two or three pillows stacked behind his back. He clutched a large mug - almost a bowl - that wafted steam almost like a freshly drawn bath in the depths of winter, and sipped from it every other second or so. He was talking with Sebastini when they walked in, but stopped mid-word when he saw Raedrick. When Julian followed him into the room, Tolburt's mouth dropped wide open.

"Nice to see you too," Julian quipped, his tone dripping acid. So much for being polite and professional.

Tolburt winced slightly at the tone and looked away, toward the wall to Raedrick's left.

Raedrick gave Julian a hard look, but he either did not notice it or pretended not to. Rolling his eyes slightly, Raedrick turned his attention fully onto Tolburt. "You want to tell us how you came to be on our lake today, Tolburt?"

Tolburt continued staring at nothing for a few seconds. Then he shook himself and tore his eyes away, looking instead at Raedrick. Something almost like relief showed on his face, as though he had been worried to be alone with Julian. Then, just as quickly that look faded, replaced by a somber expression. He sipped at his mug and was silent for a moment before he swallowed.

"Where to start?" He paused and sipped his mug again. "My friend and I found an old map that pointed to the mountains north of here." He flashed an almost apologetic smile as he added, "Supposedly it leads to a hidden cache of money and equipment." He drew a deep breath. "A *lot* of money."

Raedrick exchanged a look with Julian. Skeptical did not begin to describe his expression.

"I see," Raedrick said. "Where did this map come from?"

Tolburt shrugged. He paused for a moment, then said, "We thought about waiting until spring, but other people were looking for this place too. And besides, it hadn't gotten that cold yet…"

"Down in the lowlands, it hadn't," Julian interjected. "Up here is a different matter."

Tolburt nodded, a rueful smile flitting across his features for a second. "Should have thought of that." He sipped at the mug again. "But by the time we got up here, it would have been stupid to go back. And besides, we had it under control."

"Until…" Raedrick prompted.

"Until this storm came in. It caught us in the open, and we couldn't see where we were going. Stefan fell into a ditch and broke his leg." He shivered involuntarily, almost spilling his drink, whatever it was. "We'd seen the lights of the town, down by the lake. I got him to as good a shelter as I could, got a fire going and enough wood to see him for a while, then left to get help." He lowered his eyes. "Guess I got turned around in the storm. I didn't even realize I was on the ice at first. Then it seemed like a good idea to stay, because it was flat. After that…" He shook his head. "I don't remember much after that."

"Crap," Raedrick said to himself, softly. Sebastini glanced at him, an eyebrow quirking upward, and Raedrick fought through a momentary surprise that the older man had heard him. He was quite a bit more capable than he appeared at first glance. Or maybe the weak, hunched look was just an act, to throw people off balance.

That thought made Raedrick roll his eyes, at his own foolishness. He was just trying to not think about what he had to consider here. He cleared his throat. "Do you know where…Stefan?" Tolburt nodded. "Where Stefan is now? Can you draw us a map?"

Tolburt looked up, surprise on his face and a faint hope in his eyes. He nodded again. "I think so." He drew a deep breath. "Thank you, Corporal. You've no idea what…"

"*Constable*," Julian said firmly, but he was looking at Raedrick questioningly, and apparently not liking what he was seeing. More softly, he said, "Can I talk to you, Rae?"

Raedrick nodded quickly. "Draw your map, Tolburt." Then he gestured for Julian to lead the way back out of the room.

"Tell me you're not really thinking about doing this?" Julian demanded. They were back in the entrance hall, and he looked fit to be tied.

"Stefan is stranded out there. Injured. He could die without help." That was all there was to it.

Julian shook his head. "Well you could die trying to get to him. Have you *seen* the weather outside?" He waved at the double-doors leading outside, and just then the wind decided to howl menacingly through the cracks around their edges.

Convenient.

Raedrick suppressed a shiver as he contemplated the bitter cold, about to become all that much worse once full dark settled in, outside. "We can't just leave him out there."

"Bollocks. We don't owe Tolburt a damn thing, and you know it. You know he didn't tell you the whole truth in there. He's the kind of guy…"

Raedrick narrowed his eyes, sudden anger welling up within him. "That what?" he said, softly, coldly. "The kind of guy that what?"

Julian met his gaze for a long moment, then looked away, still scowling but some of the heat gone from his gaze.

"Whatever he is now, he became that because of us." Raedrick looked back down the hallway toward the treatment rooms. "Because of *me*," he amended, more softly.

Julian snorted. Loudly and with gusto. "You know better than that, Rae."

He thought he did. But... Maybe it was the fact that their anniversary was coming up tomorrow. Last year it was the same thing. Guilt, the weight of the burden he bore for the lives of his men. His men whom he had led into treason. They had paid the price, while he escaped and, indeed, had prospered here.

It should have been he who paid, and they who survived.

But even if guilt were not driving him, the fact remained that he could not in good conscience leave a man to freeze to death out there. Not if there was a chance they could rescue him.

Raedrick drew a deep breath in through his nose and slowly exhaled through his mouth. Then did it again. And again. Slowly, he calmed himself, let the guilt and doubt fade into focus. He knew what he had to do.

"You don't have to come, Julian," he said. "One of us should stay and keep an eye on things around town."

There was a long pause, and then Julian said, "I'm not going to convince you, am I?"

Raedrick shook his head, still looking back toward the treatment room.

"Bugger me."

PREPARATIONS

The door closed behind Julian, leaving Raedrick to ponder the situation alone for several minutes before Sebastini came back out of the treatment room.

Julian was right. This was likely going to be a futile effort, and could very well lead only to sorrow. But there was no choice. Had Tolburt not been involved, it would not even be a question whether they would send aid to a person stranded up in the mountains. So forget about Tolburt. It was not about him. Not really.

"You are going after this Stefan."

Sebastini did not pose it as a question, but Raedrick nodded in response anyway.

The elderly guildsman pursed his lips for a moment, then nodded to himself. "I shall accompany you." He held a piece of parchment out to Raedrick.

He did not notice for a second, so shocked he was by Sebastini's announcement. He was…what? No, that would not do. Raedrick shook his head vehemently. "That's not a good idea, Master Sebastini. It's going to be a difficult climb, and you…"

"I have more time in these mountains than you, young man. I can handle myself."

Raedrick opened his mouth again, to protest, but Sebastini cut him off with a raised hand.

"This fellow is injured and, by the time we find him, will be suffering from exposure. If you are to have any chance of getting him down the mountain alive, you will need my skills." He smiled, his eyes twinkling. "And besides, I've been cooped up in here for far too long. Willam will welcome my absence."

"I really think you should stay here. Send Willam with us. He can…"

Sebastini shook his head. "Willam is a capable young man, but he does not yet have the skills for a case such as this."

Raedrick looked him steadily in the eye and saw only stubborn resolve. There would be no talking him out of it.

Crap.

"Is that the map?"

Sebastini nodded and held it out to him again. Raedrick examined it by the light of one of the room's wall-lamps. It was rough. Very rough.

"I believe the large mountain referenced there is Tollard's Peak," Sebastini said.

Raedrick frowned, considering the drawing. It could be.

"Povol Gerberson climbed Tollard's Peak a year and a half ago, you know."

Raedrick blinked, surprised. He looked at Sebastini for confirmation, and the old man nodded affirmative.

"But...I thought they said it could not *be* climbed."

Sebastini chuckled. "Not by anyone but Povol. I suggest you ask him to be our guide. There is no one better in the Vale."

Raedrick blinked again.

"You *were* planning to bring a guide? Or did you magically gain knowledge of the mountains when I wasn't looking?"

Sebastini was just boxing him in on all sides. The clever old fox. Despite himself, Raedrick laughed. He nodded acquiescence.

"Good." Sebastini sounded satisfied. "We leave at first light then?"

"I was thinking immediately."

The guildsman pursed his lips, then shook his head. "It will make no difference to Stefan if we take a few more hours to get to him. But if we perish because we went blundering around in the dark, it will make quite a large difference indeed."

Again, he had a good point. Raedrick nodded. "First light then."

"I look forward to it."

Raedrick found Povol without too much difficulty. He presumed the outdoorsman would be at Holb's Tavern; for whatever reason, people of his ilk seemed to prefer it, while the fishing men and craftsmen kept to The Oarlock.

Holb, towering and bulky as ever and dressed in simple wool clothing beneath a white apron, scowled at him when Raedrick pushed aside the canvas flap that served as the entrance to his tavern. For whatever reason, he rubbed the tavern keeper wrong; Holb had actually thrown him out of the place the first time he ventured inside. Since then, relations between them had improved, but only marginally.

All the same, Raedrick had no desire to chitchat with him any longer than necessary. "Have you seen Povol?"

Holb grunted and nodded toward the corner to his left, where the canvas pavilion that enclosed the sitting area met the side of the building housing the bar. A half-dozen roughly dressed men crowded around a small table there, all talking over each other in between drinks from their tankards. They made a small cacophony that, for all its volume, seemed good-natured enough.

Raedrick nodded thanks to Holb and meandered over toward the table. As he went, he scanned the rest of the sitting area and shook his head. He could not understand how Holb or his customers preferred this setup to a properly constructed building. The only part of the tavern that had a real wall was the bar, and it was literally a hole cut into the side of a building. Braziers scattered around kept the place warm enough, but the wind whipping around made the canvas of the pavilion flap annoyingly, and every now and then a particularly forceful gust would force itself within, overcoming the braziers with a blast of cold. The place was nice enough in the summer, short as that was, but now, in the depths of winter?

The world accommodates all kinds.

That was true enough, he supposed.

One member of the boisterous group, sitting with his back to the canvas wall, noticed Raedrick's approach and raised his tankard in a small salute. Raedrick did not recognize him: a thin, almost wiry man of about Raedrick's age with short blond hair and grey eyes who wore a green coat over an off-white shirt.

"Constable," the blond man said by way of greeting, his voice cutting through his fellows' conversation easily. All eyes at the table turned toward Raedrick, and the men made quick nods of greeting. "Why do we get the pleasure of your company tonight?"

Raedrick chuckled softly at the man's tone, light and slightly teasing, then returned the nod. "Gentlemen," he said. "Just need to talk with Povol for a moment."

He had only met Povol once, a few months back, but he picked the mountaineer out from his fellows easily enough. He sat to Raedrick's right and wore clothing of nondescript homespun wool; good for braving the elements but hardly the height of fashion. He was bald, short and stocky, with powerfully muscled arms and legs: they say he could take a man lying on the ground and lift him up over his head without assistance. Of course, *they* say lots of things that most times do not end up being true.

Povol's eyebrow rose when Raedrick named him and he took a quick swig from his tankard. "I didn't do it. It wasn't me." He grinned, showing a gap in his front upper teeth where he had lost one. "You can't prove it."

The other men around the table laughed uproariously, making Raedrick feel certain he was missing something in this conversation.

But that was not important right then.

"I need your help, Povol. There's an injured man up near Tollard's Peak, and we're sending out an expedition in the morning to bring him to safety."

The smiles around the table faded immediately, the outdoorsmen's expressions becoming grim. Povol's eyes narrowed.

"What kind of a fool goes up there on a day like this?"

Raedrick related Tolburt's story and handed Povol the map. The mountaineer frowned as he began the telling. By the time he reached the end, Povol's frown had become a full-on scowl.

"Bloody idiots." He peered at the map for a long time, his scowl only getting worse. "Yeah that's Tollard's Peak all right. And the canyon to the northeast." He shook his head and raised his eyes - they were a deep shade of green, and why Raedrick should notice that right then was beyond him - to meet Raedrick's. He did not look hopeful. "I know that area well, but there's not enough here to go on. This guy could be anywhere in a ten square mile area, from what this shows."

A lump of cold developed in Raedrick's belly. Fear? Why was he afraid over this man he had never met? But he knew the answer to that question before he asked it of himself.

"Nevertheless, we're heading out tomorrow at first light. I would like to have you along to keep the rest of us out of trouble." Raedrick flashed a grin and put on a more cheerful tone. "Think of it as your good turn for the year."

Povol snorted. Loudly. "Last good turn I did almost cost me a finger." He looked intently at Raedrick, and the Constable could see the wheels turning as Povol thought it through. Finally, Povol nodded. "Fine. But I want double my normal rates." He grinned wolfishly. "Compensation for the lateness of the request and the unpleasant weather."

Raedrick blinked. He had not anticipated that Povol might demand payment. He and Julian did not have much of an operating budget. In point of fact, they did not really have a budget at all. City Hall paid them and paid for the ladies who kept up their office building. But aside from that… They had not really needed much in the way of money at all since they took over the job. What would the Mayor say about this outlay?

It did not matter. Stefan needed help, and Raedrick was going to deliver. He could worry about the financial aspects later.

"Agreed," he said, and held out his hand to Povol.

Povol's grin broadened and he took Raedrick's hand in a powerful grip. "First light then. Meet up at my place. Me and my dogs'll be ready."

Raedrick nodded, then turned and left the tavern. It was going to be a long day tomorrow and he needed to get some rest. It did not take long, after he reached his flat, for sleep to come, and with it, memories.

✿ 6 ✿

ENTRAPPED

The squad, tied hand and foot into their saddles, rode single-file under the direction of their captors, toward the divisional headquarters, Raedrick had no doubt. He rode at the rear of the column, and could only see the back of the man in front of him - Laremy - and the guards who rode on either side of them.

So this was it. This was what came from doing the right thing, refusing an unconscionable order, being true to his conscience. In spite of his best efforts, he had, in fact, only led his men to the gallows.

Had he been alone, Raedrick thought certain he would break down in tears at the injustice of it all.

But he was not alone. Even if they were only going to their graves, his men looked to him and he had to be strong, to remain true to principle. That was what they needed. Or maybe it was what *he* needed. Regardless, it was all he could allow himself to do. So he rode with his head high, eyes up and not lowered like one who has been defeated.

Of course no one noticed. His men were just focused on the road ahead, and the guards. For their part, the guards simply diverted themselves with jokes at one another's, or more often at the prisoners', expense. Then, as the afternoon wore on, they became more focused on picking out a good place to pitch camp for the night.

And so it was that the troop came to a halt with Raedrick riding like a king, at least in his own mind, but being ignored altogether. Oh well, it was the thought that counted.

For the prisoners, camp was simple. Their bonds were released to allow them to dismount, one at a time, but then quickly re-tied. And then they were tied again, onto a long picket-line similar to what the men would have done with the horses. Once they were secure, their captors set two men to guarding them while the rest erected the remainder of the camp.

Tents. Lots of tents. But not one of them for Raedrick or his men. At least they were allowed dinner. A meager dinner, far less than their captors ate, but also more than they had been able to indulge in during their time on the run. But when sentries were set and the rest of the soldiers bedded down for the night - in their tents - Raedrick and his men were left to ride out the night under the stars, along with their pair of guards.

Raedrick did not mind so much, at first. Most nights since they deserted he and his men had not had shelter for the night. But not long after sunset, clouds rolled in and with them, rain. A slow but steady rain that seemed at first nothing to complain about, but then sooner than he thought possible left him soaked and shivering.

All around him, his men tossed and turned, complaining in muffled tones but unable to get to sleep. Surely their anxiety about what lay ahead contributed to that, and the rain only made it worse. But they were hardened soldiers, and soldiers caught sleep whenever the opportunity arose. Sleep was a weapon.

Of course, knowing death was a possibility was much different than knowing it was certain. Hard to calm yourself down when facing that.

"What are we going to do, Corporal?"

The whispered words came from Raedrick's left. He could not see the man's face, but he knew the voice. Tolburt.

What was Tolburt doing here with them?

"Shut up, you traitor." That was Laremy, Raedrick was sure.

Tolburt's snorted response spoke volumes.

"Enough," Raedirck said, putting on his best command tone of voice. Or as best as he could while keeping it low enough to not alert the guards. Around him, men who were tossing and muttering went silent, and Raedrick felt a sense of anticipation from them. As if somehow he had a plan, and once he expressed it they would get out of this and everything would be ok.

If only.

Raedrick drew a breath, pondering what to say. "I don't know," he said, finally. It was the truth, but he hated it as soon as he said it. He could feel his men deflating all around him. But what was he supposed to do, lie to them? He had no idea how they were going to get out of this, if it was even possible.

Better to not give them false hope.

"You rat bastard!" The words came from further to Raedrick's left and were spoken with such fury, such fiery hatred, that Raedrick could not at first tell who had spoken them.

Tolburt cried out suddenly, surprise and pain combining to make his scream high-pitched like a woman's. He screamed again, more shrilly - Raedrick would not have thought that was possible.

What was going on?

Down the picket line, a torch bobbed closer; the guards were coming.

"Get off of me!" Tolburt finally managed to shout coherently, and there was the sound of men thrashing around in the dark.

"Here now, what's this? Stop it, you!" The guards had arrived, and by the light of the torch, Raedrick could see Tolburt and Hinderbrook engaged in a strange sort of wrestling, if it could be called wrestling with both of them trussed up as they were. Hinderbrook had most of his body atop Tolburt's, and... Raedrick did a double-take. Hinderbrook's mouth and chin were covered in blood. And Tolburt had...teeth marks?...on the side of his neck.

"Get off him!" the senior guard - a Corporal like Raedrick - ordered, taking in the scene faster than Raedrick had.

The junior man bent over to pry the two of them apart.

"You promised me special treatment," Tolburt said, looking desperately up at the senior guard as his man grabbed at Hinderbrook. "Please."

The senior man snorted, then grinned viciously. "Don't worry, you'll get it." His grin widened. "Captain says you're to hang last."

The junior man finally managed to tear Hinderbrook off of Tolburt, whose face had gone ashen in the torchlight as his mouth dropped open in shocked horror, but the struggle caused him to overbalance and he fell back atop two others of Raedrick's men. They squirmed overtop him similar to how Hinderbrook had done with Tolburt. One of them slammed his forehead into the guard's nose, and he cried out in pain.

The Corporal cried out in chagrin and dashed forward, flailing at Raedrick's men with the torch. They backed off quickly, rolling away from the downed guard, but one of them - Shermyn Raedrick thought - had a wicked burn on his right cheek as a result.

The two guards backed away, the Corporal waving his torch threateningly. "To bed, you lot," he ordered hotly, though he sounded more disturbed than resolved to Raedrick's ear. He clearly had not expected any actual resistance from them.

Raedrick's men stopped moving, their eyes lowered submissively, and after a moment the Corporal harumphed and nudged the other man with his elbow. Then the two of them left, heading back down the picket line toward where they had their little campfire for the night.

For a time, the only sound was that of a man weeping. Raedrick was sure it came from Tolburt. Then Raedrick heard Shermyn's voice, whispering. It made his heart leap.

"Corporal, I got his knife from his belt."

It took an eternity for Shermyn to cut Laremy free, and an even longer eternity for Laremy to cut the rest of the squad free as well. All except Tolburt and those closest to the guards. It would not do for those two to see Raedrick's men skulking about, not until it was too late to do anything about it.

A quick consultation later, Laremy and Kilfer crept up on the pair of guards. They were huddled around their campfire. The Corporal had his back to Raedrick's men, even.

Laremy took out the private with the knife, making quick work of him from behind. Kilfer was even quicker. The large man engulfed the Corporal in his meaty arms and snapped his neck with a quick twist of his shoulders. And then there was nothing standing between Raedrick's men and their freedom.

Elation spread through the group, and before Raedrick knew what was happening, a trio of them had gone to the campfire and retrieved brands. They set off through the camp, lighting tents ablaze while Laremy freed the last of the men.

"No!" Raedrick tried to shout for his men to stop. There was no need for this; they could just disappear into the night and no one's the wiser.

But it was no use. The day's terror and despair had given way to elation, and then raging bloodlust and a desire to make the people pay who had caused them to feel such fear. In moments, a half dozen tents were ablaze. Men screamed from within. Some tried to flee. A few made it unscathed, coughing and gagged from the smoke. Others emerged from their sleeping gear fully ablaze, their screams eclipsing the worst sounds Raedrick had ever heard, and he thought he had heard them all on the battlefield.

But there were many more tents in the Company that captured them, and within moments the rest of the troops spilled out. They were dressed in their small clothes, most of them, but they brandished weapons, one and all.

It only took a moment for them to recognize the source of the attack, and they came running. First in ones or twos, and Raedrick's men managed to overcome them. But quickly, squad leaders and officers got their men coordinated, and they advanced as a unit.

"We've got to get out of here," Hinderbrook said, standing at Raedrick's side. He bore a longsword that he had taken from one of the solitary soldiers who had come against them, but he was bleeding from a gash on his shoulder.

Raedrick nodded. "Retreat!" he called, and the closest of his men complied.

Others, too close to the advancing soldiers, were not so lucky. One fell the moment he turned to run. Two more hefted newly-liberated swords and went back-to-back, their faces grimly determined. Raedrick knew that expression - there would be no surrender; they would go down fighting. In the end they were dead anyway, so why not?

Hinderbrook grabbed Raedrick's shoulder, spinning him away from the fight. He was right; there was nothing Raedrick could do except get killed himself. It was time to go. He began to run.

"Corporal!"

Tolburt's voice brought him up short. He turned and saw the youngster, still bound to the picket line. His eyes were wide with terror, and he looked at Raedrick desperately.

"Corporal, help me!"

Raedrick hesitated.

"Corporal!" Hinderbrook shouted, from next to him.

Raedrick barely heard him. Tolburt looked so scared.

"Raedrick!"

Something struck him across the face and he stumbled a step backwards. Hinderbrook recovered from the slap and grabbed Raedrick by the shoulder again.

"We need to go now." Hinderbrook glanced back at Tolburt and spat. "He's getting what he deserves."

Raedrick opened his mouth to protest. He could not leave his man behind. But Hinderbrook shoved him backwards, shouting, "Move!"

Raedrick took two stumbling steps away, then looked back. Tolburt lay squirming in his bonds, desperately. Their eyes met. "Corporal! Please!"

His two men who were fighting back-to-back had fallen. The rest of the soldiers were advancing toward them. Hinderbrook was right. It was time to go.

He turned and ran, Tolburt's last despairing plea seeming to chase him through the night as he went.

7

RISE AND SHINE

Raedrick awoke feeling fuzzy-headed; his sleep had not been particularly restful. Those memories intruding on his dreams prohibited it. For a few seconds, as he lay there in the darkness, he considered just forgetting the silly notion of heading up into the mountains after this man and going back to sleep. But duty called, so he pushed himself up to a sitting position and rubbed at his eyes, removing the last sleep from them.

At least he did not have a headache. His mouth was dry and a sour taste lingered on his tongue, but aside from the slightly-fuzzy feeling that comes from inadequate sleep, his head was fine. Better get moving before that changed.

He forced himself up, went through his morning routine - abbreviated a bit - and snarfed down some dried fruits as a quick breakfast. In just a few minutes he was out the door of his little flat, dressed in his thickest winter coat and leggings, several layers of thinner cloth beneath each, his gloves and cold weather hat, and overtop it all his pack and a thick wool cloak. It was a damn sight more appropriate for the elements than what he had been wearing the day before, but he had no illusions that he would be anything but cold on the side of the mountains.

He considered bringing his sword but quickly shelved the notion. This was a rescue, not an assault. The sword would just get in the way and be extra weight to carry. So he left it behind, taking a long dagger in its place.

His flat lay less than a block from The Oarlock, on the same street as the Inn. He would pass it by as he set off for the Healers Circle. For a moment he considered stopping and going in. Molli and Lani were almost certainly up already, getting ready for the day, or closing out the previous one depending on how busy the place had been last night. It would be good to speak with them…with her.

He pulled his flat's door to and locked it, then turned and froze still.

A young woman, maybe twenty years old, stood outside his flat, her arms crossed over her chest, and not just from the cold. She was bundled up for the cold but even with those layers it was obvious she had an impressive figure. Only a bit shorter than Raedrick himself, she had flowing blonde hair and hazel eyes. Her heart-shaped face was marred by a frown that was, unless he missed his guess, brought on by worry...and a bit of irritation.

"You were going to go without saying goodbye?" Lani asked flatly.

He did not ask how she heard about the expedition. Lani heard everything, and oftentimes well before he did. "We won't be gone for more than a day, maybe two. It's hardly goodbye."

Her tone grew more heated. "I've lived here my whole life, Raedrick. I've seen more than my fair share of men leave on day trips in the middle of winter and never return." She drew herself up. "And you know it."

Raedrick's cheeks grew hot as he flushed slightly in embarrassment. Of course she would not buy into that argument. She knew the perils of the mountains far better than he did. He sighed. "I'm sorry. I didn't want to worry you."

She voiced a very unladylike curse in response to that. "So you thought my not knowing where you were would make me worry less?"

Raedrick had no response to that. In truth, he had not given Lani, or her mother for that matter, a whole lot of thought. His mind had been focused on his new mission, and on getting ready for it. Everything else...

But that was not entirely true. He knew Lani would worry, but he also knew - or rather suspected - that she would try to stop him. And he had not been sure he could hold out against her attempt.

Silence lingered for several seconds while he tried to get the words together to understand. Then Lani sighed.

"Why are you doing this, Raedrick?"

"There's an injured man up there who needs help."

She shook her head. "No. Why are *you* doing this? You could have hired Povol and his pals," she was good; did she know all the details of his plan? "to search the mountains and report back to you. That's what Malory always did, and it worked out fine." In the semi-darkness, she leaned forward, peering at him. "Why are you going out there personally? You don't know anything about how to get around and survive in the mountains."

That was not completely true. He had plenty of training, and more experience, on surviving in the wild, in all sorts of conditions. But the Saddleback Mountains in the depths of winter were not just any set of conditions; they were some of the harshest conditions a man could face anywhere in the Kingdom. And he intended to go right into their teeth.

Put that way, it did not make a whole lot of sense.

Raedrick took Lani's hand gently and gave it a little squeeze. "It's something I have to do." He told her about Tolburt, all of it, and her features softened. Somewhat. "I left him behind then, to save myself. If I help his friend, maybe..." He swallowed. "Maybe that will make amends. A little."

"You left him. After he betrayed you. I don't think you owe him anything."

The same argument Julian had made. They did not understand. "He was one of my men, Lani." He shrugged slightly, looking away, toward where the Healers Circle lay. "A commander does not leave one of his men behind."

She was silent for a long several seconds, absorbing his words. He did not look back at her, for fear that her disapproval would have grown worse. He was not sure he could deal with that, on top of everything else.

Suddenly, she embraced him, squeezing him fiercely. He was so surprised he did not return the embrace for a few seconds, so sure was he that she was only growing more angry with him. Finally he held her, and it seemed they stood there like that for an hour, though in truth only a few seconds passed.

Nestled against his shoulder, she spoke softly. "Don't you go and do something stupid up there, Raedrick Baletier. I could not stand it if anything happened to you."

A sound that was half-snort and half-chuckle, from behind them, interrupted before Raedrick could reply. "Fat chance of that, Lani. I don't think I've ever seen him *not* do something stupid, once he decided to get all heroic in the head."

Julian stepped into view. Like Raedrick, he was dressed in overlapping layers of wool and fur, gloves and a cold weather hat, a pack, and stout boots. Unlike Raedrick, he bore a bow and quiver slung over his shoulder. He smirked playfully and gave Lani a little wink.

She gave a little start at seeing Julian and stepped away from Raedrick, pushing a lock of hair back away from her face. If Raedrick had to hazard a guess, he would say she was embarrassed.

"Hello, Julian," she said. "Are you going off on this mad hunt as well?"

He shrugged. "Looks that way." His eyes left her and traced down the street, toward where The Oarlock lay, a small circle of light in the otherwise mostly dark street. They kept the lamps outside lit all night, and depending on the night kept serving all night as well. "Getting started early this morning?"

She shook her head. "Just getting off. The Tanlyson brothers played last night, and the crowd demanded several encores." She grinned, but the grin was overcome by a yawn a moment later. "Figured I could catch this lump before he slinked away if I waited long enough."

Julian chuckled. "She's got you figured out, Rae."

"Seems like it."

They stood in silence for a couple handfuls of seconds. Then Lani inhaled softly and nodded briskly to each of them. "Well," she said, her voice steady, tightly controlled, "be careful up there." She opened her mouth, as though to say something more, but instead just shook her head and stepped around them. "Good luck," she said over her shoulder. Then she vanished into the slowly lessening gloom.

Raedrick watched her walk away, an ache in his heart that took him by surprise. He truly did not want to cause her concern, but he had a job to do. He sighed and turned back toward Julian.

His friend regarded him with a frank expression. "You're going to have to get that figured out pretty soon, Rae. She won't wait on you forever."

Raedrick flushed and coughed into his fist. This was not something he wanted to discuss right now. Or maybe at all. He cared for Lani, but… No, this was not the time. He squared his shoulders and cleared his throat, forcing his thoughts back to the business at hand.

"Thought you weren't coming."

Julian snorted. "Last time I let you do something on your own, you almost got yourself run through." He flashed a grin that Raedrick found himself returning in kind, angst over Lani's state of mind fading somewhat to the background.

He nodded and clapped Julian on the shoulder. "Let's get to it."

8
UP THE HILL

At least the weather was better.

The wind had died down to a gentle breeze with occasional brisk gusts and the overcast had broken up. The moon was clearly visible in the eastern sky, a shining crescent a thumb's breadth above the mountains that would be its home for the day, and dawn was beginning to break, pink and lovely, in the west, illuminating only a few high altitude clouds in the sky overhead.

"Going to be a nice day," Raedrick said.

"About time. I thought that blow would never end." Julian squinted up at the rapidly brightening sky and grinned. "Maybe this trip won't be so bad after all."

Raedrick hoped he was right.

They picked up Sebastini at the Healers Circle, then hurried over to Povol's place of business.

The mountaineer had a fair-sized house in the northwest corner of town, and an above average tract of land to go with it. Behind the house, which was just a single story but seemed to loom nevertheless, he had fenced off a large area and set up a number of small buildings: the houses for his dogs.

They were already up and about as the three men walked up to Povol's property. Barks and yips, and the occasional growl, reached Raedrick's ears easily, and he immediately understood why Povol's place was as separated from his neighbors as it was. He for sure would not want to be the one who lived next to that. Not unless he had to be up extra early every day.

They found Povol around back, near his dog pens. The mountaineer was bundled up even more than they were, though much of his bulk came from his pack and the numerous tools and strands of rope that hung from a thick leather harness fastened over his outer coat. He was busily fastening his dogs to leads that were attached to long, narrow sleds. Five dogs each, for three sleds.

Povol glanced up as they approached, and nodded. "You're late, Constable."

Raedrick raised an eyebrow. "Seeing as you are just now ready to go, I'd say we're right on time."

Povol snorted out a half-laugh and stood. He scratched behind the ears of the dog he just attached and looked the three of them over for a moment. Then he shook his head. "Didn't know he was coming along," he said, nodding at Sebastini.

The guildsman replied, "I have been up in the mountains many times, Povol."

"I know that. But I've only got three sleds." He considered Julian and Raedrick then, frowning. "Either of you ever drive a dogsled?"

Raedrick shook his head. He had seen some of the townsfolk - those few who actually left town during the winter - getting around on sleds similar to Povol's. He recalled thinking them ingenious, but he had never taken the opportunity to learn about them, or ride on one.

Julian, surprisingly, nodded. "Horace's friend Lommy took me out one time and showed me how to work his."

Povol smirked. "So basically no." He sighed and ran a hand along his pate, considering. Then he apparently came to a decision, as he nodded briskly and turned to Sebastini. "You'll ride with me then, Ravi. I don't want your extra weight to throw them off while they get the hang of it."

Sebastini nodded acceptance.

"Ravi?" Julian asked.

Sebastini chuckled. "You've never asked my given name, but I *do* have one."

Raedrick could not help but chuckling in return. He had never bothered to learn Sebastini's name either. The momentary sense of humor he felt faded as he asked himself the next question: Why not?

Povol interrupted that train of thought. "Ok, let's get your bags stowed and mount up. Daylight's wasting."

The sun was just beginning to edge up over the mountains to Glimmer Vale's west, but Povol had a point. The days were very short up here, and Stefan did not have much time.

They made better time than Raedrick would have thought. Sure, he had seen others driving their sleds around, and he could tell they made a good clip. But that was always from a distance. Actually being on the sled, he was immediately impressed by the device's effectiveness.

The group set out heading due west, along the path to the ford across the North-flow, or at least along where the path may have been come the Spring thaw. For now, they simply stayed away from the largest of the rolling hills that made up the terrain around Lydelton and pointed at the rising sun.

When they stopped at the Northflow, it was clear the river still flowed. Though water along the river's banks was frozen, the middle remained free of ice, and the current gurgled along nicely. Raedrick had never used this ford before, but if it was anything like the ford for the Eastflow, they had a good foot of near freezing water to wade through to reach the other side.

So much for using the dogsleds for very long.

But Povol surprised him. When Julian voiced the same concern Raedrick had, he shook his head. "It's only about five or six inches at this time of year." Then he dismounted and pulled open a satchel that lay on the front of his sled, in front of where Sebastini sat. From within, he pulled out a number of long, narrow oilskin contraptions which he proceeded to slip onto his dogs' feet and tie in place. Then he produced similar, larger, leggings for himself and Sebastini. The old man got up and donned the leggings without a word.

When they had prepared, Povol gestured toward Raedrick and Julian's sleds. "You have the same gear. Watch where I go and do exactly what I do."

Raedrick nodded, and immediately Povol gave a little command and his dogs set off at a slow walk. Povol walked beside the lead dog, holding his - Raedrick presumed the dog was male - collar and speaking softly, reassuringly Raedrick presumed, in his ear.

Sedastini walked at the rear of the sled and helped guide it into and out of the water while Povol guided the dogs across the ford. The oilskin garments worked well, and the water never got high enough to flood them out. So when they reached the far bank and removed the leggings, both men and dogs were dry, as though they had not just crossed a river.

Or at least as dry as they could be from stomping through the snow for the previous half hour.

"You won't need to lead them," Povol called, from the far side of the river. "They will come to me, so you should stay in the rear. Just make sure the sled does not get swamped."

"Seems easy enough," Julian said, from Raedrick's right. He had a profoundly skeptical look on his face.

"Yeah."

"You want to go first?"

Raedrick looked at his friend, so fearless in so many situations, and was surprised at his hesitation. He thought it over for a moment, then nodded.

The look of relief on Julian's face - relief that he did not have to be the pioneer on this one, unless Raedrck missed his guess - said all that needed saying.

In reality, Julian need not have worried. Raedrick made it across easily and quickly. Proving their masters' word true, the dogs went right to Povol when he whistled for them. The only things Raedrick had to do was keep the sled from getting stuck in the slushy mud at the bottom of the river and wave at Julian to hurry up.

Julian made the crossing with equal lack of incident. A few minutes later, after they got the oilskin garments packed again, the group got back to making time across the solid ground and its layer of snow.

After the ford, they turned north by northwest, veering away from the Northflow and entering the western reaches of the Glamorwood.

The trees closed in around them quickly, evergreens that stood high above them and collected snow in their branches but kept the canopy beneath more free of snow than the plains had been. Except where branches had given way beneath the weight or the wind had blown the snow off. There, the area below the trees was a mess of randomly piled snow and the occasional downed limb.

There was no trail that Raedrick could detect, but Povol led them without hesitation, choosing his turns as though he had been driving this route for his whole life. For all Raedrick knew, he just may have been. Few people from outside settled in Glimmer Vale. This past year had been novel, with Raedrick, Julian, and Melanie taking up residence. And not just because they were two fighting men - Constables now - and a renegade mage. It was entirely possible that Povol had never been farther abroad in the world than the borders of this Vale. But within... Well, there was no one who knew these mountains better, or so the word around town went.

So far, Raedrick had seen nothing to dissuade him from that opinion.

They passed an interminable amount of time beneath the canopy of the Glamorwood. Raedrick found himself shifting uncomfortably after a little while over memories of his last visit to these woods. Granted, the events involving that Out-Dweller and the mad Mage Telurian had taken place on the other side of the Northflow, but the woods here looked almost identical. He almost expected to see, jutting out of the earth atop a small hill ahead, the spur of rock where, three months ago, they had found the mutilated body that set them on their course against Telurian. It was foolishness, but all the same he could not shake the feeling that events were repeating themselves.

The terrain became more hilly, and their pace slowed as the dogs adjusted to the greater incline. But the animals were well-trained and they kept on pulling steadily. And then, all at once, as they rounded the curve of the up-slope of the steepest hill they had encountered yet, they burst out from beneath the trees and back into direct sunlight.

The transition was quick enough as to be stunning. The mountains, now looming all around them and covered in the winter's snow, were nigh-on blinding they reflected the sun so well, and Raedrick had to raise his hand to shield his eyes.

Ahead, Povol stopped his sled, but Raedrick almost missed it in the glare. He jerked his contraption to the right and almost overbalanced before he was able to come to a halt. Julian, meanwhile, stopped alongside Povol without difficulty. Both men looked at Raedrick with bemused expressions on their faces. Sebastini's quickly suppressed chuckle was even worse, but somehow not as bad as the amused twinkle in the old man's eye.

"Well," Povol said after a short pause. He gestured toward the mountain directly ahead. It loomed, taller than the others around it, like a great, curved tooth from some giant predator. "That's Tollard's Peak." He frowned up at the mountain, looking for a moment like a man sizing up an opponent. "That mountain will kill you quick, if you let it."

"Sounds like my kind of place," Julian said, wryly.

Povol turned the frown on him. "No. It isn't."

Julian's expression lost its amusement, and he nodded.

"But we're not actually going up Tollard's," Raedrick said, fishing the map Tolburt drew out of his pocket and unfolding it. "Stefan is holed up to the north, from the look of this."

Povol glanced at the map and smirked. "Like I told you last night, that thing isn't precise." He turned back to the mountain and pointed to the east. "There's a deep valley, more like a canyon, that runs along Tollard's northeastern flank. That's where the Northflow runs. Can't go through there without a whole lot of climbing tackle and even more time." He swept his hand across the mountain's face, pointing to its western side. "The western face is all boulders and bad trails. Take us a week to pick our way through there. So..." He turned back to Raedrick and raised both eyebrows. "To get where we're going, we pretty much have to go straight ahead."

"Over the bloody mountain?" Julian sounded completely incredulous. "Are you serious?"

Povol shrugged. "It's that or go home. We won't make for the summit, just the shoulder above the canyon. It's not *too* bad an approach."

Raedrick looked up at the mighty peak, and the narrow - or at least it looked narrow from this distance - band of unbroken snow that led upwards and to the right, passing sheer cliff faces and obvious rocky patches across the mountain's eastern shoulder, and shuddered. This was not exactly what he had in mind.

"There's no other way?" He did not completely succeed in removing all hint of dismay from his voice.

"Not unless you want to circle way that hell around and come from another direction."

Stefan did not have time for that. Hell, he might be dead already if he was as badly hurt as Tolburt made out.

Raedrick sighed, then nodded his acquiescence. "All right. Let's climb a mountain."

Povol just grinned at him.

❦ *9* ❦

CAMPING OUT

The sun was low on the eastern horizon, only a hand's breadth above the mountains, and they were about a third of the way down the northern side of the mountain's flank when they found the tracks: a single line of footsteps that ran from east-southeast to the northwest. The unexpected discovery brought them up short, and they disembarked their sleds to investigate.

Povol frowned, crouching down next to the trail and studying the tracks with a practiced eye. "These are fresh. Definitely made today."

Raedrick was no tracker, but he had to agree. Yesterday's high winds and snowfall would have quickly filled in any tracks left then. Today's winds were less, especially here in the lee of the mountain, despite the occasional fierce gusts.

"None of your friends came up here today, did they?"

Povol shook his head and stood. "Whoever made them, he came from that way," he nodded to the east. "Not much there until you hit the canyon in a mile or so." He straightened his cloak around his shoulders and turned back to his sled. "Could be someone found your man already. Could be someone else we don't know about."

Raedrick shared a look with Julian. If someone had found Stefan, and then left... He could tell that Julian was thinking the same thing he was.

"I'm sure he is fine," Sebastini said, his tone firm despite the fatigue in his face. The day's climb had been hard on the older man, but he bore up well, not complaining at all.

Julian cast an incredulous look at the guildsman, who shrugged and spread his hands helplessly.

"Hope is better," he said simply. Then he turned around and settled himself back onto Povol's sled.

The mountaineer helped Sebastini get situated, then looked at Raedrick, an eyebrow rising questioningly. "Well?"

Raedrick nodded toward the east. "Let's check it out."

345

They found the camp in about twenty minutes. It was arranged in gap between a collection of boulders and a cliff face that came up on them seemingly from out of nowhere. One moment they were guiding their sleds down a gentle grade that curved around the mountain's flank, and the next they rounded a bend and found themselves at the foot of the cliff, which stretched a hundred feet or more above their heads.

The tracks led along the cliff face for a hundred yards or so, then vanished.

"Looks like this is the place," Julian said as they got off their sleds and followed the last of the tracks between the rocks.

Someone had obviously laid up here for a while. The area was mostly clear of snow; either cleared out or packed down to a near solid firmness. Leftovers of what looked like a meal littered the area: a few small bones and scraps of fruit skin. In the corner nearest the cliff face lay the remnants of a campfire; just blackened coals now, but Raedrick imagined for a moment that he could feel the fire's warmth. The faint odor of woodsmoke still lingered the in air, but then he was probably imagining that as well.

"Good place," Povol said, nodding in approval. "The cliff keeps most of the winds off you, and the rocks block the rest. Put a roof up and you could live pretty well here."

Julian looked askance at him. "We're going to have to discuss what you mean by living well."

Povol smirked back. "Not freezin' to death, boy."

Julian frowned, then shrugged after a short moment, apparently taking Povol's point.

"This cannot be where your man Tolburt left his friend," Sebastini said, eyeing Raedrick in confusion. "If he succumbed to the elements, his body would be here. If not, he would be here alive." He frowned, then shook his head.

Raedrick was forced to agree. All the same... He pulled Tolburt's map out again and looked it over. "This is the right location, isn't it Povol?"

Povol shrugged. "Can't say from that," he said. "Told you before it's rough. Could be dozens of hidey-holes like this around here." He paused. "Probably are."

Raedrick snorted. "You know everyone who would likely have come up here recently."

Povol nodded.

Silence followed. Raedrick just stared firmly at Povol. He really did not have to be this obtuse; what was he playing at?

Finally, Povol nodded again, sighing in resignation. "Ok, point taken. No one else was up here. At least no one from town."

"Other people live in the Vale though, Rae," Julian said. "At least as many as in Lydelton itself."

"Yes, but they are mostly farmers or ranchers. How many of those sorts of people go gallivanting around the mountains in the middle of a snowstorm?"

He turned and left the little campsite, folding up the map and replacing it into his pocket.

Julian followed along behind him. "We going where I think we're going?"

Raedrick pointed at the footprints leading away northwest from the campsite, and nodded.

The tracks led a straight path, or as straight as a path could be on the side of a mountain. They led generally northwest and downward, toward a valley between Tollard's Peak and its neighbors, mountains that only looked diminutive when compared to the monstrosity that was Tollard's.

The snow was surprisingly shallow, and well-packed. The tracks they followed were only slightly depressed, and the sleds' runners did not penetrate even as deeply as they.

"It's frozen solid beneath," Povol said when Raedrick asked about it during a brief stop to re-tie the leads on one of Julian's dogs' harness. "It never gets very warm up here, even in summer." He raised an eyebrow, glancing up at the surrounding peaks as he worked on the line. "Ever notice how many of the mountains are snow-covered year-round?"

He had, though he never thought about it before. "Yes, now that you mention it."

Povol grinned wryly. "Some melts and runs off, but most stays. New snow falls in the winter," he pulled the lead tight and stood, clapping his hands together quickly, "and the stuff beneath freezes."

"So we're standing on a sheet of ice," Julian said, suddenly looking uncertain about the situation.

Povol nodded. "Let's get back on the trail."

An hour later, with most of the sun below the mountains to the east and the temperature starting to drop, Raedrick started looking around for places to hole up for the night. It did not look promising; they had descended probably a thousand feet, maybe more, and the grade had lessened considerably, but the flank of the mountain was still just a bare expanse of snow, broken only by the occasional rocky protuberances and cliff faces. He thought he could see some trees ahead, down in the valley, but that area was already covered in shadow and it was difficult to tell for certain.

They could not keep on like this through the night, though. They would blunder over a cliff, run into a boulder, or just fall over from exhaustion and the cold.

Cold. That was something he had almost become used to. And of course, he had not thought to bring materials for a fire. Neither had Julian, and he had not seen any fuel on Povol's sled either. So it was not like they had any prospect of not being cold, no matter what.

He urged his dogs to greater speed, and after a minute or so pulled even with Povol's sled.

"We're going to lose the light soon," Raedrick said.

Povol nodded agreement. "I know a place, about a half mile ahead, where we can stop for the night."

Raedrick squatted against the growing wind and looked ahead. The shadows were lengthening, but he could see much farther than a half mile and he did not see anything that looked like shelter. "Where? I don't see anything."

Povol glowered at him for a second before turning his attention back to his sled, and his dogs. He did not say anything, but his expression said it all: *You hired me to be your guide. Why did you do that, if you already know it all?*

Raedrick ground his teeth, but bit back the anger that welled up in response to the mountaineer's attitude. He had every right to be proud of his abilities, and after all he was correct. He knew the mountains better than anyone. Or if not that, at least he knew them one hell of a lot better than Raedrick and Julian did. Or Sebastini, for that matter, though the old man had not second guessed Povol, or really any of them, during the entire trip. He was apparently content to sit back until his skills were needed.

A man could learn a thing or two from an attitude like that.

Raedrick let Povol pull ahead again and contented himself to following the guide. He knew what he was doing.

And boy, did he.

Raedrick knew he was gaping, but he could not help it. Beside him, Julian did the same, his mouth hanging open like a whore's bodice. Not that Raedrick had seen that many whores' bodices. Or really *any* whores' bodices or...

Ok, get it together.

But it was hard to listen to that particular thought.

He had followed when Povol stopped his sled near an innocuous rock outcropping and gestured for the rest of them to come along. The mountaineer's accusing look just a few minutes earlier had put to rest any doubts he may have had, or at least it had put to rest the notion of speaking them. But when Povol disappeared behind a fold of rock, Raedrick had balked, unable to comprehend what had happened.

Until he followed and saw the narrow crack, just wide enough for a man to walk through without catching his shoulders on the sides of the crack, that ran back into the rock face. Even looking at it straight on, Raedrick was sure he would not have noticed the crack from as little as ten or fifteen feet away.

That was surprising enough. But it was nothing compared to what lay within.

He stood, stunned, looking at a cavern as large as a good-sized house. Stalactites hung down from the ceiling, stopping about a foot and a half above Raedrick's head, but the floor was relatively smooth, with only a few rocks strewn around. The floor itself curled and flowed in irregular humps toward the rear of the cavern, which did not end so much as constrict until it became a crack again, far too narrow to squeeze through. The entire place was well lit by a half-dozen wall sconces that held oil lamps, and a pair of wooden shelves stood on the wall to the right, holding jugs, mugs, and bedrolls. A fire pit, with logs already laid out ready for burning, lay in the exact center of the cavern, and Raedrick saw there was another narrow crack in the ceiling above the pit that ran up out of sight. Very dimly, he thought he could see the last glimmers of sunlight at the extreme end of the crack.

"Bugger me," Julian breathed.

Povol turned away from lighting the final lamp and grinned wolfishly. "This is not my first night on this mountain, boys."

Clearly, but...

"Nice place," Sebastini said, stepping past Raedrick and Julian and giving the cavern a nod of approval. "How long have you been using it?"

Povol shrugged. "Ten years, give or take." He moved over to the nearest shelf and picked up a particularly large jug. Unstoppering it, he took a quick whiff from its contents. He pursed his lips, considering for a moment, then with a slight shrug he looked at Raedrick and Julian. "Mead? It's home brewed a couple months ago, but it's still good."

Julian grinned from ear to ear. Raedrick joined him.

10

A GALLANT RESCUE

If someone had asked him, Raedrick would not have believed it possible that he could spend a comfortable night, and get a good night's sleep, up on that mountain.

But once they got the dogs inside and lit the fire, the cavern became positively warm and festive. Povol not only had mead but also food stocked up, and very shortly they had full bellies and warm bodies. It was not long before Raedrick became extremely drowsy. He had the presence of mind to think it would be wise to set a watch, but before he could say anything about it he succumbed to the fatigue of a restless night followed by a vigorous day.

When he came to, the other men were already up and moving, though only Sebastini was visible, stowing the cavern's remaining stores and generally squaring the place away.

No one noticed he was awake for a minute or so, and he considered just rolling back over and trying to feign it for a bit, so good did it feel to just lie there, even on the cold rock. But there was work to be done, and a man's life to save.

Although, if Stefan had indeed been out there for two full nights without help, it was not likely he still lived. Unless he was the one who left those tracks. But if that were the case, it meant he was not injured, or at least not injured as badly as Tolburt claimed. That only left a couple of possibilities, and Raedrick did not like them. Not one bit.

He almost hoped Stefan was dead for a second.

Enough of that. He pushed himself up to a sitting position and rolled his shoulder to work out a kink for a moment before standing.

"Good to see you up and about," Sebastini said from over by the shelves, where he was replacing the implements of their night's stay.

Raedrick grunted. "How are we looking?"

The old man shrugged. "We can only hope Stefan found shelter as well."

"You think it was he who left the tracks?"

Sebastini shrugged again. "Time will tell."

"Not if we keep lollygagging around here it won't," Povol said, re-entering the cave just then. He looked Raedrick up and down and grinned at him. "We leave as soon as you're ready, Constable." Glancing at Sebastini, he added in the same playfully mocking tone he had used in Holb's when they first met, "If that is alright with your nursemaid."

Sebastini chuckled and passed Raedrick a plate filled with dried meats and fruits. "I would not let them wake you," he said, a half-apologetic smile on his face.

It was hard to be angry at that.

By the time he wolfed down breakfast and joined the other men outside, the sun had climbed well above the western peaks. Raedrick felt a momentary pang of guilt when he saw the time, but the rational part of his mind quickly pointed out that sleep was a weapon, and he needed to be at his best when they found Stefan. He did not let it enter his mind that they might not find him that day.

They got underway as soon as he got to his sled.

<hr>

It was a good thing the weather had continued to be good overnight; the tracks still created an easily-followed trail that continued down slope toward the valley ahead. So they made excellent time.

Raedrick began to worry more and more, though. It had now been two full days, and getting well into the third, that Stefan had been up here without aid. How much longer could he last, if he had at all? How long should they keep up the search before simply declaring him lost? And as the tracks led them deeper into the valley and trees began to spring up again, sparse at first but becoming an actual forest up ahead, a bigger question reared: whose tracks were they following?

They stopped for a brief lunch alongside a small stream, mostly frozen over except for a narrow strip in its center where the running water kept the ice from getting a firm hold, and Raedrick found he was not the only one troubled about this turn of events.

"An injured man, unable to get food or fuel for a fire, could not last very long up here," Povol said, "so how much longer do you want to search?"

Julian shrugged and took a bite of dried beef, looking at Raedrick in that way he did that said he was deferring the answer.

Raedrick frowned. He had been mulling that over for a while and he had no good answers either.

Sebastini spoke up. "A man can survive for quite a while, as long as he has water." The old man swept his arm around, gesturing at the snowfield all around them. "Which is plentiful, right now."

Povol snorted. "Bigger concern's the cold." He turned frank eyes toward Raedrick. "If he made it through last night, he'll be hypothermic. No chance he lasts a third night."

"He could have found another cave like yours," Julian said.

Povol shook his head. "He didn't use my cave or we would have seen him, or signs of him, and the next good cave that could be shelter is a couple miles west, and upslope again. With a busted leg..." He left the rest unsaid.

"The trail we're following wasn't left by a man with an injured leg," Sebastini pointed out.

Povol shrugged. "Not much else to go on. Could be whoever left this trail found him, or was carrying him, or..."

"Or there's something else going on here," Raedrick said, interrupting. He sighed and looked down toward the valley floor, now just a mile or so away and a couple hundred feet below them, and covered in evergreens. A big part of his mind shouted that they should return to town, that Stefan was dead. If he had ever been up here at all. They only had Tolburt's word on what happened, and he had lied to Raedrick before.

But not about something like this.

No, about something much worse.

It was a not a choice he relished making. If they gave up too soon, he condemned Stefan to die slowly, either of thirst and hunger or from exposure. But they only had so many supplies themselves.

And then there was that big question of the tracks. He could not shake the feeling that he was missing something here, something important.

"What you wanna do, Constable?" Povol asked again. "Don't much matter to me; I get paid regardless. But..." He spread his hands, letting the silence finish the sentence for him. There was no chance they would be able to find this Stefan, if they had not already. They might as well head back to town and save themselves the trouble.

Raedrick was just about to voice reluctant agreement with Povol's unspoken sentiment. But then he glanced down toward the valley again, and noticed something new: a trail of smoke rising out of the trees, about a third of the way across the valley floor.

It should not have been a surprise, seeing that. They were following a man's tracks, and men always build fires in the sorts of conditions that prevailed up here in the mountains, at least once they were finished moving around for the day.

If the person who left the tracks was down there, they could catch up with him. And maybe he would be able to assist them in their search somehow. Or maybe Stefan was down there as well.

There was only one way to find out.

The scent of woodsmoke lay lightly upon the forest, growing steadily stronger as Raedrick and his party drew near to the campsite. The trees here were tall and thick of trunk; it had been decades since men had felled a tree here, if ever they had. Though they were spaced well apart, the trees were plentiful enough that they obscured vision past a few dozen feet. The forest itself was quiet, the accumulated snowfall less, the flakes having collected on the bows above instead of making it to the ground. All the same, as in the Glamorwood there were areas of unexpectedly deep snow and fallen limbs, slowing the group's progress.

It may have been smarter, and less hassle, to leave the sleds - and the dogs - behind shortly after they entered the woods and came across the first obstruction, but Povol would not hear of it. He had spent too much time and effort - and money

- raising and training his dogs. He was not about to leave them out where they could be taken by a predator, or run away, or...

Raedrick looked askance at the mountaineer as he voiced that objection. "The dogs each weigh almost as much as a man. I think they can take care of themselves, maybe better than we can."

Povol snorted. "Not sure what you use to qualify a dog as a man."

Raedrick just stared at him, then repeated the request, more firmly.

Povol shook his head again, emphatically, and the look in his eyes told Raedrick to give over, because he would get nowhere with this.

So they continued on with the sleds, despite Raedrick's growing unease in doing so.

But why should he be uneasy? It was not like they were trying to be stealthy in their approach. They were on a rescue mission, not scouting out some enemy stronghold or something.

It must be the anniversary that had him jumpy...

Just like that, it struck him. He and Julian had not performed their remembrance ritual yesterday. He had meant to, but with everything that had happened it slipped away. He had not even thought about it. Guilt swept through him, guilt over forgetting to honor his men's sacrifice, and guilt over the betrayal he had lead them into.

Not that it had not been the right thing to do. He never doubted that. But doing the right thing carried a dreadful cost, a cost that he would have been fine paying himself. But to ask it of his men... And he had not even asked.

This was not the time to dwell on such things. He needed to keep his mind on the present, not wallow in the price for his actions. He shoved the guilt down, stifling it beneath a weight of will, but he was not able to make it leave completely.

Nor could he banish his own apprehension over the camp they were approaching.

From up ahead, he heard the pop of fresh wood catching fire, and then they rounded the trunks of a particularly large and closely-placed pair of trees and caught sight of the camp.

A quartet of men sat around the fire, which burned merrily and energetically within a makeshift fire pit the men made by stacking rocks of varying sizes together in a ring. They had set up a pair of spits over the fire, which held several animal corpses that sizzled and spat grease periodically, adding the pleasant aroma of meat that was nearly done cooking to the now prominent odor of woodsmoke that dwarfed the fresh scent of new snowfall that had mostly dominated the forest until now.

Raedrick halted his sled next to Povol and traded glances with him. The mountaineer gave a little shrug.

Might as well go and say hello.

The group dismounted their sleds quickly and set off on foot for the last twenty feet or so until they reached the edge of the camp.

Or at least, they meant to.

"Hold it right there," came a gravelly voice, from off to Raedrick's right.

He froze, turning his head slowly in that direction, but not before he saw the men around the fire turn swiftly toward the group, weapons in their hands and from their expressions completely unsurprised.

The voice came from a lean man who stood a head taller than Raedrick and was dressed in ragged furs and wools. He, too, was armed. And so were the three other men with him.

The man half-grinned, half-smirked, and the soft clearing of a throat from the left announced the presence of still more men.

Raedrick's group was surrounded, or near enough to it.

Wonderful.

❧ I I ❧

UNDER ARMS

The men spread out in a loose half-circle between Raedrick's group and their camp site. They numbered a dozen in all. To a man, they wore a ragged mixture of furs and wools that bore heavy grime from an extended time in the wild without cleaning. They all wore their hair long and most had rough beards that had not been trimmed in some time.

And they all brandished weapons: swords, a few axes, and two bows with arrows nocked.

A big, burly man with a protruding gut, salt and pepper hair, and a long bushy beard that reached nearly to his chest stepped forward. His left eye was fused shut by a puckered scar that ran down his forehead, across his left cheek, and to his jaw. He scowled at Raedrick and his companions, and the scar and missing eye gave the scowl a particularly menacing look. Had he never heard of an eye patch?

"Well, well. What have we here, boys? A few lost souls, wandering in the wilds, hmm?"

A couple of the men snickered, but made no other comment.

The speaker, apparently the leader of the group, spoke again. "What brings you four out here?"

Raedrick shared a looked with Julian, whose expression was flat and guarded, as though he anticipated trouble. He held his bow in his left hand and his right lingered near his quiver, which hung from his hip opposite his long dagger. He was ready to throw down, but they could not stand against this many men, not at this range.

Raedrick took a step toward the leader, but stopped quickly when he noticed the sudden tension in the other men, the way the bowmen drew halfway back on their bowstrings, the sudden creak of leather as men adjusted their stances to be ready to move. This would require great care if they were going to avoid a confrontation.

"We're looking for someone."

The leader cocked his head to the side and licked his lips as though tasting Raedrick's words. "Looking? Found someone you have, I would say, hmm?"

Right.

He cleared his throat. "I'm Raedrick Baletier, one of the Constables of Lydelton." The tension within the men went up as soon as he said the word Constables, and Raedrick realized he just made a mistake. But the die was cast, might as well keep on. "This is Julian Hinderbrook, Povol Gerberson, and Ravi Sebastini, guildsman of the Healers Circle." Hopefully Sebastini's status as a guildsman would go a ways toward easing their tension. Few and far between were the men who did not esteem the Healers Circle. Even the most hardened criminals had been known to leave guildsmen be, or even offer them assistance. You never knew when you might need the Circle's assistance, and though they were known to treat all comers, there was an unspoken implication when one dealt with them that causing them offense might tarnish one's chances with them in the future.

On cue, the leader's eye widened a hair at Sebastini's introduction. Raedrick glanced behind at the old man and was pleased to see he had let his cloak fall open, revealing his distinctive white and gold coat beneath.

"We received word of a badly injured man in the vicinity, and we've come to bring him back to town for care. We saw the smoke from your campfire and thought you may have seen him."

"That right." The leader sucked on his lower lip for a second or two, considering Raedrick with a disdainful look. "Ain't no one injured here." *Yet*, the man's tone implied heavily.

Raedrick nodded, managing a polite smile. "We'll leave you in peace then. Good day." He made to turn back to his companions, but halted when the leader spoke again.

"What happened to this poor fellow?" His tone said he felt no empathy for Stefan's predicament at all. "What's he look like?" He smiled quickly, a fake smile that never touched his single good eye. "In case we see 'Im."

Get the hell out of here. Now.

Raedrick knew he should follow the voice of his instinct, but fleeing at this point would only tip the leader's hand, forcing him to start violence if that was his real intent. And perhaps Raedrick could still get his companions out of this without having to resort to a fight that they could not win. Not with the odds as they were right then.

Readrick looked at the leader and put on a sympathetic frown. "Fell in a ditch during the storm two nights ago. Broke his leg. He friend almost died bringing us the word."

The leader nodded, pursing his lips again. Except this time, his eye twinkled with something that was almost merriment but not quite. Something more...sadistic. "That sounds familiar," he said, suddenly grinning as he looked at a man halfway around the semicircle to his right, Raedrick's left. "Don't it, Stefan?"

Raedrick's blood turned to ice water when he heard the name.

Oh no.

Stefan, a skinny man of average height and no beard, chuckled. "Guess I should have bled him, Geoff," he said. "Damn. I thought the storm would finish him off. That little bastard is a lot more tough than we figured."

Geoff nodded agreement then turned his eye back to Raedrick. His grin broadened, but it did not convey good humor, only the promise of sadistic actions to come. "I've got a problem here, Constable," he said. "See, I can't really let anyone go and let folks know what we're doing up here."

"And that is what, exactly?" Raedrick asked, keeping his voice calm despite the rapid beating of his heart.

Geoff did not answer. He made a small gesture with his left hand, and the two bowmen in his group drew their bowstrings back and released in a single fluid motion.

Then things began happening very quickly.

BURSTING FREE

Instinct, honed by dozens of engagements in as many battles, sent Raedrick diving to the right. His shoulder hit the snow, and he tucked into a roll and bounded back up to his feet a heartbeat later with his dagger in his hand. The arrow whistled past him as he rolled, close enough that he felt the slight breeze that marked its wake. That was close.

A cry of pain went up behind him, but he did not have time to see who was hit. Two men - one skinny and quick the other taller, with more muscles, though it was hard to tell for sure under their winter clothing - threw themselves at him. Both bore longswords, but only the skinny one attempted anything even approximating a proper cut.

Raedrick ducked beneath the cut with ease, but that just left him open to the bull rush from the larger man. The wind left his lungs as the fellow tackled him to the ground, his arms wrapped tightly around Raedrick's torso.

Unfortunately for Raedrick's attacker, he did not manage to secure Raedrick's arms when he took him down. The bandit squirmed spasmodically and let out a squeaky cry that was half surprise and have despairing understanding as Raedrick plunged his dagger into the little dimple beneath his ear. And then he lay still.

There was no time to relish that small victory. The other man was still there, and there were ten others after him.

Raedrick's lungs burned and he had difficulty inhaling, but he could not focus on that either, not if he wanted to live.

The quirky swordsman thrust his blade down at him, a stream of sunlight glinting off the sharpened tip for a second as it descended.

Raedrick rolled to his right, pressing upward with his arms and lifting the dead man's body as he did. He felt an impact, strong enough that it nearly forced the body back down onto him, and then the tip of the swordsman's blade emerged from the front of the dead man's chest.

Raedrick threw his whole weight into continuing the roll, forcing the body to the ground as he rolled onto his right shoulder.

The swordsman issued cry of chagrin as he lost grip on his blade and stumbled, falling to one knee on the other side of the dead man's body.

That was the opening Raedrick needed. He pressed down against the ground and forced himself to his feet, finally drawing in a lung full of air as he did so.

To his side, his attacker was regaining his feet as well. But he was unarmed.

Raedrick took only a moment to regain his equilibrium, then he sprang forward, kicking out with the toe of his boot. The attack caught the swordsman on the bottom of his jaw, snapping his head backward jarringly.

The man let out a grunt, there was a sharp cracking of bone, and then he fell limply to the ground, stunned at least.

All around, grunts, curses, and screams filled the area. And with them…growls and barks?

Off to the left, Julian loosed an arrow that took one of the attacking men in the thigh, but two others leapt past him and got within arm's reach before he could nock another arrow.

Further back, Povol was crouched next to his sled, fumbling at the ties that bound his dogs with his left hand. An arrow had penetrated his right hand. The dogs snapped and growled, but could do little else.

Three more men were closing on Povol. There was no way Raedrick could get to his aid in time to help.

But there was no need. Povol had worked those knots countless times, and injured hand or no, he knew how they worked. A second before the men reached him, he pulled the final knot and barked - almost literally barked - a single command.

The five dogs who pulled his sled leapt forward as one, and the three attacking men went down in a writhing mess of fur, fists, axes, teeth, growls, curses, and screams.

This was no time to stop moving. Raedrick dropped to his knee and grabbed up the sword that had been dropped by the man who tackled him, scanning his eyes to the right.

Sebastini stood a few paces in front of Julian's and Povol's positions between two of the attackers, who held him by the upper arms in firm grips. Though his eyes were tight, with fear no doubt, the guildsman held himself erect and wore a perfectly calm expression.

One of the bowmen was down, an arrow through his throat. The other stood next to Geoff, who surveyed the goings on with a displeased scowl on his face that only grew worse when his eye met Raedrick's.

For a second they locked gazes, and Raedrick felt he could see into the man's soul, so bright was the burning heat in his eyes.

A soul that could very well have been his own, if circumstances had been just a little bit different, and certainly reflected what some of Raedrick's own men had turned into after they parted ways. Geoff was a man past the edge of desperation, a man willing to do anything, prey on anyone, to keep himself alive and fed for another day.

Geoff broke their stare first, letting out a roar of rage. He swung his axe, a long-handled double-bladed battle axe that made Raedrick want to wince inwardly, it probably weighed so much, and pointed it at him. "Shoot him!"

The bowman pivoted so he faced Raedrick, then drew back and loosed.

But Raedrick was already moving. He shoved himself to his feet and broke left, spinning a complete circle that sent his cloak whirling around him even as he retreated. He felt the cloak tug as the arrow passed through it, but it did not strike him.

He raced past the engagement between Povol's dogs and the three men, darting left and right, crouching and jumping to make himself a hard target.

Another arrow whizzed by, just in front of him, and he again dove into a roll.

Ahead of him, Povol pulled a long piece of wood from the front of his sled. It took a moment for Raedrick to realize it was a spear. But the mountaineer would not be able to wield it properly, not with his strong hand run through as it was.

"Run, Povol," Raedrick called, waving at him to move.

Povol turned disbelieving eyes at Raedrick and snarled. "Not a chance - "

One of the dogs let out a yelp of agony. A second followed suit, then a third.

Raedrick spun around to see two of the men shove the dead dogs aside and push themselves to their feet. Their buddy was beset by the last two dogs, but he still thrashed and kicked strongly.

Beyond them, Julian lay on his back, one of the attackers' swords at his throat. He had his hands raised, open and free of weapons, in a gesture of surrender.

The other of the pair who attacked Julian was hurrying forward, toward Povol and Raedrick, and the remaining bowman was drawing another arrow back and sighting in on Povol and Raedrick.

"Run!" Raedrick shouted again, and shoved Povol in the shoulder. Hard.

This time the mountaineer offered no protest. He ducked, turned, and ran, a heartbeat before the bowman's arrow sped through the air where his head used to be.

Raedrick glanced back at Julian and Sebastini, torn. He could not just leave them to these men.

But the final two dogs were dead, the third man from that group finding his feet, his face a bloody mess from where one of the dogs and been gnawing on him and eyes burning with murderous intent.

The other three men would be on Raedrick in a heartbeat, and the longsword he bore was both heavier than his Tyrashi blade and required different techniques than he was used to. He might have been able to take them together using *his* weapon - if the bowman did not end him first - but with the longsword?

Hating the decision, but knowing there was no other option open to him, Raedrick turned and ran after Povol, ducking left and right to put as many trees between himself and the men, whoever they were, as he could.

✵ 13 ✵

TAKING STOCK

The sword against his throat increased its pressure ever so slightly and Julian cringed back. Or he would have, had there been anyplace further back he could have cringed. He could not move his throat further from the sword than it was, not without doing something incredibly stupid and easy to anticipate. As it was he lay prone, his hands raised in surrender and his eyes fixed on those of the man holding the sword.

Those eyes burned with hate and bloodlust. That did not make Julian feel good about the odds of him surviving the next few minutes.

Around him, the rugged men - he was beginning to think of them as brigands in his own mind; maybe they were the leftovers from Isenholf's band - were taking stock, licking their wounds. And those wounds were extensive: three dead and three more badly wounded, from what he could tell by listening. Not too bad for a group one third of the brigands' size, and taken by surprise, no less.

The swordsman looked away from Raedrick, back toward the campfire, where Geoff had been standing, and called out, "What ya want me to do wit' 'im?"

"Do not harm him." That was Sebastini's voice. Knowing that he lived made some of the tension in Julian's chest drain away. Some of it.

"You're in no position to dictate, Healer," said Geoff. Julian did not think he would ever forget that guy's voice.

Sebastini snorted. "Nor are you. You wish my services to see to your men. I wish for you to not harm him." He paused, meaningfully. "Like for like, Geoff. It is a fair exchange."

"Piss on that," said a different brigand whose voice Julian had not heard before. "Your guild treats everyone who comes to them."

"Indeed we do," Sebastini said. "But you did not come to us, or *request* for us to come to you. You assaulted my companions and I while we were attempting to see to the well-being of another. And now you threaten him, and myself as well." Julian could easily picture the satisfied smile that Ravi had to be wearing; it showed

365

through in his tone as he spoke. "We give our services *freely*, Geoff. I am under no compulsion to provide you with any assistance at all."

Silence reigned for a long time, though faintly - very faintly - Julian thought he could hear Geoff and the other man talking quickly to each other.

Finally, after what seemed forever, a trio of footsteps hurrying through the snow announced the arrival of three more brigands. They came to a halt nearby but outside of Julian's view and paused for a few seconds, panting, before one of them spoke.

"They gave us the slip, Geoff."

"What do you mean they gave you the slip?" Geoff asked, his voice rising abruptly and his tone dangerous. "There's half a foot of snow out there! They can't hide their tracks."

The speaker cleared his throat and spoke again, sounding apologetic. "They circled around and crossed their own trail three times, then they veered off over yonder until they found bare rock." A brief pause followed and Julian imagined the man was shrugging helplessly. "We lost the trail."

"Bugger me," Geoff said.

"Last thing we need is them interfering," another voice - Julian thought it was Stefan - said. "If they can -"

"You think I don't know that?" Geoff interrupted. He sighed, then added, "Crap."

The brigand Geoff had spoken with earlier interjected, "That's another reason to keep him alive. Information. About his friends and about the town."

The sound of general concurrence followed, and Julian could almost see Geoff sighing and nodding.

"Let him up," Geoff ordered, and a very brief period of hesitation followed for a second or three. Then the sword left Raedrick's throat and a powerful man with a trio of star tattoos on his forehead pulled Julian roughly to his feet.

Even if he would have been so inclined as to leave Ravi to these men's hospitality, Julian could not have gotten far. A quartet of men stood in his immediate vicinity, watching his every movement. Good thing he had no intention of running, not without bringing Ravi along with him.

Geoff faced Julian from about ten feet distant. His scowl contained the promise of all many of torments that would not end any time soon. But instead, he said, "Looks like it's your lucky day." The scowl became a positively malicious grin.

A couple of the brigands chuckled. One of them tested the edge of a dagger against his thumb.

Julian swallowed, hard. This was going to be bad.

———

"I think we've lost them," Povol declared, then he flopped onto the rock next to Raedrick.

"Let's hope so. How's the hand?"

Povol raised the roughly-bandaged hand and shrugged. The dressing looking positively awful. Dirty, held in place only with a quick knot, Povol had already bled through it, so the thing was basically one big bloodstain. "Willam'll fix me up good as new," Povol said.

If we get to Willam in time, Raedrick did not say.

"We need to figure a way to get close to their camp again," Raedrick said instead.

Povol shook his head emphatically. "That's nuts. What do you hope to gain from doing something like that?"

Did he really not know, or was that just stress and shock talking? Raedrick drew a breath to keep himself calm, then he spoke. "We're going to get Julian and Sebastini away from those men, Povol."

A loud snort was Povol's first response. "They're both dead by now."

It was Raedrick's turn for an emphatic head shake. "They won't harm Sebastini. Men like that need the Healers Circle's assistance far more often than most, so they will not want to offend him. And as for Julian," he sighed, "we will just have to trust in hope."

Povol looked at Raedrick like he had never seen him before. "You're mad." Povol pushed himself up to his feet then stood there for a second, leaning on his spear and looking out and down toward the forest's canopy a few dozen feet beneath the ledge they occupied. Finally, he pointed to the east, where the sun was about to begin setting. "We need to get out of here while we still can. The sun will cover us if we go now."

Raedrick sent a firm stare Povol's way. "You came up here to rescue a man, Povol."

"And it turns out he didn't need rescuing. Your friend Tolburt fed you a line of crap and you fell for it like an idiot." He shook his head again, then turned and spat in the general direction of the enemy camp.

That stung, but the words were true. He had not questioned Tolburt's story, not even once. And he should have; he remembered how Tolburt was, even before all hope was lost.

Raedrick drew a deep breath. "That may be true, but that does not change our obligation to Julian and Sebastini." He stood as well, brushing off his hands onto his pant legs. "Put it this way. You leave now without even trying to find out their status and I'll tell the Mayor you did not fulfill your part of the contract." He raised an eyebrow. "No rescue, no money."

Povol spluttered in consternation for a few seconds. "But..." He jabbed a finger - at least he could work the fingers on his injured hand; that was something - at Raedrick's face. "That was never a condition of our agreement, nor was going on a suicide mission against a group of bandits. Damn it, I'm not a warrior."

Raedrick snorted. Povol could more than handle himself. In his brief tenure as Constable, Raedrick had heard of Povol's involvement in no less than five or six bar brawls, and he had never come out on the losing end. Of course, a bar brawl is a far cry from a fight to the death with a group of trained killers. That was something Povol had not prepared for, not the way Julian and Raedrick had. It was probably not fair to ask this of him.

But there was no one else. In his gut, Raedrick sensed that, whatever reassurances he had spoken to Povol, as soon as Sebastini stopped being of use to those men, they would leave him in a shallow grave. Same with Julian, if they had not killed him already.

He did not have time to dilly dally.

He squared his shoulders and put on his most commanding expression, looking

Povol in the eye. "I am altering the deal, Povol. I only pray I don't have to alter it any further."

Povol traded glares with him for a long time. The mountaineer's nostrils flared with each breath as he clearly fought back a number of powerful emotions, but that was the only indicator aside from his scowl - and truth be told it seemed he preferred scowls to anything else so that was not much of a change.

Finally, he nodded and looked away, longingly, toward the setting sun and the safety that lay in that direction. "Alright, Constable, I'm in. But not for a suicide run, here?"

Raedrick returned the nod. "If we can't retrieve them without a good chance of success, you don't have to go on."

Povol looked sidelong at him, his lips pursing as he considered Raedrick's words. "You mean *we* won't go on with it."

Raedrick looked away from him, toward the slowly rising smoke from the brigands' campfire, now barely visible in the swiftly approaching twilight, but did not reply.

No matter what, he would not leave his men in captivity again.

❧ 14 ❧

INTO THE BREECH

I t was well past twilight and on to full dark by the time Raedrick and Povol crept their way down from their rocky perch and to the brigands' camp site.

Or what had been the brigands' camp site.

The fire still smoldered, the glowing coals and last remaining flames clearly visible in the blackness between the trees, but it had clearly not been tended in some time. The snow around the site was trampled almost to a solid block, making it exceedingly difficult to determine what happened where and when.

The bodies were easy to find, though. Three men, lined up in a row with their hands crossed over their chests, all dressed in the haphazard attire that marked them as part of the brigand party. Raedrick breathed a sigh of relief to see neither Julian nor Sebastini among them, just the two men who had attacked Raedrick - his kick must have broken the second man's neck - and the fellow Julian shot through the throat. Of course, that left the question of what had happened to Raedrick's friends, but at least they were still alive.

Probably.

From off to the right, Povol let out a strangled curse.

Raedrick hurried over and immediately saw what had the Mountaineer so chagrined. Povol's sleds still lay off to the side, where they had left the conveyances earlier. They were mostly intact, only the straps that clipped the dog teams to them having been cut. But that was not what had evoked the curse.

All of the Povols dogs were dead. Not just the five he had managed to free to join in the fight, but all of them. Their bodies lay stacked like cordwood on the other side of the sleds, tossed aside like so much refuse. And they were completely lacking in fur; the brigands had skinned them.

It was a perfectly sensible thing to do, with winter's heart fast approaching and every scrap of insulation possibly the difference between life and death by hypothermia. But understand it as Raedrick did, these were not wild animals or

369

predators who were harassing a herd. They were trained dogs, a man's friend and companion.

And looking into Povol's eyes right then, seeing how they reflected the dimming red glow of the dying campfire, Raedrick knew those dogs were as dear to him as family.

"Those bastards," Povol growled through clenched teeth. He flexed his good hand on the haft of his spear and Raedrick imagined he could hear the wood groan ever so quietly beneath the strain of the mountaineer's grip.

"I'm sorry, Povol," Raedrick said, feeling the words a bit lame.

Povol's breathing faltered for a second, then he sniffed and lowered his head. A soft sound escaped his lips, and Raedrick realized with a shock that he was weeping, weeping for his dogs, his friends.

He backed away a few steps, then turned back to the campfire, leaving the mountaineer to his grief. He would only have resented Raedrick for witnessing it.

By the time Povol recovered himself and returned to Raedrick's side, he had found the trail the brigands - and their captives he hoped - took away from the campfire. It would have been exceedingly difficult to conceal the footsteps of eleven people in the snow; Raedrick could not even conceive of a way to do it, now that he thought about it. So the trail was plain to see even in the faint light of the dying campfire and the rising moon.

"That's way too obvious," Povol said. From the tone of his voice - dry and slightly sardonic - one would never have known he had just suffered a personal tragedy, but Raedrick did not deceive himself. Beneath the surface, the mountaineer seethed.

Almost as much as Raedrick did himself.

Not again. Not ever.

Raedrick nodded. "If I were Geoff, I would leave men along my back trail to ambush us if we followed."

"Unless you thought we went back to town."

Raedrick turned and looked at him seriously. "He is not that stupid."

In the faint light, he could barely tell when Povol turned to meet his gaze. But he did, and held it for several seconds before he nodded acknowledgement. "So what do we do?"

Raedrick chuckled mirthlessly, testing his dagger in its sheath. Memories of a dozen midnight excursions behind enemy lines sprang to mind as he turned away from Povol and began following the beaten path through the snow.

"We set off the trap."

❧ 15 ❧

PLANNING

Julian cracked his eyes open and instantly wished he had not.

The light, so intense it seemed to burn into his brain, made him duck away, or at least try to. It felt like a torch literally jabbed into his head while it was still burning. But that did not compare with the fire that blossomed all over his skin, growing all the greater the more fully awake, and aware of himself, he became.

A guttural groan, nearly a scream, escaped his lips before he could force himself to silence.

Memory flooded back, knowledge racing ahead of pain to reclaim his mind before madness had a chance to take hold, and he grimaced, forcing the cries down as he took control once again. He would not give the bastards the satisfaction.

He tried not to remember that he had been unable to keep that resolve for very long last night. Better not to focus on that. Focus on the now, and the future. Resistance and survival depended on not giving in to despair, on remembering himself and his mission.

The Army taught him that in the final stages of his training before he reported to Raedrick's squad, oh so long ago. The odds of being captured by the enemy were slim, but if it happened every soldier needed to know what was expected of him, how he should behave, and how to resist betraying his fellows even under the worst torture.

He had scoffed at the training, back then. No one would be able to get to him.

But he had never been put to the test, not like that. Not until last night. Now, feeling the aftermath - and remembering how eager he had been to sell his friends out, how easily the knowledge he had came to his tongue, how hard it was to avoid saying anything - he shuddered to consider having to endure that treatment again.

He did not want to betray Rae, or his new home. But it hurt so bad.

So bad.

He did not know how long he could hold out in the face of what Geoff's men had done to him, and that had only been an abbreviated session.

Something touched his forehead and Julian swiped at it, instinctively, knocking it away. It was only after he had done it that he realized his hands were not bound. In amazement at that discrepancy, he looked around wildly, only stopping when a blurry ball of color appeared in his confused vision.

"Julian."

The word, his name, was barely understandable.

He blinked, and his vision cleared somewhat. The voice - it was a man's voice - spoke his name again, and then the colorful ball sprang into focus.

It was Ravi's head.

The guildsman looked down at him with concerned eyes. But when Julian met his gaze after a few seconds, some of the concern left his face, and a half smile appeared.

"It's good to see you awake."

Julian blinked again, and would have sat up, but something held him back. And then a new fire cut across his chest, making him clench his teeth to avoid groaning even as he sagged back against his bed. Or the ground. Or whatever it was he lay upon.

"Easy, my friend," Ravi said, laying a calming hand on Julian's chest. The fire seemed to fade at his touch. "Do not move too quickly."

Julian inhaled, then spent the next half minute coughing. He coughed so hard, for a second he thought he would be unable to draw another breath no matter how acute the need to breathe became. And then, all at once, the coughing stopped.

He gasped in air, grateful for ever scrap he could take in. Then he lay there, doing nothing but breathing, and let his muscles relax. After last night's agony and the fiery discomfort of the morning - was it morning? - It felt good just to do that.

"Where," another lesser cough stopped him in mid thought. "Where are we?"

Ravi shrugged and produced a wet cloth. As he used it to wipe Julian's brow, Julian realized that was what he had swiped away a moment ago. If Ravi noticed the look of guilt Julian tried to suppress, he did not mention it. "Our hosts' camp. Probably five or six miles northeast of where we met them."

Julian wanted to melt beneath the comforting warmth and wetness of Ravi's rag, but this was no time to lose his bearing. "That far..." He frowned, shaking his head. He had no recollection of walking that far. Or really, of walking at all. He only remembered the...treatment. And then a red haze, followed by the all-too-brief slumber that Ravi interrupted. "How did we get here?"

Ravi chuckled. "I walked. You," he winced. "You, they dragged behind on a pathetic excuse for a litter."

"Ah."

"We do not have much time," Ravi said, sudden intensity in his voice and his gaze lending extra weight to his words. "When they..."

Geoff's strong, gruff voice broke in, overpowering Ravi's soft speech easily. "How is our guest, guildsman?"

Ravi withdrew from Julian's side, turning a stern gaze on the man who had stepped into the tent - Julian only now realized that he was in fact lying within a tent, and a rather poorly maintained one at that. "Better than I would have expected, considering your definition of hospitality." His words were laced with deepest contempt, conveying a bitter rebuke.

But if Geoff noticed, or cared, it did not show from the impassive expression he maintained as he looked past Ravi toward Julian. "Good. It would be a shame to waste him."

Ravi scowled, but said nothing more. Julian noticed that he flexed his fingers in both hands, making fists and the releasing them quickly. So, he did not find it any easier to write off dishonorable or downright evil behavior than any of the rest of the civilized population did. That could be useful, for planning an escape.

Julian looked up at Geoff and tried to put every bit of contempt he could muster into his gaze. The outlaw just looked down at him, his face implacable, and if the reproach Julian was trying to send affected him in any way, it did not show.

Several long seconds went by, and then Geoff cracked a little smile, one that Julian supposed was meant to be ingratiating, or at least not menacing, but only came across as fake. "You've got spirit, I'll give you that," Geoff said. "Better to show some sense. How long can you hold out, hmm?" He leaned forward, seeming to loom over Julian's prone form. "What I'm asking isn't much."

Julian just scowled at him, trying hard not to show how tempting the notion of just giving in was.

Geoff studied him for another long moment then shrugged and turned back to Ravi. "Make sure he doesn't get too comfortable," he said. Then he turned and swept out of the tent. "We move in one hour," he called over his shoulder. And then the tent flaps fell into place behind him.

Ravi breathed a muted curse that took Julian by surprise. He did not know guildsmen ever heard that particular phrase, much less understood what it meant to use it properly. The old man, scowling, turned away from the tent entrance and back to Julian. He must have seen the surprise on Julian's face because he flushed and shrugged slightly. "Wasn't always a Healer," was all he said.

Over the next several minutes, Ravi gave Julian a long, gentle massage, interspersed with more washing with the blessedly warm water on the rag. That was all, but by the end of it, Julian felt amazingly better. He stretched, as much as he could with the bands holding his chest and thighs down - he finally figured out what they were in the middle of Ravi's treatment - and sighed expansively.

"I could swear you were a mage," he said, gratefully.

Ravi sniffed, actually looking affronted. "Please. I am a medical professional, not some overgrown adolescent who enjoys playing with shiny objects."

Julian blinked in surprise, but found himself without adequate words to respond to that description.

Ravi went on, "They did not actually cause any serious damage. One of those fellows knows his way around an apothecary. The solutions they used would have felt like they were burning your skin away," Julian shuddered at the memory, "but in reality they are not much more than a topical irritant. Easily washed away, with the proper ingredients."

"Thanks."

Ravi nodded, but frowned as he looked back at the tent entrance. "I fear it will be for nought in a few hours. Just an excuse for them to get started again."

"Let me worry about that."

Ravi looked askance at him. More than askance. The look he gave Julian screamed that the guildsman thought he must be insane.

Julian put on his best, most dashing smile and tried to adopt the most confident tone he could. "You need to find a way to get us out of here. Take note of their watch rotations, who does what in camp, how their sentries are laid out... The next time they let their guard down, or let up at all, we need to be ready to move. Quickly."

Ravi snorted. "There is an excellent chance you will be unable to go anywhere." His earnest face looked pained, and wary, as he leaned in closer to speak more quietly. "Why don't you just tell them? We really don't know much at all about them, and what they're up to."

Julian shook his head. "They're on the run. They'll never believe we don't know about them, or have a notion of what they're looking for, else why would we be up here? They have to think Tolburt told us everything about them already, and Geoff's all but certain troops will be right behind us. I'll never be able to convince him otherwise." He let out a sigh. "Besides, soon as he's decided I've told him anything, he'll kill me."

Ravi blinked at that, shaking his head in denial. "No. No, he promised your health in exchange for my services."

"Did he? *Really*?"

"Well...I thought..."

"Did he actually come out and say he would spare me, or was it just implied?"

Ravi frowned deeply.

Julian thought as much. He sighed again. "When the time comes, he won't hesitate. By then, you will have already treated his men. You've been seeing to them as well as me, yes?"

Ravi nodded, looking a bit sick.

"Well. There you have it." Julian pushed himself upward as much as he could within his restraints and fixed Ravi with his most stern gaze. "Of course, sooner or later, probably sooner, if he doesn't get what he wants, he'll decide to finish me, regardless. And maybe you as well, since you won't help him once I'm gone, will you?"

Ravi shook his head. He looked even more pale.

"In that case, we have to get out of here. And the sooner the better."

Ravi swallowed. Hard. He looked decidedly uncomfortable with the entire notion, but finally, after more than a few long seconds of consideration, he nodded acquiescence.

Julian managed a grin that he hoped looked confident. Time to get to work breaking out of here.

16

FORCED MARCH

Geoff was not kidding. Exactly one hour after he left, they were on the road again. Or they would have been, had there been a road. They trudged along in a rough line behind Geoff and another man - Stefan, Julian thought though he never got a good look at him to be sure. Three more of Geoff's men walked ahead of Julian and Ravi, blocking most of Julian's view ahead. The remaining four walked behind them, one of them with a pronounced limp from the arrow Julian had put into his leg.

Smart. Keep him and Ravi as closely surveilled, and as close to surrounded, as possible, to reduce chance of their escaping.

But then, where were they going to escape to, in the middle of the day, in the middle of the mountains? The fact that this particular problem factored largely into the plan he was trying to decide on was not lost on Julian.

The pace was brutal, all the more so because the bandits left the straps on around Julian's chest and shackled his arms behind his back using some contraption that attached his wrists to the straps. So he could not move his body naturally with his stride. He also could not pick his way past obstacles very well - Ravi ended up all but dragging him along in several places.

All that would not have been so bad if not for the fact that they were moving almost continually up hill. Very quickly, Julian was overheated despite the bitter cold of the mountain morning, and his breath came in rapid, ragged gasps. It was as though he could not get enough air down no matter how hard he tried.

The bandits did not talk much to each other, and never to the two prisoners, except to bark an occasional order or to grumble about the extra cost and reduced speed they incurred for keeping them with the group, or even alive at all.

It made Julian thankful that Geoff was in charge. He may have been a criminal, and an unrepentant one at that, but he was not uncivilized. At least not completely. Yet.

But how much longer could that last?

As they walked, Julian worked hard to keep note of where they were going, but also of what the bandits were doing, what they were saying, their demeanor and defensive posture, or really anything that could give him some advantage in planning or executing the escape. Or - and he hardly dared to dream on this one - if Raedrick and Povol were planning a rescue.

They emerged from the forest shortly after they set out and began ascending the smaller mountain to the north of Tollard's Peak. Julian had no idea the peak's name, if it even had one, and small as it was compared with Tollard's sheer boldness in stretching up to the top of the sky, it was easy to not realize that the peak was fairly lofty itself, with many cracks and crevices that could hide almost anything.

They stopped briefly near one of those cracks and crevices, a place where there must have been a rockslide at some point in the past. A number of boulders and smaller rocks protruded from beneath the snow, and the crack in the mountain face - Julian thought he recalled Povol talking about going up a chimney once and described it, but Julian had not really envisioned it well until now - was similarly filled. Julian supposed this spot would make a decent place for lunch, with good protection from the variable winds in the mountains.

But they did not have lunch. Instead, the bandits held a palaver. They crowded around Geoff and Stefan, speaking in low tones and referring to some paper that Stefan held in front of himself.

For a minute or two, it did not appear they would get anything decided until, finally, Geoff himself spoke out, loudly.

"Enough!"

The other bandits stopped talking. Geoff issued a series of terse orders, in a tone too low for Julian to fully make out more than a word or two. But what he heard was enough to figure out that Geoff was worried someone might be following them.

When the group set off again, two of their number remained behind, taking station in the crevices between some of the larger boulders. They would lie in wait and ambush anyone coming up behind.

This was potentially bad. Julian had no doubt Raedrick was following; he presumed Povol was as well. Normally, he would put Raedrick up against any two men and expect him to come out on top with barely a scratch. But he had not brought his sword with him. Julian had no idea how much experience Povol had, but he looked to be good in a fight.

That did not necessarily translate into his being good at killing, or at surviving an ambush.

He glanced over his shoulder once before they turned a corner that would bring them out of sight of the two bandits, trying to figure out a way to foil the ambush plan. But there was nothing he could do. A rough shove in the back from one of the bandits behind him confirmed that; it almost sent him sprawling, without his arms available to help him keep his balance. So he clumped along, going as slowly as the bandits would let him and hoping against hope that Raedrick and Povol would not be caught unawares.

By the time the sun reached the top of the mountains to the east, Raedrick and Povol's chances in the face of the brigands' ambush were the farthest thing from Julian's mind.

He only *thought* the previous night's torture left him exhausted and in pain. This day put the lie to that. When he was finally able to collapse onto his backside in the little bowl of rock the bandits - well, Geoff - chose for the night's camp site, he literally could not feel his legs, or his hands. The shackles that held his arms in place had dug into his wrists all day, and the awkward angle of his arms induced cramps in his shoulders and back. His cloak had flapped open early on, and by the end of the day, even with the layers he wore he could not shake the chill that seeped throughout his body. His legs... He never would have thought how much more difficult losing the use of his hands would make it to keep his balance. Especially as the grade they climbed became more steep, it was all he could do to put one foot in front of the other, and not fall over each time.

Ravi tried to help. He lingered back with Julian, giving him a hand as he could, but the guildsman was hardly muscle-bound, and the bandits would only let him help so much.

All told, it was pure misery.

On the bright side, Julian's inability to move steadily meant their pace slowed considerably throughout the rest of the afternoon. But that was small comfort. He was acutely aware of the annoyed looks the bandits cast his way. He could imagine the conversations going on with Geoff, up at the front of the column.

"Why are we keeping this guy with us?"

"He's just slowing us down."

"Best to bleed him and have done with it."

"Toss him off a cliff."

That last imagined suggestion made Julian's stomach lurch. The notion of falling and falling, for what he was sure would seem an eternity, of watching the ground come up to meet him, and knowing all the while that there was nothing he could do and his end was coming with that ground... He shuddered to think of it.

But there was a very real chance that the bandits would take that option, or another, before too long. Sooner or later it would not matter whether he gave them the information they wanted - especially since he really did not know anything. He was a liability, and they would be done with him.

He only prayed that Ravi had found out something that would help with their escape, because he had nothing.

❦ 17 ❧

AMBUSH

Raedrick squinted his eyes against the glare of the sunlight reflecting off the snow on the slope in front of them and considered the way ahead. The trail led upwards and to the right, veering around the base of a sheer cliff that stretched upward for several hundred feet. The base was riddled with fallen boulders and the cliff face itself was riven by large vertical cracks, all custom-made hiding spots, should someone wish to conceal himself.

It was the perfect place for an ambush.

He looked sidelong at Povol, who had stopped a few feet to his left and stood waiting calmly. The mountaineer had not found the climb up-slope difficult at all. He showed no signs of sweat or fatigue; his breathing was slow and regular. Whereas Raedrick felt like a raw recruit, unable to handle a run of more than a mile, sucking down air like it would run out in the next minute. Of course, Povol made a living by prowling these mountains all year round, in all conditions. Raedrick's own job was…less strenuous. Most days.

That did not make him feel particularly better about himself.

"You think they're waiting for us up there." It was not a question.

Raedrick considered for a moment, then nodded. That was where *he* would post a rear guard.

But then, they had passed several places during their pursuit that would have been ideal ambush sites, and always found nothing. Maybe this Geoff was not as clever as Raedrick had given him credit for. Maybe.

"Makes sense. Lots of good chimneys in that face. Lots of nooks and crannies. Plenty of places to hide, if you have the hankering."

Raedrick nodded again.

Povol waited for a several seconds before speaking again. "So, we going ahead or not?"

Of course they were going ahead. That was not a question. Not for Raedrick. And after the loss of his dogs, not for Povol either.

Raedrick had found it strange, at first, that the dogs' fate would move the man so, where the fate of human beings he knew and associated with on a near-daily basis apparently did not. He understood Povol's grief: the dogs had been his friends, maybe even his family. But they were still only dogs.

After last night he knew better than to tell Povol that, though.

The had followed the trail, Raedrick leading the way with his borrowed longsword in hand, at the ready. They marched for hours; he pushed on through the ever-deepening darkness, easily picking out the obvious signs of the brigands' passing despite the dark. Every moment, he expected to meet an attack from the rearguard. But always there was none.

Eventually, despite Raedrick's fiercest urgings to himself, fatigue began to get the better of him. His vision blurred to the point that he could not see where he was going. Or maybe the moon set and the darkness of night truly set in. Regardless, he was forced to admit they could not go on, not and expect to do any good while doing so.

Looking at Povol, for a moment he feared he had already waited too long. But after Raedrick managed to get a fire going, carefully hidden from prying eyes behind a small thicket and a pit dug into the snow and earth around the place he put the campfire, Povol came back around rather quickly.

The two men sat beside the fire, scooting as close as they dared to heat as much of themselves up as possible. For a while, they sat in silence until finally Povol spoke, softly.

"Never had many friends."

Raedrick poked at the fire with a stick, sending a stream of glowing sparks skyward as the fuel shifted. He looked at Povol sidelong. "Come again?"

The mountaineer just shrugged. "Me and other people don't really see eye to eye, for the most part." He smirked slightly. "You might have noticed."

Raedrick had noticed; tales of the man's many fights were hard to ignore. But he did not press the point.

Povol sighed, never taking his eyes off the heart of the flame. "Never had any family, growing up. Guess that's what caused it. But the dogs, though… They never mocked me, never let me down." He shook himself and forced his eyes away from the flame. His eyes met Raedrick's, and Raedrick could not deny the pain and loss the man felt. "I first started in the mountains because of the dogs, you know. If it weren't for them…" He sighed and looked down at the dirt and snow at his feet.

There was something about the way he looked, hunched over like that, that raised the hackles of Raedrick's neck. "What?"

Povol was silent for almost a full minute. When he spoke, it was so low as to be almost inaudible. "I had thought for months about ending it. I just that week came up with the perfect plan. I would tie a big rock around my ankles and jump off the end of one of the docks." He voice caught. Raedrick saw tears well up, but Povol held up a restraining hand, and Raedrick kept still. The mountaineer drew a deep breath. "But then one morning, my sled team finally meshed. We executed the most difficult maneuver in the repertoire flawlessly." He laughed quietly. "It was the very morning I was planning to jump. But when I got back from my morning rounds and unclipped the dogs, they seemed to know how much a milestone we had just passed. They yipped and jumped, bounded all around me. And looking at them…"

"You realized you couldn't do it."

Povol shook his head. "I realized I didn't *want* to do it."

Raedrick did not know how to respond to that at first. He had never been particularly fond of dogs himself, and though did not want to belittle Povol's obviously profound experience, he could not relate. Then again, it was clear that one morning changed Povol's life forever, and turned his dogs from just friends to family, a family far more enduring, more special than any he had known up until then.

Maybe that was not so strange, after all.

Raedrick shook himself back to the present, leaving memories of last night behind. Drawing his sword again, he gave Povol a serious look. "When they come, it will be from both sides at once. There will probably be three or four of them. If they're smart, they'll use bows so we can't get close. If not..." He shrugged. "If not, we may have a chance."

Povol scowled at him in response. "You're saying we can't win."

"Ambushes are designed to make it that way."

"So we're going forward...why?"

Raedrick grinned at him. "Because the best way to mess up an ambush is to trigger it."

He hustled up the slope, making a brisk pace but being careful not to go too fast. He did not want to tire himself too much before the fighting started.

Behind him, he heard Povol curse and mutter, "That doesn't make any sense at all." But he followed. That was the important part.

<hr>

They were only two, and they hid themselves exactly where Raedrick thought they would have. No imagination, and less thought. Taking them down was far easier than he would have hoped.

He rounded the large boulder and immediately dove to his left, tucking his shoulder into a roll and springing up onto his feet just as the first of them emerged from the crack in the cliff face where he had been hiding. The surprise on the man's face when his presumptive prey went from where it was supposed to be - an easy kill - to right in his face was classic.

Raedrick almost felt sorry for him as he thrust the tip of his borrowed longsword at his gut, and that almost cost him his head.

The bandit was surprised, but still well-trained. He hopped backwards, sweeping his own sword in a downward arc that knocked Raedrick's blade aside, then he followed up with a backhanded cut toward Raedrick's throat. Only the bandit's backward momentum saved him; the blade whistled past, maybe an inch from Raedrick's flesh.

The counter left the bandit open, and Raedrick wasted no time in pressing forward, inside the reach of the man's sword, and thrusting up with his own weapon.

The man jerked once when Raedrick's sword entered his chest, right at the point where the ribs meet. Then he went limp and slid slowly to the ground.

A cry of pain made him spin around in time to see the second bandit go down, Povol's spear buried deeply into his side.

Guess that answered the question of Povol's readiness and ability to fight with his strong hand injured and barely usable.

Raedrick exchanged a victorious grin with the mountaineer, and only then did it register just how close that encounter had come to ending him. The heat of exertion was replaced by a chill that went right to his bones, and he shivered. No matter how many battles he fought in, he never had managed to shake the after action letdown, the terror that sprang up from having faced death and survived, somehow.

Povol wrenched his spear free and gave Raedrick a strange look. "You alright?"

Raedrick drew a deep breath and nodded, making a dismissive gesture with his free hand. "Fine." He peered more closely at the mountaineer. "You?"

Povol shrugged, saying nothing.

That was either good or very bad. You never could tell how a man would react to battle. Some panic or freeze up, some come through without an issue. And some come to revel in the bloodshed.

"It is a hard thing," Raedrick began.

But Povol cut him off with a snort. "Ain't my first time in a fight, Constable." He smirked, derisively. "I'm not some tenderfoot that needs handholding."

Raedrick supposed that was fair enough. "Alright. Let's see to the bodies and get moving."

❧ 18 ❧

LATE NIGHT VISITOR

Julian awoke with a start. It was still dark; he could see only varying degrees of shadow within the little tent, but his nose told him another person was with him. That, and a looming sense of presence. His skin tingled with apprehension for a moment as all manner of possibilities ran through his mind as to what his visitor wanted.

"Julian." It was Ravi's voice, speaking just barely above a whisper.

Relief flooded through him and he let out the breath he was holding. The shadows shifted, accompanied by the sound of rustling clothing, then Ravi spoke again, closer to his ear.

"We have to get you out of here." He paused, and Julian heard him swallow. "They thought I was asleep, but I overheard them talking. The men they left to bring up the rear never returned. The others met with Geoff, and…"

He did not have to say the rest. They had to know it was Raedrick, and maybe Povol, who took out their rearguard. With enemies coming up the rear, the last thing they would need was someone slowing them down, or betraying their presence.

But on the other hand, he could be a useful hostage…

No. No, they had Ravi for that. And by his oaths as a guildsman he would do them no harm. He might refuse to treat them if they tried to force him, but he would not harm them. The brigands could not count on Julian to do that.

That left only one answer as to what to do with him.

"When?"

"First thing in the morning."

Julian licked his lips, but his mouth had suddenly gone dry. "Ok," he said, "what's the plan?"

"I found a knife," Ravi said, his voice trembled slightly, and he sounded uncertain. "I think I can cut you free."

Julian nodded, though he knew Ravi would not be able to see it. "Get started."

Ravi moved again in the darkness, and Julian felt the old man's hands on his chest, feeling around where the straps crossed his body and attached to the bedding beneath him. It was actually a fairly clever piece of work, when he thought about it. If...

Wait a minute.

"Ravi, how did you get in here?"

"What do you..." Ravi trailed off, the dismay in his tone making it clear that he saw it too.

Why had the bandits left his tent unguarded? There had always been a guard on Julian the entire time he had been there. And, for that matter, on Ravi as well.

Ravi froze. "Should I...?"

Julian shook his head vigorously. The die was cast. The only way was forward. "Do it," he said. "Quickly."

The old man's hands resumed their groping in the darkness for what seemed hours. In reality it was only a few seconds, tops. But at the end, after several strong tugs and more than one painful poke when Ravi slipped with his knife - Julian hoped it did not draw too much blood, but right then blood loss was the least of his concerns - the pressure on his chest let up and then fell away altogether.

"I think I got it," Ravi said.

Julian took a deep breath and tried to sit up, trying not to hope that the old man was right.

The relief he felt when he rose, unimpeded, bordered on ecstasy. "Yes!" he said as loudly as he dared, exulting in his newfound freedom of movement. "Well done, Ravi." He rolled his shoulders and twisted his torso back and forth to work out the kinks. It was as comfortable as rolling over gravel.

No time to gripe about it, though. "Help me up," he said, and found Ravi's hand. Holding on to the old man, he forced himself to his feet. There he stood wavering for a few seconds while he found his equilibrium.

If he remembered right, Geoff had his tent in the center of the camp, with the others arranged in a ring surrounding his. Very much like the patterns Julian had used during his time in the Army. Not for the first time, he pondered whether Geoff and his men were deserters. It seemed likely, from how they acted.

Hard to hold that against them, all things considered. Julian was not *that* much of a hypocrite.

"I think there is one man on watch," Ravi said quietly. "I heard him walking around out there."

Julian nodded. It made sense. Without the two men they left as rearguard, there were only seven of the bandits remaining. Putting two men on watch at a time would mean three shifts, since Julian would bet his next ten paydays Geoff was not going to stand any watch. That would leave them all strung out on not enough sleep, as opposed to just a few of them.

Come to think of it, that was probably why there was no guard at his tent, as well. Not like he was going anywhere.

One sentry ought not be too difficult to avoid.

"Ok, let's go. Keep low and stay in the shadows. We'll head out the side of the camp opposite the sentry, then double back to the trail. We keep going until we meet up with Rae and Povol, and then we get ourselves back to town, quick as we can."

"And just leave these criminals to their business?"

Julian paused. He found that idea troublesome as well, but they were not exactly in the position to take up a crusade for justice here. "Way I see it, we would not have known about these guys at all if Tolburt hadn't come to town. They weren't out here hurting anyone but him." He scowled in the darkness. "And that, they are welcome to do."

With that, he parted the flaps of his tent and looked outside.

$\mathscr{H}$ *19* $\mathscr{H}$

ESCAPE

The camp was arranged as Julian recalled: a clustering of small tents surrounding a larger tent in the center. A communal fire smoldered in its pit outside the entrance flaps to Geoff's tent, the coals giving off a dull red glow as they cooled. The smell of woodsmoke and burned meat hung in the air, and soft snores issued from several of the tents.

It was a restful sight, as long as one did not know who the camp's inhabitants were.

Julian slipped out of his tent and around the corner, crouching in the shadows between his tent and the next. And boy did that make his thighs scream in protest.

Ravi came close on his heels, still clutching his knife in a trembling hand.

Julian reached out his hand to the old man. "Let me take that."

Ravi blinked, then after a second, nodded understanding and passed the knife over. Its weight, though slight, brought Julian a bit of reassurance. At least he was not completely unarmed, although he held no illusions about his chances if he had to face one of the bandits, armed as they were.

"I need to get a sword," he mumbled.

Ravi frowned at him and opened his mouth to speak.

The sound of two rocks striking together from behind them and to the left stopped Ravi's words. Julian turned to look that way, but only saw the shadows of night. He held his breath, waiting and watching.

Another sound, softer than before but still noticeable, issued from the darkness. Then again.

A man walking through the snow. He was being careful about it, but there was only so much one could do to be silent in conditions like this; snow and ice will crunch underfoot, whatever you do.

It was the sentry. It had to be.

An idea sprung to Julian's mind. It was risky, very risky. If he botched it, the entire camp would know what was going on, and then they would be finished. But if he pulled it off…

He needed a sword. It was worth the risk.

"Wait here," he whispered to Ravi, who blinked in surprise. A moment later, his eyes widened, and he gave a vigorous shake of his head. Julian raised a finger to his lips. No time for arguments.

Then he set off into the darkness, toward the sentry.

Stepping out of the ring of tents, Julian took a moment to let his eyes adjust to the deeper darkness. It came as a bit of a surprise that the deeper darkness really was not all that deep. The ground was blanketed in snow, except where protruding rocks had been cleared by the wind, and between the stars and the glow on the western horizon that announced the moon's imminent rise there was a bit of light for the snow to reflect. So after only a very short time, Julian found he could see passing well.

The light was good enough for him to see the sentry, a dark spot against the slightly brighter background of snow, moving away from him, about thirty feet off.

Julian took a deep breath to calm himself and flexed his fingers on the hilt of Ravi's knife. He was already beginning to feel the chill; the bandits had taken most of his outer garments when they tied him and left him in the tent. Another reason they did not bother with a guard. And yet another reason that he had to risk doing this. Now that he was out of the shelter provided by the cluster of tents, Julian felt certain he would not be able to make it down the mountain without some more layers.

Moving as quickly as he dared, he pushed through the snow until he reached the sentry's footprints. He took a step, and grinned. The sentry's stride was about the same length as his.

This was working out better than he had hoped.

He moved forward, stepping from footprint to footprint and being careful not to punch through the snow any place else - that was the sound that he had heard from back by the tent, and he did not want to risk giving himself away.

Which was not exactly a way to walk quickly. Fortunately, the sentry was not exactly brisk in his movements either, and Julian gained ground fairly rapidly.

Of course, it would only take the sentry turning around, and the gig would be up.

Twenty feet.

How could this guy be so stupid that he had not even stopped walking, or checked his rear, at all?

Cursing himself for questioning his good fortune, Julian picked up the pace.

Ten feet, and the sentry stopped.

Julian tried to stop as well, but he stumbled forward and ended up crunching through the snow right behind the man.

"What the - " the sentry began, turning around.

Their eyes met, and the sentry's widened in shock. He reached for his sword.

Idiot should have called out. Julian hurtled forward, slamming bodily into the man and forcing his sword arm into his torso. They went down, and Julian grabbed the back of the man's neck with his left hand and stabbed upward with the dagger in his right.

Only then did the man think to cry out, but it was too late. He only got out a short shout before the knife sliced through his Adam's Apple.

The man squirmed, rolling the two of them over. Julian worked hard to keep his grip on the knife, then continued the roll, bringing himself up on top of the sentry.

Growling a curse, he put all his weight onto the knife's hilt. The blade crunched against something solid, and the man spasmed.

Then he lay still.

Julian rolled off of the body and lay panting for a long moment. It had only been a short burst of activity, but it had drained him completely.

Price you pay for a couple days of torture, forced marching, bad sleep, and almost no food.

Finally he pushed himself up to a sitting position and took a look at the dead bandit.

He was dressed as they all were: in furs and wools, though the furs had been augmented recently, by Povol's dogs if memory served. Julian would not be taking those, and not just because, uncured as they were, they had begun to stink.

The rest, though, was fair game.

Julian worked quickly, unbuckling the fellow's sword belt and pulling off his outer layers, then donning them himself. Finally, he strapped the sword on and cinched the belt tight.

Good to go.

He took one last look down at the fallen sentry, and suddenly realized who it was. Stefan.

Julian felt his eyebrows climb high on his forehead. If he had…

He squatted down and patted the man down. Sure enough, there, tucked into a pocket of his breaches - Julian had not bothered with them before - he found that piece of paper Stefan had been consulting all day. He unfolded it carefully and held it up, so the reflected light of the stars could illuminate it a bit better.

He could not see much, but it looked like a map.

Julian grinned from ear to ear.

Ravi shivered, and not just from the cold. He had not been this nervous, frightened really, in years. His position as a guildsman of the Healers Circle had functioned better than any suit of armor, shielding him from potential harm, and he had taken it for granted.

But here, now, doing this… This was different. His status would offer no protection from Geoff and his men if they learned what he had done this night.

Although truth be told he was not sure how much protection it really would have offered him anyway. This bunch seemed like the types to get rid of anyone who was of no more use. They had done it already, with Tolburt and now Julian. What was to say Ravi would not be next?

That did not make this evening's deeds any easier to deal with.

His eyes darted around from tent to tent. He imagined that at any moment Geoff's men would come storming out, wise to what he had done, and string him up, and Julian with him. Every minute that passed without that happening seemed an eternity, and a miracle.

At one point, he heard a noise from outside the circle of tents, almost like a man's shout, but muffled, cut off too quickly. He stiffened, pressing himself against the side of Julian's old tent, his heart suddenly pounding in his ears. If he had heard that, surely one of the men in the tents would have as well. It must have roused one of them from his slumber, and he would be out to investigate, and then they would be caught.

Oh Gods, why did he get himself into this? He could have sent young Willam. He was more than up to the task. But no, Ravi the foolish had to go off on an adventure, because he was bored. Stupid old fool.

What are you saying? Better Willam than you?

Chastened, Ravi forced his thoughts back into order. He was no coward; he would not wish his troubles off onto someone else, especially not a fine young man like Willam.

No, he would see this through. And when he got back…

If you get back.

When he got back, he would have a big pot of tea and never again dream of going off on an exciting adventure. He was far too old for this sort of thing.

"Ravi."

The voice, coming from the dark night behind him, made him jump. He almost cried a surrender, hoping against hope that they would still honor his protected status.

"Ravi, come on."

He recognized the voice. Julian. Ravi breathed out a sigh of relief, then crept out into the darkness to meet him.

It was time to go.

✥ 20 ✥

REUNION

Raedrick and Povol spent an extremely uncomfortable night crammed between two spurs of rock, with the nighttime winds howling all around. There was little rest to be had, at least not for Raedrick's part. Between the bitter cold and Povol's far too close proximity - the man truly did stink, though Raedrick was willing to admit he probably did as well - he only managed to doze on and off most of the night.

At least it was a clear night, and the stars shown brightly. That made Raedrick's interminable wakefulness not completely unbearable.

It was with a fuzzy head, a growing headache, and a gnawing belly that he set off further up the mountain the next morning.

"Wish there was some game," Povol said at one point as they trudged onwards.

Raedrick was inclined to agree. The two brigands who tried to ambush them had only a meal's worth of supplies on them. It was the first food he or Povol had eaten in a day, and it did not go far toward relieving their hunger. And that was yesterday afternoon.

It was going to be a very long, very uncomfortable day.

Raedrick had almost become used to the glare of the sun off the white snow, pristine save for the tracks of the passing brigands and their captives. Even still, Povol put him to shame a couple hours later.

"Someone's coming," he said, pointing his spear toward the trail ahead.

Raedrick squinted, trying to see through the glare. He could barely make out two forms walking toward them. Just barely. How in the hell did Povol do that?

He looked around for cover, but they were well out onto the snowpack. The closest thing approaching concealment was a small depression about fifty feet to their right.

Povol must have noticed him looking around, because he shook his head. "They've got the sun in their eyes, but they'll see us any minute now, if they haven't already."

Raedrick nodded. He had pretty much figured that out himself. But it was good to hear the expert say it, all the same. Or a least that was what he told himself.

"Spread out, and be ready for a fight."

Povol shrugged and took a couple steps to his left, taking hold of his spear in both hands, though he carried it the way a left-handed man would. Raedrick noted he still was only able to lightly close the fingers of his right hand around the haft. That would be a serious disadvantage in a fight.

Then again, just yesterday he had proved more than capable of overcoming that disadvantage, so maybe Raedrick was just picking nits for the sake of having something to worry about.

He snorted at that thought, drawing his longsword and taking a step to his right.

Then he settled down to wait.

The two men ahead spread out, lowering into ready crouches and brandishing their weapons. Any other time, that would make Julian nervous. But with this pair? A spear and a longsword. An awkwardly-wielded longsword at that. That could only be Raedrick and Povol.

He kept his weapon sheathed and picked up his pace, grinning broadly.

"I would have thought you'd be more happy to see us, Rae," he shouted, when he and Ravi were close enough.

The effect on the two men was most satisfying. Raedrick gave a little jerk and straightened, leaning forward slightly as though trying to see them better. Povol...

Povol snorted and spat onto the snow at his feet, then straightened and raised his spear, resting it over his left shoulder. "Thought sure you'd be dead by now," he called, earning a reproachful look from Raedrick. Povol returned the look and shrugged. "What? It's true."

Raedrick slipped his sword back into place behind his belt - he did not have a scabbard - and hurried across the distance between himself and Julian, smiling in what appeared to be a mixture of relief and joy. They clasped hands and Julian returned the grin.

"How did you get away from them?"

Julian shrugged and gestured toward Ravi. "All his doing."

Ravi smiled sheepishly. "It was nothing. Truly." But the twinkle in his eyes told another tale completely.

Raedrick clasped hands with the old man, and Povol gave him a respectful nod.

"Well," Julian said, "Let's get on home."

Raedrick frowned, peering back up the slope and the bandits' trail. "How many remain?"

"Six," Julian said with resignation. He had been afraid of this; Raedrick was about to get obstinate. Julian dug into his pocket and produced the map, "I took care of Tolburt's little buddy. Look what I found."

Raedrick took the map and unfolded it. One eyebrow rose as he looked it over, then he gazed at Julian questioningly.

"Those guys are out of luck without that," Julian said. "I'll bet you a mark against a penny they're here for that treasure Tolburt talked about, and that's the map to it."

Povol perked up noticeably. "Never heard of buried treasure in these parts."

Julian shrugged. "Me neither, but that's the story."

Raedrick handed Povol the map, and the mountaineer began looking it over. All of a sudden, Raedrick had one of those expressions on his face that told Julian he was about to volunteer them for something stupid, and dangerous.

"What are you thinking, Rae?"

Raedrick pursed his lips. "They will still cause trouble out here, map or no."

Julian shook his head. "That treasure - if it even exists - is the only reason they're here. Without a way to reach it, they'll fold up tents and go home. Or turn on each other and take care the problem for us."

Raedrick gave him a level look. "Do you really believe that, Julian?"

Julian frowned, hating where Raedrick was going with this one. He wanted to believe what he had just said. But he had to admit it was just as likely Geoff and his men would choose the other path, the one that involved becoming enraged, following them back to Lydelton, and wreaking havoc.

But hang it all, the four of them were neither equipped nor prepared to deal with that bunch out here. At the least, they needed to get back to town, resupply, and get a few more strong backs at their side. He had heard Gilroy and the other fishing men who fought against Isenholf's band last spring bragging over their mugs on many a night. At least a couple of them, or barring that dozens of other local men who had not participated and now wished they had, would likely stand up to help take down Geoff and his bunch. There were only six of them, after all.

He opened his mouth to say all this, but right then Povol erupted with laughter. All eyes went to the mountaineer, who was slapping his thigh with glee.

"Povol?" Ravi said, carefully.

Povol looked up from the map wearing the biggest smirk of amusement Julian had ever seen, and he had seen plenty. "Bloody fools went the wrong way!"

Julian blinked, confused. He exchanged glances with Raedrick, who did not look much better. "Come again?"

Povol shook his head and held up the map so they could all see. "See here? This is Tollard's Peak. And this," he pointed on the map to another mountain to the northeast that sat right up against the Northflow, "this is that mountain over there." He pointed away from the map, toward a smaller ridge off to the east.

Julian looked at the peak, but it just looked like one more mountain to him. "Are you sure?"

Povol glared at him. "I'm been roaming these mountains longer than you've been chasing skirts. I'm telling you, that's the mountain from the map. Look." He jabbed his finger at the peak. "See the river running past it, to the north?"

Julian squinted. He could just barely see a dark squiggle running to the north, past the mountain. He shrugged. "Guess so."

"That's what it is." Povol shook his head. "Those fools have been slowly veering north for the last day and a half. They climbed the wrong damn mountain!" He spat into the snow. "If they'd bothered to hire a guide, someone who knows the land, they'd have gotten to their precious treasure already."

"And that guide would likely be dead," Ravi said, solemnly.

That took some of the fire out of Povol. He paused, shut his mouth, then nodded, looking down at the ground. "Yeah."

"That's very interesting. Let's get moving home."

"Julian."

"No, Rae." Julian wagged a finger at his friend. "We need food, weapons, and people if we want to take on these guys and win. We don't have any of it." Well, they did. Sort of. "Ok, not enough of it. If you want to come back and find this treasure later, fine. But…"

"It's actually on the way," Povol interjected.

Damn him. "What do you mean? No it isn't."

"Well," Povol pointed back down the slope they stood on, and toward Tollard's Peak. "We could head back down into the valley, then up Tollard's Peak, then back down again. Or," he swept his hand around to point due east, toward the southern slope of the little mountain next to the river, "we could descend this way, cut across the lower portion of that mountain, and follow the Northflow to the lake."

"I thought you said it runs through a gorge and we couldn't walk it, when we came up here," Ravi said.

Povol nodded. "It does. But I happen to know a hunting lodge not far from the base of that mountain. Folks keep it stocked with supplies and have a couple canoes tied up, to use for paddling upstream."

Crap. That solved half of Julian's objections right there.

Raedrick nodded. "I think that takes care of that." He turned to give Julian a grin that was just a bit too smug. "Don't you?"

Julian sighed. He could probably think of more problems with this plan, but he was out-voted and he knew it. He nodded, conceding defeat. "How long to get there?"

Povol squinted up at the sun for a second then shrugged. "A bit after sunset, if we're lucky."

"Well then," Raedrick said. "Let's be off."

❦ 21 ❦

RIVER LODGE

Night was fully upon them by the time they reached the lodge, and with it cold that rivaled any they had encountered so far on this venture. Several times, Raedrick thought they might have to stop early, so bitter the night was. But there was no place that looked appealing, or even promising. Oh, there were rocks and cracks in the sides of the slope, a thicket or two once they got back down into the tree-filled valley, and once a collection of fallen logs that lay over a gully, but after the previous night, he did not relish the notion of stopping in any of those places.

Neither did anyone else, or at least no one suggested a stop. He supposed the notion of spending the night indoors with a fire fueled them as much as it did him.

He almost did not see the lodge when they arrived. In the dark, it looked like a particularly large boulder, or a bushy tree. But as they drew near, the straight lines of the structure became more clear and they were able to behold the goal of their trek.

It could more appropriately be called a shack. It stood on stilts about five feet tall and appeared roughly constructed of hewn logs that were probably sealed with mud. It had no windows, just a small chimney rising from the thatched roof.

Raedrick had seen worse hovels, but this one came close. Maybe it would look more welcoming in the daylight, but he doubted it.

"Why the stilts?" Julian asked as they approached.

"During the spring thaw, the river runs pretty high up here," Povol said. "The place flooded out a few times before we decided to raise it up."

That made sense.

The door to the lodge was locked, naturally, but that proved no difficulty, as Povol produced a key from one of his pockets.

They stepped inside and Povol lit a lamp that hung from a hook on the wall to the right.

The lamp's soft glow illuminated a well-stocked and orderly place, much nicer

395

than Raedrick would have thought based on the exterior. The lodge was a single room, with three sets of bunk beds along the rear wall. Off to the left, a stone fireplace dominated the wall, with half a cord of split wood stacked neatly in a cast iron bin next to it. A simple wooden table, flanked by a pair of benches, sat in the center of the room. The right-hand wall was dominated by a long counter, which held a collection of tableware and two tapped casks. Cabinets below the counter no doubt held all manner of supplies, if Povol could be believed. The entire place smelled pleasantly of wood, woodsmoke, and some manner of incense or other. All told, it was a more than passable place to hole up.

"Nice," Julian said, approvingly. He wasted no time in heading to the fireplace.

"Who owns this place, Povol?" Ravi asked.

Povol closed the door, shutting out the wind. The place seemed strangely silent, and Raedrick suddenly realized just how used to the constant whistling of the wind he had become. It almost seemed unnatural to not have it in his ears.

"It's not owned by any one person," Povol said as he walked over to the counter and picked up a mug. "A bunch of us who drink at Holb's chip in to maintain it. Holb manages the till and makes sure everyone pays their due." He opened the tap on the nearest cask, and amber fluid flowed into his mug for a moment. Shutting the tap, he turned to the rest of them and took a swig. His contented sigh as he lowered the mug spoke volumes. "Mead, boys?"

Raedrick could not help but grin in response.

Ten minutes later, everything was just a bit brighter. Julian got the fire going. Ravi found dried fruits and meat in the cupboards, and Povol poured them all a round from the cask. They sat around the table in a state of warm contentment, and right then it was easy to forget about their problems.

Of course, that could not last.

"Do you think they're following us, Constable?" Ravi asked. He had only sipped at his mead but already he looked flushed, as though the drink was going right to his head.

Povol snorted and took a long draw from his mug. "They'd have to be blind to miss our trail. I'd be after us if I was them." His eyes narrowed and he added, "Sooner the better," in a dark tone. The good cheer he expressed earlier was gone, replaced by a hard scowl that spoke to his anger and loss more than his words could have.

Raedrick exchanged looks with Julian, who was watching Povol carefully. "Best if we can avoid any more contact with them," Raedrick said slowly. "There's been enough blood spilled."

Ravi nodded emphatic agreement.

Povol just snorted again.

Silence settled around them, the cheery mood broken, and they sat for a time just drinking and thinking. After a few minutes, Povol stood, mug in hand, and turned toward the cask. That would not do.

"Keep it to just one, Povol. We need to keep our wits about us."

The mountaineer stared at Raedrick for a moment, his scowl darkening. Then, with a sigh, he nodded. Instead of the tapped cask, he strode to another barrel that stood near the fireplace and opened the lid. He stood there for a few seconds, scowling. "Still frozen."

Well, that was hardly a shock. The water in the barrel was likely frozen solid from the weeks of winter before they had arrived. An hour near a fire would not make up for that. Raedrick though about making a run to the river with a bucket, but that would be treacherous in the dark; it could wait until morning, and then they would be off anyway.

Povol suddenly smacked his right hand down into the barrel, his fist curled into a hammer. Or mostly curled; it was hard to see under his bandages. A solid thump as his hand struck the solid ice preceded a loud curse form the mountaineer by a second or so. He dropped his mug and cradled his injured hand against his chest, drawing in deep breaths in through his nose while he clenched his teeth. His face was a rictus of pain.

Ravi was on his feet in an instant. "Povol, what are you doing?" He rushed over to the mountaineer, reaching out toward his injury.

Povol pushed him away with his good hand and a fierce glare.

But Ravi would not be dissuaded. "Let me have a look at it," he said, his tone insistent, forceful. He and Povol locked eyes for a few seconds. Then, finally, the mountaineer looked down and nodded.

Ravi led him back to the table and bad him sit. Then he gently took Povol's hand and unwrapped the bandage. The mountaineer winced at every turn of the cloth.

Ravi unwrapped the last layer of bandage and his breath caught. His eyes widened in alarm, flicking from the wound to Raedrick and back. "Oh. This..." He licked his lips, concern written all over his face. "This is not good."

Raedrick stood so he could get a better look, and almost immediately wished he had not.

Povol's hand was swollen and discolored. In the immediate area of the wound, it was almost red, fading to a dull pink at his wrist and fingers. The wound no longer bled, but it oozed a yellowish puss, and there was an unpleasant odor. Raedrick had smelled that before; the smell of infection.

"Son of a bitch," Raedrick breathed.

Povol just scowled, his brow furrowed, and Raedrick realized that what he had taken as anger for much of the last couple days was mostly pain. In must have been maddening, but Povol hardly let on to it. Tough fellow.

And stupid. If he had told someone earlier, they could have... What? There was nothing to be done, not out here.

"Is it..." Julian did not finish the thought, but Raedrick knew they were all thinking it. Is the hand savable?

Ravi frowned, turning Povol's hand over to look at the other side of the puncture. "Can you move the fingers at all?"

The mountaineer shrugged and tried. All five fingers moved, but only a little, and Raedrick could tell it was only with great difficulty and pain.

"What do you think?" Raedrick asked the guildsman.

Ravi shook his head. "It is badly infected. I had medicines and ointments that may have been able to help, but Geoff's men took them when they captured us. There are more back at the guild house. But..." He looked from the hand to Povol's face, his expression pitying. "If we don't get to them soon, I'm afraid it'll have to be amputated."

"Crap," Julian said. He stood and pulled his coat back on, along with his gloves and hat. "The canoes are stored under the lodge, right?"

Povol nodded. "In racks."

Julian nodded. "I'll go check and make sure they're still there, then we're getting you out of here at first light."

"No."

Julian stopped halfway to the door and looked back at Povol, surprise and consternation competing on his face.

Raedrick concurred. "Povol, this is serious."

Povol looked at all three of them challengingly, his scowl renewed in its forcefulness. "Damn right it is. Those bastards took my dogs, and I'm not…"

Ravi broke in, his voice gentle but firm. "Do you want them to take your hand as well?"

Povol just glowered in silence.

"Because that's what will happen if you remain out here."

The mountaineer looked down at his injured hand and his stubborn scowl faded, replaced by acceptance. He sighed, but it was more a groan. Then he nodded.

22
EVACUATION

First light came sooner than Raedrick's body would have liked. It seemed he had only just closed his eyes when Julian was shaking him awake. He blinked away the sleep, fighting off the urge to just lie back, shut his eyes, and get a few more minutes of rest. Just a few more minutes.

With a grunt, he forced himself to sit up, only remembering that the ceiling was low above the top bunk where he lay when he hit his forehead on one of the ceiling timbers. That knocked the sleepiness right out of him.

"They just put that there," Julian quipped as Raedrick clutched at the swiftly-growing lump, but from his tone his heart was not in the jibe.

Who could blame him. A hard day lay before them. Even harder than Julian knew.

By the time he managed to get past the ache in his head, chomp down some dried breakfast, and get his gear squared away, the other men were already clothed and mustered outside. Raedrick felt like one of the walking dead as he clumped down the stairs from the door, but they did not look much better - especially Povol - so there was no sense complaining about it.

"The canoes are in the water, ready to go, Rae," Julian reported.

Raedrick nodded. "The river gets fairly rough in places, or so I've heard." He looked at Povol, questioningly.

The mountaineer shrugged. He looked decidedly pale this morning. "In the spring, it will. These days it's mostly frozen except for the middle and the water's low. Shouldn't be too hard."

Raedrick nodded again. He did not need to order them to make haste.

There were racks for four canoes between the stilts that held the lodge aloft, but as they trooped toward the river, Raedrick could see two of them were empty. He presumed Julian had taken those two for the group's use. A dozen paces later, they pushed through undergrowth that was little more than bare twigs and branches and came to a small inlet that was separated from the river proper by a series of boulders that looked as though they had been rolled into place by some great giant's design, so well did they create the sheltered cove.

It was frozen over now, of course, but Raedrick could see in his mind's eye how the area would look in the middle of summer: all green undergrowth, with flowers interspersed here and there, birds alighting in the trees that in places grew right up to the water's edge, and the cove itself calm and flat like a mirror reflecting the beauty around it. It was easy to tell why the outdoorsmen had chosen this place to build their lodge.

There was just one thing wrong.

"Where are the canoes?" Ravi spoke the question before Raedrick could.

Julian smirked bemusedly at the guildsman. "Can't really put them in here, can we?" He gestured for them to follow, them set off around the boulders, moving quickly but carefully down a beaten path in the snow, where he had clearly gone before.

It only took a moment to round the rocks, and Raedrick beheld the Northflow itself. The river was more narrow than he thought it would be. Down where it joined with Lake Glimmermere, the Northflow was well over a hundred yards across, but it was very shallow, even away from the ford. Here, it was maybe a hundred feet from shore to shore. Thinking about it for a moment, though, it made sense. The river was probably deeper here. Or something.

As Povol predicted, the river was frozen over except for a portion about twenty feet wide in its center, where the current was great enough to prevent the ice from growing any further. The canoes were, true to Julian's word, in the water, but nestled in a hollow of broken-out ice that allowed the current to eddy around without carrying the boats away.

Raedrick frowned; that hollow was not natural. He cast an accusatory gaze at Julian. "You should have woken me to help you."

Povol snorted out a half-laugh. "Tried to," he said. "Julian practically shook the teeth out of your head, but you did not stir a whit."

Raedrick blinked. That never happened; he was a very light sleeper. Always had been.

"Guess you were pretty tired," Julian said, grinning at him teasingly. Then he shrugged. "It's ok, Povol and me managed it without too much trouble."

Raedrick rather doubted that, but there was no point grousing over it.

They carefully walked out across the ice to where the boats lay waiting. It was a disquieting experience, actually. Sure, Raedrick had been out on Lake Glimmermere a time or two, at Lani's insistence every time, and he knew that Julian and Povol had been out here earlier, so there was every reason to believe the ice was more than sufficient to hold them. All the same, the thought of all that icy cold just beneath his feet, and the knowledge of exactly how little time he could survive in it, sent preemptive shivers up his spine.

Finally they reached the boats.

"Are you good with a canoe, Ravi?"

The guildsman gave a little shrug. "I paddled a little, in my youth." That was not saying much, but the confident smile on his lips as he replied belied the humble words.

"That makes one of us," Julian said.

There was no need to ask Povol about his skill level. He was likely better in a boat than any of them, but he could not paddle, not with his hand injured.

"Alright." Raedrick pulled out the map Julian had retrieved from Stefan and unfolded it. "Let's see. Povol, correct me if I'm wrong, but we're right here."

He pointed at where he presumed the lodge to be, and the mountaineer nodded. "Thereabouts, yes."

Raedrick nodded, the possibilities churning in his head. It would be a relatively quick trip down river to the lake, but a longer walk back to town; they would not be able to paddle the whole way, not with the lake frozen over as it was. But there was no reason to expect any major difficulties, and they ought to have Povol to the Healers Circle well before nightfall.

But there was that other matter.

"What about this?" He pointed upstream, toward where the spot marking the treasure was inked, and looked Povol in the eye.

The mountaineer blinked in surprise. "I'd say it's just a couple miles upstream. Why?"

"Rae, what are you doing? We have to get Povol back to town." He could just about feel Julian's accusing stare boring through his head.

Raedrick drew in a deep breath and nodded to himself, the decision made. "And you will."

Julian's eyes widened, and he shook his head emphatically. "No, Rae. We're all going if -"

He cut off at a sharp gesture from Raedrick. Their eyes locked and Raedrick could see the defiance, the simmering frustration, even anger, within his friend. He drew in a slow breath and let it out before replying. "It makes sense, Julian. Povol can't paddle, and Ravi will need your help to steer the boat downstream. You don't need me to get Povol to help, but if I can get to this cache before they do -"

"You'll what? Destroy it? Carry it back to town yourself and hope they don't catch up to you and cut you to ribbons? What *exactly* is your plan, Rae?"

Put that way, he was forced to admit it did not sound like the most rational scheme ever. But it had to be done. "I'll get anything valuable and use the other canoe. I can make better distance on the river than they can ashore, and it will remove any reason for them to remain here, or for others to follow in their footsteps."

Julian threw his hands up in frustration.

Raedrick continued on in a rush before he could get a word in edgewise. He leaned forward, speaking in his best command tone. "I'm doing this, Julian. And you're getting Povol back to town for treatment." He paused, then added, "That's an order."

Incredulous did not begin to describe the expression that came over Julian's face. He snorted. "Bollocks. You're not my Squad Leader anymore, Rae. We're *partners*, remember?"

"Then do this in the name of our partnership. If we wait to come back, Geoff and his men may have already retrieved it - "

"Let them. Who cares?"

Raedrick sighed and looked away. "It's not theirs."

Another snort. "No? Then whose is it?"

"They conned it out of Tolburt."

A long second passed before Julian responded. When he did, it was quietly, barely more than a whisper. "Are you...?" He stopped, cleared his throat and looked around as though unable to believe he was actually someplace real. "Are you nuts?" he said in a more normal tone. "What is it with you and him? He sold us out, would have seen us on the gallows to save his own skin, and you act as though you owe him something." Julian spat on the ice. "That's what you owe him Rae, right there. So he got conned. Serves him right. And you..." He shook his head. "You don't need to go getting yourself killed over his sorry ass."

Julian was right, of course. In a fashion. Tolburt had betrayed them, but only after Raedrick had led him into a far greater treason first. Could he really blame the man for trying to do right by himself, in those circumstances?

Yes, a part of Raedrick's mind replied.

He forced that voice down, and with it a flash of bitterness that he thought he had put long behind him. No matter if he had or not. Tolburt had been one of his men - still was one of his. And he had left the man behind, to his fate.

Not this time.

Raedrick reached out and clasped Julian's shoulder, giving it a gentle squeeze. He looked his friend in the eye for a long moment. "I need to do this, Julian."

Julian returned the gaze in silence for a small eternity. Frustration and incredulity battled in his expression until finally they gave way before acceptance. He was not going to talk Raedrick out of this, and he knew it.

Julian nodded and laid his hand atop Raedrick's. He returned the squeeze and cleared his throat. "Povol, Ravi, get in the boat. We're casting off."

The two men exchanged doubtful, confused looks, but complied in silence. No doubt Povol was eager to be off, and the elder Guildsman knew better than to rekindle the argument. The wisdom of age.

Raedrick released Julian's shoulder and took a step back. He nodded once and tightened the straps of his pack. Then, adjusting the fit of his sword belt, he turned and made his way back to the riverbank. Behind him, he heard the soft scrape of ice against the canoe's hull as his friends cast off into the Northflow's current.

He hoped he would see them again.

✷ 23 ✷

UNDER A ROCK

Raedrick pushed hard, keeping to the river's edge as best he could, to keep his bearings. But Julian had been right: there was no time to lose. Geoff and his remaining men were certainly heading this way, their minds fixed on revenge, and Raedrick had no illusions about his ability to take them on and live.

Maybe if he had his own sword...

No. He still was not proficient with the Tyrashi blade. At least not to the standards he expected of himself. More than once he had considered just giving up on it and returning to his trusty saber. He knew that weapon inside and out, and he knew it was no boast to claim he was a master with it.

His new sword, a gift from his late comrade-in-arms Selam, was another matter entirely. The weight and balance were different, the grip different, the curve of the blade, and the sharpened edge on the back-edge. Even one of those elements would have meant weeks of training to adjust properly. But all of them together... It was a monumental change, requiring different stances and movements than he was used to. And he had no one to teach them to him; the only pattern he had to follow was the memory of how Selam had moved in battle, and he had only fought beside the man for a short time.

It was hopeless. But he could not dishonor Selam by setting his family's sword aside; he had passed it to Raedrick because he lacked a son and his family was dying with him. How could Raedrick refuse a request like that?

And so he had to live up to the man's wishes, learn to wield it in a manner worthy of the honor Selam had displayed, and that he had payed to Raedrick on his death bed.

Not that that would be helpful at all under the current circumstances.

Bloody fool. That bull-headedness of yours is going to get you killed one of these days.

Raedrick chuckled at the little voice in the back of his head. It was probably more right than it knew.

The riverbank twisted and turned as it cut through the mountains to the north, and Raedrick found himself almost reversing course several times. That and the steady uphill grade, shallow as it was, made for slow going even as he pushed himself to greater speed.

At least the snow cover was less along the bank. The terrain was more often bare rock, or covered in ice, and what snow there was had become packed over the weeks of winter, so his trail was less obvious than it would have been in the loose powder deeper in the woods. Small comfort, that.

The sun was a third of the way to its zenith when Raedrick paused and pulled Tolburt's map out again. He studied it for a time, frowning as he pondered. The Northflow was plain on the paper, winding its way past mountains on either side until a small dotted line broke away, toward a strange symbol on the third mountain on the west side: an X within a circle.

X marks the spot.

The problem was, where exactly was it? Raedrick looked around to get his bearings again. To the east, across the river, lay the northern flank of the mountain he had been trudging past all morning. To the north, more hills and mountains were visible ahead, but just as to the south he could not see far along the river itself before a bend cut off his view.

To the west, though…

The woods along the river obstructed much of his view; he could have marched well past his aim point by now, and not realized it. Povol had said the marking on the map was just a few miles upstream. If he had passed it by, he would be forced to double back, and that could be beyond hazardous with Geoff and company on his trail.

He needed to get to higher ground, take a look around.

Raedrick stuffed the map back into his pocket and made for a nearby tree. Tall and sturdy, it had a few low-hanging limbs that should offer good purchase for climbing.

Ten minutes later, he wedged himself into a nook between a limb that was probably a bit too narrow and the trunk, which was also a bit more spindly at this height - about thirty feet - than he would have preferred. But it held, and he had a commanding view of the area; only a few other trees nearby were as tall as the one he had picked.

From his vantage point, Raedrick could clearly see the slope of the mountain he had been walking past. Though from this distance the peak seemed to scrape the top of the sky, it was quite a bit smaller than the others nearby; Tollard's Peak dwarfed it easily. On this side, the peak was almost completely wooded, the tree line only cutting off on the mountain's top third. In places, the trees were broken by cliff faces and the occasional pile of debris from some ancient rock slide. But that was nothing unusual, and he could see nothing special that would point him one way or another, nothing that hinted at the map's hidden secret.

Wouldn't be much of a secret if it was just lying around, easy to spot.

True enough, but it still irked him. Time was running short; he needed to find this cache, whatever it was, and get out of here. Fast.

But where?

Raedrick took the map out and unfolded it. He spent a long while looking at it, trying to see something - anything - in its simple lines that might help. But there was just the dotted line running from along the river bank, up the flank of the mountain, then around a bend to the circle and X...

He blinked, then looked up at the mountain again.

A bend in the side of the peak. It had to be something prominent, something recognizable...

There. A bit less than a mile further north and a third of the way up the slope - a rocky protuberance that thrust out from the trees. It looked as though maybe it curled back on itself. Maybe there was a little canyon on the other side?

That had to be it; there was nothing else Raedrick saw that could even be close.

Unless you already passed it.

He forced the doubting voice down and re-pocketed the map. Then - slowly, carefully - he made his way down from the tree.

When his feet were back on solid ground, he took a minute to gather himself. Then, trying not to feel the surge of excitement that threatened to well up, he turned away from the river, toward that wall of rock, and set out.

He probably got turned around a half dozen times before he finally stepped out from under the forest's canopy and into the clearing at the base of the protuberance. It could not have been more than a mile from his tree, but it had taken nearly three hours, best he could tell, to get there. It was upslope, sure, but still it should not have taken that long.

Raedrick cursed his lack of bearings, feeling more than a bit disgusted with himself. But then, he should not have been surprised. Orienteering had never been his strong suit, and he did not even have a compass with him for this venture.

Which was stupid in and of itself.

"No sense getting worked up over it," he said aloud to himself.

That only helped a little.

He took a moment and just stood there, breathing deeply to lower his heart rate after the strenuous climb and looking up at the rock face. It certainly was impressive. Craggy, offering many good hand and footholds for someone who had the notion of climbing it, the protuberance thrust up over a hundred feet above him. High up, he thought he could see clumps of branches and twigs in some of the crags - bird nests of some sort, he thought. Here and there, a hardy tree or bush had managed to take root on the side of the cliff as well.

Turning around, he could see the river flowing below, in the valley between the mountains. Further south, the gorge leading down to the lake was more clearly visible.

In all, it was quite a beautiful view. Too bad he did not have time to bask in it.

He followed the rock wall, moving to his right and stepping carefully around the boulders and smaller rocks that littered its base, not a particularly easy task considering many of them were buried in snow and he only learned of their presence when his foot came down and did not go as far into the snow as he expected. After a few steps, he gave up and retreated back to the tree line. At least at the edge of the canopy he could be reasonably sure to avoid the worst of the trip hazards.

The wall continued on, gradually curving away from him so it veered more north than east. And then, all at once, he reached the end. As though someone had sliced the rock with an axe and heaved the excess aside, the wall simply stopped, leaving just the not-so-gently rising slope of the mountain to rise past it.

This had to be the place.

Raedrick gingerly left the trees and made for the end of the rock wall, feeling his way carefully with each step. But for whatever reason, here there were not as many rocks to snag his feet, and within a minute he found himself standing beneath the cliff.

Now what?

The cloven edge of the cliff extended back a good ways, but then seemed to end as it met the mountain's slope. As far as Raedrick could tell, there was nothing else to it.

He frowned. He had been so sure this was the place. There was nothing else that even resembled the drawing on the map. Maybe…

Raedrick flashed back to the cave Povol had led them to during their first night on the mountain. That had been nearly impossible to see. Unless you knew it was there, you could easily walk right past it. If this was similar… He slid his hand along the cliff face and slowly walked back toward where it met with the slope, looking closely at the ground and the cliff itself as he went.

Finally, he saw it. About thirty feet back, concealed by a small bush that grew near the base of the cliff and by the fold of the cliff itself: a small hole, maybe three and a half feet wide and as many tall, leading back into the cliff face.

Raedrick crouched down and peered into the hole, but the early afternoon sun did little to illuminate the interior. After only a couple feet there was nothing to see but shadows and blackness.

Well, what did you expect?

Raedrick snorted and shrugged his pack off, then went back to the tree line. A few minutes later, he came back with a stout branch. He opened his pack and pulled out a scrap of cloth - the remnants of his old shirt - and wound it around the branch. Then he set to with flint and steel.

It took longer than he would have thought, but eventually he got the makeshift torch burning. Replacing the flint and steel into its pouch, he pulled his pack back on then, hefting the torch, he got down on his knees and looked into the little cave mouth again.

Still nothing. The torch would not illuminate anything from out here.

Raedrick took a deep breath, then crouched over and, moving carefully to avoid burning himself in the face, half-crawled into the cave.

❧ 24 ❧

HIDDEN GEMS

T he cave widened slowly as it burrowed into the cliff face until, after about twenty feet, it stretched a good six feet across and five high. Raedrick could walk normally, albeit with a stoop, but that was a far sight better than it had been at the opening.

The walls and ceiling were rough, jagged, but the floor was smooth, as though many feet had tromped through here over the years and wore it down. Or perhaps paws more than feet.

That was a distinct possibility, now that he thought about it. Bears and other animals sought shelter for the winter in caves. Raedrick imagined they would not be pleased to have their slumber disturbed by the likes of him.

He paused mid-step and almost turned around to leave, the thought of an enraged bear tearing him limb from limb giving him pause. But there was no sound, aside from the soft crackle of burning cloth and wood from his simple torch, and the only odors he could detect were woodsmoke - again from the torch - and his own grime from the last several days in the wild. Surely if a creature had made this cave a layer, there would be some sign.

Raedrick drew a deep breath and continued forward.

The passage bent to the right ahead. Raedrick followed and, after two paces, stopped dead in his tracks again. But this time from amazed surprise more than nervousness.

No sooner had the passage completed its bend than the cave opened wide on all sides, becoming a semi-circular chamber probably thirty feet across and twenty tall at its center. All over the chamber, stalactites hung down from the ceiling, nearly meeting stalagmites, lesser in number, that rose to greet them from the floor. But that was not what amazed him.

There was light here, above and beyond the flickering of his torch. It streamed down from a crack in the ceiling and cast a soft glow over the entire chamber, but particularly on a still pool that sat in the center of the floor. The light struck the water and reflected all around the chamber in glistening waves that seemed to shimmer and move of their own accord.

Strange that, considering the water itself was perfectly smooth.

"Gods be good," Raedrick found himself murmuring. The silent beauty of the place - and it was silent still, except for the noises Raedrick brought with him - seemed to warrant it.

This had to be the place, but he could see no sign of any cache. No structures or furniture. No chests or bags. Nothing to suggest that men had ever set foot here.

It had to be here. But where?

Raedrick frowned and made a slow circle of the chamber, being careful to avoid the pool. The last thing he needed was to get wet, as cold as it was. Although now that he thought of it, it was not nearly as cold here in the cave as it had been outside. That did not change the fact that he would have to head back out, and soon. Getting wet could be a fatal mistake.

But as he completed his circuit, he still could see no sign of the promised cache.

"Damn it," he muttered.

This must be the wrong place. He must have passed the spot. He pulled the map out and unfolded it, then spread it out on the floor and crouched down, holding his torch to fully illuminate it. What had he missed?

Nothing.

He could see nothing in that map to indicate anything he had overlooked outside. The rock face that held this cave was the only formation that fit the drawing on the map. Or at least, the only one he had come across so far. It was possible he had not passed the place up, but had instead stopped to early.

"No, no," he said to himself. That could not be it. This place was too perfect: a well-concealed cave in the cliff face. How many other places like this could there be?

At least one, he thought, recalling Povol's cave again.

Raedrick snorted and pushed himself to his feet, crumpling the map in his hand in frustration as he stood. He did not relish the notion of tromping even further north through the snow and ice, especially with Geoff and his men very likely drawing nearer by the second. But there was no other choice. If this was not the place, then he must...

He stopped, midway through turning back toward the cave entrance. Something glinted at the edge of his vision. What was that?

Slowly, deliberately, he turned to his left, carefully sweeping his gaze over every inch of floor, wall, and ceiling in his field of view, trying once again to see the...

There it was.

Son of a bitch.

It was so obvious, and he had overlooked it completely.

There, in the center of the chamber where the stream of light hit the water from the crack above, something metallic glinted from the bottom of the pool. He moved slightly forward, and the glinting ceased. Slightly back, and it started up again.

Now that was clever. Whatever it was down there had been placed so it would only give itself away if someone was looking for it at exactly the right angle. Lucky that Raedrick had done the circuit, otherwise he would have missed it.

He snorted. He very nearly had missed it anyway.

His heartbeat quickening with sudden excitement, Raedrick moved to the edge of the pool and squatted down with narrowed eyes. Now that he knew where to look, he could see it plain as day: a small wooden chest, fully submerged in the water - it was hard to tell how far down it was - with brass or gold fittings holding it together. Probably gold, considering it had not tarnished.

A grin spread over Raedrick's face. "Gotcha," he said.

He had found it alright. But how to get to it?

The pool was a good ten feet across, and the chest lay at its exact center. Worse, it lay completely underwater, and the more he looked at it the more certain Raedrick became that it was deeper than arms-reach.

His initial elation - hell, exhilaration - over the find faded as he considered the logistics of it. There was no way he was going to get that thing out of the pool, not without getting soaking wet. And that was not really an option, not if he wanted to keep on living; he did not have time to spend drying off before heading back out into winter's cold.

"Son of a bitch," he said softly.

Now what?

He pondered for a long several moments, but could not think of any way to retrieve the chest short of hopping in the pool. He shook his head. It looked like Julian was right. He might as well leave it and head back; he was never going to hear the end of this one.

The silence of the chamber was broken. A scuff of boots against rock from behind, followed by a shuffling sound caused Raedrick to stiffen.

"Well. Isn't this a cozy place," a voice said from behind him.

25

MEET-UP

Raedrick spun as quickly as he could, dropping his torch to the ground and withdrawing the longsword from his belt in one smooth draw as he rose to his full height. In that half-second he forced himself to calm and focused. He could not win, not alone. But he could go down fighting.

His brain fully registered the voice that had spoken at the same instant he completed the turn, and he brought his sword down. He felt the embarrassed scowl growing on his face before he could stop it.

Julian grinned back at him, amused.

"Hi, Rae," he said, eyes flicking up and down over Raedrick's form. "A little jumpy, aren't you?"

Raedrick let out his breath in a rush, letting the last of his tension flow from his body with it. He let his shoulders sag as he grounded the point of his sword, but could not stop the sudden shaking of his limbs from the surge of adrenalin.

Chagrin over being caught by surprise - and being so slow to recognize his friend's voice - chased relief through his psyche. He eyed Julian askance. "What the hell are you doing here?"

Julian shrugged and stepped fully into the chamber, throwing his cloak back over his shoulders as he moved. He carried a torch in his left hand, makeshift like Raedrick's, and wore an unconcerned expression. "Turns out Ravi is quite a lot better with a canoe than he let on. After a few minutes I realized you would probably need my help more than he did, so I had them put me ashore." He looked around the chamber, pursing his lips for a moment, then grinned at Raedrick. "You didn't *really* think I was going to let you do this alone, did you?"

All manner of protests leapt to Raedrick's mind. Reasons beyond number why Julian should not have done that. But right then none of them mattered worth a damn; the gratitude he suddenly felt toward his friend overwhelmed them all.

He opened his mouth to speak, but Julian beat him to it. "This is the place, huh?"

Raedrick cleared his throat and nodded, tucking his sword back behind his belt. "In the pool."

Julian raised an eyebrow and walked over to stand next to him, squinting as he peered into the pool. After a moment, he nodded. "Clever. Sort of. Hope whatever's in that chest holds up well in water."

Raedrick grunted. "The more immediate problem is how to get it out of there."

Julian looked askance at him and almost appeared about to laugh. But then he peered at the pool again and his lips turned downward into a frown. "If we had time, we could build a fire to dry off afterward. But..."

"We don't have the time," Raedrick finished.

Julian nodded emphatically. "We really don't. I'm pretty sure I saw Geoff's men up on the mountain, a few miles back. They're still a ways off, but heading downslope." He left the rest unsaid.

Raedrick bit back a curse. It had only been a matter of time before the ruffians caught up to them; their trail would not be difficult to follow in the snow. It would have been nice if they had a bit more time, though. "Any ideas?"

Julian looked around again, still frowning. "Short of getting a few branches and trying to fish it out...?" He shook his head. "Of course, they can only come at us one at a time through there." He gestured toward the cave entrance. "We could hold this place against them for a year."

Raedrick considered Julian's words for a moment. He did have a point. They could get the chest out and take all the time they needed drying off, and all Geoff could do about it was block them from leaving. It was not like he could come in and take it from both of them, the way the cave was configured.

But then, he did not have to, did he? Merely preventing their escape would be enough. It would not be a protracted siege. Raedrick shook his head. "If we had food we could. For a short while."

"Well then," Julian said, nodding concurrence. "Let's go get some branches."

<hr>

A quarter of an hour later, near as Raedrick could figure it, they made their way back down the entrance tunnel and into the cave's main chamber, several branches, ranging in length from four to six or seven feet in length, carried between them.

Once inside, they took a moment to examine the pool again, then they both hefted sticks and walked to the water's edge.

The plan was simple enough: push the chest out of the center of the pool with the longest branches, then keep on poking and prodding it until they could get it within arm's reach of the edge. By then, it would be mostly out of the water, and the two of them would just snatch it up.

Raedrick was not entirely sure the notion would work. The pool's bottom looked smooth enough, but in the dim light it was hard to tell for sure, and there could be holes that the chest could catch on. But he did not have a better idea.

Julian hefted his branch and flashed one of his nigh-eternal grins. "All set?"

Raedrick nodded. "Let's see how this does."

He pushed his branch into the pool...

And it skittered atop the surface of the water, not even penetrating an inch.

Shocked, Raedrick dropped the branch, and it clattered to the ground, two thirds of it resting atop the surface of the pool as though it were made of rock.

"What the...?" Julian began, then stopped, his mouth hanging open in astonishment.

Raedrick merely shook his head, at a loss for words.

Julian pressed his own branch into the pool, with the same effect. He raised his hands helplessly and looked at Raedrick in confusion. "How does that work?"

"It must be an enchantment of some kind," Raedrick said, his mind awhirl. It had to be a magical effect, but it was like nothing he had ever seen or heard of. Not that he was an expert on the subject by any means, but he had seen enough to have at least a passing familiarity with what a mage could do.

"Great," Julian muttered. "Where's Melanie when we need her?"

Raedrick shared the sentiment. The presence of Lydelton's mage in residence certainly would be helpful right then. But that was not going to happen. Raedrick scratched at his chin, then crouched down at the edge of the pool and reached down to the water.

"Whoa, Rae," Julian said, the sharpness of his tone bringing Raedrick up short. "If that pool's got spells on it, I'm pretty sure you don't want to be reaching your hand in there."

Raedrick paused, considering Julian's words. He had a good point. Mages could be tricky; there was an excellent chance whoever had laid these enchantments had also spun a number of other magical traps. He had seen their like before. If he were lucky, it would only burn his hand. If he were unlucky... The possibilities for mischief and harm were almost literally endless.

All the same, they needed to find out just how far the enchantment went.

Slowly, he stretched his hand back out toward the water. Next to him, Julian breathed a curse under his breath and took a half-step away. Just in case.

Raedrick's fingers touched the water...

...and slid in effortlessly. The water was beyond frigid; it was the essence of cold itself, unquenchably greedy for any and all warmth. He could feel the heat from his body siphoning out through his fingertips and into the water. Intuitively, he got the sense that the depth of cold within the pool could never be changed; even if it took all of his and Julian's body heat, it would not have warmed up even a hair. The chill began to spread up his arm, and for a moment he almost felt paralyzed.

Then he came back to himself and he jerked his hand away, out of the water. Cursing mightily, he shook the residual water off. Except no water flew from his hand. Not a single drop.

Raedrick blinked, confused, and raised his fingers to eye level. His hand was completely dry, not even a hint that it had just been submerged. Aside from a greenish-blue color in the tips of his fingers, he could not have told anything had just happened.

That color, and the frigid chill that lingered even still.

"Well that didn't work," Julian said, from behind him.

Raedrick cleared his throat. "Almost."

Julian snorted. "You didn't get any farther than that branch did."

It took a minute for Julian's words to sink in. When they did, Raedrick whirled back to him so quickly Julian took a half-step back in surprise. "What are you talking about? I got in the water just fine. It was just," he shuddered slightly, "so cold."

Julian's eyebrows rose, and he stared at Raedrick in silence for a moment.

"What, you didn't see it?"

"Rae, your fingers splayed out like you had just hit a brick wall and you all but bounced off."

Well, that was odd. Raedrick shook his head. "Strange. I could have sworn…" He peered back at the pool, its surface still completely smooth, undisturbed. "It was like the pool was sucking the warmth out of me through my hand. If I had stayed there for just a few moments more, it would have drained me of heat completely."

Another long moment of silence followed, then both of Julian's eyebrows shot upwards again. "It took your body heat." He sounded excited.

Raedrick nodded.

"But it did not wet you at all."

Another nod.

Julian grinned. "I've got it." He turned around and bounded a few steps away to where their lone remaining torch lay smoldering where he had left it, leaning against the cave wall. He hefted it and loosely wrapped another scrap of cloth around the smoldering torch head, then carefully blew onto the torch head in long, slow breaths. After a minute or so, the flame kindled back to life, and Julian grinned at Raedrick. "Let's see what this does."

Raedrick was about to ask him what he thought he was doing, but before he could say a word Julian had crossed the distance to the pool and thrust the burning torch head into it.

As with the dried sticks, the torch did not penetrate the pool at all, and Raedrick almost snorted out a laugh. But then the flame flickered and faded, and a second later extinguished completely. The torch head stopped releasing smoke and, when Julian had withdrawn it, little flecks of frost glistened atop it in the dim light of the cave.

"By the Gods," Raedrick breathed, and Julian nodded in agreement, but his eyes remained fixed on the pool.

"Is it just me, or is it a little bit shallower?"

Raedrick turned his gaze away from the extinguished torch and beheld the pool. At first, it looked exactly the same as it had before Julian hit it with the torch. But then, looking at it more closely…

Feeling his eyes widen, Raedrick nodded, sudden excitement rushing through him. "It is! Hot damn, Julian."

He reached over and clapped his friend on the shoulder. Julian just grinned in satisfaction.

Raedrick was not sure how much time passed. It could not have been long, but time has a way of running past a man when he's busy. And he and Julian were busy indeed, for the next little while, breaking up the branches they had gathered, stacking them into a small pile next to the edge of the pool, and then working the flint and steel on the last of their cloth to get the fire going.

Then they sat back to wait until the branches had well and truly caught.

"Now *that's* nice," Julian said, holding his hands out before the little blaze and grinning again. "All we need now is some sausage and brandy and we could have ourselves a merry afternoon."

Raedrick chuckled, shaking his head. He could not deny the appeal of that idea. If only they had time.

And sausage to roast.

Instead, Raedrick grabbed out a branch that had well and truly caught ablaze - there was not much to hold on to - and cast it onto the pool.

As before, the flame flickered and quickly died, but it took a bit longer than it had with Julian's torch. And this time, the pool was definitely more shallow. It was working.

"How about we just push the whole thing over onto it?"

Raedrick blinked, then nodded. He should have thought of that.

That just left how to go about doing it. Eventually, they just pulled out their swords and pushed at the campfire the same way they had thought to push the chest free of the pool using the branches. It was far from elegant, and the fire lost its carefully constructed geometry, but it worked. Mostly.

At once, Raedrick saw the utility of doing it that way. The fire flickered and faded, but continued to burn, the self-sustaining nature of the burn seeming to resist the heat drain from the pool. Or maybe as the pool was reduced, it lost some of its appetite for heat. Regardless of why, the fire did not go out all at once, but slowly began to dim and fade.

Excitement surged through Raedrick again. He could see the pool shrinking by the second, more rapidly now. The top of the chest was almost clear.

"More wood!" he said, automatically reverting to a tone of command. "Quickly!"

Julian, to his credit, did not question or hesitate. He could see what was happening just as well as Raedrick. At once, he turned and hurried out of the cave entrance.

He was not gone long, though it seemed to take forever as Raedrick watched the fire gradually die despite all his efforts to sustain it: blowing on it, feeding it what few burnable objects he could find, and hoping. When Julian finally returned with a moderately-sized bundle of branches tucked under his arm, there was not much left burning in the formerly bright and cheerful blaze.

"Hurry," Raedrick urged, not taking his eyes from the dying fire. "We're almost out of time."

Julian dropped the branches with a clatter and began breaking them into smaller pieces. "Seems like I always pull your chestnuts out of the fire," he said with a smirk as brought the first stack over to Raedrick.

Raedrick could not help chuckling. Carefully setting the new wood atop the dwindling fire, he sat back on his heels impatiently. The wood was cold, partially frozen and likely entrained with water. It would take a while to catch. If the pool drained the last of the fire's heat before it could light the new wood...

He need not have worried. Before long, the new wood caught. He and Julian fed larger and thicker pieces of wood and soon enough the fire was blazing merrily again. He looked to the side, judging how long the new stack of wood would last.

"We're probably going to need more. How much light do we have left outside?"

Julian shrugged. "Maybe an hour." He met Raedrick's gaze for a moment, then he sighed. "Alright, alright." He turned toward the entrance again, with a dejected slump to his shoulders that Raedrick just knew was fake. "I'll be back in a bit."

He slipped out, leaving Raedrick alone with the fire once more. There he sat, his back to the entrance, and watched, periodically adding another piece of wood to the fire as it faded. But his eyes never left the steadily lowering fluid of the pool, and the treasure sitting in its center.

26

FOOLS GOLD

By the time Julian returned again, the remaining wood was nearly gone, but virtually nothing remained of the pool.

Raedrick had had to shove the fire further down into the pit twice, each time fearing he would douse the flames by moving it too quickly and scattering the fuel. But each time it remained lit, as much as it could while in contact with the heat-draining enchantment.

"Almost there," Julian said, sounding relieved, as he dropped the fresh wood next to Raedrick and began breaking it up.

Raedrick nodded, grabbing up a piece and snapping it in two before dropping it onto the fire. "Shouldn't be long now." He frowned, gauging the pool's remaining depth. "We could probably reach the chest and haul it out now, actually." There was one rock in particular that now protruded from the surface of the pool. If one of them got onto that, he could reach the chest easily enough.

Julian looked sidelong at him, then shook his head. "If it's all the same to you I'd rather not. No telling what else that stuff will do." He pointed toward the pool's remaining fluid with a stick.

Raedrick considered for a moment. He had a point. You never knew what an enchantment might do, and their process was working. No sense rushing if they had the time. But did they?

"Did you see any sign of Geoff and his men?"

Julian shook his head, but frowned. "The sun'll be below the mountains soon, though. Can't imagine they're that far behind."

"We may have to risk it."

Raedrick stood and walked slowly around the pool to the closest point to that rock near the chest. About three feet away from where he stood now, and maybe a foot from the chest itself, it was rounded, but large enough to stand on easily, and looked to be completely dry. Strange that. Or maybe not. Memory of how the fluid felt came rushing back: cold, endless cold, but not wet. Not at all.

"I really don't think this is a good idea, Rae. It'll only be a few more minutes with the fire."

Raedrick nodded. "Just don't say I told you so if this doesn't work." Then he hopped over onto the exposed rock.

Naturally, his right foot slipped on the rounded surface of the rock and he lost his balance. For a second, he flailed about, trying to reclaim his balance, then seemingly slowly, he fell forward.

Julian cried out, "Rae!" and rushed forward, but he could not get close enough to help, not in time.

Raedrick was going over. He was going to fall into that bottomless well of cold, and it would devour him. There would be no pulling himself out if his entire body fell in, he was sure of that. He flung out his hands, seeking something, anything, to cling on to.

And they came down on the chest.

Abruptly, his fall stopped. He stood balanced on his left foot, with his hands atop the chest, but he was no longer falling.

He let his breath out in a rush, relief flooding through him. Then a chill deeper than the deepest winter night ran up his right leg. He looked down in chagrin to see his boot partially submerged in the pool. The heat rushed from his body, through his leg, and he felt himself growing weaker. He began to shiver and...his breath frosted in front of his face, despite the warmth of the cave.

Oh Gods, he had caught himself, but not in time. The cold. It was eating him alive. Consuming him.

He had almost no strength left, but maybe he could...

Raedrick pulled upward on his leg with all his might. For a second, he could not move it. Then, all at once, as though he had been pulling on a tense rope that parted, his foot sprang free of the fluid.

He almost overbalanced again, but he managed to bring the boot down atop the rock. It was glossy - covered in a film of ice, and Raedrick found he could not move his toes.

"Son of a bitch," he groaned, but it was weak; he could barely hear his own words.

"Rae, are you ok?"

He just perched there for a moment, shivering uncontrollably and not daring to move. Then he managed to croak out, "Yeah" in a loud enough tone to carry. He drew in a deep breath. "Fire," he said, and then his voice failed him.

Julian nodded, then hurried away, out of Raedrick's line of sight. He heard his friend bustling around busily for several moments that felt like an eternity. Then, slowly, he came back into view. Under his left arm he carried a small bundle of wood. In his right hand he carried a burning stick; he must have fished it out of the fire.

"Hold on, Rae," he said, and he set the burning stick down at the edge of the pool nearest Raedrick, then carefully piled the other wood atop it. An eternity later, another little fire burned there, sending heat Raedrick's way.

It burned like the sun, it was so hot. But he knew that was only in comparison with the infinite cold he had just felt. Slowly, ever so slowly, his shivering slowed and he felt strength returning to his limbs. He managed to raise his ice-logged boot to hold it closer to the fire. It hurt, Gods did it hurt, but it was good also. He imagined he could actually feel the blood thawing in his foot, the capillaries expanding, and circulation returning.

He set his foot down on the rock again and drew a deep breath, then let it out and tried to tell himself he did it without a sob.

Julian crossed his arms over his chest. "I told you - "

Raedrick shot a glare at him, and he stopped. He merely shook his head with a wry expression on his face that did not extend to his eyes, which were still deeply concerned. Raedrick sighed. "I'll be alright," he said, more forcefully. "That fire works wonders."

"How about you let it work back over here, away from that...whatever it is." Julian waved his hand at the remaining fluid in the pool. There was now maybe an inch of the stuff left, but after his last experience Raedrick did not fool himself that it was anything less than deadly.

He pushed off the chest and forced his weight fully back onto his feet. His right foot was still mostly numb, the parts that were not were a mass of pins and needles, so he nearly lost his balance again. He forced himself to stay in place. "We don't have..."

"Rae, get back here. I'll get the damn thing out, ok?" From the tone of Julian's voice, he was about ready to jump the distance himself, throw Raedrick over his shoulder, and haul him back. And to blazes if there was enough room for that.

Raedrick sighed and nodded, turning away from the chest. He winced as he bent his knees to make the short leap across the pool. But when he got there and sat down next to the fire, he had to admit Julian was right - it was far better there, and the fire warmed him far more quickly.

Julian sat down next to him. He said nothing; just watched the pool as its liquid level continued to lower steadily. Across the way, where their first fire had been, a veritable bonfire was burning; Julian must have tossed all the remaining wood onto it before coming to help Raedrick. No wonder the liquid level was dropping as quickly as it was. For that matter, the fire was not fading as quickly, either. The enchantment must have almost run its course.

Julian noticed his gaze and smirked at him. "That's right. We're waiting until the fire does the job on the pool for us. I'm not as dumb as you are."

Raedrick felt himself scowling before he could stop himself. Julian was right. This time. He thought about protesting anyway, but the fire's restorative heat felt too good. Instead, he said, "We need to hurry."

Julian looked at him as though he were daft, but nodded. "Sun's almost down and they'll have a hard time following our trail after dark dark. Moon won't rise for a long time still." He stood and brushed his hands off on the thighs of his leggings. "Now that I think about it, we're probably ok. If they haven't found us yet - "

He broke off talking as a metallic clank issued from the entrance passage, followed by a soft curse.

"Ah hell," Julian muttered.

Raedrick was forced to agree.

27

THE DREAMS OF AVARICE

Raedrick tried to push himself to his feet, but found his right leg would still not support his weight very well and he stumbled back to the ground. He gritted his teeth to try again; he needed to be up and ready for action if that was one of Geoff's men coming through the passage - and who else could it be?

But Julian beat him to it, bounding past the little fire and actually giving him a little shove back to the ground. "Stay there," Julian ordered, skirting around one of the few stalagmites on this side of the pool and pressing his back to the wall of the cave. Then he slid slowly toward the entrance and pulled out his knife.

Raedrick understood at once. The person coming in would have seen the light of their fires reflecting down the passage. He knew someone was there, but not how many. If he rounded the corner and only saw Raedrick...

The light from a torch appeared in the passage and a burly man dressed in furs - dog furs no doubt - rounded the corner. Not just burly - the man was tall. Huge. Raedrick recognized him immediately as one of Geoff's men; his height was distinctive, and his face was crisscrossed with tears and bite wounds - the calling card of one of Povol's dogs. He carried a lit torch in his left hand. He wore a longsword on his left hip and the straps of a backpack were visible on his shoulders.

Their eyes met across the cavern and the thug grinned, showing more missing teeth than not. Then he turned his head and bellowed, "He's here," back down the passage.

So much for silencing him before he could make a report.

The thug stepped into the cavern, keeping his eyes locked on Raedrick. His free hand drifted down to the pommel of his sword. "Constable, you've got a world of hurt coming your - "

The rest of his words were cut off in a grunt of surprise that became a yelp of pain as Julian moved on him. Striking from behind the big man and to his right,

Julian grabbed the bandit by the side of his neck and plunged his knife into the his side.

The yelp became a bellow and the big man went down, hard and without a semblance of grace. His gloating expression faded completely, replaced by a grimace of pain as he rolled over onto his back clutching at his injured side. His eyes, wide with confusion, swept around, finally coming to rest of Julian as he wiped the blood off his knife.

"You bastard!" cried the stricken thug from between clenched teeth.

Julian shook his head and drove his boot into the big man's temple. The bandit's eyes rolled in his head and he fell limp. "My parents were married," Julian said, coldly. Then he wiped his knife off and sheathed it. He looked over at Raedrick, his expression all business. "Can you walk? We need to get moving."

Raedrick shrugged and pushed himself up off the ground. Moving more slowly, he found he was able to gain his feet without overbalancing. Gingerly, he moved his so-recently frozen foot forward and shifted his weight.

A hundred little knives shoved themselves into the foot, and he gasped. But the foot held up and he was able to keep his balance as he finished the step.

Julian frowned. He did not need to say it; they were going to have to move faster than that if they were going to get out of this. Geoff's band numbered five more. Long odds under good circumstances. Odds they had faced and overcome before, but they were weary, hungry, and he had a sword he was not used to. That just made the odds worse.

Julian ducked into the entrance, keeping his back against the rock wall, and peeked around the corner. Whatever he saw made him cringe back, quickly.

"They're not coming in," he said as he moved quick to Raedrick's side. "Yet. But there's at least one more of them right outside the cave. He shouted for our friend there," he gestured at the unconscious man, "wanted to know what was going on."

"It won't be long, then."

Julian shook his head.

He was right; they needed to go. Raedrick looked aside, at the chest, now all but completely free of the pool's fluid. Less than a quarter of an inch looked to go before the chest would be out. They were so close; it would be a shame to leave without what they came for, to leave it to the scum who conned Tolburt.

Julian groaned softly, shaking his head. Then he walked over to the unconscious thug and, grasping him by the shoulder, rolled him over onto his side. The movement revealed his wound, and Raedrick could see blood still flowing. Slowly; not spurting, but it still flowed. He would be in trouble in a few minutes if the bleeding continued like that. But Julian paid that no mind. He set to work getting the man's pack off.

"Can't lug that chest around very quickly," he muttered as he pulled the man's first arms out of the shoulder strap. Then he pushed the man over so he lay face-down on the ground. "But we don't really need to, do we?" He made short work of the other strap, then he stood and hurried over to the rock Raedrick had nearly fallen off earlier.

The pool was much reduced and Julian had no trouble stepping on to the rock. Then he crouched down and rummaged through the thug's pack for a moment. He pulled a small implement of some kind out and unsheathed his knife, then he leaned forward, obscuring Raedrick's view of the chest.

"What are you doing?"

"Laremy," Julian stopped speaking and muttered a curse softly, then resumed whatever it was he was doing, "showed me how to open up a lock once."

Raedrick blinked, surprise preventing any response. "Ah," was all he could manage after a moment. He had not realized any of his men had such... eclectic...skills.

No time to worry about it now. Laremy was long gone and Julian...Julian was not his subordinate anymore, was he? And besides, they had moments at best before the rest of Geoff's thugs came charging in.

Raedrick picked up his longsword from where he had set it when he went to work on the fire, seemingly so long ago, and stepped over toward the cave entrance. It was getting easier to move; each step brought less pain - more like pins and needles than daggers now - and his balance was less awkward. He stopped next to the fallen thug and listened carefully. Julian was making enough noise with his tinkering, but if anyone was coming into the cave, Raedrick ought to hear it.

Nothing.

It was too much to hope the man outside had left. At best he was waiting for the rest of his companions to reinforce him before he came in after them. At worst... At worst they were all there concocting something dreadful for him and Julian.

Raedrick adjusted his grip on his sword and settled into a ready stance. His left foot slipped on the ground, and he looked down to find the rock at his feet slick with blood from the unconscious man.

That would not do, not at all.

***

It took Julian longer to get the lock open than he thought it would. Granted, he had not even tried to pick a lock in quite some time; certainly not since he became a law man. Just try explaining that one to the mayor.

He snorted softly at that thought.

His knife caught on something inside the lock and twisted in his hand, and he nearly dropped it into the whatever it was that made up the pool. He was not going to go into *that* stuff after the knife. No way. Gritting his teeth, he adjusted his grip and re-inserted the slender blade, then held it steady as he fished around with the narrow metal file he had found in the thug's pack. He must have been handy with a lock, too, that one.

He heard Raedrick pacing around behind him, and Julian could practically hear it in his friend's footsteps: hurry up!

And he was right. The longer they remained here the more likely they were not going to get out at all.

The knife slipped again and Julian almost gave up right then and there. Whatever was in this chest was not worth their lives. Best they get rolling.

He looked over his shoulder to tell Raedrick as much and saw that he was crouched over the fallen bandit. What was he - ? Oh, he was bandaging the man's wound, where Julian had stabbed him.

Always the softy, Raedrick was.

Julian found himself chuckling, and he shook his head. Then he turned back to the chest, his thought of leaving going unspoken. Just like he would not just let that bandit bleed out, Rae would not go without Tolburt's loot, whatever it was, and to blazes with being smart about it.

Better get this stupid thing open, so we can get out of here.

He set to the lock again, jabbing the knife in a bit harder than he intended to. It caught on something and stuck fast.

Julian frowned. That was probably not good. He probed with the file around where the knife's blade was sunk and felt something he had not noticed before. A little protuberance. He twisted the file counterclockwise, and…

The lock clicked and the lid of the chest shifted, ever so slightly. It was open.

For a second, Julian sat there in surprise. That was…easy. Sort of. Easier, in the end, than a chest like that had a right to be.

But then again, the magical pool was more than lock enough, wasn't it?

Julian yanked the knife out and examined the blade; it was notched in a couple places, but not too badly. Nothing a bit of time with a whetstone would not cure. He slipped it into his belt and put the file away. Then he gripped the chest's lid with both hands and lifted it open.

He looked inside, and found himself frozen in place by shock.

❦ 28 ❧

BESIEGED

"Um… Rae, you want to take a look at this."

Raedrick pulled the makeshift bandage tight around the thug's belly and looked back at Julian. He sat crouched on the rock island, such as it was, and had the chest open. But his tone said what was inside the chest was not good.

Raedrick pushed himself to his feet, suppressing a grunt as the pins and needles stabbed into his foot again. He hobbled, still more slowly than he would prefer, over to the edge of the nearly-vanished pool.

"What is it?"

Julian rose to his feet and hopped off the rock and back to the edge of the pool. "Tolburt wasn't the only one who got conned." He held out a folded piece of parchment.

Curious, but with a sinking feeling in his gut, Raedrick took the parchment, yellowed with age and torn about the edges, and unfolded it. "What is…"

He stopped speaking as he saw, written in a firm hand, a simple message on the parchment. "You've done well to get this far, Kalem, but this was just the first step. Your birthright awaits you at the Falconer's Stairs, if you prove worthy." There was no signature.

"There is nothing else in the chest," Julian said as Raedrick looked up from the note. He jabbed his finger at the parchment. "Just that."

"You're kidding."

Julian's scowl would have knocked over a bear at ten paces. "Do I look like I'm kidding, Rae?" He threw up his hands and stalked away from the pool. "I *told* you not to get involved in this. Tolburt didn't deserve it, and it was trouble we didn't need. But *no*. You had to go and be all *noble*." He whirled around again, facing Raedrick fully, thrusting his index finger at him like a lance. "All of this, the fighting, nearly getting ourselves killed. And *this* is what we get for it? A bloody riddle?"

His last question ended in a shout that echoed around the cavern for a couple seconds.

Raedrick had no response for a moment. He looked back down at the page, reading it over again. He frowned. "Who's Kalem, I wonder?"

He looked up to see Julian looking at him incredulously. "Who cares?"

"Well there's clearly something to be found. Looks like this was part of a right of passage for this Kalem, and coming here was just the first step. If we can find out who he is…"

Julian cut him off. "We'll do what, go off on some loony quest for," he waved his hands around aimlessly, "whatever his birthright is? *Was?*" He snorted. "Probably a half acre of rocky ground with a couple sheep on it."

Raedrick opened his mouth to reply, but Julian kept right on going.

"Not that we'll get a chance, because Geoff and his boys will probably gut us in a few minutes. How - "

Just then the fire they had lit atop the pool's fluid popped and went out, leaving only the little fire Julian had lit to warm Raedrick after his near miss, and the thug's torch where it lay on the cavern floor. The comparatively dim illumination was like evening compared with midday. Julian snarled a curse and turned away from him, stalking over toward where the torch lay.

He was right, of course. Whoever Kalem was, and whatever this birthright of his might be, it would have to wait. The priority now had to be getting out of there with their skins intact. Raedrick again drew a breath to speak, and was again cut off.

"Everything all right in there, Constable?"

Geoff's voice came from through the entrance passage, and Raedrick stiffened. Julian spun toward the entrance, drawing his sword. They waited for a long moment, but neither Geoff nor his men came into view.

Raedrick moved even with Julian and, stuffing the parchment into his pocket, hefted his sword. He tried to feel confident in his prospects with the unfamiliar blade, but given his lack of mobility…

"Constable?"

Closer to the entrance now, it was obvious to Raedrick that the thug had not come inside; he was shouting from outside the cave.

"He's just trying to spook us," Julian said, softly. "Make us do something stupid."

Raedrick shrugged. "He knows we're in here." He raised his voice. "We're doing great, Geoff, thanks. Your friend says hi. He's taking a nap right now."

"I'm surprised to hear that." His chuckle sounded more than a little disturbing as it echoed down the passage. "So we've got a little problem here. You've got what I want. I could take it, but frankly you've cost me too many men already."

Julian grinned wolfishly. "We can cost you a few more if you'd like," he shouted back.

Speaking of doing something stupid…

"Didn't realize you had someone else with you, Constable." Julian blanched a little. "How about this? You come on out, nice and quiet, and bring me what's mine, and we can all go about our business. Nice and easy, no more trouble."

"Yeah right," Julian muttered. "I believe that as much as one of Horace's sea stories."

Raedrick chuckled. "Horace's fishing stories are more honest." He raised his voice again. "How do I know you'll keep your side of it?"

"You don't," came the reply. "But I can sit out here 'til spring if I have to. We could have a right fun time of it, eh boys?" He paused, no doubt waiting for his men's response, which did not travel as well down the tunnel. "How long can you last in there, Constable?"

And that was the question of the day, wasn't it? Raedrick looked back at the little fire beside the pool and the torch, both already beginning to dwindle as their fuel burned away. Before long he and Julian would be left completely in the dark. And then what?

Julian saw it too. His frown spoke volumes. "There's some food in that guy's pack," he nodded at the still prone thug. "But..." He let the rest go unsaid.

They could not stay here long. The longer they waited, the less tenable their position became. Geoff's offer, dishonest as it likely was, was their only option.

"Give us a minute to talk it over in here," Raedrick shouted.

"Of course," came the reply. It positively dripped with gloating superiority.

❧ 29 ❧

COMING TO TERMS

"**Y**ou ready?" Raedrick asked Julian, and received a shrug in return.

"Don't see any point in waiting." Julian tugged at the strips of cloth he had fashioned into a rope. It would not do for those knots to let go. "How 'bout you, big fellow?"

The thug who had attacked them in the cave grunted and tried to say something, but all that came through the gag Julian had forced into his mouth was a muffled bit of gibberish.

Julian looked back at Raedrick and flashed a nervous grin. "Let's do it," he said. Then he gave the thug a shove between his shoulder blades to set him to walking, and followed him into the tunnel leading outside.

Raedrick paused only to pick up the chest. It was not particularly large, but it was solidly built and heavier than it looked; good thing he would not have to carry it far. Then he followed.

The thug had begun to come around almost immediately after their exchange with Geoff, and it was then that Raedrick had come up with the plan.

Plan. That made it sound like something more than what it really was: a desperate gamble. But it might work.

They had made quick work of tying the still stunned man up and gagging him, then Raedrick went back to the end of the tunnel to banter with Geoff, hoping to delay him long enough for Julian to get the chest out of the pool completely.

It had almost not worked. The chest had proven impossible to lift until Julian had just tossed the last of their fire onto the surface of the fluid. Praise the gods, there had been enough fuel left for the fire to reduce the pool to just below the bottom of the chest, and he had managed to lift it up and out of the depression where it had lain for who knows how long.

And now they were slinking their way through the tunnel out of the cave, Julian and the thug leading the way and Raedrick bringing up the rear. Julian had his knife out in his right hand and the torch in his left, and he kept the thug moving with gentle - or not so gentle - prods with the knife.

"We're coming out," Raedrick yelled. Geoff and his men had certainly seen them coming, but it could not hurt to give a little warning as well. The plan was simple, but delicate. Any number of things could go wrong, almost from the start, but there was no other course open to them.

The real difficulty began when the ceiling had lowered to the point they all had to crouch down. Julian could still urge the prisoner ahead, but for Raedrick, carrying that chest while doubled over... It was a relief when they finally emerged into the open air.

Almost.

Julian and the prisoner got out first, and Julian promptly tossed the torch to the ground and grabbed the big thug by the back of his shoulder, pulling him back against his body and placing the knife against his throat. "No one come any closer," he ordered in his battlefield voice.

Raedrick hurried to follow, and found himself facing a semicircle of five armed men, Geoff in the center. The men were rather worse for wear. One of them, standing immediately to Geoff's right, had a bandage wrapped tightly around his thigh, where Julian had shot him earlier. The two to the right wore bandages on their arms and lower legs, the other victims of Povol's dogs. Besides Geoff himself, only the bandit to Raedrick's extreme left, a fellow who was little more than skin and bones, bore no injuries, but even he looked haggard; they had passed several unpleasant and wearying days. Good to know he and Julian were not the only ones.

The sky to the east was pink-orange with the last vestiges of sunset; overhead, the first stars were visible. A short way away, under the forest canopy in the direction of the river, a fire was burning and Raedrick could make out the outlines of tents. He had a flashback of their first meeting for a second, except Geoff had no falsely magnanimous look about him this time.

Geoff was just opening his mouth - to retort no doubt - when Raedrick emerged. Geoff's lone good eye widened noticeably when he saw the chest Raedrick carried. All around the semicircle, Geoff's men grinned. The skinny one nudged his neighbor with his elbow and said something softly, causing the other man to chuckle.

Geoff's glare put an end to that. "Thought you'd go looking for it," he said, turning his attention back to Raedrick. He grinned broadly. "Couldn't resist the thought of all that gold, could ya?"

Raedrick did not bother to contradict him. "Here's how this works. I'll leave the chest here. We'll go that way." He nodded toward the south. "Once we're clear, we'll let your friend here go, and everyone leaves happy."

"Very generous of you," Geoff said, mockingly.

Raedrick took a step forward and dropped the chest, then rolled his shoulders to relieve the kinks that had developed while he was bent over. "No good to us anyway," he said. "Damn thing's locked."

The group of bandits laughed at that.

Julian began inching to the right, pulling at the prisoner to keep him close, and

Raedrick moved to join him, trying to ignore the pins and needles in his foot and walk normally.

"Yep, that's mighty generous," Geoff said. "Problem is, you killed some of my friends." His grin turned vicious. "Can't let that lie." He nodded. "Boys."

As one, the thugs began to close in.

❧ 30 ☙

MELEE

Here was only a second to respond before the bandits fell on them, but Julian did his part without hesitation. He drove his knife into shoulder muscles on the side of the prisoner's neck and shoved him forward into the path of the closest bandit on the right. The wound would not kill him, but it would bleed like crazy; hopefully seeing their comrade bleeding from a neck wound would make at least one of Geoff's men stop to tend to him.

Raedrick had his sword out and was moving before Julian finished, leaping toward the next bandit on the right.

The man was not expecting him to charge, that much was plain from the look of baffled surprise on the man's face. But he was not unskilled either. He veered to Raedrick's left, getting out of the path of his charge and cutting downward viciously.

Which was just what Raedrick was waiting for.

He shifted his sword into his left hand and dropped his weight onto his rear as he went to the ground, sliding through the snow beneath the bandit's cut. No sooner had the bandit's blade whistled past his ear than Raedrick stabbed upward with his own weapon. The man's eyes widened in shocked surprise that turned to pain as Raedrick's sword punctured his left leg at the hip.

The bandit went down, clutching at the wound and screaming, and Raedrick kicked himself up to his feet.

He very nearly went down again when his right foot caught most of his weight. For a second it was as though his ankle had lost every bit of support structure it had ever had and he was going to go down. Then he got his other foot beneath him and managed to stumble into a mostly balanced stance.

He looked behind himself and saw Julian bounding away from the re-wounded prisoner. The prisoner was firmly entangled with his comrade, who had apparently ran straight into him and taken the two of them down in a tangle of limbs.

The two bandits who had been to their left when they came out of the tunnel were moving forward, but one of them - the skinny one - had eyes only for the chest, and the other was hampered by his wounded leg.

Geoff... Raedrick expected him to be enraged, but the bandit leader looked calm, even amused. His eyes met Raedrick, and Geoff raised his finger to his brow in a little salute. Then he stalked forward toward the chest.

Apparently his lost comrades were not all that important, after all.

No time for wondering about Geoff's motivations. Raedrick turned and followed Julian into the quickly darkening forest.

Of course, it was never going to be as simple as that.

No sooner had he passed the first of the trees than Raedrick heard Geoff's voice rise in a loud cry of anger. He must have opened the chest and seen the nothing that resided within. That did not take long.

Raedrick cursed under his breath and pushed himself to greater speed, but there was only so fast a man could run in ankle-deep snow. If only they could have found a way to lock the cursed chest again...

No time to dwell on that.

"Won't be long now," Julian said from a few paces ahead. He ducked beneath a particularly low tree limb, then came to an abrupt halt. "Ah hell."

Raedrick followed suit, stopping at his friend's side, and immediately mirrored Julian's curse.

In front of them, the terrain fell away a good thirty feet or so in a sheer cliff. He could just make out boulders in the growing dark, clustered around the bottom of the drop-off.

"Won't be going that way," Julian muttered.

Raedrick looked left and right. The cliff face ran as far as he could see, which admittedly was not very far. What was this? He did not recall any cliffs like this when he walked up to the cave before. He looked up and realized the problem immediately: instead of running more or less south, they had bent eastward, going more directly downslope toward the river.

"We'd better head back a ways," Raedrick said, turning his back on the drop-off. "I don't want to stumble back onto this after it gets full dark."

Julian grunted, scowling, but he did not voice an objection. There was none to make.

Raedrick took the lead, pushing past the low tree limb and hurrying upslope about fifty feet. There he turned left and set out to the south again, more slowly this time. The light was all but gone, and the danger of falling into some hidden hazard loomed large. With luck, maybe the thugs would follow their first trail to the drop-off and...

Behind him, Julian cried out, and there was a muffled thump of a body falling to the ground.

Raedrick spun around, bringing his sword to bear, and saw his friend lying face-first on the ground. One of the thugs, the fellow who had tripped over their prisoner Raedrick thought, lay atop Julian where he had tackled him.

Raedrick froze for a second, surprise stealing his initiative as he pondered how the man had gotten to them so quietly.

Of course, he would not have had to be terribly quiet; they were making plenty of noise. And he had probably just been following their trail when they appeared right in front of him, and it would not have taken much to sprint across the intervening distance...

Julian twisted beneath the thug, but the man had the advantage of leverage and he forced Julian back to the ground. "I've got them!" he bellowed, and drew a knife from his belt.

Raedrick snapped himself from his reverie and hurled himself forward toward the thug. The thug had no sword; his knife would be poor defenses against Raedrick's attack, so Raedrick simply thrust straight at the thug's heart.

He should not have been surprised when the thug saw him coming and leaped to the side, avoiding his attack, but he was. The man had not looked all that nimble earlier.

Raedrick took a second to regain his footing. That was all the time the thug needed to regain his as well. The two stared at each other over the span of six or seven feet. The thug wet his lips, and Raedrick could just see the man's eyes flicker from Raedrick's sword to his own small knife, then to the ground to Raedrick's left. Raedrick took a quick glance in that direction and saw a sword - the thug's apparently, where he had dropped it during the tackle.

Idiot.

"Better run," Raedrick said, turning his attention back to the thug.

Off to the side, Julian found his feet again and picked up his own weapon.

The thug looked between the two of them and swallowed.

"Go," Raedrick said, nodding back toward the cave, and the thug's comrades. Hopefully the fellow would choose discretion over valor. Raedrick had no doubt he and Julian could take him, but the other men could not be far behind.

It was as though the thought had summoned them. The shadows to the left moved, and with a loud cry, skin-and-bones bounded forward. The last remnants of the sunset flashed off his blade as he crossed in front of his comrade and sent the cutting edge toward Raedrick's neck.

Raedrick hopped backwards and the sword whistled harmlessly through the air in front of him, then he advanced, his own weapon dipping quickly downward before becoming a rising thrust at the man's solar plexus.

Steel met steel with a loud CLANG as skin-and-bones knocked the thrust aside. His lips twisted into a sneer of contempt, and he shuffled forward, swinging backhanded at Raedrick's face with the pommel of his sword.

Again Raedrick backpedaled, but the thug was coming on too quickly; Raedrick would not get away by retreat alone.

So he dropped to the ground and kicked his feet upward.

The thug's eyes widened as his own momentum drove himself into Raedrick's kick. He half-coughed, half-groaned and stumbled off to Raedrick's right, all thought of the fight gone as he tried to recover the breath that had completely left his lungs.

Raedrick shoved himself to his feet. He glanced at the stumbling, coughing thug and dismissed him as not an immediate threat, then peered around to find the other fellow.

In the deepening gloom, he could only see two shadows grappling at each other, each trying in vain to gain an advantage over the other and force him to the ground. Raedrick was reminded of the wrestling matches his Army unit had engaged in during the long months of relative inactivity before the war had really caught fire. He recalled Julian was pretty good at wrestling.

He was also exhausted and still harboring the wounds of his previous captivity, though he was loathe to admit it. This was not going to end well.

Raedrick hurried toward his friend and the first thug. As he drew nearer he was able to make out more details. Julian with his left hand on the thug's right wrist, working to keep the knife away from himself. His other arm entwined in the thug's where the man had gotten inside Julian's sword swing. He would not last long with his weaker hand against the thug's stronger.

The two wrestling men turned, bringing the thug's back to Raedrick, and he raised his sword.

Suddenly the thug gave a jerk, twisting his torso away from Julian and wrenching Julian's shoulder. Hard. Raedrick heard the pop a split second before Julian cried out in sudden pain. His right hand went limp and his sword dropped to the ground. His left arm seemed to lose all strength, and the thug's knife moved inexorably plunged toward Julian's body.

There was no time to think, so Raedrick did not. He simply thrust.

The resistance when the tip of his sword entered the thug's back was less than Raedrick expected; it must have slipped between two ribs. But the result was immediate. The knife fell from fingers that were suddenly limp and the thug sagged, forcing Raedrick's blade down with the weight of his body as he breathed out a long gurgling breath. Then he fell forward at Julian's feet, slipping off the sword as he went.

Julian staggered backwards, his left hand moving to his throat as though to make sure his flesh was still intact. Then he gave a little shiver and slumped back against a nearby tree. "That was close," he murmured.

Raedrick nodded, pausing to wipe his sword free of blood and shove it back behind his belt. Then he picked up one of the swords lying on the ground and offered Julian his hand. "We need to move."

Julian glanced aside at skin-and-bones, who was had still not begun to recover his bearings. Raedrick could not see it in the gloom, but he was sure Julian raised a questioning eyebrow at him. Raedrick shook his head; no need to harm skin-and-bones further, not if they could help it.

Julian shrugged. Or tried to; the movement instead produced a hiss followed by a groan of pain.

Raedrick helped his friend away from the tree then, supporting him with one arm wrapped around his good shoulder, the two of them set off south.

"I think," Julian said through clenched teeth, "it's well past time we went home."

Raedrick was forced to agree with him.

❦ 31 ❦

EVASION

They walked for a time, slowly at first. But after a few steps, Julian regained his equilibrium and he was able to make a better pace. They soon lost sight of the fallen thug and his stunned companion, but not before the latter managed to regain his feet. Raedrick looked back and saw him, a shadow against the lighter shadow of the snow-covered ground, stumble over to where the other man lay. He checked on his companion then stood, looking at Raedrick and Julian. For a moment, Raedrick thought sure he would charge after them. But instead, skin-and-bones turned and hurried away, back toward the cave and their camp.

"He'll be back with his friends," Julian said. He too had stopped to look back.

Raedrick shook his head. "Only five remain, and two are too injured to fight effectively." The fellow who had taken the arrow to his thigh would not make a difficult opponent, and the man they had held prisoner would be in no shape for fighting for a long time. "I think Geoff's band is done for this fight."

Julian gave him a skeptical look, but did not press the subject.

———

A few minutes later, Raedrick decided they had put enough distance between themselves and the camp that he could afford to take a look at Julian's latest injury. He did not protest that he was fine when Raedrick suggested they stop. That was a bad sign.

He did protest while Raedrick helped him out of his pack, coat, and shirts - all four of them. Quite vociferously, if not particularly loudly; even in the pain of moving his injured limb, Julian remembered the need for as much stealth as they could muster.

It could have been worse. Near as he could tell, Julian's right shoulder was dislocated. Raedrick had feared he had a broken bone; there would be little he

437

could do about that. But he knew a fix for a dislocation. Julian had performed a similar service for him not so long ago. He recalled it hurt like mad, but it worked.

"This is going to hurt," he said as he grasped Julian's arm.

"What doesn't?" Julian said weakly in reply. For a moment Raedrick considered not doing it, but Julian would need to be able to at least move both his arms to make the trip back. Their eyes met and Julian rolled his, then gave a quick nod.

Raedrick pushed. Hard. Julian cried out, his eyes rolled back in their sockets, and he passed out.

A couple minutes later, when Julian had come back to his senses, Raedrick helped him back into his clothing. It was slow going, with a lot of wincing and muttering on Julian's part, but at least he had some range of motion in the injured arm now. Once Julian was settled, Raedrick helped him to his feet.

Raedrick considered for a moment whether to bother with Julian's pack, then decided to just leave it. All of their meager remaining possessions fit easily into Raedrick's own pack, and he did not want to put any more weight onto Julian's shoulder than he had too. So instead, he took a moment to bury the pack under the snow. Then they set out to the south, Julian's arm over his shoulder as Raedrick supported him so he could walk.

Very quickly they lost the light entirely. Oh, there was some small amount of light from the stars overhead that filtered down through the canopy, but it was far from sufficient. And when - not if, but when - the clouds rolled through, that would be gone completely.

The memory of the drop-off that they almost ran into weighed heavily on Raedrick's mind as they walked. There were any number of hazards, many as bad or worse than that drop-off, that they could potentially meet here in the wild. And he could barely see his hands in front of his face.

Continuing on was madness. They needed to wait until light, or they both could die in some mishap that would be easily avoided during the day.

But he dared not stop. Geoff and his men were back there, not a mile distant. Skin-and-bones had to have reported back by now. Geoff would know he and Julian had escaped him, yet again.

Raedrick and Julian were well past a nuisance to Geoff. He almost had the prize in his hands, the thing he had lied, cheated, and killed to obtain. And Raedrick had cheated him of it. Or at least, that would be how Geoff saw it. Maybe losing yet another man, with two others wounded, would convince him to leave over, let them go, but Raedrick, regardless of what he had said to Julian earlier, rather doubted it. Geoff was the vindictive type; he did not let things go.

But there was vindictive anger and then there was sheer stupidity, and Geoff was not stupid. He would probably wait until it was light to set off after them again. And they could not be anywhere near the cave when that happened. They would be easy enough to track through the snow. No sense making it easier still.

And so they had no choice but to walk through the woods in the dark, on the side of a mountain.

At some point, Raedrick fell asleep.

He had no idea when, or how long he and Julian had stumbled along through the night. Hell, when sunlight on his face made him blink his eyes open, he for a moment did not remember that he was out in the wild, in the depths of winter, alone except for an injured friend, with a group of men bent of vengeance probably right on his heels. For a moment, all he thought was how pleasant the sunlight felt, and how its refraction through a nearby icicle really was something to behold.

He smiled, drew in a deep breath.

And remembered.

He sat upright with a start, frantically turning his head left and right as he sought to get his bearings. Where was he? And Julian. Where was Julian?

The answer to the first question was simple enough. He sat in the middle of a thicket, dense except off to the right, where the underbrush had been roughly broken aside. The trees and brambles on all sides were bare, their leaves long since fallen to the earth and buried by snow or, in the case of the evergreens, high enough above him that they did not impact his initial look around. And yet the snow was less here than elsewhere; a quick glance past the broken brambles to the world beyond showed that. And there was less wind than Raedrick remembered. Even bare branches can help with that, it seemed.

But how had he gotten here? He had no memory of finding this place, or of stopping at all. One moment he was trudging along, trying to ignore the deepening cold, the numerous aches of his body, the crushing fatigue threatening to flatten him with every step, and the danger that forced him to keep taking that next step. So what had happened?

And, again, where was Julian?

He could not have left Raedrick, gone on alone. He was in no condition to do such a thing. That just left a few possibilities, and they were all bad.

The sound of footsteps in the snow brought Raedrick's attention to the rear. He spun around, or rather tried to, but even the lesser snow within the thicket was enough to make turning slow and cumbersome. Apprehension combined with the familiar feeling of adrenalin surging through his body as he readied himself for a fight...

Looking haggard, weary, with bruises showing all over his face, Julian nevertheless managed a half-smile as he pushed aside a branch and stomped into the thicket. The smile slipped as he settled his weight onto his forward foot, becoming a wince as he struggled to hold back a groan. "Morning, Rae," he managed, through clenched teeth.

Raedrick sprang to his feet, relief fighting with concern as he went to help his friend. "Take it easy," he said. Julian accepted his help, allowing Raedrick to support him as he lowered himself down into a seated position. "What do you think you're doing?"

Julian coughed. Winced. Then held up his right hand. Raedrick had not noticed it earlier: he was holding a dead rabbit. "Getting you breakfast," he said, and grinned again, slightly.

Raedrick blinked in surprise.

He must have looked as baffled as he felt, because Julian barked out a laugh that ended abruptly in a spasm of coughing, followed by a very colorful oath. "Set a snare last night," he said, finally.

How's that? "Julian, we were... It was..." He paused, trying to make sense of what Julian had said. "What?"

Julian grinned again, but though he looked amused enough to laugh again, he managed to restrain himself. One coughing fit in as many minutes was sufficient, Raedrick presumed. "You got downright delusional last night. I thought *I* felt bad, but you..." He shook his head. "Half of what you said made no sense, and you kept changing direction. At some point, we blundered in here," he gestured at the thicket all around, "and you said something about a snare, then just passed out."

"So you set a snare."

Julian nodded.

"In the dark."

Another nod.

"In your condition."

Julian just looked at him with a long-suffering expression on his face.

"And the damn thing actually caught something?" This was the most ridiculous thing he had ever heard, and if he had not seen it with his own eyes... Raedrick sighed. "What time is it?"

Julian shrugged. "I make it about eight in the morning," he said, and began clearing some of the snow from the ground in front of him. Or trying to; he paused after moving a couple handfuls, wincing as his left hand moved quickly to his right shoulder.

Eight in the morning. They did not have much time then. Raedrick stood reluctantly, his knees popping from the sudden movement of limbs that had gone stiff from the night spent on the ground, in the bitter cold. He was surprised they had made it through at all.

"We don't have time to cook, Julian," he said. "Geoff and his men will..."

Julian snorted. "I think you were right last night. He's not stupid, and his men are probably just as tired as we are. They're done with us for now. Maybe forever."

Raedrick was not so sure. Geoff would not let what happened slide, not that easily. Of course, from the look on Julian's face he did not want to hear that right then. No matter, there were other reasons to move out. "Regardless, we need to get you to the Healers Circle."

Julian shrugged. Shallowly. "Sleep did me good. I'm right as rain."

Raedrick looked at him levelly.

Their eyes met for a moment, then Julian lowered his eyes. He nodded, then slowly, with obvious effort, stood. He kept the rabbit in his hand. "Fine. I'll cook it when we get back."

Raedrick chuckled. "Come on. We can't be far from the cabin."

Raedrick was right. Once they descended the rest of the way down the hillside, which they accomplished in about a quarter of a mile, they turned downriver. Maybe a half-mile further on, they approached the little curved spit of land that formed the northern edge of the cove near the cabin. Their tracks from the other day were easy to see.

He grinned and slapped Julian on the back - he had gone back to leaning on

Raedrick for support after the first few minutes of walking. He was no where near as well-off as he had tried to claim in the thicket.

Julian grinned as well, but did not speak. His eyes said all that needed saying. Thank the Gods, now let's get in that boat and get out of here.

Raedrick found he concurred completely.

He made to retrace his earlier steps out to the canoe, but the breeze shifted, bringing the smell of woodsmoke to his nostrils. He stopped cold, casting about for the source of the smoke.

"Rae," Julian said, urgency in his tone. He pointed west, toward the woods along the riverbank where Povol's cabin lay.

A thin trail of smoke, growing thicker by the second, rose there. There could be no doubt what was burning.

"Son of a bitch," Raedrick said in unison with Julian, then they hurried toward the cabin.

❦ 32 ❦

ON ICE

By the time they pressed through the woods to the small clearing where the cabin lay, it was too late. The whole structure was ablaze, the heat intense enough that they could not come within thirty feet of the place that had sheltered them so well just a day ago. Smoke billowed from the blaze, and all around loud popping noises began issuing from the trees and undergrowth. Ice that had coated, and in some cases penetrated, limbs was melting or splitting, taking some of the limbs with it. It would not be long before the closest trees were free of snow entirely, and then...

"This whole part of the woods is going to go up," Julian said. He was holding a hand up, shielding his face and eyes from the blaze as he peered around at the trees, some practically right on top of the burning cabin.

Raedrick nodded. Julian was right, and there was not a damn thing they could do to stop it. Maybe if Melanie were there, she could use some bit of Magery to quench the flame, but short of that... Anger welled up within him, more like righteous fury. "Geoff did this," he said through clenched teeth.

Julian looked sidelong at him, and for a second Raedrick thought he would disagree. But instead he nodded.

They stood there for a long moment, just watching the fire consuming Povol's cabin. The flames' movement as they whipped about in a frenzy was mesmerizing, the heat, intense as it was, lulling. It would be so easy to just stay there and watch, then continue to watch as the trees on either side caught fire as well, and then...

A thought struck Raedrick, and he jerked out of the brief reverie. "The canoe!"

Julian blinked, then groaned. "That bastard better not have."

They turned as one and rushed back toward the river and the boat Raedrick had left in the ice the day before.

———

The cold hit with renewed fury after a dozen steps, seeming doubly eager to trample them underfoot after their brief respite in the heat of the blaze and playing counterpoint to the cold sliver of fear that run up Raedrick's spine. If Geoff had destroyed the canoe, or taken it, they were screwed. It was a long walk back through the wooded valley then over Tollard's Peak to the Glamorwood. And shortly the valley's forest would be aflame; that would not make for a pleasant hike. Between the cold without and its twin within, Raedrick went from sweating to shivering in moments, and it seemed he would freeze between one running step and the next.

They made it along the north side of the cove and out onto the ice, and that sliver of fear became a lance.

The canoe was still there, but it was not alone. Geoff and two of his men, skin-and-bones and a swarthy, burly fellow with a black beard long enough he had braided it, stood between Raedrick and Julian and the boat, weapons drawn.

Geoff's vicious grin appeared immediately as the friends stepped into view. "Thought we'd find you here," he said, pitching his voice so it would carry easily across the twenty feet or so between them. "Like what we've done with the place?" He gestured with his battleaxe past Raedrick's shoulder, toward the burning cabin.

"Have you gone mad?" Raedrick demanded. "The entire forest is going to go up! It'll cook the men you left back at your camp, and us too unless we get out of here." He presumed Geoff had left the wounded back at their camp and marched these fellows down during the night.

"My men'll be fine. As for the forest," he shrugged, "that's on you, Constable. Now." Geoff lowered his axe, resting its head on the ice, and he laid his hands atop the weapon's handle. "That was pretty clever last night with the chest. How about you give me what's mine, and save us all any more trouble and unpleasantness."

Raedrick looked aside at Julian, who wore a scowl that made thunderclouds look bright, then sighed. "Geoff, the chest was empty. Someone else beat us all to it."

Skin-and-bones snorted loudly. "That's rich," he said, dripping derision as though he had forgotten how easily he had been beaten the night before. Raedrick found himself regretting that he let the man go.

"Have it your way," Geoff said, then hefted his axe. It was large, far longer than the smaller battleaxes the heavy infantry companies in the Army used. Those had been designed to wield one-handed, allowing the use of a shield as well. Geoff's axe looked almost a third longer than Raedrick's sword. He did not relish the thought of going up against that weapon.

Geoff nodded to his men. "Kill his friend. The Constable's mine."

The thugs advanced.

Typical. Raedrick had almost begun to believe that just this once they were going to make it out of this without a showdown. He sighed as he drew his blade and sidestepped to the left, putting some distance between himself and Julian so they would not interfere with each others' movements.

Why, oh, why did there always have to be a showdown?

33

SHOWDOWN

The footing would be treacherous. Snow covered the ice, lessening the danger somewhat, but if he was not careful, a poorly-placed foot would send Raedrick sliding to the ground, or even out into the frigid water. As battlefields went, this was about the worst one Raedrick would have picked.

Of course, Geoff and his men would suffer the same peril. If anything, they possibly were at more of a disadvantage than Raedrick and Julian. The two moving toward Julian would have to be careful of how they attacked, to avoid striking their partner or sliding into his attack. Julian would have no such limitation.

Which was all well and good, but it was not Raedrick's immediate problem.

Geoff's axe, dual-bladed and heavier than Raedrick would have ever considered wielding, whipped through the air in smooth arcs as he advanced. They were flourishes, not attacks, but Geoff performed them with effortless aplomb that bespoke great strength, as well as an intimate familiarity with the weapon and how to employ it.

Raedrick had no such bond with the longsword in his hand.

He swallowed, backing up a couple steps to maintain a comfortable distance between himself and Geoff.

Off to the right, skin-and-bones reached striking range of Julian, cutting downward at his injured right shoulder, but Julian easily avoided the blow, ducking outside the arc of the sword's cut and getting to the thug's quarter before he could pull back from the attack. A boot to skin-and-bones' hip sent him sprawling in front of his bearded comrade, who had to leap to avoid tripping over him.

And then Raedrick had no more time to spare noticing the details of Julian's fight. Geoff snarled, a ravenous light in his eyes, and lunged forward, the great axe cutting toward Raedrick's belly.

The straightforward attack caught Raedrick by surprise; he had expected something more...elegant. But while the attack was not fancy, it was effective, and Raedrick was almost too slow in his defense. He brought his longsword down in a descending arc intended to knock Geoff's blade aside and set himself up for a riposte.

And found that the great axe was no longer there.

Oh, it was still present, but it no longer veered toward Raedrick's gut, but instead whipped upward toward his throat.

Raedrick spat out a curse and hopped backward, tilting his head backwards and whispering a quick prayer in his mind; there was nothing else he could do, the feint had tricked him so.

The axe's passing came with its own gentle breeze, and then it was gone as Geoff recovered from his swing and pulled back to a guarding position. Raedrick thought the cut had missed for a second, then he felt the ache starting. He raised his left hand to his chin, and his glove came away bloody.

Geoff smirked and spun the great axe in his hands. A few drops of blood splattered onto the snow-covered ice between them. "I reckon I'm going to enjoy this," he said.

Julian grimaced as he brought his sword up. His shoulder still throbbed, despite Raedrick's first aid the night before, and his arm did not move as well as it normally did. He was barely able to get the parry up in time to meet the incoming attack.

Steel met steel and the two blades rang as one for a moment. The attack had been a clumsy back-handed swing, the best braid-beard could do with his balance off after leaping over his fallen comrade. But he managed to put a fair amount of force behind the cut, and Julian's arm buckled, bending involuntarily at the elbow and allowing the encroaching steel to come mere inches from his neck.

Braid-beard grinned and pressed his advantage, throwing his weight against his sword.

Julian laid his left hand overtop his right on the grip of his blade, trying to reinforce his failing arm, but slowly, surely, he was losing it. The angle was wrong and the brigand had all the leverage. Any second now, Julian's sword arm would give way altogether, and then he was done.

"Time's up," Braid-beard taunted. He pressed forward even harder.

Julian relaxed his sword arm and twisted, letting the force of the brigand's shove turn his body clockwise and backward. Julian gave one last shove against the brigand's blade as he twisted, not opposing his force but redirecting it, and then his body was out of the way of the attack. Spinning completely around, he returned the braid-beard's backhanded cut with one of this own.

Braid-beard moved forward with the momentum of his push, then staggered as Julian suddenly was no longer there. Julian's sword swept through next as he completed his spin, and Julian felt the telltale resistance of the steel cutting into the brigand's flesh above the hip.

Braid-beard lurched forward, stumbling as the wound began to register. His left hand went to his hip, where blood had begun to flow, and a confused expression came over his face. He made as if to take a step. And then his leg buckled and he fell in a heap into the snow. His sword landed, uselessly, next to him. Only then did he cry out, a long loan moan of pain that sounded as though it came through gritted teeth.

Julian rose to his full height and nodded in satisfaction. One down.

He turned back toward the other brigand, and his satisfaction faded quickly. The scrawny fellow was back on his feet, moving toward Julian with much greater deliberation than he had at first. Scrawny's eyes flickered between Julian and his fallen comrade, and he licked his lips, from nerves hopefully.

Julian stepped back, giving himself some distance from the fallen man, and made to lift his sword to a guarding position.

His right arm would not move.

Or at least, it would not move past about twenty degrees from pointing straight down. This was not good, not at all.

Scrawny saw his difficulty and any nervousness faded. He grinned hungrily and advanced.

The cut was bleeding badly; it must have been pretty deep. But Raedrick's chin merely ached; it did not burn with the pain that such blood flow would seem to dictate. He had suffered deep wounds before, so he was pretty sure he knew the difference.

Time to worry about that later.

Geoff advanced again, his too-long axe spinning a circle that reflected the sunlight, causing Raedrick to blink for a second. Only instinct and a desperate dive to the side prevented him from being chopped in half by the attack that followed.

Raedrick rolled over his left shoulder and sprang to his feet, only to see the cutting edge of Geoff's weapon descending toward his head. Moving with a speed born of desperation, he sidestepped to the left and flicked his sword right. Steel met steel with a sharp clang, and Geoff's axe rebounded from Raedrick's sword, continuing its descent past Raedrick's right shoulder. Raedrick kept moving, sidestepping further to his left and flicking the cutting edge of his sword toward Geoff's right shoulder.

Geoff began moving as soon as the parry deflected his cut, drawing his right leg back and twisting his body out of the way of Raedrick's counter. It was almost as though he knew what Raedrick was going to do before he did it, he moved so smoothly.

Raedrick retreated a step, drawing a deep breath and raising his blade back to vertical in front of himself. His heart pounded in his ears from the exertion of the duel, and his entire body felt as though it were going to fly apart, he was charged up so.

Geoff paused and, frowning slightly, removed his left hand from the grip of his axe. He raised it to his right shoulder, and the fingertips came away red. Geoff sniffed and raised his eyebrows at Raedrick.

Raedrick glanced quickly at the end of his sword. The tip - the very tip - was lightly stained with blood. A small drop pooled and began running down the blood groove in the middle of the blade. So his cut had not been completely ineffectual after all.

He had not realized how much the speed and efficacy of Geoff's initial attacks had put a damper on his spirits. But seeing his opponent's blood on his blade - however little - the confidence Raedrick had not realized was fading rebounded within him. He returned Geoff's raised eyebrows with a quick grin - *that* hurt a *lot* - and rolled his shoulders, settling down into a more relaxed ready stance.

Then it was his turn to advance.

He darted forward and to the right, thrusting straight ahead with his sword ever so briefly before cutting straight down at Geoff's left thigh.

Again the thug moved as though reading Raedrick's mind. He did not even try to deflect the feint; he merely hopped backwards a half-step, allowing Raedrick's cut to pass harmlessly through the air where his leg used to be.

Then he countered with a sweeping cut at neck-level.

Gotcha.

Raedrick stopped his rightward movement and, crouching low, slid his left leg far out to the side and shifted his weight onto it. Geoff's decapitation strike whistled harmlessly through the air over his head, close enough that his hair billowed softly in the breeze of its passing. Raedrick countered immediately with an upward cut, angling to the left so that it would open Geoff up from left hip to right shoulder.

Again the thug was not quite quick enough. He moved out of each of Raedrick's sword, but not before Raedrick scored a cut on his hip.

The big man stumbled as he retreated and the pain of the new wound registered, but he regained his balance quickly. Again his left hand left his axe's grip and went to the wound, but this time it was no mere scratch; the blood began flowing immediately, staining his furs with a quickly-growing circle of red.

"You're right, Geoff," Raedrick said in his most derisive tone. "This is fun."

Geoff's nostrils flared and he barked out a curse. Then, the pain of his new wound apparently forgotten, he launched himself forward.

Julian backpedalled, ducking beneath a high cut, and countered. But though he had trained to fight left-handed - that was simply a prudent thing for a fighting man to do - his swing felt almost as awkward as it looked, and Scrawny sidestepped it easily.

This was not going well at all.

The brigand wasted no time, but instead pressed forward with his own attack. A smile wrought from the assurance of victory bespoke the man's outlook on the fight more than any boast could have. He was going to win out, and soon. Trouble was, Julian tended to agree with him.

He half-stepped, half-slid to the side and sucked in his gut, just barely getting his belly out of the way of Scrawny's sword. For a second, the brigand was wide open for a counter attack from above, but Julian's sword was out of position still. And he did not feel confident in pressing the attack. So instead he retreated.

Several quick shuffle-steps backward put about ten feet between himself and Scrawny, and Julian paused to take his bearings.

Off to his right, Raedrick still had his hands full with Geoff. The two men danced around each other, Raedrick barely avoiding being gutted by that extra-long axe twice in as many seconds. To the left, the nearly frozen river flowed through the channel it had cut in the ice. That channel was close now, just a dozen feet away. To the front, past Scrawny, the smoke from the cabin fire still rose from beyond the little rocky cove. And more; the smoke column was wider, thicker. The trees must have caught fire.

Julian's opponent rolled his shoulders, the movement drawing Julian's attention back to the brigand, who grinned again and advanced, more quickly this time.

Probably wants to get this over with in a hurry.

Bloody fool.

The attack was simple, a thrust straight toward Julian's navel. He made a show of failing to parry it and hopped backward instead, giving ground again to avoid the attack. Then he countered with a backhanded cut toward Scrawny's neck. It was far from steady, but it was the best cut he could manage right then.

Once again, the brigand avoided it easily, simply batting it aside with a nearly contemptuous parry before shuffling forward again, this time cutting straight down toward Julian's uninjured left shoulder.

Julian pivoted on his right foot, spinning out of the way of the descending blade and drawing his body perpendicular to his attacker - a fine stance to minimize the target area he presented, except that it placed his injured shoulder, and not his sword, closest to Scrawny.

The thug could not fail to take advantage of that opening, so Julian did not give him the chance to. Quickly shifting his weight onto his left foot, he snapped the edge of his right foot out.

The sole of Julian's boot met the side of Scrawny's left knee with a dull popping sound. Scrawny's eyes widened in sudden pain and shock, and he stumbled and fell, the leg giving out completely beneath him.

The brigand hit the ice, his sword, forgotten, clattering down beside him as he clutched both hands against his injured knee and let out a high-pitched shriek of pain.

Julian let his own sword fall to the ice and, gritting his teeth through the pain, forced his right arm to move. Squatting down and grabbing the thug's right boot with both hands, he growled something even he could not understand at the man, then forced his legs straight and spun his body around, clockwise.

The pain in his shoulder flared, and spots of light appeared in Julian's vision. He gritted his teeth and a new pain lanced out as he bit down on his tongue, but he forced himself to continued pulling Scrawny along.

The snow layer atop the ice was thinner here, near to the flowing water, and it proved little impediment to the momentum Julian managed to build up. Scrawny spun slowly at first, but very quickly he was moving at a good clip in a circle centered on Julian's body. He cried out again, in surprise as much as pain Julian presumed, and released his injured knee, reaching up toward Julian's hands where they gripped his ankle.

Julian released the boot.

Scrawny slid across the ice toward the flowing water, only a few feet away. The hapless man recognized immediately what was happening, and he clawed desperately at the ice to slow his progress.

But it was too little too late. With a cry even more shrill than the one he had made when Julian broke his knee, the man reached the edge of the ice and went over.

He came up briefly, his hands, shaking horribly even after such a short immersion, grasping at the ice's edge. He croaked out a feeble, "Help me!" And then he lost his grip and submerged fully.

He did not bob up to the surface again.

Julian, out of breath from his exertion, fell to his knees and inhaled deeply. Relief flooded through him, almost enough to eclipse the pain of his shoulder. Almost. He raised a trembling left hand to the injured joint and probed it, and the pain increased immediately.

"Damn it," he muttered.

A cry of pain from behind drew him from his inward focus, and Julian turned to see Raedrick stumbling backwards away from Geoff. The thug's battleaxe was stained red; a particularly nasty cut on Raedrick's left shoulder stood out in Julian's view.

He needed help. Now.

"Always the hero," Julian muttered to himself. Then he picked up his sword in his left hand and forced himself to his feet. The change in posture caused more pain to shoot from his shoulder for a moment, and he tasted blood. He spat red; he must have done his tongue really well.

Then, hefting his sword in his bad hand, he trudged forward as quickly as he could.

The pain in his left shoulder eclipsed his other wounds as Raedrick retreated quickly. It was all he could do not to fall over as he scrambled away, barely avoiding yet another cut from Geoff's great axe.

He had thought he was getting the upper hand after scoring that last cut on the burly man, but if anything it only seemed to infuriate Geoff all the more. He came at Raedrick in a blazing whir of steel that almost overwhelmed him completely. It was only through sheer luck that he had only escaped with the cut on his shoulder.

But it could not last. He had no illusions there. Soon, quite soon, he would falter and Geoff would take him.

He tried a counter attack, but Geoff merely attacked in kind and the longer reach of the thug's weapon forced Raedrick to abandon his cut and dive to the side to avoid being eviscerated. He came up in a roll, facing Geoff, and brought his sword up between them.

The thug grinned, again. "You're done, Constable. Might as well save us both the trouble and admit it."

Raedrick swallowed hard and returned the grin with the hardest glare he could muster, then he spat at the thug's feet.

Geoff's grin widened and he advanced again.

Raedrick ducked beneath the shoulder-level cut and surged forward, lowering his shoulder toward Geoff's injured hip. If he could just get him off balance...

Geoff became a blur of motion and something struck Raedrick in the side. Hard. He went reeling, and almost passed out from the pain as he landed hard on his injured arm. He let out a groan and flipped himself onto his back. Then he found he could move no more, and he just lay there, looking up at the morning clouds wafting across the sky.

Geoff's face abruptly blotted them out. He looked down at Raedrick in silence for a moment, then he shook his head and raised his axe. "Bye, Constable."

The axe began to fall.

It moved in slow motion. Raedrick could not take his eyes away from it. Somewhere in his brain, Raedrick shouted at himself to evade, to get his own blade up to parry. Something. But he could not force himself into motion.

This was it; the end.

Then Geoff's face went slack and his eyes rolled back in their sockets. The great axe, which had begun the killing blow, faltered, then fell from Geoff's suddenly limp hands and clattered to the ice harmlessly.

Geoff fell like a sack of potatoes, landing with a solid thump on the ice next to Raedrick.

A moment later, Julian looked down at him from where Geoff had been. He shook his head with a sardonic grin. "I'm *always* pulling your chestnuts out of the fire, Rae." Then, chuckling, he gingerly wiped his sword clean, slid into his belt, and held his left hand down to Raedrick.

Raedrick accepted the hand up and could not help laughing himself. Right then it seemed very appropriate.

34

HOMEBOUND

"**Y**ou look like hell, Rae. Gonna be one nasty scar."

Raedrick wanted to scowl, but that would just make his chin hurt worse. Turns out that first cut had sliced clean through to the bone, leaving a flap of his skin dangling from his chin. It had taken Julian a long time to get that bandaged up, wrapping his head in what felt like miles of cloth.

Raedrick grunted and replied, "Can't be helped." He pulled the knot he was tying snug and straightened, checking his handiwork.

Geoff lay on the ice before him, tied hand and foot with strips of cloth they had torn from the thug's cloak, a bruise on his left temple that seemed to grow larger and darker by the second. He breathed shallowly, actually snoring softly as he lay there.

Raedrick shook his head and glanced aside at Julian. "You hit him hard enough. Lucky he's not dead."

Julian shrugged noncommittally. "Meant him to be. Next time I'll try harder."

Raedrick snorted. "Then why didn't you just run him through?"

Julian shrugged again but did not respond otherwise.

Raedrick grinned, not pushing the issue. Let Julian keep up the hard act if he wanted to; he was honorable and respected the law as much as Raedrick did. More maybe. And he wanted to see Geoff publicly tried and punished too. A violent death out in the wild might have been acceptable if the conditions warranted it, but stabbing the man in the back? Raedrick had never seen Julian come close to doing that, even while protecting another. He had always found a way to at least make it sporting.

"Let's get him to the boat."

Julian sighed, but he nodded and bent over, grabbing hold of the bindings around Geoff's ankles with his good arm. The other hung in a sling that Raedrick had fashioned from the rest of Geoff's cloak after they had bandaged their various wounds - and Geoff's - with it. Julian must have cut the other thug deeper than he thought; by the time they had come around to him, he had already bled out. Which was just as well, as they had about ran out of cloth for bandages, anyway, after binding their own wounds.

Raedrick grabbed Geoff by the shoulders and they lifted together.

Gods, was he heavy! It took a seeming eternity to move him the few tens of feet to the boat. They had to stop several times to rest, and even with that it was almost too much for them. Getting him situated in the canoe, in the center between the two bench-seats forward and in the rear, and then tying him in place was almost as difficult as the carrying; twice they almost capsized the boat in the struggle. But eventually they managed it.

They paused for a long minute, breathing heavily from the exertion.

"Guess it's too late to change your mind about this," Julian said, but his tone was teasing; he did not mean it. Or at least he knew Raedrick's mind was set.

Raedrick nodded.

"Best get to it then."

Raedrick chuckled and cuffed Julian lightly on his good shoulder. "Thought you'd never ask."

With that, they settled into the canoe, Julian in the front - with his injured shoulder he could hardly paddle, let alone steer - and Raedrick in the rear. They shoved off and very quickly, the current carried them away downstream toward Lake Glimmermere.

Gods willing, it would be a smooth ride, and then an easy hike, all the way home.

35

WRAPPING UP

Geoff glared at Raedrick from behind the bars of his cell, the scowl on his face enough to knock a deer over at fifty paces. "You'll pay for this, Constable. Mark me."

The cell was the center in a set of three similar units that ran the length of the corridor behind Raedrick and Julian's office in the Constabulary. Opposite them, three more cells of identical make stood empty. For that matter, the other two on Geoff's side were devoid of occupants as well. Few in Lydelton actually caused trouble, and most of those who did were just men who had consumed too much at the Oarlock or Holb's; after they slept it off they were generally all right to set loose, minus the fine the judge always demanded of course.

The last time more than one of the cells had been used for any length of time had been in the aftermath of the battle with Isenholf's brigands, when Raedrick and Julian first came to Glimmer Vale almost a year ago. The surviving brigands, and Isenholf himself, had packed the cells full for a couple weeks while awaiting the Judge. With that crisis long in the past, Raedrick did not expect to ever fill them all again, not from the town's inhabitants anyway.

It had been more difficult getting back to town than it should have been, with Geoff in tow, but it could have been worse. He had awoken a half hour after they got underway in the canoe and promptly set about trying to upset the boat. A whack over the head with Julian's paddle - light enough to not actually hurt him but hard enough to leave an impression - and a stern reminder that he would go in with them and he hadn't even a prayer of swimming to safety tied as he was put a stop to that quickly.

When they reached the solid ice of Lake Glimmermere they had a hell of a time getting him out of the boat and onto his feet. But eventually, they convinced him it was follow along with them or die right then and there, so he went along, if not willingly, then with little enough fuss.

They took Tolburt's route: straight across the ice toward the town. It was more direct, flatter, and promised a quicker trip than going to the shore. The ice was certainly thick enough to hold them all - Raedrick reminded himself of that every dozen paces or so - so the decision was easy to make.

They made it to town shortly after sunset, moving on stiff legs against a bitter breeze that blew in from the east. Raedrick had wanted nothing more than to throw Geoff into a cell and go home for a long night's sleep.

But there were other matters to attend to, and he spent a while after getting Geoff situated checking on Ravi and Povol. The latter was under the Guildsman's care in the Healers Circle. For his part, Ravi had developed a cough at some point. Every couple minutes the old man had to pause to hack forcefully, but when Raedrick asked about it, he waved it off as nothing of import. Povol was the greater concern. And he was; his hand looked even worse than Raedrick remembered, despite Ravi's treatments. The Guildsman suspected he would lose at least one finger.

Luckily, Povol was not awake to hear that.

Ravi insisted that Raedrick and Julian remain at the Circle long enough to properly dress their wounds before they turned in for the night. It took a dozen stitches to close up the cut on Raedrick's chin and half again as many for his shoulder, but sick as he was, Ravi managed it so deftly that Raedrick hardly felt the pricks of the needle. Julian was not so lucky when Ravi re-set his shoulder. He howled even worse than he had when Raedrick set it out in the wilderness. Ravi extracted a reluctant promise from Julian to return first thing in the morning for a check-up, and then they were done.

Raedrick finally walked - more like staggered - to the little flat he called home. He did not even manage to remove his boots before he fell onto his bed, exhausted, and slept until the long hours of the morning.

When he awoke, all he wanted to do was pull his blankets over his head and go back to sleep, but his responsibilities forced their way into his mind and would not shut up. So, reluctantly, he got up and, pausing only to change into fresh clothes, he headed back to the office, and his prisoner.

And so his first conversation of the day began with Geoff's surly words of warning.

Raedrick raised an eyebrow at Geoff's comment, then gave the cell door a tug. It rattled in place, but did not move. "Perhaps," he said, "but not today."

Geoff opened his mouth to respond but Raedrick kept right on rolling.

"Nor tomorrow, I expect. Tomorrow you go before the judge, and I don't think he'll take kindly to your activities here. Confidence games," he raised one finger, "assault," another, "attempting murder," a third, "vandalism," a fourth, "theft," his thumb, "kidnapping." Raedrick shook his head and whistled ever so softly.

Geoff shut his mouth, his scowl growing darker.

"Breakfast will be here in a few minutes," Raedrick said, turning away from the cell and its occupant.

In fact, the food arrived almost as soon as he returned to the front office, shut the door to the cell block, and settled into the chair behind his desk. The door cracked open, admitting the wind, which was cold and energetic this morning and threatened to overwhelm the heat the stove in the corner put out. The delivery man from The Oarlock, clad in a thick coat, matching leggings, and a cowled cloak, shut the door quickly and stamped his boots to clear them of snow, then pushed back his hood.

Raedrick blinked. *Her* hood. Or more in particular, Lani's hood. He rose to his feet in a rush, smiling in greeting. "Lani," he began.

She silenced him with a look that put the wind to shame in its chill and set a small satchel, containing Geoff's and his breakfast no doubt, onto his desk. "Your order, Constable," she said in a level businesslike tone that would seem perfectly professional to someone who did not know her.

What was going on here?

"Thank you," he said. "It's good to see you."

She snorted, then turned and headed toward the door, his shoulders set in the posture Raedrick had seen her use a time or two, when she was furious.

"What - ?"

She stopped at his question, her hand partly raised to the door latch. She stood there for a few seconds, then she drew in a quick breath that almost sounded like a sob. "I was so worried," she said. "When you didn't return after two days, I knew something horrible had happened. And then when Master Sebastini and Povol got back..." She shook her head, still not looking at him. She sniffled, and Raedrick knew she was crying.

He stepped around the desk to go to her, but she whirled around, raising her hand, palm out toward him in a stopping gesture. Tears ran down her cheeks and her lips trembled, but her eyes burned with fury - she was probably at least as angry that she had lost her composure as anything else, if he had to make a guess.

"And then this morning I find out that you returned last night. I found out from a *messenger*." She drew a deep breath, wiping her eyes with the back of her glove. "We were open until two o'clock last night. You did not bother to come tell me yourself?"

Taken aback, Raedrick did not know how to respond for a second. He had been so tired last night, he had not even thought...

He had not even thought.

He hung his head, shame flooding through him as he realized what he had put her through while he was so absorbed in his own issues. "I'm sorry."

She looked at him, at his bandaged wounds, and tears welled up. "I told you I could not bear it if anything happened to you, and look..." She gestured toward his face and her voice caught. Her fingers curled into a fist that she raised before her mouth, to cover the beginnings of a sob.

Before he could say another word, she turned, opened the door, and left. The cold wind that entered the room with her passage seemed fitting, just then. It matched the ache in his chest.

He started toward the door, intending to follow her, to explain. But he held short before he had covered half the distance. What was there to say? He had his responsibilities, and he had put them before her. Hell, he had put them before everything - before his own safety, that of his friends. She was right to be angry with him. He would find a way to make amends, but it seemed clear she did not want to hear about it just then.

Sighing, he turned away from the door and picked up the satchel of foodstuffs, but paused as he heard through the door leading back into the cell block - just a collection of wrought iron bars, like the doors to the cells - Geoff's mocking laughter.

$$\maltese \quad 36 \quad \maltese$$

PENANCE

"I'm such a fool." Tolburt hung his head, refusing to look up at Raedrick, or even at anything except his own lap. After a second, his breath caught and it sounded as though he was weeping, or trying very hard to keep from doing so.

They sat in the treatment room at the Healers Circle, and Raedrick had just finished telling the events of the last several days. He tried to keep a stern, calm face while doing the telling. But especially now, as Tolburt broke down, he had to work hard to maintain his bearing, so he thought of other things to keep himself calm: the sound of wind through the trees, the taste of finely mulled wine on a crisp autumn day, the pleasant ache of his muscles after a hard workout in the sparring ring with Julian.

Finally, Tolburt got himself a bit more under control. He wiped his nose on the back of his left hand and glanced quickly up at Raedrick. "How could I have not seen Stefan was playing me?"

Raedrick shrugged, but said nothing. This was the sort of thing Tolburt was going to have to figure out himself. It was well past time he grew up, truly grew up.

Tolburt must have seen the disapproval - the disappointment - in Raedrick's gaze because he lowered his eyes again. "Thank you for..."

"Do not thank me."

Tolburt recoiled at the rebuke in Raedrick's tone. He had used his best dressing-down voice; that had always worked wonders with subordinates who stepped out of line, and now with subjects of his - infrequent - investigations around town.

"You caused a lot of trouble for my town, Tolburt. Julian will be a long time recovering from his injuries. His shoulder may not ever be the same again. Povol lost two fingers, all of his dogs, and his dogsleds. Master Sebastini developed a bad cough, and at his age..." Raedrick trailed off, letting the rest go unsaid. He prayed Ravi did not take a turn for the worse. He was a gem of a man, and almost more important than that, the town could ill afford to lose its Guildsman in the middle of the winter. He drew a breath, putting that worry from his mind as he continued on. "And then there's the destroyed cabin and the forest fire. You have a lot to answer for."

"Me? But I…"

"Yes, you. Oh you were led astray, conned by Geoff's man." Raedrick jabbed a finger at Tolburt and he sank even further back into his pillows than he had already. "But you should have known enough to see through it. Instead you went willingly to be fleeced, and then you dragged us into it as well."

Tolburt's mouth opened and shut wordlessly for half a minute as he struggled to find some way to reply. His expression said he could not believe what Raedrick was saying, that he was being wronged. After everything that had happened, that was what angered Raedrick the most. He really did not see how he was responsible. Well, he would have time to figure it out.

"I've spoken with the Mayor and the Judge, and this is what's going to happen."

Tolburt went pale. Good.

"You will stay here and get well. When you're better, you'll check into a room at Bigsbe's Boarding House. You'll work at Holb's Tavern until the thaw, doing anything and everything he tells you without complaint. Your pay will go toward the supplies to rebuild the cabin and toward replacing Povol's sled dogs. After the thaw, you'll help Povol and the other men who owned that cabin rebuild."

Tolburt's mouth dropped open wide. He looked speechlessly at Raedrick, his eyes unbelieving.

"When everything that's happened has been put right, I'll give you the note we found in the chest. You can leave the Vale, follow the note to wherever it leads, whatever. But not before." Raedrick stood from his chair and took a step to the edge of Tolburt's bed. He was looming, and it was working. "Do you understand?"

Tolburt nodded silently.

"Good." Raedrick managed a half-smile that he hoped was at least a little comforting. "Welcome to Glimmer Vale, Tolburt. If you play your cards right while you're here, you may find you've finally become a man." He held Tolburt's gaze for a moment, then nodded briskly and turned away.

When he pulled the door shut behind him, Tolburt still had not said a word.

Raedrick met Julian down at the docks, as they had planned before Tolburt came to town and threw things out of kilter. He trudged through the snow past the Covington Brothers' warehouse, his head down and his hands shoved into the deep pockets of his coat in anticipation of the bitter wind that blew in off the lake. But for whatever reason the breeze was still this afternoon, and when Raedrick stopped in front of Julian, one of his eyebrows drifted upward in droll amusement. Or at least Raedrick presumed it was amusement; the rest of his face was covered by a thick red, yellow, and brown scarf so it was impossible to tell. But Julian being Julian…

"I believe the world is about to end, Rae." He gestured around at the lack of wind.

Raedrick nodded. "Surely that scarf is one of the prophesied precursors."

Julian snorted, or maybe laughed briefly. "A gift from Molli." He stamped his feet as though unwilling to stay still for too long lest the cold overcome him. Not a bad thought, actually. "Lani still mad?"

Raedrick nodded again. "We talked again last night, but..." But he was going to be in trouble for a while over this one.

Julian sighed, and the tone of the sigh carried worlds of commiseration. For a second Raedrick thought he was about to offer some manner of advice or other. Instead, he simply said, "We going to do this?"

"Aye," Raedrick replied. The situation with Lani could wait. Raedrick forced down a resigned sigh, then turned and led the way past the first two docks.

At the stairs leading up to Dock One, a familiar older man with thick grey hair to his shoulders and a beard of nearly the same length stood waiting for them. As always, he wore his battered old wool cloak. The only other concession he made to the bitter cold was the furred clothing he wore below the cloak; he did not even wear a hat. Years - hell, decades - of work out on the fishing boats had hardened him against the ravages of the elements, or at least that was what he wanted others to think.

The old fishing man looked the two of them over as they approached and inclined his head in greeting. "Constables. My boys got things set up as you asked."

"Thank you, Horace."

Horace shrugged. "No skin off my back. Can't see why you'd want to do this, but it's your funeral."

Raedrick tried to grin in response to the teasing tone the old fishing man took at the end, but the stitches in his chin warned him against it. Instead he just nodded then mounted the steps to the dock.

Julian remained behind for a moment, exchanging a few low words with Horace. The two had made fast friends when Julian and Raedrick first came to town, and Julian almost never passed up a chance to exchange words - and usually more than enough drink - with the old man.

Raedrick did not wait, but continued down the dock toward the end, where a small table had been laid out, along with two chairs. As he had asked, a single bottle lay uncorked on the table, and three glasses were set out, waiting for them. Just as it had been this time last year - well, almost as it had been anyway. It was far more cold here than it had been on the tropical docks of Qoramyr, and, of course Lydelton had no taverns on the docks themselves. But he and Julian had promised each other to do it like they had every year, and this was the best they could do.

"I told you before," Julian said from behind him. "We can do this just as well indoors."

Raedrick gave him a level look and settled down into the east-facing chair so he could watch the approaching sunset. "No we can't. This is our penance, Julian." He picked up the bottle - good whiskey all the way form Tol Guldor, very hard to come by - and poured two fingers' worth into the three glasses. "Part of it," he added softly, not meaning for the words to reach Julian's ears.

Julian sat opposite him and tugged the scarf down from his mouth. That eyebrow raised again. "Penance?" He shook his head disdainfully.

He did not understand, but Raedrick did not expect him to. Julian felt the loss of their comrades, and maybe felt a tinge of conscience over their desertion - their treason. But if he did, he never showed it; in fact he had tried on more than one occasion to set Raedrick's mind more fully at ease over the whole thing. They had done the right thing. To stay would have been the true betrayal, of all the principles they had sworn to uphold when they joined the Army. Of the reasons the war had begun in the first place.

And he was right. But he was also wrong. He had the luxury of only focusing on that part of the picture, but he had not been in command. In the end, it was Raedrick's decision that set them on the course that had resulted in so many of his men's deaths - and of Tolburt's fall. It had been the right thing to do, but the cost...

He took hold of his glass and raised it high between them. Julian followed suit.

"To our lost brothers, and those who cannot be with us."

Julian clinked his glass against Raedrick's. "One too few lost," he murmured softly before throwing the whiskey back in one smooth swallow.

Raedrick froze for a heartbeat. That comment could only refer to Tolburt. He knew Julian disapproved of allowing him to remain in town any longer than it took for him to recover fully. Patch him up and send him off, he had said. In truth, Raedrick had been tempted to do just that, except it would have been tantamount to an execution; there was no way Tolburt could make it through the passes before thaw, not alone. And there would be no caravans for months yet, if at all. And there was the possibility that this could help Tolburt finally get himself squared away.

But that was not the only reason. Raedrick had re-read the cryptic note they found within that chest half a dozen times. Something about it tweaked at his memory, but he could not lay his finger on what. It piqued his curiosity. Having a few more months to ponder its meaning would not be a bad thing.

Raedrick let Julian's words pass unanswered, instead downing his own whiskey just a hair slower than Julian had.

Julian smirked; he was no fool. But he said no more, just picked up the third glass and flung its contents over the railing of the dock and onto the frozen lake.

They sat there for a time, trading tales of their lost comrades and sharing drinks, just the three of them - Raedrick, Julian, and the ghost of the past. Finally, the bottle empty, the two men stood and stumbled back to the shore, leaning against each other for support against the swimming of their heads.

And somewhere during all of that, Raedrick realized the other side of his decision of two years ago. It had resulted in tragedy for too many of his men. But some of them had found new lives, and he and Julian made it here, to this place. There was a lot of good here, a lot of good people, and they were helping to make it better. They had built a home, a place where they could do some good and turn away from their past. And maybe that was enough. If nothing else, it was a good start.

They left the dock and went their separate ways, Julian grumbling about needing to turn in early because of an early appointment with Ravi. Raedrick watched him go and could not help but laugh and the drunken annoyance in his friend's tone. Then he turned on unsteady legs and headed toward The Oarlock. Lani was working again tonight, and he found he was no longer content to let their reconciliation happen on its own schedule.

He set as strong a pace as he could muster without tripping over himself. On the way there, he passed several townsfolk who were trudging through the streets on business of one sort or other. Each and every one of them looked at him askance, and it was not until he turned into The Oarlock's stable yard that he realized why.

He had been whistling the whole way there.

Raedrick placed his hand on The Oarlock's front door and managed a smile despite the lingering pain of the cut to his chin. Yes, this was a good place. And if he had anything to say in the matter, it would remain so for a good long time.

Squaring his shoulders, he pushed the door open and stepped inside, out of the cold.

MESSAGE FROM THE AUTHOR

Thank you for reading my book. I hope you enjoyed reading it as much as I enjoyed writing it.

Every review helps an author out, so whether you loved this book, hated it, or something in between, please take a minute to tell other readers what you thought. All of the online retailers make it very easy to do, and I would really appreciate it.

Feel free to come say hi at my website or on Gab. I always enjoy hearing from readers, especially since you all are, collectively, my boss.

I also have a weekly podcast, Story Time With Michael Kingswood, where I read stories and talk through some of the latest goings on in my world. I'd love to see you there.

Thanks again. My best to you and yours.

Warm Regards,
Michael Kingswood

MAILING LIST

If you enjoyed this book and would like word on new releases and special deals from Michael Kingswood, sign up for his newsletter on his website. Guaranteed to be spam-free, you can opt out at any time. And you can rest assured he will not share your information with anyone, for any reason.

https://michaelkingswood.com/newsletter-signup/

MEMBERSHIP

Michael would like to invite you to become a supporting member of his website. Similar in concept to Patreon, a few dollars a month will give you access to exclusive content, and help him to focus more of his time to writing fun and exciting stories for your enjoyment.

Sign up at his website:

https://www.michaelkingswood.com/membership/join/

ABOUT THE AUTHOR

Michael Kingswood is 20-year veteran of the US Navy submarine force and a life-long fan of science fiction and fantasy literature. His work has appeared in numerous collections and anthologies, to include the Fiction River Anthology series from WMG publishing. He holds a bachelors degree in Mechanical Engineering as well as a Master of Engineering Management and a Master of Business Administration. He has four children and currently resides in San Diego.

Find Michael Kingswood online at:

www.michaelkingswood.com
www.gab.com/michaelkingswood
rumble.com/michaelkingswood

MORE BOOKS BY MICHAEL KINGSWOOD

GLIMMER VALE CHRONICLES

Glimmer Vale

Out-Dweller

Tollard's Peak

Robbed Blind

The Falconer's Stairs

Campaign Season

Glimmer Vale Chronicles Books 1-3

STORIES FROM GLIMMER VALE

Legacy

Hidden Magic

Captive Hearts

Wedding Gifts

Lost Credit

THE PERICLES CONSPIRACY

Passing In The Night

The Pericles Conspiracy

DAWN OF ENLIGHTENMENT

Masters Of The Sun

NOVELLAS

What Lurks Between

The Necromancer's Lair

The Champion

Veritas Morte

SHORT FICTION

Michael has also published a number of shorter works, links to which can be found on his website.